MW00716709

Back to Lmuma Mine

Three Young Men Mature

A Young Adult Novel by

Al Allaway

Al Allaway

Published by AllawayBooks, Yakima WA
www.allawaybooks.com

ISBN 978-0-6152-0674-5
Printed by Lulu in the United States of America
www.lulu.com

Back to Lmuma Mine

Other Books by Al Allaway

Snowbirds Guarding the Gold

Mystery of the Lmuma Mine

Jonathan of Scots

E-Praise 4 Gifting

Treasure in the Park

ALL-Ways the Rebel

E-Praise (1)

E-Praise Two

All-Ways an ALLAWAY Family (2 volumes)

Memories (Short Stories & Poems)

Contents

ILLUSTRATIONS:

Preface

Soaring, born of wind, a Golden eagle drifts lazily over an immensity of shattered rock. Just as in eons past. Always and afterwards, sharp eyes scan the contours of geological rift.

Shifting light and lengthening shadows create new vistas. Scrubby conifers, wind shaped, cast their scraggly like shadows in contrast to the grey-white granites. What is obvious before is not seen an hour later. Time causes new things to appear with each passing minute. Slick wet puddles reflect an azure sky and create an illusion of things that are not there.

Below, stone chills to freezing from last winter's dirty snows; creatures seek to escape into the warmth of underbrush or sunny exposure. Scintillating wavy lines confuse the eye; shimmering temperature ripples mixed cold and warm. But the eagle sees all.

If one listens carefully, small pebbles or grains of crushed sand whisper from steep talus slopes, loosened by expansion of heated rock, grinding, growing, contracting, freezing.

Further still, more than a mile below the eagle, a thin sliver of movement creeps like a silver coated worm winding its way over the still snowy Donner Pass, guided by two ribbons of steel. It appears placid from this height, barely creeping, hiding its Herculean diesel strength. Both power and time stand still, and then marches forward.

* * *

On the westbound silver streamliner, *City of Chicago,* Ron Martin could feel the bulge of his wallet in his back pocket. It contained $550 in cash, more money than he could earn in a whole year. He was in a dream like trance, wildly imagining spending or saving, or power, further hypnotized by the clickity-click rhythm of the rails.

As the train cautiously picked its way through numerous wooden snow sheds still dripping with spring thaw, Ron could not believe his phenomenal luck. For a teenager, by 1947 standards, the money was a fortune, all legally obtained. His two companions, Rex Franklin and Tim Caruthers had exactly the same amount because the three boys divided all the money equally. Part of it was in the original fifty-dollar bills they had secretly plucked out of the Central Nevada sagebrush, blown there by the winds. That alone would have been the adventure of a lifetime, but their triumph in the Lmuma Mine had topped it. They had actually captured a spy who had been reporting on military munitions movements to the Soviet Union. The Russian had been using an unused tunnel in the mine to spy on the valley below. Cold war espionage was a fact of life all over the world as it recovered from the terrors of World War II, and the United States was no exception.

All three boys were honored at a military reception and then the mine owner, Forrest Williams, paid an unexpected but handsome bonus for their volunteer time.

Now, the glory bubble burst, the train trip back to boarding school in Sacramento offered nothing more to high-school sophomores than the boring ritual of the

LaSalle Christian Brothers Catholic High School, which would start promptly at 5:30 a.m. the next morning.

"What time does the train get in to Sacramento?" asked Rex.

"I think the conductor said around five," answered Ron.

Tim, sitting in the next seat, asked, "Will Brother Felix meet the train?"

"Dunno."

"Suppose we'll get back to school in time for dinner?"

"Yech!"

"I'd rather find one of those new McDonald's."

A cloud of gloom settled over an already foreboding, cheerless future.

Mesmerized by the hypnotic effect of equally spaced power poles as they flashed in the train windows, Ron dozed briefly, dreaming about life's new prospects. After high school, he hoped to obtain a Bachelor of Science with a major in photography. All through grammar school he'd been mesmerized by dreams if Aztec and Mayan culture, ruins and gold. His explorer hero was John Lloyd Stephens, whose footsteps he hoped to follow someday, with a camera lens.

Rocking to the sway of the train, Tim dreamed of his future. He had his eye on

LaSalle College for a teaching degree. He would be the "Brother Prefect" of the future. He figured that his mom would divorce again, but Tim considered that as no loss.

Rex was still torn between a career as an officer in the Navy, like his father, or joining a fire department with a degree in Fire Science Engineering. His step-mom's cerebral tumor would probably take her life within a year. He knew he had matured enough in his internal strength to be able to cope.

Three young men advanced toward maturity very fast in one short week and learned a lot about the rewards of being honest. And they learned another valuable lesson, that broken dysfunctional families can still produce winners, despite the odds. Considering all that had happened, the bottom line of their future lives was still basically the result of their own actions. A good prayer based faith in God reflected in everything they did.

* * *

The coyote walked slowly up the trail, created by countless footsteps, from the mine to the plateau, her sensitive nose testing every air. She was hungry again, with only vague memories of all things past. She checked the hiding place under the rock slab one more time, as she often did, finding only another of those green-grey papers the humans placed so much importance on. Feeling only pangs of hunger in her belly, she turned and complained to the full moon.

* * *

Ron Martin, Rex Franklin and Tim Caruthers miraculous triumph was gone forever, except for the memories.

Grumpy old Brother William met the train, only three hours late and escorted the boys back to the LaSalle Christian Brothers boarding school. Brother William wore his clerical black gown and cassock. And, of course the car was black to match the boys' somber mood.

Further, the Sacramento rain dampened more than their skin. Back at school, the dining hall was closed; peanut butter sandwiches its only offering. Their dormitory was dark, after hours and they had to feel their way into cold beds. Any use of lights would bring instant demerits.

Life for three fourteen-year-old kids plummeted from high adventure to the black nightmare of boarding school discipline. No talking, no thinking, no laughing, recite by rote, no fun! Study, go to Mass, study, eat, march, study hall, no talking, memorize Scripture, march, sit up straight, clean your plate, do chores, more study hall, no whispering, back to chapel, lights out!

Student weekdays started as early as 5:30 a.m., followed by an hour-long chapel, including daily Mass, then breakfast. Breakfast was always followed by an hour-long mandatory study hall before classes started at 8:30. The classroom schedule ended at 3:45, allowing outdoor playtime until dinner at 5:30. At 7:00 it was time for Vespers followed by another hour-long study hall. Lights out at 9:00 didn't allow much time for any personal endeavors.

Before Easter vacation, all their dormitory mates had been full of questions about the pending trip to a Nevada gold mine. Now, on their first day back, there would be many more questions. The first day would be the worst. Ron, Rex and Tim felt tall and important, itching to share parts of their adventure. The tension and wait for the right opportunity overwhelmed the entire community. It could be said that even the faculty felt the tension.

Marching single file into the chapel for morning Mass, the prefect, Brother Felix broke his customary silence more than once.

"No whispering!" he would admonish repeatedly, adding a stern prophecy, "One more warning and I will unload demerits on everyone."

Ron and friends bit their lips to the point of bleeding.

Brother Felix was a large man, his size multiplied by the loose flowing black robe that hung all the way down to within an inch above his black shoes.

If he ever smiled, it would cause wrinkles to assemble in his neck just above his too-tight white medieval clerical collar. It looked like something the Old Dutch Masters once wore. The horizontal starched flats of the collar would flap like the wings of a bird as he spoke.

The chapel was divided down the center aisle, the left side for boys; the right reserved for faculty nuns, brothers and occasional guests. A gleam entered the eyes of Brother Felix. He grasped Tim and Rex firmly by the shoulders and steered them to the front.

"You are going to help Father O'Connor serve the Mass," he said.

"But Sedgewick is on the Alter boy list," complained Tim.

"Schedules can change," said Brother Felix.

"But, I've never served before," said Rex, sure that he had an out.

"No time like the present to learn." Brother Felix winked. "Tell Sedgewick that he gets the morning off." Next, the Prefect turned to Ron, steering him to the right side.

"To keep you from talking, you will sit here with Sister Berniece." Ron took one look at the aged, wrinkled nun and knew this was not going to be a good day. She smiled ever so sweetly at him and leaning back off her kneeler, motioned him to go around her so he sat now between two nuns!

Forty other boys, across the aisle, anxious to hear about the adventure, also felt part and parcel to Ron's frustration. And so the day began. Proud information would remain bottled up until classes finished at 3:45

Al Allaway

Book One

Ron
(1953-1986)

Chapter One ~ The Big Lie

Six years later~~

Ron Martin was in a quandary. How could he ease the burden of what he must tell his mother? One thought was to wing it or play it by ear. Perhaps it would be better not to rehearse anything, but just blurt it out.

He studied his mirrored reflection for a long agonizing moment. Ron was tall, had an angular face, a full head of blonde hair, tan complexion and a square jaw. One might even consider him to be handsome, especially now decked out in cap and gown.

"C'mon, Ron," it was Tim Caruthers, a voice interrupting the deep concentration, "We're gonna be late!"

They filed out of the dressing room, joining a procession of forty other young men graduating from St. Mary's College near Oakland, CA. Above the podium a huge banner proclaimed the message: *Congratulations to the Class of 1953!*

Ron quickly glanced through the crowd of proud friends and relatives gathered for the graduation ceremony. He made easy eye contact with his mother and aunt sitting in the second row.

His trepidation returned and he looked away. Words of the college psychologist returned to haunt him, echoing repeatedly, *"Tell your Mom you found out the truth about your father... It's the only way!"*

Mrs. Martin had always been vague whenever Ron asked about his father. It became a sore subject so Ron simply stopped asking. The only "truth" he could get from his mother was that his dad was dead and there was no reason to keep bringing up the subject. As a teen-ager, Ron easily accepted whatever he was told without question, but now, as a young man about to graduate from college, the shadows of the past had been addressed.

It happened in a goofy strange sort of way, almost by blind circumstance. So it had been, on a rainy San Francisco day the week before, he found himself in the downtown library researching something for a college paper. Taking a fun break, he thought he could pump up his ego by seeing his name in print in the Portland <u>Oregonian</u> birth announcements, for which he searched diligently through dusty reels of microfilm, but in vain.

One listing was really close; it contained the right date, right first and middle names, right hospital, right parents, but wrong surname.

"Something is haywire here," he told the elderly microfilm librarian. He knew that he had the right date and location.

Then it happened! Armed only with the real surname, she scratched her head briefly, and said, "Follow me to the Reference Section."

Ron could imagine the gears grinding in her head like a well-oiled clock. The Reference area in the main library is in a huge complex of rooms, perhaps a city block in size. The librarian certainly knew her way around and marched straight to the last bookcase in the far corner. She then adjusted a rolling ladder and climbed up to the very top shelf.

"Ah, here it is," she said, as she pulled a dusty old book off the shelf. It was an "Index to The New York Times," over 20 years old.

She wore her age well, except for the quaver in her neck and the tongue moistening her old dry fingers in order to turn the pages.

Better than any high-speed computer, she went right to the correct surname, unveiling a dozen stories and articles about the crime, the fugitive, the arrest, indictment, trial and conviction. Through the blur of moist eyes, Ron could make out a familiar surname, his own! Mom's lie became crystal clear.

God bless librarians!

Mom would hate her guts.

His dad turned out to be a fugitive felon before he met and married Ron's mother, using a made-up alias surname. The birth was recorded under that fake name, which his mom later had the Courts correct. His dad meanwhile had served a long term in Sing-Sing prison for embezzling funds from an exclusive New York society women's club where he had worked as accountant.

In High School and the first three years of college, Ron knew nothing of this. He bought his mother's lie that his father died before he was born (She was too embarrassed to tell him the truth).

Now, she would not be able to deny the truth, evidenced by reams of copied news clips and photos. Ron loved his mother and had no desire to upset her, especially on this day of achievement and celebration. As the final strains of *The Graduation Song* faded, he made up his mind what he would do, and he was at peace with his conscience.

Ron felt Tim jab him in the ribs, as the master of ceremonies husky voice amplified out over the audience, "And now, our

Valedictorian, Ron Martin from Hawthorne, Nevada..."

Shortly thereafter, it was time for friends to part.

"Do you suppose the three of us will ever get back to Lmuma for some kind of a reunion?" The question had been bugging Tim, for years.

"I'd like that," said Ron, "if we work at it, I'm sure we could pull it off."

"Has anybody heard from Rex?"

Rex Franklin joined the U.S. Navy right after high school, trained in underwater demolition, and was now part of an elite Frogman team serving somewhere near Korea.

"Not a word since the peace talks started at Panmunjom in April," said Ron.

"I've heard there's better than a 50-50 chance the cease fire will happen in less than a month." Offered Tim, "Maybe then we'll hear something from our buddy. The last I heard, he'd been promoted to Petty Officer."

"Well, turkey," kidded Ron, "I've got the photo studios offer. What'r ya going to do?"

"Ha!" exclaimed Tim, "I decided against being a Christian Brother so I applied and I've been accepted by a Portland area Fire Bureau. Training begins next week.

Ron hugged his friend without any sign of embarrassment.

"Keep in touch, turkey butt! See 'ya someday at Lmuma."

* * *

A large manila envelope had been stuffed with all the copied evidence Ron had gathered about his dad in the San Francisco downtown library the week before graduation. The envelope now took up residence on the bottom shelf under the household bath towels in the Martin house. Ron placed it there the day after St. Mary's College commencement exercises. Ron was not a coward, afraid to confront his mother with her lie. Instead, he felt the shock would be easier on her if she "accidentally' stumbled onto his packet of information. He knew this would eventually result in her opening up the conversation. It would go better for her, if she felt in control. All he had to do was to wait.

It didn't take long.

"Ron, come sit with me," she said, "We need to talk."

"Yes, I know."

It didn't turn out nearly as traumatic as he imagined. True, Mrs. Martin cried, but not because of the deception. She had bottled up her anger against Ron's father for too many years, and now with the secret out, the dam of emotion burst like a major flood.

"The bastard was arrested when you were only five weeks old and left us with a mortgage, no money and no job," she sobbed, "And no chance of a job because of the Depression."

"I know how hard that must have been on you," Ron said, giving her a comforting hug. "You must have sacrificed much."

"I'm glad it's out in the open, now," she said, regaining some composure. "He's out of prison and I'm surprised he hasn't tried contacting you." She took a deep breath and continued, "Did you know that he abandoned another family back in New York before us? Did you know that you have a half sister who is seven or eight years older than you?"

* * *

All through college, Ron held a work scholarship as University photographer, which paid for much of his tuition. He also honed his photo skills as a free-lance, selling news photos to local newspapers.

After covering a very serious auto accident one day, a lawyer contacted him and offered a hefty sum of money for an exclusive right to all his photos and negatives. It was an offer Ron could not refuse, and it opened up a whole new world of possible income. In his darkroom at the college, Ron set up a police scanner so he could respond to other car wrecks, knowing there was demand for this service.

One thing led to another, and the first thing he knew, he was working part time for a private investigator, sneaking pictures of unsuspecting people who were plaintiffs in damage lawsuits, sometimes requesting millions of dollars. Before Ron would take on any case, in was necessary for his boss to convince him that they were both on the right side of "justice," ridding the world of cheats and scoundrels. Ron's conscience dictated nothing short of this.

So it was on August 20th, during summer break before his final year at college, Ron found himself hidden in the dense foliage of a nursery, armed with a 16mm movie camera and long telephoto lenses. He was waiting and watching a house across the street, hoping for the suspect to appear. It was a sagging old house, in sad need of repair belonging to one Nicholas Tomasini.

Tomasini's bother, John had filed a huge workman's compensation claim, demanding monetary support for the rest of his life because of an injured back. Steve, Ron's boss had been hired by the insurance carrier, who insisted John Tomasini was a faker and a fraud. This day's stakeout had been set up because somebody snitched on John, telling the investigators he had been seen helping his brother repair the house.

There was activity at the house across the street and Ron could not chance being seen. He lay cramped on his belly in the bushes. Ants and flies began to investigate his sweat and he was very uncomfortable. He had been waiting in this cramped position for several hours, when finally, John drove up and parked his car.

Ron's camera was rolling before John opened his car door to exit, then panned following him as he ran, bounded up the steps two at a time and into the back door of the house.

Great, thought Ron, *If I don't film another frame, that should be enough to prove he's faking!*

Ron was able to stretch his aching limbs and restore blood flow. He was tempted to stand or maybe leave, but thought better of it.

That had been the right thing to do, because less than five minutes later, Nicholas came out the back door and set up a ladder then climbed to the roof. Right behind him, John peeked out the back door, looked up and down the street, all around.

Convinced nobody was watching, he descended the steps, bent down to pick up a 4x6 ridge timber and hoisted all twelve feet of it onto his shoulder, then amazingly carried it up the rickety ladder to his brother on the roof.

All the time this went on, Ron's camera was grinding out movie frames at 24 to the second. *Holy smoke! There's no way this guy can be disabled.*

Discretion held Ron in hiding for another hour; otherwise any surprise in the trial would be thwarted. After more exposed film, the two workers quit for a coffee break inside, and Ron slunk quietly out of the area.

"How much do you figure that timber weighs?" asked Steve, as they viewed the film.

"I'd guess at least 140-150 pounds," said Ron.

"There's no way he can be disabled."

"Or win his lawsuit."

The evidence at hand spoke volumes about how the case would turn out, if it went to trial. But, the fickle finger of fate had not yet thrown her last curve ball.

"Copy and archive the film," Steve said, "Protect it with your life."

"You keep a copy, also," suggested Ron. "I have to go register for the final semester. Let me know if this ever goes to trial."

So far as Ron was concerned, the film was safe and the matter was ended, and forgotten.

A couple of months later it happened that Ron's mother dissolved her partnership in the Hawthorne department store, and moved into a retirement home in the Bay area to be near his college. The retirement facility was smaller than she expected so she had extra furniture to dispose of, including a small color television.

A classified ad coincidentally attracted a young lawyer named Benjamin Brown who visited Mrs. Martin to buy the TV.

Unlike most attorneys, he seemed to be in no hurry; they sat talking over tea for several hours.

Jeri Martin asked, "And what do you do for a living?"

"I try insurance cases in court," Brown answered.

"What a coincidence," Jeri exclaimed, "My son Ron works for a private investigator as a photographer disputing insurance claims."

"Yeah?"

"In fact, he has to testify at a trial a week from Tuesday", she said.

"Yeah?"

"Yeah! He caught some guy with a bad back hauling heavy beams up a ladder."

It wasn't much, but it was enough. Jeri didn't even suspect that Brown was there for purposes other than buying her used TV.

The tea and conversation dried up fast and suddenly Mr. Brown was in a big hurry; late for an appointment, he claimed.

* * *

Lawyers throughout the Bay area still talk about the "Case won by TV" which apparently set some kind of a record.

Ron Martin and Steve the Private Investigator were all set up to show movies to a skeptical jury. It was intended to be a huge surprise; a totally unexpected *rara avis*.

Instead, Benjamin Brown called John to the stand.

"Have you ever done any major labor since your accident?"

John Tomasini: "Well, yes, my brother's roof was leaking, but he and his little kids all had the flu. I had to help fix his roof one day. It hurt like hell, but I had to do it."

Brown: "And when was that?"

Tomasini: "Uh, sometime in August, I think about the 20th."

Brown: "Was that the only time?"

Tomasini: "Absolutely, positively!"

Steve, the investigator glanced over at Ron and groaned. Their defense attorney stood quickly to his feet, as if to object, had second thoughts and sat back down, a look of gloom settling over him. "Damn!" he mumbled, just loud enough for Ron and Steve to hear. Their case was busted wide open. All element of surprise was gone. Showing the film now to the jury would simply reinforce the plaintiff's testimony.

When the Court recessed, a heated discussion developed between the insurance attorney, Steve and Ron. They decided to go ahead and show the film. In the end, Tomasini was awarded his requested disability, and the "Case won by TV" became famous all over the state. It was the last investigation Ron worked, out of choice.

Jeri Martin was kindly spared the knowledge of the trial outcome. Steve and Ron concluded that Benjamin Brown had to have some prior information about the filming and photographer. It was just too coincidental that he "just happened" to buy Jeri's TV. Most likely, nobody except Brown would ever know.

* * *

The last year of college, Ron took a part-time job with a major wedding-portrait photography firm in the Bay area and had advanced to a respected administrative position. Upon graduation, it had been planned for him to open two branch studios in nearby cities, partially franchised, partial owned by Ron. With help from Mom plus all the Lmuma money that had been wisely invested, Ron could now claim 50% ownership in the new businesses. Success was coming at him from all directions; perhaps coming too fast.

Chapter Two ~ Father Larry

After the first year, Ron was already beginning to weary from the two studios. True, he enjoyed the management aspect and the respect he could earn from his employees, but he felt handicapped; his talents being wasted in the hum-drum of routine weddings and portraits. He started looking for more challenge.

It came one day from the most unlikely source, in the form of Larry Martin, recently released from Federal prison; yes, Larry Martin, the father Ron believed to have been dead until his encounter with the computer librarian the previous year.

It started with a phone call from the Sausalito police department.

"Ron Martin?" queried the voice, "This is Sgt. Perkins from the downtown precinct."

"Yes, how may I help you?"

"We've got a drunk in the tank who claims to be your father. Do you know a Lawrence Martin? He's asking for bail money."

Ron cursed under his breath.

After an overly long pause, Sgt. Perkins asked, "Sir, are you still there?"

"Yes," said Ron, recovering. "How long have you had him?"

"A little over 24-hours. He just woke up."

"I thought he was still in the pen," offered Ron. Do you know anything about that?"

"No," said the Sgt. "Are you coming down?"

Ron answered in the affirmative and hung up the phone.

There are memorable moments that happen every now and then in everybody's life; they are never the same; sometimes anxious, not always good. Ron felt a chill and an immediate conflict. *Could he help this man who had never contributed a dime to his growth? Did he even want to know him, let alone talk to him?*

This was one of those rare moments of conflict and Ron wondered why he had said "yes" to the policeman.

My God, did you have to send him to me? What can I say to him?

It occurred to Ron that God indeed knew what He was doing, and did indeed send Larry. Ron knew that he had no choice but to follow the lead and see where it went.

Turning his next three portrait sittings over to an assistant, Ron pointed his '49 Chevrolet hatchback toward the center of town, six miles away. It was late afternoon and traffic was heavy and moving slow.

He suddenly remembered a long forgotten incident. Back at Christian Brothers School, Brother Felix, the boarder's prefect awakened him in the middle of the night for an urgent phone call. He was escorted to the phone up in the front office, and left alone in the half light.

"Hello?" Ron queried.

Silence

"Is that you, Mom?"

A gravelly voice with a deep slur said, "Ron? (pause) This is your father. How are you?"

"Huh?"

The voice sounded very far away, "This is your father..."

Ron thought that he was dreaming, hung up the phone and walked back to his dormitory, fell into bed and promptly forgot the whole incident, until now.

Funny that I should recall that right now, he thought. He pulled in to park at the cop shop. A light drizzle was falling through the fog. Twilight was waning and street lights were coming on all around him. Ron felt confused, needing to think and in no hurry. He sat there in his car in the dark seeking time. All thought vanished and he allowed his mind to wander.

Back at Christian Brothers, the boys had figured out how to cheat Ma Bell out of her telephone change. They quickly learned how the only payphone would accept Neco candy wafers in lieu of nickels. After gumming up the works, the phone company replaced it with a newer model and phone calls dropped until some wise kid figured out the turn dials were nothing but a series of clicks, which could be duplicated by clicking the cradle up and down in rapid succession. Until the procedure was perfected, a lot of wrong numbers were reached. It was probably the only dishonest thing Ron could remember doing.

Now he was faced with a much more serious problem. If his father needed charity, there was no question that Ron would give it. He was more concerned with meeting the man face to face; not knowing if he wanted answers to many questions or not.

Might as well get it over with. Ron entered the police station and asked for Sgt. Perkins.

* * *

Lawrence B. Martin was well known to the Sausalito police. He'd spent half a dozen different nights in jail, usually for drunkenness but occasionally for vagrancy or disturbing the peace. He was an alcoholic with a short fuse and no money. On this night, he was relatively sober, slouching on a corner cot. His grey-white hair was straight and tousled over a narrow sallow face sporting a week's growth of beard. Brown eyes were sunken deep into his skull. His small weak frame supported filthy sun tans and a torn checkered shirt. He wore no shoes and his socks allowed large toes to peek through the holes.

Larry looked up when he heard the guard rattle his keys. Behind him stood a handsome tall young man who seemed to be staring straight into Larry's soul.

When the iron door screeched open, Larry slid off the cot and extended a quivering hand to the newcomer. Both were visibly aware of the palsied shaking.

"Ron Martin?" Larry was first to speak.

Ron nodded, turning over in his mind how pitiful this shell of the man looked.

Before Ron could speak, Larry continued, "This is one hell of a way for father and son to meet for the first time. I am so utterly embarrassed, but I have no one else to turn to for help." His eyes were pleading and moist with tears.

Ron turned to the guard, "What is the bail situation?"

"No bail," replied the officer, "He's free to go, but only if you can keep him off the street. Otherwise, he'll be bound over to County rehab."

"Well, Pop," Ron said with sarcasm, "I guess we're going to get acquainted. I've a spare bed in my apartment; no booze, deal?

"Deal," replied Larry, fingers crossed behind his back.

Ron continued to have qualms about this stranger in his house and constantly had the need to convince himself that the wiry little man was his own flesh and blood. There was no love, no respect, nothing between them. It was only Ron's charitable spirit at work; he'd dry out, feed and get this guy a job; he'd loan him some clothes; then, get him out of his life.

Ron had another think coming; just as it appeared that God had other ideas as well.

Larry was a convicted felon, what one might call a mild-mannered crook. He was never a violent man, though he had been penned up with murderers and rapists. All convicted felons, whether violent or non-violent, bore the same stigma of "ex-con."

Ron's first step was to get Larry bathed, shaved and into some clean clothes. A scraggly shrunken soul sat before him and Ron knew nothing he had would fit. Sometime tomorrow he would have to take Larry to be fitted with some decent clothes. The next step would be to find him a job.

"How long since you've eaten?" he asked Larry, whose eyes were roaming around the room, especially the upper cupboards.

"Three days, maybe," replied the old man.

Ron, following his eyes, reminded him, "No booze." The rheumy glaze reappeared and Larry seemed to shrink even more.

The apartment was a roomy three level condo on the waterfront of Richardson Bay. Across the Bay a little over a mile away was Belvedere Island containing upscale homes slightly higher priced than those of Sausalito. Beautiful Angel Island State Park could be seen peeking out just beyond Belvedere and the Tiburon Peninsula.

To the south, the view widened to golden San Francisco. When the fog was absent, Alcatraz Island screamed out in stark contrast to the beauty around it.

On this night, millions of lights twinkled like fairy dust on all sides of the bay. Larry strolled over to the picture window while Ron got busy preparing dinner.

"Anything you can't, or shouldn't eat?" he called to the old man.

"Nope. Anything will do, thanks."

Ron made mental note of this first mention of thanks or gratitude for anything he had done so far. No matter what his Christian conscience would dictate in the future, Ron had doubts if he would ever be able to accept Larry on a permanent basis, let alone, feel any love for him.

He fixed a healthy dinner of chicken stir-fry and a green chef's salad, including extra egg, meat and cheese, as it appeared Larry was run-down from lack of protein.

They ate in silence.

When Ron started to clear the table, Larry said, "Can I help?"

"Sure," Ron replied, "Do you want to wash, or dry?"

Larry would dry dishes and put them away, and conversation was finally open.

"What kind of a job should we look for?" asked Ron. "Mom told me you used to be an accountant."

"That would be good. I used to keep books for the warden, too. How is your mom?"

And the ice was broken.

"My bookkeeper is looking for extra help." Offered Ron, "Shall we try him in the morning?

Ron didn't sleep well that night, chiefly because he was unsure of his new house guest. Larry was up, prowling around the condo at least three times during the night and Ron lay there hoping his dad would not steal from the hand that fed him. Fortunately, there was no alcohol of any kind in the apartment. If Ron heard the front door open, he would get up and follow Larry, otherwise he lay in bed listening to the night sounds and worrying.

* * *

Walter of Cascade Accounting was out of town for a couple of days, so the job interview was postponed. Meanwhile, Ron's studio was in a panic. Someone had double booked two weddings and he was scrambling to get a qualified cameraman from one of the other studios. That didn't leave much time to think about Larry, alone all day in the condo. The weddings were both the next day and Ron felt swamped.

He was two hours late getting home that night and the worst of his fears were realized when he found his front door unlocked and no sign of Larry. *Guess I should have offered him a key.*

Larry staggered in, quite drunk, at about 2 A.M.

"This isn't going to work..." Ron opened the conversation, like he was talking to a young teen.

"Tomorrow..." slurred Larry, "I'm too sick to talk, tonight..." He staggered into his bedroom.

Ron wondered if he had made a mistake or if perhaps the situation could turn out more positive. Life on this earth is similar to an undeveloped photograph. His thoughts turned into a pragmatic parable:

Under a darkroom safelight everything is gray. My hands are drained of life. Stop bath settles in my nostrils and stomach like formaldehyde. Maybe that's the way it should be, because what a photograph does is embalm something into a framed box and stilled forever.

A darkroom is a place where our failures come to light: a wrong combination of f-stop and shutter speed, a misjudgment of depth of field or right exposure. Or we make new errors. We don't check the temperature of the chemicals; something spills; we turn on the white light too soon; or somebody flushes a toilet next door changing temperature balance of the wash.

But sometimes, everything happens just as it should. I rinse the print in the darkroom's red light, and there in my hands is the perfect photograph I hoped for.

Ron had known other alcoholics and not one ever recovered. Could it be any different for Larry?

The next day was Saturday, and after the weddings, Ron came home to a repeat of the previous day. It was still daylight. The third neighborhood tavern Ron checked produced a depressed and beer sodden Larry, propped alone on a high stool.

"Where'd you get money for beer, Pop?" Ron was angry and his demeanor showed it.

"I.. cannot.. tell a lie," Larry answered, "I... borrowed some coins ...out of your ...desk."

"My Mercury dime collection?"

"Well, uh..."

"So, you are still a thief?" Ron accused.

"No I'm not... I'll put 'em back. I jus needed a drink."

Ron's decision was instant.

"C'mon, we're going for a ride."

"Where to?" asked Larry, draining his beer.

"You'll see."

* * *

The Sundown AA Ranch was north on Hwy 101 just outside San Rafael. It was the newest in private dependency clinics. There was little conversation during the 10 mile trip. Larry was feeling penitent and Ron was angry. Pulling into the parking lot, Ron spoke for the first time. "You do know why I'm doing this?"

"Yeah, 'spose so."

"Walt at Cascade Accounting won't want to talk to you until you're dried out."

"Yeah, 'spose so."

"And you have to have and keep a job," Ron continued.

"Yeah, 'spose so," repeated Larry.

Sundown AA staff admitted Larry, confining him to a four week treatment period.

"How much does this cost," asked Larry, just as Ron started to leave.

"Plenty."

"I can't pay you back."

"Don't worry about it, except to replace my Mercury dime collection."

"Thanks, son."

After Ron got home, the real depression set in. It was the first time Larry called him son and he wished that he hadn't.

In most circles, Ron Martin was thought to be an eligible and wealthy bachelor. He had plenty of lady friends, but felt that running two studios was a burden that could not be confused by the addition of the permanent responsibilities of marriage. Perhaps he would wed someday, but not now. His family life was otherwise limited. Jeri, his mother, tired of the retirement home confinement and bought a park model mobile home in Phoenix, Arizona. The only other family was Larry, and he unwanted.

Ron suspected that any mention to Mom about taking Larry in, could result in losing her altogether. She was that bitter. It was an unforgiving bitterness that Ron prayed daily she would not take to her grave. He firmly believed what Jesus said in the book of Matthew, *"...If you forgive those who sin against you, your heavenly Father will forgive you. But if you refuse to forgive others, your Father will not forgive your sins."* (Ma 6:14-15 NLT).

Midweek, Sundown AA staff called Ron at the studio. "We've stopped two attempts to breakout," they told him. "If he keeps resisting, we can't guarantee continued confinement."

"He committed himself," reminded Ron, "but if you need a Court order to hold him, Sgt. Perkins of the Sausalito police has the judge all lined up. Larry's only freedom is contingent upon you keeping him off the street and out of the bars."

Ron waited for a response, hearing none, he continued, "Now, if you'd rather give up your fancy fee, I'll come get him and turn him over to County Rehab, where the judge wanted to send him in the first place."

The threat worked, Ron hung up the phone and returned to a mess of other problems in the studios.

Things were changing for Ron. He was thinking more and more that he had jumped into the portrait-wedding studio too fast. His heart had always been fascinated with capturing the beauty of more inanimate objects, flowers, scenery, wildlife; objects of grace and majesty that could not talk back. He was a first class photographer; a free spirit needing a daily change of challenge.

When the pressure at the studio let up, he would find himself daydreaming, more and more often. He regretted the waste of time and credits in college. His minors had been in anthropology and archeology and his childhood dreams were of finding lost Aztec or Mayan treasure. During his third year of college, he applied for and was accepted into a Nationale Geographica excursion training program. His sponsor was a kind professor, a Dr. Chester Crowell. Ron remembered with sadness how disappointed Dr. Crowell was when Ron cancelled his application in order to accept the studio job.

"Nationale Geographica will be losing the potential of a fine photographer," he said, "If you ever change your mind, you know how to reach me. Good luck!"

Things were steadily deteriorating at the studio and tension was growing between Ron and his employees.

Larry seemed to be a new person after fulfilling his one month term at the Sundown AA Ranch. After the first week, he had settled in for some serious rehabilitation.

A day or two after his release, Ron took a clean, smiling and sober Larry to the interview with Walter, the owner of Cascade Accounting Service. Walt and Larry hit it right off and Larry was hired, to begin work the next day.

"Let's celebrate," suggested Larry as they left the office.

"No way!"

"Aw, come on, son. I'll buy," insisted Larry, "but it will have to be Starbucks."

Ron found a studio apartment only two blocks from the accounting office and showed it to Larry.

"This will do fine," said Larry, "I hope it is still vacant when I get my first paycheck."

"How about I pay first and last and move you in right away?" said Ron.

"Thanks, son."

There, he said it again! This time, Ron reacted with a hug.

Later that day, Ron moved Larry into the small apartment. He furnished bed linens and whatever kitchen stuff Larry thought he might need. Ron forked over two months rent and co-signed for all the utilities. He moved in a small television, stereo and bookcase full of books. Larry was beaming, happier than Ron had ever seen him, but Ron was still worried.

Was Larry cured enough to be trusted living alone, with the constant temptation to buy booze?

It wasn't long before he had an answer. Larry reported for work the next day, and Walt called Ron with stories of praise and thanks.

Ron felt he had done all he could for his dad and could now turn his full attention to other pressing matters, namely how to get out of the dead-end he had placed himself in by buying the photo studio.

When his presence was not demanded by a weekend wedding or bar mitzvah, Ron found himself more and more in the company of friends out on hiking field trips, naming birds and photographing the raw beauty of nature. At these times he felt a peace and a closeness to God; a peace like no other. He joined the local Native Plant Society, the Cascadian Mountain club, Audubon, Green Peace, and the National Wildlife Foundation. Evenings were often volunteer time given to outdoor youth groups, such as the Boy Scouts. He looked for any opportunity to share his love of nature and to promote ecological conservation.

* * *

Alcoholics are seldom cured as easily as Larry's apparent successful journey. Most people with addictions are masters of deception. There are unimaginable and ingenious places to hide drug substance and facial emotions to fool the most astute case worker.

Social workers assigned by the Court, working with Sundown AA staff followed Larry for months, frequenting asking questions of his fellow workers, neighbors and landlord. At the end of three months, their reports were all positive and some of them scratched their heads in unbelief. It appeared that Lawrence Martin was permanently cured and "on the wagon" for life. They all closed their case files and moved on. The judge sent a congratulatory and positive letter to Ron.

One day, Ron stopped by Cascade Accounting to take Larry to lunch and found his cubicle empty and his desk cleared off.

"Where's Dad?" he asked the receptionist.

"Let me buzz Walt," she said, "He wanted to talk with you if you came in."

Walt was in conference with some corporate clients and Ron had to wait. After five minutes, Walt took a short break from his meeting in order to talk with Ron.

"He called in sick, this morning," Walt said, "and he missed three days last week, also."

"You should have called me."

"I would have, Ron, but he said it was only a cold and he was taking time off so as not to spread it around to the other accountants." Walt had over forty-five others working.

It was a cold, bone-chilling damp drizzle that only the Bay area can produce, when Ron knocked on Larry's door. He could hear opera music playing inside, probably loud enough to generate complaints from neighbors.

He knocked three times. Getting no answer, he tried the door, which opened easily to his touch. The music flooded out to the street.

Along with the music, came a flood of stale alcohol and cigarette smoke (or was it marijuana?).

Ron's heart was saddened even before he saw Larry cuddled up on his day-bed with a strange lady. They were half naked and quite drunk.

He turned the stereo off and tried to waken Larry, who only stirred and groaned, then drifted back into la-la land. The woman, however, sat up on the edge of the bed, exposing her bare breasts.

Ron threw her a bath towel so she could cover up, and said, "Who are you?"

"You must be Ron." she slurred, "My name is Toni and I moved in here to take care of Larry."

She was a sagging mid 50s, but looked 80 years old with straight long grey hair. Her overly applied makeup was smeared and her teeth looked like an unpainted picket fence with every other picket missing. Sober and with a closed mouth, she might be slightly pretty.

"Is this how you take care of him, by getting drunk?" Ron was disgusted. He poured what booze he could find down the drain.

"I've got to get some fresh air," he almost screamed at her, "Have him call me when he wakes up." Outside, the cold drizzle hit Ron like a snowball and he realized he had left his coat inside.

Well, she'll need it more than me, he thought as he drove off.

Chapter Three ~ Geographica

It was a call from Dr. Chester Crowell that broke the back of Ron's depression. Back in college, Ron had applied for work with Nationale Geographica through his friend Dr. Crowell, but had later rescinded his application in lieu of taking the photo studio offer.

His love for the studio life had long since waned. He would jokingly tell his Native Plant Society friends on fieldtrips how he hated fussy brides and primping self-indulging models.

"I've never heard a wildflower complain." was one of his favorite lines used to justify his desire to change professions. "A feeding beast could care less if the truffles ordered for the wedding reception come from South France or Northern Scotland."

Dr. Crowell was forming up an expedition deep into the Yucatan and wanted to give Ron another chance.

Pleased he had studied archeology and anthropology in college, Ron gave Dr. Crowell and affirmative answer.

"How long do I have in order to sell my share in the studio?" asked Ron.

"With training and preparation I'd say we should be ready to mount the full expedition in about eighteen months."

Larry, of course, fell hard off the wagon and was drinking steadily with his new found "friend", Toni. Somehow he managed to put in two and a half days each week at work. It was enough, with Toni's contribution to pay the rent and keep them in booze. Toni made a few dollars dressing hair for neighbor ladies.

Ron knew he had done all he could short of full hospital commitment, and until Larry had another run-in with the Law; he would remain a free man, doing whatever he chose.

* * *

The decrepit DC-3 circled the ancient Yucatan city of Merida, barely visible through a dark brown smudge of air pollution. Ron Martin stared out his window and frowned; his first sight of the land of the Mayans? It wasn't a very inspiring view.

"Feces," said the lady from the seat across the aisle. She was leaning over him, craning her neck for a look out his window. She was younger than he was, red-haired and beautiful. Ron had noticed her slim tight figure several times during the flight but had been too bashful to open a conversation.

"Pardon me?" Ron answered. He was in his late twenties, sandy-haired and dressed like an explorer.

"Feces," she repeated. "That's the first thing you notice when you get off the plane. The whole town smells like crap, an open sewer."

Great opening sweetheart! Ron thought. "Thanks for sharing," he said.

The lady grinned, her whole face brightening. "Every city has its own particular smell – have you ever noticed that? Cairo smells like urine. Paris smells like an old ladies shoes. Edinburgh smells like scotch whiskey. Green Bay like ripe cheese and London like old wet cigars."

"I've only been in San Francisco, Los Angeles and New York airports," replied Ron

"That would be sulfur mud flats, a giant car ashtray and rotting garbage, in that order," she said with a twinkle and a laugh.

"Amazing!" he said, "I'm Ron Martin, on a International Geographica assignment."

"Sayra al Schcla, I'm pleased to meet you."

"Yours is a most unusual name," replied Ron. "It's romantic, almost poetic."

"It's Arabic. I work for the Egyptian Consulate," she smiled most sweetly. "I'm here to deliver a diplomatic pouch to the Mexican legation at Merida."

She leaned over again for a last look out the window, her breast brushing his forehead.

Ron could smell her exotic perfume and feel the heat from her body.

"Where are you going, next?" she asked.

"When the rest of the crew arrives," he said, "we'll head inland to the mountains on the south Yucatan Quinana-Roo border. There's a train to Tzucacab, then horseback and donkey cart and finally we will hike the last twenty miles through jungle."

"What in the world for?"

Ron could think of no reason to evade the question; he was not aware there could be anything secret about his expedition. "A new tribe has been discovered, living completely apart from any civilization. Hidden back in the mountains the way they are, it is believed they could be a true blood remnant of the extinct Mayan peoples."

"That would shake up the scientific world," she replied, boldly adding, "Are you free for dinner?"

* * *

At the train cabana in Tzucacab, Ron told his companions "Wait here, while I find our horses." He headed in the direction of the town square.

There was a sudden gust of wind and Ron squinted into the small hurricane of blowing dust. He blinked and cleared his throat and blinked again, eyes watering. He smelled the market before he saw it, a rank sweet scent of death and offal that cut through the ever-present stink of rotting garbage and raw sewerage that flowed along the narrow gutters. He heard the market as well, a mad mixture of sheep and goats and snuffling pigs and crowing roosters. Dogs barked and monkeys chattered.

He was looking for a Guatemalan named Sergio in order to arrange for the next stage of their journey. Ron had no reason to watch his back trail, so failed to notice the tall European who rode the train all the way from Merida and who now walked a discreet distance behind him. His face was immediately forgettable. It was a round face, waxy in texture, without a hint of any passions, set with narrow eyes behind steel framed spectacles; a face so featureless it gave the impression of not being there. A precise bristly moustache went with his precise, toy-soldier gestures; the only evidence of his Teuton ancestry. His hair was combed in greasy snakes across his scalp.

When Ron found his wrangler, Sergio, the tall European slipped unseen behind a market stall, but close enough to overhear any conversation between Ron and the wrangler.

Horses and wagons were inventoried and driven back to the train depot to load expedition supplies.

The Expedition leader, Dr. Chester Crowell was not scheduled to arrive for two days. In his absence, Ron was in charge of two International Geographica interns and Sergio the Wrangler who would also serve as Chief Guide.

The Interns were Hugo Bunch, a Maya student, and Nick Peters, a Mesoamerican researcher from USC

When their three wagons were packed and secured, Ron turned his attention to the village's little hostel, a one-story adobe structure of six small rooms, each with a loft reached by a rickety pole ladder. Each loft contained two hammocks. There were no beds. For three and a half Pesos, Ron rented one room for two nights. Sergio would sleep with and guard the wagons, Hugo and Nick in the loft, while Ron rolled out his mat on the dirt floor.

With two days to kill and their gear secure, Ron felt like a little recreation. His trusty Roliflex in hand, he announced he wanted to check out the local wildlife, "Anybody want to tag along?"

"Sure, I need to stretch my legs," said Nick, "I'll go with you."

Nick Peters was a muscular, well-proportioned post-graduate who had played three years of Trojan football. He was full of questions about nature. Ron took an immediate liking and adopted him as a protégé.

They wandered through the village to a large white water river, noting birds and native plants and photographing as they went. Nick was like a six year old with a million questions.

Ron tutored Nick on the river, explaining about eddy lines and hydraulics, as well as the watershed's plant and wildlife; how mountain laurel leaves were glossy and rhododendron were not; how mink tracks included the claws, but otter tracks showed only the paw pads.

When they encountered a new mystery, Ron would simply shrug and say, "We're going to learn together a lot of new stuff about this jungle climate."

"I'm grateful that you are a part of this trip and are so willing to share," Nick said.

"I enjoy sharing with a willing student," said Ron, "We're going to be good for each other."

They hiked on for another hour, deciphering the beauty of the Yucatan jungle.

Ron photographed an ocelot up close and a huge boa constrictor before heading back to the village.

Sergio had hired two native guides, Q'echan and Tixq'al, each versed in different native dialects. These men appeared always to be smiling and very friendly. Their pure white teeth were in stark contrast to their light ebony skin and black hair. Tixq'al bore a scraggly, thin but long beard that wobbled in a funny way whenever he spoke. Q'echan was a little taller and always chewing some kind of a nut and spitting out a vile black juice. Ron wondered how his teeth could be so white. From something he once read, he was reminded of beetle juice.

Next day, Ron tried to get better acquainted with Hugo Bunch, the other intern. But Hugo was a different prototype; he was exactly the opposite personality from Nick. Hugo preferred sitting alone and appeared very introverted. Like Nick, he too was well built and muscular and would be a valuable asset on the expedition. One side of his head was badly scarred including most of an ear missing. Hugo offered no explanation, and none of them had the courage to ask. When Hugo did speak, which was seldom, it was more of a beast like growl than a human voice. It was reported he was taking a sabbatical from Columbia University where he was a post-graduate protégé of John Lloyd Stevens, a nineteenth century explorer and expert on Mayan culture.

Hugo had been hired by Dr. Crowell, but could not produce any positive references from Columbia University.

They passed one more day in the stifling jungle heat before Chester Crowell arrived to begin the expedition.

The trail east out of Tzucacab was supposed to lead to the imaginary border between the Mexican states of Yucatan and Quinatana-Roo, estimated to be about 40 miles, somewhere beyond an unnamed, but huge snake shaped lake. Aerial photography has shown the lake to be over seventy miles long, shaped like an "S", but less than a mile wide. Perhaps it was an ancient river bed. The unknown tribe was supposed to be living in uncharted jungle on the other side.

Chester Crowell was a short overweight man with white mustache and white mutton chops. Ron had never met the man face to face; had only known him as a telephone friend. So, their meeting was somewhat of a shock to Ron, who had always imagined him as a kind old professor, somewhat taller. His monocle made him appear kind hearted, but his eyes would dart quickly everywhere, giving the impression of knowing exactly what anyone was thinking. He was commanding and an obvious leader, but also a disciplinarian, to be feared by those under his command. There was also a sinister quality about him that Ron could not quite put a finger on.

That evening, Sergio sought out Ron who was sitting down by the river, camera in hand. In broken English he explained that something was not right.

"The hombre, Hugo tell me go away," he started, "b'cause heem guard d wagons. I say okay, 'n go piss 'n get somtin to eat. Later cum back but not seen. Beeg tall hombre stranger crawling under d tarps lookin' fer somtin. Hugo helping heem. Seem strange. I cum tell you."

"Who is watching the wagons, now?" asked Ron.

"Q'echan," replied Sergio.

"Thank you for telling me," said Ron. "Tell no one else, for now, okay?"

"Okay."

Ron considered the situation by turning thoughts over and over in his mind.

Who could the tall stranger be? What could he and Hugo have been searching for?

He decided that he would have to keep an eye on Hugo, but didn't consider any of this important enough to trouble Dr. Crowell.

On the following morning, the small expedition wound its way through the dusty streets of Tzucacab. There were three wagons, each pulled by two horses. Sergio and Ron in the lead followed by Chester, Hugo and Tixq'al. Bringing up the rear was Q'echan and Nick. Seven souls, six horses and three wagons in all. Most of the cargo consisted of trinkets to give or trade with the natives. One wagon was loaded with tents, personal gear and camp making necessities. Another contained food, hay for the horses and tools.

Because travelers were so rare, natives were always aware of any movement and seemed to appear from nowhere to watch any procession. Some of the younger ones waved and some of the old ladies held their rosary beads in prayer as if to bless the trip.

Was it an omen?

Within a mile, the wagon road turned into a narrow track with dense jungle infringing on all sides. Vines dangled from overhead and the men riding the wagons had to dodge and duck to avoid a slap in the face. Some of the vines sported long sharp thorns, capable of destroying an eye. Once, a little green snake fell into one of the wagons.

Tixq'al was instantly on his feet, hollering something in his native tongue. He stomped and kicked as fast as lighting. The snake went flying out of the wagon bed, back into the jungle.

Sergio stopped the lead wagon and spoke with Tixq'al.

Then so the others could hear, "Bad, he say. Mucho muerto! No cure."

The wagons moved on, more watchful and Ron was thinking, *Another omen?*

Their progress was slow the first day, covering only eight miles. Camp that night was made in the center of the trail; armed with machetes, the men slashed additional space from the jungle growth.

There was little in the jungle palatable for horses, so Sergio broke open half a bale of their hay and a bag of oats.

All day, Ron took notes and many photographs and after camp was set up, he had time to take a closer look at the fauna and flora.

"Can this jungle get any denser?" he asked Dr. Crowell.

"In a couple of days, we should break out of the rain-forest into open savannah."

he answered, and if it is a clear day, we'll see our goal, the three spires of Chiapeche."

"That's strange," Ron said, "I thought we were going south east. The Chiapeche are south."

"Crowell flinched, cleared his throat and said, "Sorry, my mistake." He walked away signaling the end of the conversation.

They had been traveling through fairly level land averaging about 100 feet above sea-level, but now had reached a slight escarpment of low hills, some up to 700 feet in elevation.

This world of the ancient Maya contained around 8,000 species of plants with flowers. Geological faults had caused many earthquakes which changed the land by compressing it, elevating and sinking. This combination determined such a wide variety of vegetation. Moisture and climatic conditions caused dense and entangled plant growth during the entire year, there being little change of seasons as we know in more northern climes.

Anyone who wandered far off the trail, could be instantly lost. The overhead canopy was so dense, no sunlight penetrated to the forest floor, and a man could not tell directions without being able to locate the position of the sun. Mosses grew on all side of trees, offering no help.

Ron was in paradise, wondering if he might run out of film too early. The bird life was spectacular as the area supported over 900 species, with more being discovered every year.

Dark comes rapidly in the tropics; fires were built for cooking and for light. Howler monkeys, noisy all day, were now quiet; replaced by strange grunts and growls of unknown jungle creatures.

Dr. Crowell insisted on directing sleeping order.

"I planned to bed down on the wagon," Ron complained.

"You'll sleep in a tent, with Nick and Sergio," he commanded. "Hugo and I will take the other tent, and the Indians together in a third. No one will be outside, and that's final!"

What difference does it make, Ron thought, *Chester Crowell isn't himself!* Did he bear watching? Time would tell. That night passed without further incident.

Passage through the dense hot humid jungles made for slow passage. Each day gained between six and eight miles. At noon on the third day, they broke out of the jungle onto the sandy banks of a long narrow lake. The lake was some 70 miles in length according to reconnaissance aerial photos examined earlier. Fortunately, their course brought them to within a mile of the southern end of the lake and that mile passed quicker than any other when the wagons were driven on the hard-packed sand.

Leaving the lake, their route led back into the dense jungle. At camp that night, Chester warned everybody to keep a sharp vigil, as they were now inside the borders of the mysterious tribe of their quest.

The twilight of the fourth dawn came suddenly, and when camp was broken, they were trudging forward again, south east by the compass.

Toward mid day, a definite change in the foliage began to be apparent. Now and then, the lush jungle would thin and patches of sun warmed their dank spirits. But as soon as the sun appeared, the jungle would regain dominance, plunging them back into twilight. The jungle would then close back in on them like a wet sponge.

Ron had an uneasy feeling that they were being followed. He kept glancing over their back trail. Once he thought he saw motion, but could not be sure.

When they stopped for a brief lunch, they were in the largest clearing yet; it was almost a meadow, filled with sunshine and tall grasses. More animals than usual were apparent in both the undergrowth and trees.

Ron photographed a jaguar stalking a white-tailed deer. Peccaries, iguanas, rabbits, tapirs and monkeys were everywhere.

Dr. Crowell insisted on changing the wagon order for the balance of the day. He and Hugo now took the lead. Sergio and the two Natives were in the middle, while Ron and Nick brought up the rear.

"I thought we hired Sergio and his friends to be guides," said Nick. "So why is Chester leading?"

"I've wondered that also," said Ron. "Hugo certainly doesn't know the area."

At the next open meadow, they stopped in order to rest the horses. Chester and Hugo wandered off several hundred yards, using the excuse to stretch their legs.

Ron was following the action of a strange bird through a high powered telescopic lens when he noticed Chester reaching up to pick a red flower from a vine. After he lost the bird, he realized there was something wrong with the picture he had just seen. Dr. Crowell had never been interested in blossoms, and on second thought, Ron realized the flower was the wrong shade of red. When he focused back on the distant scene, Chester and Hugo were examining the item, like they were reading a note. *Impossible* thought Ron and shrugged it off.

When the wagons started off again through the open savanna, Ron thought they were steering a little more to the south, not much but out here, a couple of degrees variation could result in ending up miles away from the intended destination.

"Is it just me, or have we changed course?" Ron asked Nick.

"I feel it too, but our leader knows what he's doing."

Ron didn't tell him yet about seeing Chester and the red note.

The rest of the day, the landscape remained savanna like, interspersed with brush and evergreen shrubs. An occasional sapodilla or mahogany tree towered 80 feet above the plain.

The terrain was gradually rising, occasionally interspersed with rocky outcrops from some ancient lava flow. Hills to the south rose four to five hundred feet and look like they were clothed with some type of pines. Visibility was almost unlimited.

When the sun was two hours above the horizon, the dark green of lush jungle again appeared ahead of them as well as to the north and the south. They were being led into a vegetative "box canyon" and as the call of the jungle creatures grew nearer, Chester called for a stop.

"We make camp here," he said, "Same sleeping arrangements as before. Tomorrow, we enter the jungle again."

The need for water conservation was on them, as no stream had been found since the lake and the water barrel was quite low. Ron warned everyone of this.

The day had been a tiring one, as all hands were required to spend the morning whacking jungle, making paths wide enough for the wagons to pass; the evening rest was welcome, and as soon as tents were deployed, snores could be heard.

In the prelight of dawn, Ron awoke. An uneasy feeling was gnawing at him and he lay in his sleeping bag trying to identify the emotion. Sergio and Nick were snoring in loud harmony. Maybe that was what wakened him. A wind had come up in the night and he noticed the sides of the tent were rising and falling. Then he noticed the flicker of flames.

That's funny, he thought, *the campfires should have gone out long ago. ...FIRE!* He was on his feet in a flash.

Jerking the tent flap open, he hollered to his companions, "Get up! The wagons are on fire!"

And they were, but only two. It soon became apparent the third wagon and all the horses were gone. Gone too was Chester and

Hugo, apparently gone in the middle of the night, abandoning five men with no food, no water and no equipment except two tents and the clothes on their back. The two wagons were now reduced to glowing coals and all their supplies with them.

Chapter Four ~ Jungle Heat

"Perhaps they'll be back," suggested Nick, knowing how ridiculous the words were even before they left his mouth.

"If they comin' back," said Sergio, "Why dey take all my horses?"

"They're not coming back," Ron said, "If they burned our stuff that sounds like a pretty final 'good-bye' to me."

"We be good as dead," added Sergio.

The two Natives, Q'echan and Tixq'al returned from a brief scouting mission and talked to Sergio. Their native language was a Nahuatl hybrid of the ancient Aztec, and only Sergio could communicate with them.

"Dey say wagon tracks go sout, den meet up w' another wagon, still there."

"How far?" asked Ron.

"About one an half kilometers."

Ron's plan was to gather up everything of any use, take inventory, and then go take a look at the mysterious new wagon.

Meanwhile, he instructed Sergio to ask his two side-kicks to hunt down some game, and also to look for water.

Q'echan and Tixq'al seemed to like the idea of hunting. They promptly cut some long spears and sharpened them with a machete retrieved from the ashes, and bounded off into the brush, happy as children.

"What do you make of there being another wagon?" asked Nick

"First," said Ron, "It would appear Chester and/or Hugo made earlier arrangements to meet somebody else here.

"How would they know exactly where?"

Sergio spoke up, showing them three small axe slashes on a nearby tree; a signal easy to see if one was looking for it.

Then Ron remembered the red note incident, and it all started to come together. He mumbled, "I had warnings something was afoot, but I ignored them."

The three counseled briefly about what they should do next. By Ron's calculations, they were well across the border into Quintana Roo thereby much closer to the coast of the Caribbean and probable civilization. Trudging back through the jungle to Tzucacab would be suicide.

"Well, we're not quite lost," joked Nick, "But we're on foot, with no water, no food and a long way from anywhere."

While waiting for the hunters to return, packs were examined and contents divided into three piles: (1) Items absolutely essential for survival, (2) Items of probable survival value, and (3) Personal stuff having no communal value. This included Ron's cameras and a hundred rolls of film, half of it exposed.

"The pictures are too valuable to just destroy," said Ron. "I think a small plane would be able to land here, assuming we ever get out."

It was decided to take one tent with them. All five could crowd inside if needed, the other tent would be used to wrap and protect stuff too valuable to carry that had no survival value, to possibly be picked up later.

In their personal packs they counted up three canteens, one compass, some pocket knives, about 10 energy bars, a bag of Tootsie Rolls and a small jar of peanuts.

The ashes of the wagons produced a small steel handled hatchet, a folding saw, a couple small aluminum pots and another machete.

After another hour, the hunters returned with only one small coney. They would save it for later.

The Indians, Q'echan and Tixq'al carried no packs, didn't use sleeping bags, didn't care to sleep indoors, in fact, and didn't even have shoes. They would take turns carrying the tent. Ron, Nick and Sergio each had backpacks to carry what little supplies they had gathered between them.

It was about midday when they started out, following the tracks of the hijacked wagon.

Ron hoped the quick side trip would find clues and information; he hoped to discover why Hugo and Chester chose to abandon their mission and their crew.

True to the report, about a mile due south, they found another wagon. It was not the same wagon Chester and Hugo had been driving, but was much smaller, more like a donkey cart. Tracks indicated it arrived from the west and was pulled by one horse. There were footprints of at least three men, apparently transporting several heavy objects from the small cart to the larger wagon. Tracks of the wagon and seven horses then headed in a southerly direction. The leftover cart had been left with a smashed wheel and a broken axle; deliberately sabotaged.

"I think he intends to have us die," suggested Nick.

"That would be murder," said Ron, "But what's the motive?"

"We too tough to die," quipped Sergio, "We find way out!"

"Right! All we have to do is believe we can do and to keep our heads," said Ron, "I'm going to fall on my knees for prayer to my Father in Heaven. Any who want to join in, please do so." And three men knelt in humility.

The Indians watched in awe.

Five men headed due east, by Nick's compass, filled with high hope of reaching the ocean before the jungle could claim their lives.

* * *

After three days tramping through the steaming jungle, there was not the slightest indication they might be close to reaching people, let alone the seashore.

One day Ron stared at Nick's compass, cursed and in a rare fit of rage, slung the thing deep into the jungle.

"It's been tampered with," he cried, "and reset over 90 degrees off."

No sunlight penetrated to the floor of the jungle and without a good compass, directions were pure guesswork.

Moral was at an all time low and something akin to despair was setting in. Ron and Nick were both slowed by fever and walked as if in a twilight dream.

Occasionally, a teaspoon or two of water might be found high in the trees, captured in the base of air plants called bromeliads. But something sinister was usually in the water, insect larvae or secretions, probably the cause of the fevers.

The coney had long since been eaten. All they had since was two parrots between them.

Mosquitoes covered bodies, but Ron soon learned if he killed one while it was sucking, the place swelled as if stung by a bee; so it was less painful in the long run to endure the sting and let them drink. Most were near naked as most clothing had rotted or been torn by thorns.

They had no feeling for time. Their legs were deadweights that dragged along, one step and another and another. Any pain had long since gone numb. Vision blurred again and Ron trudged with his head down, following the tracks of the men in front of him. He no longer thought ahead, or even thought much at all. They had all fallen into a merciful trance of half consciousness, moving bodies by reflex and instinct. Ron's tongue had swollen like a cotton boll so that it almost filled his mouth, and at times he felt as if he would choke on it.

He lapsed into a dreamlike state and seemed to float away like some bodiless spirit, back to his Nevada home. He thought that he heard Forrest Williams back at the

Lmuma mile hollering "Fire in the hole." Everybody duck! He then splashed barefoot into a fresh water pond, not realizing what it was.

It was their salvation.

"Water!" exclaimed Nick, the sound falling on others numb and deaf ears. Ron's fog slowly faded before his senses realized it; he was taking a dive face first into the clear and refreshing liquid.

It had been eight days.

Someone climbed a tree, and called down that he saw smoke. Soon afterwards they all heard a shot fired, then a rooster crowing and knew that civilization could not be far off.

Suddenly, fiercely painted natives sprang up out of the brush all around them. Most were armed with spears or bows, but two or three pointed ancient muskets. Their gestures left no doubt that Ron's small group were prisoners.

Attempts at language were futile; they tried English, Spanish, Portuguese, Tehuante and Q'eqchi'. Their captors roughly shoved the five along a well traveled trail leading into a primitive village.

Once in the village, they were jerked apart and each lead into a separate hut bound with vines and left alone.

Ron's prison was dark and no bigger than a pigsty. He had no idea where his comrades were located or even if they were still alive.

After what seemed hours, his hatch was pried open by a huge fat man, naked from the waist up. He wore chains of feathers and animal parts. Assuming him to be a leader or medicine man, Ron again tried communication and learned the man was the Chief and knew a little broken English.

The Chief threatened to hang them all, shouting they were thieving dogs. Ron tried to explain they were lost scientists and offered him a gold chain and asked for a medicine man to attend those who had wounds. The Chief replied that no surgeon was needed because the hangman would soon heal all. But he kept the chain.

Chapter Five ~ Cross and Double Cross

The old crone shared the decrepitude of her lodgings. The skin hung loosely from her skull; pale, dry scalp showed through her thinning hair; her eyes were sunken, hard and glittering behind loose snakeskin-like folds. If age softened what had been hard, it hardened what had been soft, turning her high cheeks gaunt and hollow, her mouth into a cruel slash.

Hers was the face of a survivor.

Ron Martin's bounds had been removed and he was sitting in the midst of this squalor the old crone called her home. He had been condemned to be her slave.

Similar fates had been decreed for the others, and Ron was glad to know they were at least, still alive, being fed and their wounds dressed.

Ron's 'lord & master' was apparently the widow of some high mucky-muck chief or medicine man and was highly respected by her village. Guards were stationed outside the hut and they accompanied Ron on his menial assigned tasks, such as hauling water, burying sewage, etc. Any chance of escape was limited and should he be lucky enough to escape the village, where could he go? They had been so turned around in the jungle with a phony compass, they could now be anywhere on the Yucatan peninsula, or even as far south as Belize or Guatemala.

After several weeks, Ron began to pick up a few words of the native dialect. Nothing remained to remind him of his own civilized culture, except a gold cross and crucifix the old lady wore around her neck. When he motioned a question, she replied with her only word of English.

"Meeshunie," she said.

It took Ron several tries before he finally understood, and he laughed it out loud, "Missionary! Praise God!"

There is always hope, only believe!

And believe he did. Three days later, there were shouts and people running to the opposite end of the village. The old crone motioned him to follow.

Three Catholic monks, dressed in long brown robes and riding burros were making their way through the cheering crowds into the village plaza. It was a scene identical to an artists renditions Ron had seen in museums of the Spanish Conquistadores in 1551, except the monks wore wrist watches.

One of the monks spotted Ron, dismounted his burro and walked over to him.

"*Engleesh?*" he asked.

"*Si!*"

"*Que es llame?*" asked the monk.

"*Me llama es Ron Martin,* and I need help," he finished in English.

"I am Father Paul from Chetumal," the man said in perfect English. "When you failed to report, the Geographica sent out search parties."

"Praise God," said Ron

"Are you all here? ...Dr. Chester?"

"We are all prisoners," said Ron, "and, no, Dr. Chester and Hugo abandoned us five in the middle of the Yucatan."

"We're here to rescue you," said Father Paul, "First I must talk with the Chief."

* * *

"They are not the lost Mayan tribe you were looking for," Father Paul explained, "but only a rebel spin-off from the Surgeo Buitron tribe. We have some converts there, and once we convinced Chief Rutu you were not the thieves he assumed you to be, he agreed to let you all go with his apologies."

Ron, Nick, Sergio, Q'echan and Tixq'al had developed a bond of fellowship and were now riding a donkey cart with the three monks. It would be a half days ride to their Mission at San Christobal a couple of miles north of Chetumal, located on the border between Quintana Roo and Belize. Their thoughts ranged between freedom, sirloin steak, feather beds and dreams of hot showers.

Contrast was the key word in everything they did for the next few days; returning to civilization was more than a dream, it was reality.

Chetumal had a major airport with conveniences equal or perhaps better than Merida where Ron first landed in the Yucatan.

Geographica agreed to supply an immediate rescue mission, thinking Dr. Chester was perhaps lost. Ron chose not to argue with authority, agreeing to lead an expedition, primarily to retrieve his photo gear and film.

When he broached the plan to Sergio and Nick, they agreed immediately to go back with him. Sergio had hopes of recovering his stolen horses.

"Supplies will be on the morning plane from Miami," Ron told them, "and this time we will have firearms, good compasses and powerful radios. Geographica has purchased five horses also for our use."

"Five?" queried Nick.

"Si," answered Sergio, "Me good Indians, Q'echan and Tixq'al go wherever I go."

It was agreed.

Fully provisioned, the five set out in the chill wind of dawn. Before them, they saw the distant hills kindled. Day leaped into the sky. The red rim of the sun rose over the flat shoulders of the eastern Caribbean behind them. Before them in the northwest the world lay still, formless and gray; but even as they looked, the shadows of night melted. The colors of the waking earth returned: gold tipped the tops of palms, green flowed over the tall forests; the white mists shimmering in the water places; and far off to the left, fifty miles or more, blue and purple stood the higher foothills flushed with the rose of morning.

Ron felt a glow of adventure and a satisfaction of being able to bring to a conclusion what he started.

Before leaving Chetumal the capital of Quintana Roo, Ron and Nick sought the sanction of the Mexican government. Officials seemed pleased, but offered none of the requested help.

Nick observed, "They are holding something back like guilty kids caught with their hands in the cookie jar."

"Yeah, I noticed it too," said Ron, "Something is fishy,"

Government rebuff behind them and forgotten now, they made good time and in four days, were standing in the grassy savanna by the remains of the two burned wagons.

Ron recovered his cameras. They did not appear to have suffered damage, well wrapped as they were in the buried tent.

The area was again surveyed. No evidence was found of any human activity.

"Chester never came back, did he?" asked Nick.

"There's no sign of anybody," said Ron. "We camp here tonight, and then try to follow his wagon track."

During the night, Ron had difficulty sleeping. There were too many questions and not enough answers. *Why in the world would Dr. Chester and Hugo take off like that and abandon human lives to probable death? Maybe he was searching for something. What could it be? Who met him with another wagon? Was the cargo saddles? Where were they now?*

Ron thought of all the possibilities and came up with no definite answers. He searched back in his memory for any possible clues. Perhaps something Chester said could be of help. He finally fell into a fitful sleep, filled with weird dreams.

In the morning, while camp was broken down, he still had no positive solutions.

The first mile led to the place where Chester rendezvoused with the new wagon. Another search was conducted to no avail.

"Is there anyway we can repair and use this wagon?" asked Nick.

Sergio the hostler was already at work doing a more extensive examination. He shook his head, sadly, "Weeth axle busted, she be fini."

"So be it," said Ron, "It should be easy to follow tracks of seven horses and a wagon, even if they are over a month old."

The track led south and a little west for perhaps five miles, and then faded on top of a lava flow. The tracking skills of Q'echan and Tixq'al were put into use, they walking slowly ahead looking for rock chips, evidence of horseshoes striking rock.

After a bit, the terrain changed back to grasslands and softer soil. And the Indians returned to their saddles.

Tixq'al on the lead horse, suddenly reined in and held up his hand, signaling a stop. He dismounted, joined by the others. There before them, plain as day was yet another wagon track, joining the main trail from the south.

Tracks indicated it was drawn by two horses and was about the same size as the one Chester was riding.

The Indians scouted around a bit, and then spoke to Sergio.

"Dey say second wagon follow first mebee two weeks after," Sergio told Ron & Nick.

"So Chester wouldn't know he was being followed," concluded Ron, "Very interesting!"

"It could have been planned," said Nick

"Or it could be a total surprise," added Ron.

More questions!

To make matters worse, the tracks now led into dense jungle.

As it was midday, Ron called for a lunch break.

"Send a man up one of those tall trees to scout ahead," he told Sergio.

Ron was still concentrating, trying to recover an elusive thought, when two things suddenly came to mind.

Something Chester said earlier and a comment made by one of the Mexican officials in Chetumal gave Ron two new clues to where Chester might be. *Why didn't he recall this earlier?*

Ron stood up with a shout, "I know where they were going!"

Sergio and Nick moved closer.

Ron explained the conversation when Dr. Crowell said, "In a couple of days, we should break out of the rain-forest into open savannah and if it is a clear day, we'll see our goal, the three spires of Chiapeche."

"I told him Chiapeche was south, no where near where we were going, and he dismissed the conversation as a mistake.

Then, at Chetumal, that Mexican official said, "Perhaps they go to Chiapeche and look for the little golden man! Ha, ha!"

"Was the official serious?" asked Nick

"He acted like he let something slip because a grey shadow fell across his face before he recovered his composure with the 'ha-ha'," said Ron. "Chiapeche is the mythical site of an unknown Mayan treasure trove. Hundreds have searched but found nothing."

Q'echan and Tixq'al returned from their climb and talked to Sergio.

"Jungle not thick, mebee two kilometer, den foothills, easier travel," he said

"Ask about three needles of Chiapeche," instructed Ron.

Sergio interpreted, "Yes, ahead, mebee twenty kilometer."

"That's it!" exclaimed Ron, grateful to finally have answers.

Chester, Hugo and whoever was with them hacked a clear path through the remaining jungle, a trail that was reinforced by a second wagon two weeks later. Ron and his team had no trouble following.

Well into the foothills, they stopped for the night. The site had been used as a camp by those who went ahead.

Just before dusk, after everybody had been fed, the wind shifted bringing with it the cloying smell of decayed flesh. The stench was too severe to be ignored. Ron and Nick took electric torches and followed to its source.

What they found turned their stomachs and Nick retched his dinner.

It was the badly bloated body of a man, instantly recognized by them both. Covered with maggots, it was Hugo, stripped naked with three bullet holes in his chest and one in his temple. Obviously, he had been murdered.

And the plot thickens!

Ron tried to raise the Geografica office at Cancun in order to report the murder, but no one was manning the radio at this late hour.

That night, Ron again drifted off to a troubled sleep. His last thought was: *Maybe we should start posting a guard at night.*

In the morning, Ron could still not make radio contact. They buried Hugo in a shallow marked grave. After breaking camp, they proceeded on, now at a much slower pace. Ron sent Q'echan and Tixq'al about 100 yards out to right and left flank. With himself and Sergio at point, and Nick guarding the rear, they moved forward, making a little over a mile an hour.

Presently, the terrain forced the flankers to move closer and closer in to the main body. They were in an ancient river bed, fairly clear of vegetation and the low side hills got closer forcing the flankers, Q'echan and Tixq'al to within 25 yards. The three spires of Chiapeche loomed dead ahead, less than a mile away.

"Stay alert," warned Ron.

They kept moving forward until finally they reached the entrance to the canyon. The opening was barely fifty feet across, one side jutting out a little more than the other so that in anything less than full sunlight shadows would make the opening virtually invisible.

The rock cliffs rose claustrophobically on either side, narrowing so that the wagon tracks they still followed came to within a foot or two of the side walls.

"Still seeing two distinct wagon tracks, one on top of the other," whispered Ron, "I think we might be getting close."

They could see for a hundred feet along the canyon where it suddenly took a sharp turn to the right and out of sight.

Ron dug out two low-frequency walkie-talkies and handed one to Nick. "Wait here while I reconnoiter," he said, then walked straight into the narrow opening.

Around the first turn, the canyon straightened, and then became narrower still. As quickly as it straightened the canyon curved again, this time to the left. A few vines had been hacked away and lay withered on the ground. A hundred yards farther on the narrow gauntlet broadened into a small high-sided valley. All was in deep shadow, as no sunlight could penetrate this deep cleft, except at high noon.

Nick heard his speaker crackle, "They're here, I'm coming out." Ron was whispering.

In two minutes, he was back, heart pounding in his chest. "They're here," he repeated, "At least I saw two wagons and a corral full of horses."

"Me horses?" queried Sergio.

"Looked like them," said Ron. "There's withered vegetation that indicates no one has been in or out this way for at least three or four days. It's a narrow, sandy valley with brush only along the canyon walls. The wagons and the corral are out in the open about three hundred yards from the opening. The only way we can reach them unseen is to wait until nightfall. I saw no sign of people."

Sergio interpreted for Q'echan and Tixq'al who nodded their assent.

Now, in this moment of truth, Ron was not sure of his own motives. Would they be going after Chester out of revenge or out of justice? He certainly needed answers to questions that only Chester could give. A Scripture verse from Psalm 24:29 popped into his head: *"Say not, I will do so to him as he hath done to me: I will render to the man according to his work."* Ron knew he must avoid revenge, at all costs.

"We wait here until dusk," Ron said, "Make yourselves and the horses comfortable, eat something but keep a sharp lookout."

They pulled their horses back away from the canyon entrance, partially hidden and sat down to wait about four hours until dusk. Holsters containing .45 caliber semi automatic pistols were now being worn by Ron, Nick & Sergio. They had guns for Tixq'al and Q'echan, but the Indians refused to carry them.

Ron had Tixq'al climb the tallest tree they could find to run up his antenna wire, and was able to reach a station in Cuba. He asked them to relay information to Geographica about their location and that Hugo Bunch had been found murdered. Also, that new players had joined the game.

Dusk came on fast and Nick & Ron both could hear their own pulse pounding in their ears. This was a job for military or policemen, not scientific explorers, but they had little choice.

Leaving Sergio and the Indians, they moved through the narrow canyon shoulder to shoulder, breaking out into the open basin. Eyes quickly adjusted to the dark. They moved forward together along the right side of the wall, partially because of the seclusion offered by the sparse brush. There was no moon, for which Ron was thankful. The stars provided just enough light to see that the basin was now quite wide, perhaps a half mile across. They were close enough to the corral to hear the horses rustling as they fed, but still against the canyon wall.

Ron, feeling his way along the wall suddenly tripped over something large and soft. He chanced a sheltered use of his penlight. It was a body of a man, not yet stiff. He gently rolled it over.

"My God," he whispered to Nick, "It's Dr. Crowell." He felt for a pulse and found none; the body was cold, but drool and other body fluids told Ron that the corpse had just been placed in this location within the past few hours.

"He's dead," he said to Nick, "Let's keep going."

The wall took a 90 degree turn to the right and opened into another valley, forming a "T" with the first. A flicker of firelight was reflecting off the wall, perhaps a hundred yards in front of them. Crouching down in the dried grasses, they observed a tent and two people sitting by a campfire. One of them appeared to be a woman. The other was an overly tall skinny man with spectacles and a moustache.

Ron tugged on Nick's arm, signaling a retreat. Back around the corner, out of sight of the campfire, he said, "That's the same man that Sergio caught going through our stuff in the wagons back at Tzucacab."

"But who is the woman?"

"She also looks familiar," said Ron. "Let's make sure that no one else is here. We'll stake the valley out all day tomorrow, then strike tomorrow night."

From high above the southern rim of the valley, Ron and Sergio could see most of the cleft below. The horse corral was at the apex of the two canyons. High walls were pock marked with caves. The two people from the campfire, now looking like ants, proceeded to place ladders and entered and explored three caves, one after the other. Ron counted over thirty caves and assumed they would all be searched if not already. The two people were highly intent on something, presumably Mayan treasure. But the little valley bore signs of others who probably also searched and found nothing.

From where he observed, Ron could see the body of Chester. They could not tip their hand by moving it. A couple of vultures were circling overhead.

Ron calculated there should be nine horses in the corral, but it only contained six. *Why?*

The answer came about sundown when the tall man with the moustache led three horses out one by one and shot them with a single bullet to the head. It made no sense until Ron considered the contents of one wagon which contained three saddles and only a partial bale of hay. *They're running out of hay and can't afford to feed all the horses.*

The killing upset Sergio, but Ron promised that the Foundation would replace all he lost and then some.

More vultures joined the first two, as Ron and Sergio climbed down the backside of the cliff and returned to their own camp.

The plan of attack was simple as it appeared the two felt confident enough that they kept no watch. There was only one tent in use which meant the man and the woman were both in the same tent, probably sharing one sleeping bag. Ron, Nick and the two natives would circle around and come up to a few feet behind the tent and wait. Sergio then, from behind a large boulder fifty feet away, would holler something in Spanish. When the two exited the tent, they would be taken from behind by Ron's team.

They waited until after midnight. The plan went off like clockwork with no shots fired and no injuries. Tixq'al and Q'echan searched and bound their prisoners, while Sergio built up the fire.

It was time for some answers.

The woman was first to speak, "Good evening, Mr. Ron Martin."

At his name, Ron's mouth fell open.

"Sayra?"

"Yes, Sayra al Schela from Egypt. We talked on the airplane and you took me to dinner in Merida."

Bitterness flooded over Ron and he asked sarcastically, "What does this place smell like?"

She was not smiling now. "Double-cross," she said and hung her head.

"And you?" Ron looked squarely at the tall man.

"I am Oliver, brother to Hugo. We, Hugo Sayra and I planned to double-cross Dr. Chester Crowell, but he killed Hugo, so I had to kill him.

"Sounds to me like a triple-cross," broke in Nick. Chester and Hugo abandoned us, joined up with Oliver who conspired with Sayra. Chester eliminated Hugo, incurring the wrath of Oliver who then killed Chester. As soon as Chester led you here, you planned to do away with him anyway, keeping the treasure for yourselves. You hadn't planned on Chester killing Hugo or we five surviving against all odds and knowing how to find you."

"Great speech, Nick," said Ron, "Sounds like you've got it all together."

"What we do now?" asked Sergio.

"We've got a full bag of oats, so the horses can survive on that plus local grass," said Ron. "I'm for looking around for a day or two before hauling these guys back to jail."

Chapter Six ~ Mayan Gold

With nothing left to lose, Sayra and Oliver cooperated by telling Ron which caves they had searched and which they had not.

But Ron had other ideas.

Tixq'al and Q'echan were given the responsibility of guarding the two prisoners, and they took the job with vigor; they found pigments and painted themselves with horrible looking warpaint. They also agreed to practice shooting and wear the sidearms in addition to spears they had been carrying.

They made such a terrifying sight that Ron took pictures of them.

Sergio would supervise and backup the jailers.

Ron and Nick carried a long ladder and went to the south end of the canyon complex where there were no caves. All the evidence of previous searching was in the northern end, where Oliver and Sayra had been seen, and Ron had other ideas.

Halfway up the far side slope of the canyon was a jutting overhang of darker sandstone, and directly beneath it something that looked like a broken vertical line of shadow that was simply too geometric to have been an accident of nature.. Climbing the slope, they reached an almost invisible ledge, barely two feet wide, and the narrow remains of a cave entrance that had been bricked up and sanded over long ago. Somewhere along the line, hundreds of years ago, there must have been some kind of seismic activity and one side of the mud brick wall had crumbled and collapsed, leaving an opening. Later a sandstorm or a small collapse of the overhang had disguised and almost flossed the entrance once again.

"What d'ya think?" asked Nick

"Positively positive," declared Ron. "Lets get some lanterns and tools and have a looksee."

Returning with another ladder and tools, they carefully brushed away some of the outer veneer sand, exposing ancient clay brick. A little chisel work loosened some of the crumbling clay and made an opening into a hollow black void beyond the wall.

"How sturdy do you think this wall is?" asked Nick, "If we cut a hole large enough to climb in, could the whole cliff face collapse?"

"It has stood up to the test of time of many centuries," suggested Ron. "Let's enlarge the hole enough to put two hands inside, holding a mirror and a flashlight."

"That makes sense," said Nick picking up the chisel and hammer.

After a few taps, the hole was large enough. Ron was surprised at the coolness of the exiting air. It felt as if he was looking into the fan of an air conditioner, blowing cool air at least thirty degrees below the outside temperature.

Inserted lights showed a low cavern, perhaps less than four feet in height and maybe eight wide. The ends of two sarcophagus type ossuaries could be seen along each side wall.

"Jackpot!" exclaimed Ron.

"Let's check the structural integrity," suggested Nick.

He inserted the mirror and turned it in order to inspect the inside of the wall. "It seems safe enough," he said, "There appears to be a reinforcing doorframe, peaked at the top and about two feet wide at the base. Nick scratched an outline indicating where they could safely remove stone.

While Ron chiseled the old rotten mortar, Nick stood back a couple of feet, watching for any sign of cracks in the masonry above. In short order, they had a fourteen inch square hole, large enough to wiggle through.

Their next concern was to watch for vipers. A poisonous snake bite this far from civilization would mean instant and painful death.

"Looks clear," announced Ron as he took several pictures before he slithered head first through the tiny hole. Inside his voice echoed back as he spoke to Nick. "C'mon in, the air is fine."

There were four stone boxes, lined up, two against each wall, and what looked like a bricked up wall in the back. Each box had a two inch stone slab on top, forming a tightly sealed lid. Each box was about five feet in length and about fourteen inches in width, just big enough to hold a small person.

"I think we are on the verge of a major cultural discovery," said Ron, "and we have to be extremely careful what we do." He proceeded to photograph as much of the room as was possible in the confined space.

"I think we might try opening only one of these and leave the rest to the professional archeologists," Ron continued, "What do you think?"

Nick nodded and begun to clear away debris from the top of the nearest ossuary. They both assumed that the stone boxes would contain mummified remains.

It was also obvious that another opening existed to the chamber because the cool air was fresh, breathable and slightly moving.

"If there are human remains inside," Ron warned, "we must be alert to possible toxic fumes and avoid breathing any stale gasses that might be present."

"Agreed," said Nick who continued to move dirt.

It took another five minutes to clear all the dirt away from the top of the stone box. Sticking his machete into the faint crack between the box and its heavy top, Nick twisted slowly and the top slid fractionally to one side, releasing a puff of stale, dusty air. Ron passed a lit candle flame slowly over the crack. The flame did not flicker, so Nick widened the crack another inch. The flame continued to remain bright.

Crouched at each end of the box, they each twisted their blade enough to move the lid another two inches. Shining his flash into the opening, Ron said, "I see gold! Keep sliding."

Together they heaved the heavy lid revealing a hideous carved mask hiding a few bones. If it had been a mummy, it was too far deteriorated to be recognized. Ron took photos from several angles. The casket contained some woven materials, feathers, stone pots and a seven inch solid gold statue of a little fat man. Nick lifted the object out of the box, estimating its weight at over twenty-five pounds. Ron wasn't sure if they should take the statue or not. It would be seen as positive evidence of a genuine Mayan treasure and perhaps a new culture. Leaving it available for other fortune hunters could be a mistake. He decided to take it direct to the Geographica Foundation. From there, they would mount an expedition to properly explore the site.

"Let's close the lid," he instructed Nick and they both strained to move it back to its original position.

After more photos, they carefully backed out of the small catacomb. Ron carefully wrapped the little gold man and hid it carefully in his pack. Then, they carefully piled as many broken pieces of brick and rock as they could to partially hide the hole they had cut. Fortunately, the cliff face was facing enough toward the south to not be seen from the more popular part of the canyon.

"It should be safe, until the archeologists get here," said Ron.

"Yeah," agreed Nick, "That should be within a month."

They removed the ladders and all traces of their activity. Ron took one last photo and they returned to their companions.

"We pull out of here at first light," Ron told them. Nick filled them all in on what had been found. Meanwhile, Ron was on the radio, making a full report to Geographica.

* * *

It was a somber procession making its' way back toward Chetumal. Ron, Nick, Sergio, Q'echan and Tixq'al were each on horseback. A wagon pulled by two horses carried Sayra al Schela and Oliver Bunch securely bound and tied to opposite ends of the wagon with the wrapped body of Dr. Chester Crowell lashed between them. Tethered to the wagon and bringing up the rear, was the last horse carrying the exhumed rotting remains of Hugo Bunch tightly wrapped in one of the canvas tents.

Food was running low and Ron allowed only one meal a day. Often Q'echan and Tixq'al would run with the caravan, sometimes hundreds of yards on the flank, hoping to pick up the trail of game.

So was their formation one day out from Chetumal when Ron signaled a halt. Two Mexicans on horseback were standing on each side of the trail.

"Ah, senor," said one, his wide smile showing white gleaming teeth, "We have come to relieve you of the gold." In a flash, they both pulled old Navy Colts from under cover and pointed them at Ron's forehead. "We also request the release of madam Sayra and the Bunch brothers."

"Hugo Bunch is dead," countered Ron, biding his time.

"Do not joke with me, Senor. He is our leader."

"See for yourself," said Ron, waving to the rear. As the man turned to this distraction, he was hit hard from behind by Tixq'al and the Colt pistol went flying.

Simultaneously Q'echan hit the other bandit who then fell face-first into the dirt. The Indians looked up at Ron with comical grins spread ear to ear, looking for his praise.

"Good job," he said and they understood.

One of the Mexicans was the same official who had given them a bad time earlier. Mexican officialdom was full of graft and corruption, as these two proved.

"Two more prisoners to turn in," laughed Ron, "Tie them securely to their horses," he instructed Sergio, adding, "And, it might be a good idea to continue to keep our good friends a few yards out as outriggers, in case we run into any more of these crooks."

The next day in Chetumal, they were met by the American consul and officials from Geographica. Reports were made, charges were filed and Sergio was rewarded with all the horses plus free barge transportation all the way around the peninsula back to Merida. His native friends were paid well and would accompany him.

Ron thought about all the double-crosses and how many perfectly beautiful people turn out to be crooked, like Sayra, for example. Who could have guessed that she knew who he was and where he was going even before he boarded the plane to Merida?

Greed is an awful thing, but conspiracy can be worse. A Scripture verse occurred to him from Ecclesiastes 1: 15 (KJV) *"That which is crooked cannot be made straight: and that which is wanting cannot be numbered."*

Chapter Seven ~ Shangri- la

The International Geographica Foundation was very pleased with Ron's find. They dispatched a team of archeologists back into the hills to claim the rest of the Mayan secrets.

Ron and Nick worked so well together, it was decided they should continue as a team.

They worked on Geographica assignments all over the world during the next fifteen years, each becoming famous in his field. Ron also turned into an effective best-selling author and provided much input on important wildlife preservation committees.

He helped write <u>The International Code of Ethics for Wildlife Photographers</u>.

Animal enthusiasts all over the world benefited; the animals even more so. The idea was to make hard and fast rules that no photo is worth disruption of wild animals lives or destruction of habitat. Stress on animals must be minimized by observers and photographer alike. The codes applied equally to insects, birds, reptiles and plants.

Ron once captured a Sidewinder rattlesnake in Arizona, Cooled the snake briefly in the refrigerator before photographing it, and then returned it promptly to the exact same spot he found it. This had to be done in order to obtain extreme close-ups (one inch or less) of the snake's heat sensing organ for a scientific journal.

Another time, in Africa, he lay in the brush on a moonless night, less than three yards from the feet of the biggest tusker he'd seen in all his wild life pursuits, manually focusing in the starlight on his occasionally glinting tusk and *Damn!! The flash refused to go off when I pressed the shutter release!!*

He was hoping the small ditch between him and the giant would keep him from squashing Ron into a permanent fixture on mother Earth, just long enough for him to get a few shots. It was an awesome specter. His tusks were definitely longer than Ron was. They were almost like those seen in history books on mammoths, shaped like huge bows made of ivory.

Got it! he thought as he pulled the flash off the camera body, shifted the camera exposure dial to "B", put the flash on the test mode and then hoped for the best.

As the elephant tore down a tree right before his eyes, he waited patiently for his tusk to shine once again in the starlight so he could refocus the camera.

There it was!! I think I got it focused. How he wished it hadn't been a moonless night but the starlight was quite bright too. He just hoped for the best and pressed the shutter release. Hearing the familiar click, keeping the button pressed to keep the shutter open, he triggered off the flash test switch. It worked!! *Yes!!*

This was followed by a few moments of absolutely undiluted tension spent trying to gauge the reaction of the elephant to the flash. It had paused in its demolition of the tree for a few seconds. Ron remembered wishing he could stop his heartbeat, which sounded too loud for comfort!

Then the giant elephant resumed his meal. Ron heaved a sigh of relief and took a few more shots before Nick, waiting behind a bush thirty yards away, urgently whispered in his radio earpiece, "Let's get outa here, NOW!"

The next morning when they went back to the same spot and looked at the ditch he relied on so much, Ron almost did a back flip and died.

Later he confessed to Nick, "I think I was very lucky I'd come across an extremely hungry elephant more intent on his meal than on a man at his feet flashing light every now and then. I remember hoping he drove some sense into my head. I lay there and just stared a while at this awesome creature and it's raw display of power, then reluctantly crawled away before it pulled me off the ground and wrapped me around whatever was left of the tree."

Nick replied, "The beast probably thought the flash was lightning but why would lightning flash from the ground!! I guess you do have to be a little nutty in the head to be a wildlife photographer.

Nutty but still keep your wits around you to work your way around problems and get yourself out of dangerous situations which could turn ugly very suddenly. He had been charged and chased by elephants on four different occasions and twice by tigers.

Nearing retirement, he would often say to newcomers, "If these things aren't for you, don't even think of getting into wildlife photography. But," he would continue, "I'd rather face a wild elephant any day instead of a vain old actress or a fussy bride."

* * *

Ron Martin had been married only to his work for almost 40 years until physical problems forced him to retire. He had both fame and fortune when he hung up his trusty old Roliflex in order to further pursue a writing career.

Over the years, close contact had been maintained with Rex Franklin and Tim Caruthers, companions from school years at Christian Brothers.

Ron perceived the idea of writing a young-adult novella about their earlier adventures in Forrest William's Nevada gold mine. It would be his first attempt at fiction; writing for the sheer joy of entertaining kids and he dove headfirst into the project with enthusiasm.

He wrote Rex and Tim, proposing the idea of a reunion at the old mine. That is, if they could ever find it again. He already learned that Forrest long since passed on, and the Nevada Mining records could find no record of a "Squaw" mine ever existing anywhere in Mineral or Esmeralda counties.

Another mystery? Or did they dream it all?

Al Allaway

Book Two

Rex

Chapter Eight ~ Naval Attraction

After the adventure in the Lmuma Mine, the glory bubble burst; the train trip back to boarding school in Sacramento offered nothing more to high-school sophomores than the boring ritual of Christian Brothers Catholic High School, which would start promptly at 5:30 a.m. the next morning.

"What time does the train get in to Sacramento?" asked Rex Franklin.

"I think the conductor said around five," answered Ron.

Tim, sitting in the next seat, asked, "Will Brother Felix be there to meet the train?"

"Dunno."

They were all fairly stuffed with Aplets and Cotlets, a sugary dried fruit sold on the train for exorbitant prices.

A cloud of gloom settled over an already foreboding, cheerless future.

Rex was still torn between a career as an officer in the Navy, like his father, or joining a fire department with a degree in Fire Science Engineering. His step-mom's cerebral tumor would probably take her life within a year. He knew he had matured enough in his internal strength to be able to cope with that.

Three young men advanced toward maturity very fast in one short week and learned a lot about the rewards of being honest. And they learned another valuable lesson, that broken dysfunctional families can still produce winners, despite the odds. Considering all that had happened: the bottom line of their future lives was still basically the result of their own actions. Also, a good prayer based faith in God reflected in everything they did.

When classes resumed after Easter vacation (We call it Spring break, now), Rex's only extra curricular activity was the Christian Brothers Gael's swim team. He excelled in every event and brought home many trophies to his school.

True to predictions, his mother, Sarah Franklin succumbed to the nasty growth inside her head. It happened right at the end of Rex's final year at Christian Brothers. In fact, the call came during final exams.

Brother William, the Principal, pondered whether he should pull Rex out of class during finals, or let him finish first.

The call came from Lt. Cmdr. John Franklin, Rex's dad. He said that he was in mid flight over the Pacific somewhere between Guam and San Francisco

Amazing what some of these military electronic gadgets could do, William thought, *Imagine, a telephone in an airplane!*

He broke in just as the exam was finishing, spoke briefly to the instructor, escorted Rex out the door and was gone.

Imagine the rampant wild thoughts which that action caused among his fellow students, Ron and Tim especially.

Classes did not let out for another hour, and by that time, Rex had packed up all his stuff and was headed to San Francisco in the Navy staff car that had been sent for him.

Ron and Tim entered their otherwise empty dorm room, still full of questions.

"Wha-a-at?"

"Did they haul him to jail?"

"What for?"

"Dunno!"

"Look here, his locker is empty."

"Let's ask Brother Felix..."

The funeral for Mrs. Franklin was on Saturday at the Hunter's Point Navy chapel. One of the Brothers attended with a carload of any of the boys who wished to go, Tim and Rex included.

Later, the three comrades had a brief moment together; Ron and Tim were crushed when Rex announced he would not be joining them at college the following September.

"What will you do?" asked Ron.

"I'll be joining the Navy, attend diving school and see if I can't get in that new Frog Man program we've been hearing about. Also, I can gain college credits through the Navy's correspondence programs."

"Why now?" asked Tim.

"Russia tested her first A-bomb last year and Communist Korea is about to boil over. If the U.S. gets involved, I want to be in on the action."

"Makes sense," said Ron, "We're all eligible for the draft and this way, you'll have your choice of service instead of induction into the Army."

Tim said, "Jeez...Aren't you even coming back for graduation next week?"

"No! Brother William already gave me my diploma."

"Well, I guess this is good-bye," said Ron with a sly smile, "Maybe you can capture another Russian spy. Ha!" He was referring to the incident three years before at the Lmuma Mine.

* * *

The day Rex entered the U. S. Navy as a Seaman Recruit was the same day North Korea crossed the 38th Parallel, invading South Korea, June 25th, 1950.

Boot camp in San Diego held few surprises for Rex, who by all definitions was a true "navy brat." Before high school he lived on Navy bases all around the world.

He fell right into the drill routine and quickly gained platoon leadership, followed shortly by recruit company commander. Recruits spent long hours marching, learning close order drills with rifle, seamanship, handling small boats and firearms. Classroom work included memorization of the Uniform Code of Military Justice, among many other subjects.

He had most of the sailors 'bible', *The Bluejackets Manual* memorized by graduation day.

For his small stature, Rex was wiry and quite strong for his size. That could be attributed to years of intense competition in swim meets. What might be lacking in size, he more than made up for in aptitude and intelligence. Rex Franklin was a born leader.

Chapter Nine ~ Korea

In the grand American tradition, much of the equipment and experience of the military in World War II was discarded promptly after VJ day, only to be reinvented a few years later when North Korea started rattling swords.

For Underwater Demolition Teams, that came in September 1951 with the audacious amphibious landings at Inchon, Korea.

Fresh out of basic training, Rex applied for UDT dive training and was amazed when accepted. Normally, raw recruits were sent to sea for a minimum six months before any specialty was ever considered, but Rex had some pretty high recommendations that got him a billet in the Self Contained Underwater Breathing Apparatus School. (SCUBA) Three months later he was temporarily assigned to a UDT unit headed for Inchon.

However, there was no glory. Rex was still scheduled for long arduous underwater training, temporarily postponed due to the urgency of the invasion. Instead of UDT duties, he was assigned as ordinary seaman aboard one of the high speed patrol boats used for deployment.

Good enough, for now!

While swabbing decks and scrubbing the head, he felt important supporting the warriors, and learned much by watching their repetitious drills.

With United Nations forces trapped in a shrinking perimeter at the southern tip of Korea by a rampaging nearly victorious North Korean army, General Douglas MacArthur and his staff designated an "end run" operation on the enemy, with the port city of Inchon on the western coast of the peninsula, near the already fallen capital of Seoul, as the target.

The harbor at Inchon is a treacherous one, with an extreme range of tides that would make the timing and execution of any amphibious operation extremely critical. To minimize the danger, UDT was used to provide detailed information about channels, docks, tides and defenses. They cleared channels of mines the hard way, by hand, swimming in line-abreast and attaching charges to the mines as they were encountered.

Rex's unit was assigned to take down a communications tower near the Naejin Harbor, ten miles north of Inchon. The night before the scheduled invasion found their patrol boat, slightly larger than an old WW2 "PT," in the East China Sea, creeping silently as close to their objective as possible. About eight miles from Naejin, they disembarked two rubber life rafts, each with four Frogmen. Only five men remained aboard the boat: the coxswain, a radioman, an engineer, a gunner and a surplus body named Seaman Rex Franklin. They were to avoid enemy patrols by vanishing into the night, returning before dawn to pick up the frogmen before hightailing it for home.

A good plan, in theory!

The approaches to Inchon Harbor are filled with hundreds of tiny island reefs. As the tides were high, Coxswain Roberts plan was to hide the boat between two small uninhabited islands, quietly idling and wait for the time of rendezvous. Except for keeping the crew supplied with hot coffee, Rex was ordered to be on deck, keeping watch using night-vision binoculars just like the rest of the crew.

In order to maintain position against an outgoing tide, it was necessary to keep the propellers engaged and about 0200 hours, the starboard prop suddenly struck something and began to cavitate and vibrate.

"All stop!" Roberts shouted into his voice tube, and the engineer disengaged both props.

"What the 'ell was that?" he called back.

But Roberts didn't reply, instead he asked Rex, "Have you qualified with SCUBA yet?" Rex nodded affirmative. "Then get suited up and see what we've tangled up with."

With a brief, "Aye," Rex bounded below for the equipment locker. He was the only odd man without specific critical duties and knew much depended on him.

Heart pounding in his temple, Rex slid over the side and into the murky water. The boat was now drifting with the tide and exposed in the open harbor, helpless to evade any enemy action.

Rex fastened a safety halyard to one shaft so he could concentrate on the problem. A mine cable had hooked itself around the top of the starboard shaft, and as the boat drifted on the tide, the shaft acted like a pulley. Rex followed the incoming cable with his light and discovered a true horror. The mine attached to the cable was inching closer and closer. In less than three minutes it would be in contact with the boat.

Keeping a cool head, Rex knew he had to cut the mine from its cable and do it quickly. The cable cutters carried for just this kind of emergency were too small to do the job, so he was forced to cut one strand at a time. The mine kept inching closer and closer.

Adrenaline flowed!

He cut the last strand and the mine bobbed up to the surface, less than five feet from the boat. Unhooking his lanyard, Rex swam hard for the side ladder, and even before leaving the water, he hollered, "Full forward, we're inches from a mine!"

Fortunately Roberts heard him in time.

Whew! That was too close!

"Damned good job, Franklin! You saved the whole mission. I'll be sure the Captain knows."

The rest of the mission went like clockwork. By 0400 hours, all Frogmen and their gear were safely aboard and the patrol boat was racing for home port.

After the Inchon invasion totally changed the complexion of the war, with the North Koreans reeling back, the UDT units were used again, but not just for beach recons and clearance missions. Their skill and experience earned them assignments to blow bridges, railroads, tunnels, and similar targets well away from the beaches.

Korea was the first of a series of nasty little wars that didn't conform to the expectations of the strategic planners in Washington, but that didn't prevent soldiers, sailors and Marines from having to fight and die.

* * *

Who could not resist a quiet walk along the beach on a winter morning in southern California? The salty mist swept in from the sea, and the pale blue sky's reflection bounced off the tides gently rolling up the sandy shore. The tranquil ocean deceptively made a swim seem plausible even for this time of the year, but the chilly nip in the air restored perspective.

A harsh wind, on the leading edge of the coming storm, flattened the clacking dune grasses and churned the waters of Imperial Bay into froth. The wounded morning sky, as lackluster as midwinter of more northern climes, grew duller rather than brighter with the coming day.

Rex Franklin was also battling his own internal storm. *Karen or Carol?* He loved them both and could see neither during the next twenty-six weeks. Special Ops training camp was located on the Coronado Peninsula just north of Imperial Beach, California, south of San Diego, less than three miles from Mexico.

Once he entered the gate before him, he would begin one of the most challenging and brutal training camps in the country. There would be no liberty, no outside contact except written letters for the entire duration of the course. This was where all Frogmen were born and most who tried flunked out. The course was so physical and mentally demanding that less than 10% ever made it halfway. Some even died trying. The only reward at the end of this hell was the awarding of Frogman flippers.

Perhaps his long interment would settle the lady friend question. A half a year away with no phone or visits would certainly have an effect of proving "stick-to-it-iveness" or commitment.

Rex knew what was ahead. Glancing over his shoulder, he took one last look at the approaching storm, showed his papers to the gate sentry, and entered a new and forbidding world.

Good-bye freedom!

One of the first and most terrifying tests to earn their flippers was called "Drown Proofing." This involved spending a half hour vertically suspended in a ten foot deep pool with hands tied behind the back, floating at the surface, coming up for a breath, then completely relaxing underwater until sinking to the bottom then being able to push off the bottom and up for another breath. After that, students had to retrieve their face mask resting on the bottom of the pool while their hands were still tied behind.

Men fell out every day because the stress was cranked up so high that only the fittest could survive.

The drill instructors motto was "The only easy day was yesterday" which they kept shouting at the students. And it was true because whatever high standards a man achieved on one day, had to be better the next day.

Another common proverb, heard over and over was: "This is high risk training. And we define that as anywhere there is potential for serious injury or loss of life..."

Men spent a lot of time in the water and the water is cold, even in summertime; hypothermia is a fact of life. Obstacle courses training soldiers on land are difficult to say the least, but Special Ops courses are mostly underwater nightmares.

Finally, after 25 continuous and arduous weeks, came the worst of all, aptly called "hell week."

The trainees began five and a half days of constant activity. They received an average of about twenty minutes sleep per day, if lucky. They went from one event to another, continually running in the soft beach sand, doing boat drills, swim, crawl in slime, roll in the surf or doing "Log PT," which requires boat teams to lift and maneuver logs weighing up to 600 pounds.

Although they don't get any real sleep, the trainees get plenty of food, consuming about 7,000 calories a day and still lose weight.

Flippers earned, it was off to Fort Benning Georgia to be parachute jump qualified and another six week separation.

In the end, it was Carol who still waited for Rex Franklin and they began making wedding plans.

Chapter Ten ~ Free Fall

After Fort Benning, Rex was granted a short one week leave, before being ordered to SubPac2 in San Francisco where he was to undergo advanced diving operations, including escape from submarines.

But, for this week in July, 1952 at least, his active young mind was on other things, opposites of war: peace and love; a whole week in which to romance his lovely Carol back in San Diego.

Carol was one of those elegant little angels that appear only once in a lifetime in each young man's dreams. Bangs of golden hair flowed like silk on a perfect forehead which shadowed her baby blue eyes. Her slim neck towered above an elegant figure.

Rex could pick her out of a crowd anywhere by her bouncy but purposeful walk. She excelled in tennis as he excelled in swimming. It was the tennis that probably caused her to appear always walking on the balls of her feet, like a ballerina.

Carol's energy was only exceeded by her intelligence; a major in psychology desiring to study law.

Rex was in love, looking for a permanent commitment. Carol, too was in love, perhaps seeking a delay from permanence in order to fulfill her desired profession; not yet sure.

Of course, there was the question of Rex's tours of duty; no new wife wants to be left home alone for months at a time.

For now, however, this precious week of togetherness would abandon all questions of the future and just allow time to enjoy each others company.

"Where should we go?" asked Rex.

"How about the beach?" she suggested, realizing what his answer would be even before it was uttered.

"Please, no," he said, "I've had it with ocean beaches for awhile."

"I understand."

"Would some camping and fishing in the mountains interest you?" he asked with a degree of hope.

"Perfect!"

Larger Navy bases support a Welfare and Recreation division where sailors and marines can check out camping, fishing, hunting and boating equipment free of charge, so it was that within two hours time they were headed into the hills east of San Diego.

"I know a perfect secluded camping spot between Campo and Lake Morena," he told her, "and it has a stream full of nice trout."

They found an idyllic meadow well off the road. The peace and tranquility of the next few days was an experience Rex had not felt for almost a year.

Here the Red-tailed hawk soared in the sunshine, silhouetted sharply against the blue sky. Vivid colors were everywhere, butterflies and flowers, deep greens and purple shadows. Soaring, born of wind, the hawk drifted lazily over an immensity of God's creation. Just as in centuries past, sharp eyes scanning the soft places

And here, hearts met and souls searched, becoming one, tears flowed and voices laughed, joy winning over all. Rex Franklin and Carol Jeffers tumbled together in the ecstasy of free fall.

Shifting light, passing time and lengthening shadows brought a return to the reality of war; the situation in Korea had been steadily deteriorating. President Truman's dismissal of MacArthur seemed to stall progress; the Communists again captured Seoul and peace talks were further stalled.

Carol followed Rex to San Francisco.

The next six week course was designed to "scare hell out of you" if it hadn't happened already. Even more Frogmen were weeded out. Rex learned more than he ever wanted to know about the nasty things that happen to people who make mistakes underwater.

Many of the lessons of early life at Christian Brothers suddenly began to make sense. Like Father O'Connor, the only live-in Priest at school. Short and chubby, round faced and balding, the resident boys avoided him like the plague. He had this nasty habit of pinching nerves in wrist, elbow or shoulder joints. He had an iron grip and it hurt. Once he had a boy in his grasp, he always delivered little sermonettes or jewels of advice, smiling the whole while.

"I don't think he realized how much pain he causes," Rex had once told Tim.

"Yeah, he says all boys' sin and he does it to cause penance," replied Rex.

Anyway, Father O"Connor's lasting advice on the last occasion was that Rex not even think about marriage until he was 21 or 22. The funny thing was, he never forgot the pain, or the message.

Then there was the old cook who sometimes sat outside the pantry door smoking his tailor-mades. A tailor made is a roll-your-own from a tobacco pouch of Bull

Durham. He was a real funny geezer with sunken eye sockets and no teeth. He'd talk funny and entertain the boys by making faces. His favorite was hanging his lower lip up and over his nose. It always got a laugh. His advice to Rex was to never take up smoking, and Rex never forgot that advice, either.

Rex, who was now 20, and Carol, 18, decided to ignore her parent's advice to wait with marriage. Rex's mother had been deceased for over a year and his father was presently serving aboard a carrier squadron in the Mediterranean command. He thought of old Father O'Connor and chuckled.

* * *

U.S.S. Carbonero (SS-337) was a Balao class diesel-electric submarine with a crew of 10 officers and 70+ enlisted men. She often carried 10-12 frogmen trainees in addition.

SubPac2 (Submarine Pacific Command) was now to be Rex's home for the next six weeks. Carol rented a flat in nearby Alameda so Rex could spend weekends with her.

In 1952, the *Carbonero* was fitted with a new Fleet Snorkel modification package. She operated off the California Coast, and occasionally in the Hawaiian Islands. Later, *Carbonero* was fitted with control equipment which enabled her to guide a missile once it passed beyond the range of the firing ship. She performed in various phases of this program including the launching of Loon missiles and the evaluation of a Regulus missile guidance system.

U.S. submarines have a small chamber, the "escape trunk," installed forward of the sail (conning tower). This little chamber has two functions; the first allows trapped submariners to escape, usually four or five at a time. The second allows for the deployment and recovery of combat frogmen, without having to surface.

Rex and other trainees became very familiar with this little cramped space.

In actual combat, the sub will slither in as close to shore as the skipper will allow, still retaining deep enough water for escape.

The six weeks passed quickly and Rex heaved a big sigh of relief as he stepped off the deck of *Carbonero* for the last time. A jeep transported him to the dockyard parking lot where his Chevy Impala waited. It was Friday and all thought was on Carol who had waited patiently for his return.

He was assigned back to Coronado. Rex and his beloved Carol were married in San Diego on May 5, 1953. Invitations were sent to Ron Martin and Tim Caruthers, his closest friends, but they were set to graduate from college and could not attend.

Rex had few family members who could attend. His dad, of course, was there. Carol Jeffers, on the other hand, had family and friends enough to fill the large church.

Rex got a two week leave and they honeymooned in Hawaii.

"Wanna go scuba diving?" he asked Carol and just about destroyed the marriage before it started.

Some bad people were out to hurt Tim Caruther's mother, Helen so Rex and Carol agreed to have her hide out with them in San Diego.

Rex's UDT worked all over the Pacific on various short hop jobs.

In September, 1954 Rex got word that Carol was due to give birth to their first child and he got permission to fly home early from a mission.

When he showed his ID at the exit gate, he was in for a rude surprise.

"Petty Officer Rex Franklin?"

"Yes."

"We have orders from the Admiral to intercept you. You'll be flying to Washington at 0100 hours. Pack for four days and be back here before 1100 hours tonight."

"What's it all about?"

"No idea, sailor. Just be sure you're on time."

Dang!

* * *

CIA, Washington D.C., 0900 Saturday:

"Room 308, upstairs." the Marine MP told Rex as he was deposited in front of an impressive marble building inscribed, 'Central Intelligence Agency.' Another Marine guard at the entrance examined his identification extensively. Ordinary enlisted men were not customarily allowed in the building without officer escort.

"Standby," the guard said. He took two steps back and made a brief telephone call from a small call box set into the marble wall. Presently a uniformed Lieutenant Commander appeared. Rex and the Marine both saluted.

"I'm Commander Peter Banks," he said.

Peter Banks was a tall, thin man in his early fifties, he grinned cheerfully as he warmed Rex's hand. His bony, intelligent face creased into deep folds beside his mouth, and lines radiated out like spokes around his eyes. They were blue, magnified slightly by rimless glasses that had a tendency to slide down his aquiline nose.

"Welcome to Washington, do you know why you are here?"

"No, sir," replied Rex.

Banks escorted him into an elevator and when the doors closed, said, "Did you know that your dad is here?"

That was a shock to Rex. "My dad, here? I thought he was in the Mediterranean.

Banks said nothing, simply nodding.

The elevator doors opened on the thirteenth floor. Rex casually remarked, "The Marine told me third floor."

"Aha," said Banks, "Numbers make no sense in this building. It's that way to confuse any attacking enemy."

Walking down a long highly polished hallway, Rex continued to make conversation, trying to relax. "I've never seen a high-rise with a thirteenth floor, Commander. They usually skip the number."

"You can call me Pete," Banks said, "We'll be working together without any rank."

Rex had to bite his lip in order to avoid asking more questions.

They paused outside a door marked Conference 308, Pete knocked, then ushered Rex inside. There was a small conference table with twelve chairs, four being occupied. There were two Admirals, a Captain and a civilian. Rex started to come to attention in order to render the required salute, but Pete grasped his arm whispering, "Not needed."

What kind of crap is this? thought Rex.

It was not until the Captain stood up and walked over to Rex that he recognized him.

"Dad," he cried, "You've been promoted!" Captain John Franklin gave his son a hug, "We'll meet after this for a drink." Turning to the others, he said, "Gentlemen, this is my son, DV2 Rex Franklin." Others introduced themselves as Rear Admiral McCann and Vice Admiral Parker. The man in civilian clothes seemed a little shy, stating his name was Homer Pickens. He was on loan from the French Air Force.

Admiral Parker growled, "Sit down and let's get to it."

The lights were dimmed and a map was projected onto the end wall.

"In the north part of the East China Sea, lies a series of over a hundred little islands, just offshore from the border between China and North Korea. The southernmost of these is called Taehwa-do, about two miles by two in size. About a mile to its southwest lays a tiny uninhabited island of less than a thousand square yards. Surveillance photos have discovered considerable construction on it. It is named HaiDao."

High definition aerial photos were projected on the wall.

The Admiral continued, "Submarine recon has detected huge undersea communications cables just being laid from Communist China to HaiDao and from the island into North Korea. Intelligence believes the cables support telephone and telex lines."

"But that doesn't make any sense, with today's sophisticated electronics and radio systems," said Homer.

"Yes it does," said Peter, "Radio and satellite transmissions and codes can be compromised. Courier dispatches can be intercepted, but a secret underwater cable nobody knows about can transmit top level information with no risk."

Admiral McCann spoke for the first time, "Intelligence indicates they have built a gigantic bunker to house teams of switchboard operators hooking the entire Communist world together at the touch of a secure telephone."

All this time, Rex sat quietly wondering how any of this could relate to him. Finally, he could bear it no longer. "Excuse me, Admiral," he said, "What have I to do with this top-level planning stuff?"

McCann looked miffed, "Hasn't anybody informed him yet?"

"Apparently not," said Parker, looking at Peter Banks.

Banks, sitting next to Rex, smiled and said, "Your Father and I picked you and Homer to be part of my team. We're going to sneak in there and take it out."

McCann cleared his throat and demanded, "May I continue now?" And he drummed on with details, of which Rex heard little.

The attack was urgent because the center had to be destroyed before a planned secret invasion of North Korea at Haeju and Nampo.

"It has to be completely destroyed within two months," said McCann, finishing his part of the presentation.

The whirlwind of events was catching up with Rex, who now sought comfort from his father over a scotch in the Commissioned Officers club.

"I'm confused, dad," started Rex, "Why me? I'm barely off Frogman probation."

"There are circumstances that I can't share," said Captain Franklin, "but relax and know this: Senior and more qualified Frogmen in the area are under investigation."

"For what?"

"You know I can't say."

"Who is this Homer Pickens character?"

"He's a telephone engineer from France," answered Rex's dad, "Because the Commies bought all their exchange equipment from a French company in Vietnam, he knows the equipment and will show you where to place the charges."

"Can we trust him?"

"I've not run clearances on him," answered the Captain, "He's Peter Banks nominee."

* * *

Back in San Francisco the following month, Peter Banks and Admiral Parker held a briefing for Rex and Homer, who had been drilling together in preparation for this difficult mission.

The unique details of the mission needed to be discussed such as radio frequencies, rendezvous points, routes in and out of the objective, recognition codes and the commander's intent.

"Why not bomb it?" asked Pickens. Homer had a perfectly round face with light sandy hair and pudgy lips. His nostrils had an unusual flair, resembling that of a hog.

"Bombs are too risky," said Parker, "The job has to be 100% successful on the first try. The bunker appears to be too heavily reinforced. It can resist the biggest conventional bomb."

At the briefing: Peter Banks was thoughtful. "Well, we could destroy the common equipment racks. But the damage could be repaired. You need to knock out the manual exchange, the automatic exchange, the long-distance amplifiers, the telex exchange, and the telex amplifiers, which would probably all be in different rooms.

"Remember, you can't carry a great quantity of C4 explosives with you. There must be some equipment common to all those systems."

Homer answered, "Yes, there is: the MDF: The main distribution frame. Two sets of terminals on large racks. All the cables to and from the outside come to one side of the frame, all the cable from the exchange come to the other, and they're connected by jumper links. Ideally, you'd want a fire hot enough to melt the copper in the cables."

"How long would it take to reconnect the cables?"

"A couple of days, but only if the repairmen have the record cards that show how the cables were connected. They're normally kept in a cabinet in the MDF room. If we burn them too, it will take weeks of trial and error to figure out the connections."

"This is sounding good," said Rex, "What about getting into the building?"

"Should not be a problem. It's on a tiny atoll in their complete control, heavily mined at sea, good low level radar and heavy shore batteries; but completely defenseless against attack by two frogmen. You might have to ace a couple of guards, but that should be easy for trained people like you."

"If you free fall to 500 feet in their one blind spot, the swim to the island should be a piece of cake."

They would have to carry sticks of yellow plastic explosive with a dozen detonators, an incendiary thermite bomb and a chemical block that produced oxygen for setting fast hot fires in enclosed spaces. Weapons are standard M-16 with two or three 30 round cartridges.

* * *

Rex Franklin had nothing good to say about airplanes. The ground was better than the air, but water was where he felt most at home, thanks to both instinct and long training. Right now he and Homer were at thirty thousand feet above the East China Sea, the setting sun brushing scattered clouds as they secured their jumpsuits. In approximately one hour and six minutes they'd hit the plane's jump door and drop into a two minute free-fall.

Commander Peter Banks asked, "Are you clear on those codes we went over? 92 for visual on any hostile forces in the area, 699 for sighting of the island fortress."

Rex shifted his parachute slightly, straightening the line of his oxygen mask. "Good to go on the codes, sir." His face was calm as he slipped on the thin highly tensile gloves that had become a staple during his long covert training. From now on his skin contact would be limited. His senses were too special to risk sensory overload.

"One minute to drop zone, gentlemen."

Rex felt the drum of the plane's engines and the howl of the wind beyond the jump door. The world seemed to slow down, every atom in his body focused on the here and now. He felt his pulse spike. His breath tightened to compensate for the adrenaline surge.

"A RIB (Rigid Inflatable Boat) will pick you up at the rendezvous point. Good luck."

Show time!

When the jump light went on, Rex moved to meet the air's frozen fury, hammering his body with below zero temperatures, as he fell into the dark void.

Chapter Eleven ~ Sabotage

At 600 feet, Rex felt a sudden jerk as his chute automatically deployed. Except for his penlight illuminating the altimeter dial, there was no other light. There was no moon and the stars were blotted out by high level clouds.

' The waters of the North Korea Bay came upon him suddenly; there was an unexpected shock of colder than anticipated water, almost frigid. He quickly shed the parachute and harness, sinking them out of sight.

Searching around with his penlight, he located the white aluminum container that had been launched with him. It had also experienced a free fall, slowed at 500 feet by a six foot parachute, activated by the same type barometric switch that deployed his chute.

Removing scuba gear and tank, he then retrieved a twin pack of C4 explosives with detonators, cord and timer. A quick compass check provided the correct bearing for him to search and at 300 yards, he saw the low silhouette of the fortress outlined against the black sky. Sinking the mini chute and aluminum container, he set "699" into his mini transmitter and set it to send three bursts at thirty second intervals.

Rex started swimming on the surface toward the fortress. About halfway, he met up with Homer. No spoken words were necessary. Each was fully aware of the dangers inherent with the next phase of the operation. Access to the fortress was only available to them under water, over 120 feet down. Passage into this submarine pen would be fraught with problems. The chances of them setting off some type of alarm were higher than 50 percent.

The first obstacle was a cable submarine net. The mesh was wide enough to swim through, but close examination by feel revealed fine copper wire interspersed between the steel cables. Rex took a chance and turned on his penlight for closer examination.

Funny, he thought, *If the wire has been mounted to sound an alarm if broken by a swimmer, why wouldn't large fish be causing many false alarms?* Homer nodded as if he understood Rex's concern.

Could the fine wires be a ruse? They swam along the net to the side of the pen and found one opening without the wire.

Homer started to swim through, but Rex grabbed his ankle and pulled him back.

Rex couldn't understand why his partner was being so careless; why was he forging ahead without proper reconnoiter?

Homer signaled a question, but Rex pointed upward and motioned Homer to follow. Imbedded in the ceiling a foot behind the opening used to mechanically raise the net, he pointed out an underwater laser beam, shining straight down, intersecting the middle of all the side net openings. A swimmer could not get through the opening without breaking the beam of light, thereby probably setting off an alarm somewhere inside the fortress.

Further examination showed a similar beam on the opposite side of the pen, but no beams in the middle. So, it appeared the copper wires were there to fool any divers into searching for other routes in.

Tricky! It was a cheap, but effective alarm system.

They swam through the center part of the net, ignoring the wires, fairly certain of continued stealth.

A few feet further and they surfaced in a huge manmade grotto like cave with a cement dock on each side, just wide enough for a submarine to nestle between for loading and unloading supplies. Two bare bulb lights were the only illumination. The submarine pen was empty except for one lone guard patrolling the dock. From the look of his uniform, he was North Korean.

Rex conferred with Homer in whispers how they should eliminate this guard. The guard was not particularly attentive, more interested in smoking his cigarette, so it would be an easy job; Rex waited for Homer, who was closest, to take action, but instead Homer delayed as if waiting for the opportunity to pass. Rex wondered what the man's problem was before he himself sprung into action and used a garrote. Then in no time, the man was floating face down in the water.

"Why didn't you take him out?" Rex whispered. But got no answer, instead Homer indicated he would check to be sure there were no other guards. This puzzled Rex for a brief second, until more pressing matters had to be dealt with.

On the dock now, Homer barged ahead. Rex spotted a thickly bound book on a desk the guard may have been using. It looked like a code book and might be useful later. He shoved it inside his wet suit, and followed Homer.

Inside the first door, Rex encountered a double-cross, a nightmare: Homer!

He had a pistol in one hand, knife in the other with a craving for death lighting his eyes. Words with the Frenchman were unnecessary; Rex could instantly tell that he had done more with the Communists than merely sell them telephone equipment. Homer had picked up a pistol from someplace, acting like he was in familiar surroundings.

He was not four feet distant. Rex's instinctive hesitation at what he saw was almost fatal. Held at arm's length, Homer lunged with incredible quickness; the blade drove in straight as an arrow and slammed into Rex's chest.

Homer gasped as the point slid off, gouging black rubber with a tearing sound, deflected by the soft lead cover of the code book tucked against Rex's chest under the wet suit top.

Rex tripped the release buckle on his weight belt. The heavy nylon strap studded with cast lead slipped off his hips. Rex took advantage and altered the momentum by whipping it around to the side of Homer's head. Lead impacted bone like a sledgehammer hitting a hollow log. Bone cracked with a loud pop and Homer went down at once, grey matter oozing out of the side of his skull. The gun hit the deck with a clatter, and it was over as quickly as it started.

* * *

The basement of the fortress was at the same level as the submarine pen. It contained storage warehouses, kitchens, security offices and all the equipment Rex had come to sabotage. Exchange switchboards filled the main floor, while the second and third floors contained dining, recreation and sleeping quarters. An elevator joined all this self-contained community together.

Rex quickly moved all his and Homer's equipment into an unused room. He knew he was fighting time because sooner or later, someone would come to relieve the dead guard. Homer's body was now in the water drifting toward the net with the outgoing tide.

He was glad he paid attention at the earlier briefings because he certainly could not now rely on Homer's advice where to place the charges. The main distribution frame was easy enough to find. Another guard was sometimes patrolling the area. Other times he was seen at a desk, feet propped up, leafing through the latest Playboy magazine. Rex couldn't get close enough to see if it was printed in English or

Chinese. The guard followed an established timetable, like a night watchman on a keyed clock, he walked the entire basement area, recording various stations on the clock tape which he carried on a strap around his neck. The entire route took fifteen minutes and he made his rounds once each hour. That gave Rex a full thirty or forty minutes out of each hour to set and mold his C4 explosive into well hidden places throughout the many equipment frames. During the fourth hour, he carefully joined each explosive package to the primer cords and hid the detonator clock out of sight on the top of the main frame. In ninety minutes all the charges should go off at the same time, reducing the whole installation to a pile of rubble.

Time to split!

Retracing his steps back to the grotto, he was just about to slip into the water when a klaxon sounded, flood lights came on and machinery engaged to begin lifting the anti-submarine net.

Rex disappeared under the surface and swam deep toward the entrance. The net had been lifted and just as he started to enter the tunnel, a large black object propelled through the water, straight at him. He could hear the purr of electric motors and the ping of close range sonar. The sonar hurt his ear drums, but it kept the incoming submarine from scraping the side walls. Rex had to flatten himself against the wall, less than three feet from the passing sub. He was counting the seconds to escape the coming explosions, and did not appreciate this unexpected delay.

The sub continued to creep by so slowly, Rex felt time was standing still.

Ten minutes lost!

As soon as he broke the surface, outside the fortress, he dropped his mask and scuba tanks, lightening him for a fast power swim to the next island to the northeast, a full mile away, where the rendezvous pickup was scheduled. At least 60 minutes had passed since he set the timer, and he began to have doubts if he could make it on time.

It is no feat to swim a mile, as long as the swimmer can pace himself. A full-strength power swim in cold water was another thing. The ice cold water was seeping inside his wet suit where Homer's knife blade had deflected, and the extra weight was slowing him down.

He shut down his mind and his doubts and put all his effort into his cold aching muscles. *Ten minutes to zero hour!* Still there was no sign of the island goal. He should at least be hearing surf crashing on its beaches. Rex stopped for a moment to catch his breath, now coming in violent gulps. He had to rest. Checking his compass, he worried he might have swum right past the second island.

Four minutes left!

He bumped into something soft and rubbery, and several pairs of hands jerked him out of the water and into the rubber raft. It was the Navy's latest high speed inflatable. There were three men aboard, a coxswain and two ordinary sailors.

"Where's the other man?" asked a sailor, "We're supposed to pick up two."

"Get us out now," chattered Rex, "He's dead." They wrapped a warm blanket around him.

Dawn was just showing on the eastern horizon.

The inflatable boat powered by twin oversized outboards took Rex almost flying back over the waves. The rain had eased off, the squall-clouds moved on. It was smoother headed downsea. Small brown birds soared and dipped, flinging their wings over at each crest as if they too were enjoying themselves.

The sea was more nearly smooth than it had been for the last few days, the wave heights one to two feet, no more. The sky shone the clearest blue he'd yet seen it in these parts of the ocean. Bubbles rocked along its surface as the boat sped on, Far to the north fluffy white clouds hovered, their upper works glowing like heated silver.

Then the horizon lit from one hand to the other in a searing flash that tracered silent sparks, like ascending meteors, through a whole quadrant of the sky behind them. There was no sound, only silence for a full second and then a muffled thud rolled out of the dark followed by a ripple of detonations, sharp and dull, drumming and popping like the finale of a fireworks display. Scarlet fire arched and then faded, leaving a dull red glow like the embers of a dying campfire. The fortress island southeast of North Korea's Taewa-do should now be rubble. Rex's debriefing would surprise them all. In addition to the communications center, he had also nailed an enemy submarine.

Rex settled into the seat next to the coxswain, feeling proud that his luck had allowed so much to be accomplished.

The inflatable boat was to rendezvous with a submarine almost ten miles south in the Yellow Sea where water was deep enough for evasive maneuvers.

"What sub are you from?" he asked the coxswain.

"I didn't think you recognized us," the man said, "We're from your previous station."

"Carbonero!" exclaimed Rex, "I saw you in San Francisco only ten days ago. How'd you get out here so fast?"

"We're the super U.S. Navy," he replied.

Aboard the sub now, Rex had a chance to rest and to file detailed reports through channels to Peter Banks and the team of Admirals.

Carbonero sailed south out of Korea Bay, down the west side and around the end of the Korea peninsula and east into Sasebo, Japan. Protocol forbade Rex to talk with the sub's crew about his mission.

By the time they reached the Sasebo Naval base, he was basking in his own self achievement; looking forward to his formal debriefing with Lt. Cdr. Peter Banks.

At the dock, he expected friendly escort. A smile, perhaps and a handshake. Instead, he was met by two swarthy Shore Patrolmen and clamped in irons and taken straight to the base brig.

No explanations.

It was New Year's Day, 1955.

IF I have a son, he thought, *He'll be more then two months old...?*

Chapter Twelve ~Peter Wolf

Rex Franklin sat in the base brig at Sasebo for two days, wondering what could possibly have gone wrong. What kind of misunderstanding could have been heaped on him? Guards bringing him food would not talk.

"Is Lt. Cdr. Peter Banks on the base?" he would ask at every opportunity.

"He'll be here later this afternoon," the guard finally revealed.

"Please tell me why I'm here?"

"You're to be charged with murder," the guard said.

Impossible! I should be awarded a medal for completing a hazardous mission and that against impossible odds.

Rex had been wearing standard navy blue dungarees when so rudely snatched off the pier. The first thing the brig Master at Arms made him do was stencil a huge "P" in black paint on the back of his shirt, and white paint on both legs of his dungaree pants. He was allowed no belt or shoes.

Alone in a cell, separated from other prisoners, Rex had much time to think. The

153

only pleasant, healing thoughts were of his little wife, Carol. *How would she take all this? Did we have a son or a daughter?*

He was recalling some Scripture from the Acts of the Apostles, Chapter 12 about Peter's miraculous escape from prison, when he heard the key rattle in his cell door.

Maybe that's my angel come to take me away, he chuckled to himself.

Instead it was a young Lieutenant from the JAG office.

"I'm Lt. Fitch," he said, "I'm to prepare you for your Courts Marshal."

"Whoa, whoa, back up," pleaded Rex, "I've been held here incommunicado for two days and I haven't the slightest idea what you are talking about."

"You mean Cdr. Banks hasn't told you?"

"Nobody's seen me! You're the first."

The lawyer scratched his head and said, "Something's fishy here."

"You're telling me!" said Rex

The resulting conversation revealed that Cdr. Banks had filed charges against Rex for killing Homer Pickens.

"That's stupid," said Rex, "It was self defense; he's a Commie and he tried to sabotage the operation. Has my dad, Captain John Franklin been advised of this outrage?"

"No, Banks has requested a gag order."

"Well, well well!" said Rex, "If you're serious about defending me, find out why he wants everything hush hush. Something is rotten here."

J.A.G. is a Navy acronym for Judge Advocate's General and the young attorney had copies of Rex's detailed reports of the mission that had been transmitted while he was still aboard *Carbonero*. He agreed with Rex that there were many discrepancies in Cdr. Bank's action.

"We'll have to somehow prove that Homer Pickens really was a planted agent.

"Remember," suggested Rex, "He was chosen from the French army personally by Banks."

"...and by your father," interrupted Fitch.

* * *

Senator Abram Collins was involved up to his eyeballs in the conspiracy.

"Get to Franklin; make sure he won't break. He's our weak link." He slammed the phone down after finishing a conversation with Admiral McCann.

"Damned idiot," he muttered. Then he screamed into his intercom, startling the poor receptionist, "Get Rob in here, NOW!" Rob Schoen was Chief of Staff for the Senator.

"I'm sorry, sir," quivered one teary-eyed and very shook up lady, "He's in Atlanta."

Urgent situations often lie stagnant under conditions where no one has any control.

* * *

Lt. Wiley Fitch, the J.A.G. lawyer seemed to be the only friend Rex had at the time.

"You did get word to my dad, Captain John Franklin?" Rex asked for the third time.

"Right, he said he knew all about your case, but was tied up with other problems of national security."

"Did you tell him that we desperately need his help and intervention?"

"Yes, Rex, I've already told you," replied Fitch. "It's pretty obvious to me that your dad has some ulterior motive to avoid you."

Fitch had other reservations about this case. Unusual things were happening including threats to his own family; things that could only be caused by military officers with lots of pull. He had been "asked" several times to quit the case, but the more opposition there was, the more determined he was to follow through.

"Attempts to thwart the justice system really piss me off," he told Rex. "Prepare yourself for a hard and long fight."

"Aye, aye, sir!" said Rex, "That's what Frogmen are trained to do." *A little out of context,* he thought, *but I'm ready to fight.*

Navy defense lawyers were limited in many ways, especially if their commanding officer puts on his "stingy hat." Fitch could not get allocations approved for out of jurisdiction investigations. He felt that his hands were tied which made him all the more persistent. By pooling some of his own finances and Rex's savings, they were able to hire some outside investigative work. The Courts Marshal was scheduled to begin within a week, and time was of the essence.

Wiley Fitch had so many meetings with Rex inside the Sasebo brig that he was accused of taking up residency there.

That was all well and good. Let the nay-sayers have their jokes. Long hours of research into every detail of the raid would pay off on the bottom line. His persistence was to become legend.

One of their greatest problems was the liberal media and a government that thinks war is somehow fair and subject to rules as in a basketball game. Many government legislators probably should not get into any conflict in the first place.

Nothing is fair in war, and sometimes the wrong people get killed. It's been happening for millions of years. There are always murderous cut-throats who are not fighting under the rules of Geneva. The only real counter offensive against them are the rules of Article 223, that's the caliber of the Frogman's M4 rifle.

We have always had rules, and our opponents use them against us. We try to be reasonable and fair; they will stop at nothing short of torture, beheading and mutilation.

Rex observed, "It's funny that the Chinese and North Koreans have not screamed to the world media about the hundreds of people who died in that explosion at the communications center. Plus another estimated 80 in the submarine."

"They did," Fitch answered, "but they lied about the date. They are demanding apologies for the outrage, or else..."

"What date?"

"They claim the explosion took place a whole week earlier. That made it easy for the navy to claim that you read the story and then made the whole thing up for your defense."

"Well, the truth will come out in the Courts Marshal tomorrow."

Chapter Thirteen ~ Courts Marshal

The Judge Advocate General's office assigns qualified lawyers, naval officers who have proven their mettle, to both the prosecution and defense of military personnel who have been charged with a crime.

Jonathan Proctor was a full three stripe Commander. His impeccable reputation preceded him into the court room. In smaller commands, he had already earned his stripes as Judge Advocate, but had been flown into Sasebo primarily to prosecute this poor petty officer named Franklin, that one, "That had murdered one of our allies, the French engineer and tried to blame it on the Chinese and North Koreans in order to start another war."

"What a crock," whispered Fitch to Rex. They were sitting at the defense table waiting to see who the judging court would be. Much pressure had already been brought to bear to allow Rex to be in dress blues without leg irons, although he was still handcuffed.

"Attention on Deck!" called out the Chief Clerk. Everybody rose to their feet, as five distinguished officers filed onto the bench.

There were two Admirals, two Captains and a civilian. Enlisted men's Court Marshals were usually conducted by junior officers, seldom anyone higher than Commander. This Court comprised of: Fleet Admiral Moore, the leading judge, a three striper; Vice Admiral Parker, a Captain Johnson from the Atlantic fleet, a Captain McVey from Hawaii and the civilian, a retired Air Force Colonel named Lee Clark. It was the brassiest of the brass.

As soon as the panel was seated, Lt. Fitch was on his feet.

"Objection," he cried, "One of the judges has a conflict of interest."

"Who is that?" demanded Moore.

"He knows full well who he is, sir," answered Lt. Fitch, "It's Admiral Parker."

The head judge looked at Parker, "Well, Admiral?"

Parker flushed several shades of red bordering on purple, and excused himself.

"One down," whispered Rex to Wiley Fitch, "The trial hasn't even started and they are attempting collusion."

Admiral Moore had no choice but to postpone the hearing until an alternate judge could be found to replace Parker.

It was another full day before Wiley showed up in Rex's jail cell.

"Good news, me bucko!" he announced himself while the guard unlocked the cell. "We drew a gorgeous redhead."

"Huh?"

"Colonel Ruth Loring, a Marine will be the fifth judge, Lt. Fitch said, "We'll convene after lunch today at 1330 hours."

The afternoon session accomplished little, except the routine announcement of rules. Judge Moore asked the attorneys to produce a list of their expected witnesses to be shared with opposing counsel. Basic charges were read along with outlines of procedure. Opening statements were read. Court was adjourned at 1645 hours with the Prosecutor Jonathan Proctor to call witnesses and begin arguments at 0900 the following morning.

* * *

The wind had risen even more and the sky was black as a seam of coal. A band of charcoal clouds dangled tendrils that occasionally twisted into spirals, like the business end of a corkscrew. They ran from one horizon to the other. The seas, kicked steep by the shoaling shelf, were short and already breaking. This was not cyclone season and nobody paid much attention to the weather alerts. Typhoon Ayisha was the first of the season, and five months early. She was just off the Ryukyu Chain and headed due north, straight into the shallow bays of Nagasaki or Sasebo. Hurricane flags were flying all along the south and west coast of Japan.

* * *

At 0700 hours on Friday morning, Fleet Admiral Adam Moore studied the weather reports and decided the trial would have to be postponed. The U. S. Naval base at Sasebo was only 10 to 12 feet above sea level, and because of the geographic features of the harbor, meteorologists were predicting a possible storm surge of 18 feet. If that happened, the courtroom used for Rex's Court marshal would be flooded under three feet of water.

Lt. Wiley Fitch welcomed the delay, as he still had a few loose ends to clean up for Rex's defense.

"Where's the pilot of that old C-119 that carried Homer and I to the drop zone?"

"Excellent question, Rex," replied Wiley, "Banks had him shipped to Alaska, thinking we couldn't find him to deliver a subpoena, but I tracked him down and he'll be here. Not a word to anyone about it. He's going to surprise the prosecution and make our case."

"Is he safely hidden?" asked Rex. "They will go to any length to keep him quiet."

"Got it covered, lad got it covered."

Typhoon Ayisha took a ninety degree left turn on Saturday and headed west to slam on the Chinese coast near Yancheng in Jiangsu Province, approximately 150 miles north of the Yangtze River.

At 0900 hours Monday a hush fell over the courtroom as prosecutor Jonathan Proctor rose to begin his case against Rex Franklin for the murder of the French Engineer, Homer Pickens.

Lt. Cdr. Peter Banks was first on the witness stand. Rex could not help glaring at this so-called friend who was now preparing to stab him in the back.

His lying testimony was nothing new. They had heard it all before. All he did was reinforce Proctors opening statements, i.e. Rex and Homer were dropped at a specified location in the North Korea Bay for a brief recon mission. All they carried was normal scuba gear and parachutes.

On cross examination, Fitch pressed Banks as hard as he could, "You're certain they weren't also issued C4 explosives and detonators?"

Peter Banks denied there was any such possibility.

"Who do you suppose blew up the Communist communications center near Taewa-do?" Wiley asked.

"Proctor was instantly on his feet, screaming an objection as immaterial.

Wiley let it rest and said, "nothing else for this witness."

Next, the prosecution called Admiral McCann, who harrumphed up to the stand, letting everybody know he was bothered. He outranked most officers there and wanted to be sure they all knew he had more important things to do.

Proctor kept his questioning brief, probably because he was intimidated by the Admiral. Wiley, on the other hand, felt no such compassion, and he battered the old admiral without mercy. If his career was in jeopardy, his love of justice overcame any fear.

"You testified that you met in the Pentagon in conference room 308 on September 19th with the defendant, the victim, Cdr. Banks, Adm. Parker and Capt Franklin. Who else was there?"

"Nobody!"

Wiley Fitch pushed harder, "Come on, sir, you know there was another person... the photographer's mate who ran the slide projector."

"Oh, yes, I forgot about her."

"Her?" Wiley kept digging, "Why isn't she here to testify?"

"She was pregnant and is home on maternity leave."

"Is there a name," asked Wiley.

"I don't remember," said the Admiral.

The senior Judge, Admiral Moore, rapped his gavel and adjourned for the day.

Next morning it was Admiral Parker who sailed through the Prosecutor's questions with ease and braced himself for Wiley's cross-examination.

But Defense Wiley had only one question, "Why did you dismiss Captain Franklin from following his subpoena?"

Parker smiled at the ease of the question, "Obvious, you idiot, no father wants to testify against his own son."

Admiral Parker thought he had scored a point for the prosecution, where, in fact, he opened up the way for a wily defense. Time would tell.

The Prosecution would have one more witness after lunch: A French Air force Officer.

All afternoon they listened to the witness extol the virtues of Homer Pickens. He brought personnel records from France and was asked to read every line. Proctor did not bother to have a French interpreter on hand to verify that what was read was truly accurate.

Wiley cross examined the man, but could gain nothing. Rules would not permit him to bring in a new witness during cross examination, so he made a motion to hold the man over, or to enter his records into the exhibit file. The man had to leave, but the record stayed as part of the trial.

And that ended day three of the trial.

Than evening, Wiley and Rex burned the oil late into the night preparing final details for next day's defense.

"I still think you should let me testify," said Rex.

"Remember," Wiley reminded him, "That prosecutor Proctor can be most vicious and his cross-examination will flay you like a filleted herring."

When Wiley entered the courtroom on Wednesday morning, he was grieved to see that Rex was back in leg irons.

"What's the meaning of this?" he asked the Clerk.

"His honor, Adm. Moore ordered it."

Wiley sat down next to Rex, and smiled, "I think the old man has already made up his mind that you are guilty as charged. Today we will surely change his mind."

His first witness was a French school teacher who testified the document read the previous day about Homer Pickett was not what was read. The judges had the court stenographer read back the sworn testimony of the French Officer. There were many discrepancies.

"What else do you see?" Wiley asked the witness.

"Parts of the document have been erased with bleach and written over with a different ink and typewriter," she said.

"And what does the new writing say, right here," Wiley pointed to a sentence.

"The king then hung the Cross of Honor on him and kissed him..."

"So you think that it's forged?"

"Obviously," she said.

"Objection!' screamed Proctor.

"Overruled," said Judge Moore. "Call your next witness."

Wiley was smiling, "Next, I call Photographer's Mate Warren Venable.

"Objection," called Proctor, there's no Photographers on the witness list.

"Begging your pardon, sir, but Admiral McCann's testimony allows it. He is the slide projectionist that was supposed to be pregnant. The room erupted in laughter and Judge Moore had to restore order by pounding his gavel. When things quieted down, Wiley asked, "What slides did you show on September 19th in Conference Room 308?"

"They were maps of islands in Korea Bay and some other photos that are classified."

"Can you share the classified pictures with Senior Judge, Fleet Admiral Moore?"

Before he could answer, he was interrupted.

"You damn right, bring them to me, Petty officer," commanded the Admiral.

The room fell deathly silent except for the riffle of paper photographs being passed around to members of the panel. They were aerial photos of the communications center, the same fortress Rex had been sent to destroy, but that Cdr. Banks insisted had nothing to do with Rex's mission.

Admirals Parker and McCann and Cdr. Banks had departed from the area the previous day, and had no idea that their integrity was now under question. The only remaining member of the original conference sitting in the courtroom was Rex's dad, Captain Franklin.

"I'm not done," said Wiley Fitch. I have two more witnesses."

"Proceed."

"I intended to call Lt. William Ford, the C-119 Pilot, earlier, but he was kidnapped and later found bound and gagged in Senator Abram Collins motel room, here in Sasebo."

The courtroom erupted again and reporters went running out to find phones. Judge Moore almost broke his gavel until order was restored. "I hope you have proof. These are pretty wild accusations," he glared at Wiley.

"How about you hear it direct from the pilot? I call William Ford to the stand."

Lt. Ford then proceeded to tell all.

Wiley asked, "What besides parachutes and scuba gear were Rex and Homer carrying?"

"Over 35 pounds of explosives plus detonators and some kind of oxygen generator," said Ford.

"That's enough for me," broke in Judge Ruth Loring.

Senior Judge Moore called a recess until the following day.

"Your honors," broke in Wilcy Fitch, "Can you at least order the leg irons be removed?"

"So let it be done," Moore said, "but he still is to remain in custody."

On Thursday, the word came down that the recess was extended, and for all parties to be prepared to reconvene on Friday.

"It's not over yet," said Wiley, "We still have not taken our best shot."

"What's that?" asked Rex.

"Your code book you took from the fortress. After that is introduced, there can be no doubt that you were there."

"But what about the actual charge of murder?" pleaded Rex, "I did kill the man, and there's no witness."

"Yes there is," said Wiley.

"Who?"

"You! I'm putting you on the stand when we resume."

They did not receive a call until after lunch on Friday. The court room was packed, mostly with reporters from around the world.

Judge Moore was the first to speak, "I have an important announcement, ladies and gentlemen," he began, "Certain Naval Officers and a United States Senator are under full investigation. Apparently the United States of America did in fact blow up a North Korean-Chinese communication center, killing hundreds, for which we have no regrets and make no apology. As long as armed aggression threatens the United States and her allies, these things are going to happen. Regretfully, they are the spawn of war.

"Now, back to the case at hand. We still must have proof that Petty Officer Franklin was in fact, the instrument used in this destruction of enemy forces, and you (He looked straight at Jonathan Proctor) must prove murder with forethought of the Frenchman. So far, you have failed. We will now hear the rest of the defense."

Wiley stood facing the panel. "First, your honors, I would like to introduce into evidence this North Korean code book, which would now be in the hands of Intelligence if this silly charge against Franklin had not been filed."

That really stung Proctor, who started to object, but thought better of it.

Wiley continued, "I call Petty Officer Franklin to the stand." When Rex was sworn, Wiley asked, "Do you recognize this code book, and if so, where did you obtain it?"

"The guard in the submarine pen had it on his desk. I picked it up after I put him out of action."

"You killed him?"

"Yes sir. We had no choice. Homer was supposed to do it but he held back."

"Then what happened?" asked Wiley.

"Homer came at me with a knife. We fought and he tried to stab me. He would have succeeded, except his knife deflected off the code book cover. If you look you can see the gouge mark." Rex was sweating. He did not enjoy reliving the memory.

"And then?" said Wiley.

"Then my Frogman instincts took over, and I don't remember exact details, except I loosened my diving weight belt and swung it at him. It hit the side of his head and knocked him out."

"Kill him?"

"I don't know. I didn't check. He had become my enemy and I had to finish the mission. The Navy Frogman program taught me the reflex action." Rex was visibly shaking.

Just then, an observer from the back of the room stood up and said, "If your honors please, I can clear this all up."

"Who are you?" asked Judge Moore.

"I am Captain John Franklin who Admiral McCann earlier excused. I am Rex's father and I am damned ashamed of what we put him through.

Wiley said, "We? Who are we?"

John traded the witness chair with Rex.

Captain Franklin outlined the whole conspiracy and named all names. Reporters were busy scribbling notes. No press photographers were permitted in the room.

"I didn't know that Homer was not who he said he was. I accepted the word of Cdr. Banks and Admiral McCann. They and the Senator had reasons for the mission to fail. They did not share those reasons with me, except that it had to do with high level national security. They said the CIA was involved and I believed them.

"I approved using Rex because of his inexperience; we all thought he would fail. Homer was supposed to disable Rex, but not harm him, and then abort the mission.

"Now that Rex spoiled their plans and had killed Homer in self defense, the French Communists were pissed, the Chinese were pissed, the Senators were in fear of being exposed, the officers were basically doing as they were told, because Banks had financial ties to the construction, and I was being blackmailed because of a female indiscretion which could have affected my future.

At this point, Wiley interrupted. "You mentioned Senators in the plural. Did you mean that?"

"Yes, there are others involved, but I don't know who."

More reporters dashed out of the room.

Chief Advocate, Admiral Moore rapped his gavel, "Will the stenographer please read back the testimony of Admiral McCann from Monday."

"Yes sir," she replied, "It will take only a moment." The room was so quiet that one could hear a needle drop.

"Here it is," she started, "' There was no such thing as a Communist communications center, except in the imagination of this young frogman. He was only dreaming of achieving glory. He and Homer Pickens were sent on a routine reconnaissance mission in the Korea Bay, nothing more.'"

"Well," said Judge McVey, "We certainly know that there was a communications center that got destroyed, so why did Admiral McCann perjure himself?"

"I think we've heard all we need," said Admiral Moore to his panel, "Do you want to discuss anything, or shall we vote now?"

Four voices in unison declared, "Innocent."

Judge Moore rapped his gavel, "All charges dropped. The prisoner is to be released."

And that was it!

Rex Franklin could finally meet his son, Nathan now almost 3 months old.

* * *

Rex was back in the Frogman's Navy, at Coronado, as if nothing had happened.

"My love is too strong, to let a little thing like a charge of murder change it," Carol laughed, kissing him passionately.

"It's good to have it over," he said, entering their apartment and closing the front door.

Fifteen minutes later, there was a loud knock. It was an Admiral's aide. His long limousine waited at the curb.

"DV2 Rex Franklin," he asked. "You are wanted back in Washington. A Navy jet is waiting for you this instant."

Damn!

Chapter Fourteen ~ Will the Axe Head Float?

Eight hours later, Rex was called to the White House.

President Dwight D. Eisenhower was most cordial and seemed like he wanted to talk forever. After pinning the Navy Cross on Rex's proud chest, he rambled on about the world situation. He asked Rex if he thought General so-and-so was doing a good job, or if he should be replaced.

Rex was taken aback, "The peace talks at Panmunjom defined a still shaky 38th parallel," was all he could think to say.

"You know that you really opened a big can of worms," said the President, "The media has named it *"The Schoen Conspiracy"* after Senator Collins aide. Your action wiped out two Senators and one Congressman and ended the careers of three traitorous Naval officers. The Nation will be eternally grateful."

When the conspiracy started to unravel, it collapsed like a house of cards. The Senators were impeached. Both

Admirals received dishonorable discharges and lost their pensions. Lt. Cdr. Banks was tried and hung for treason. Captain Franklin was dishonorably discharged, but was allowed to keep his pension. Criminal charges were still pending on the Senators, the Congressman and the two Admirals.

Rex had memories, how could one lone sailor cause all that? He had been awarded the navy's highest Medal of Honor, pinned on him by the President himself, yet he felt no honor. His beautiful America showed her true colors, like a basket of half rotten apples. It was the first time the thought of changing careers entered his head and he was scared to death.

After lunch with the President, he was excused, and had to arrange for his own transportation back to Coronado. He was dogged by the media all the way.

Cameras flashed in his face when he least expected it. He quickly learned the best evasive maneuvers to avoid reporter's questions.

Later, back at home, he was faced with a dilemma: to stay in the Navy or not? He loved the challenge and adventure of the Frogman motto and ethics. *But can I trust those in command?* He kept questioning himself.

Carol was no help. She had what it took to be a sailor's wife, but no woman is going to commit to weeks or months of loneliness. The best she could do was to convince Rex she wanted stay in San Diego, near the Frogman Special Ops Center at Coronado.

This convinced Rex to stay on at least until the end of his current hitch, to see if the political situation changed.

By Christmas, Rex was back with his unit, somewhere in the Pacific and Carol waited patiently for his return. She was pregnant again.

Rex's dad, John also settled in Coronado and was waiting. He had an idea of financing a scuba equipment partnership with Rex, but only if he could convince him to leave the Navy.

Friend Ron Martin was somewhere deep in the jungles of the Yucatan on some National Geographic photo shoot, and Tim was in the middle of a huge brush and forest fire and could not be spared.

* * *

While Rex could be called for duty anywhere in the world, he could be sure his home base would remain at Coronado. He and Carol settled into the enlisted housing at San Diego. Rex was now earning more as an E-5 and Carol kept busy raising babies and working part time in the base commissary.

For the next year, his duties involved a few recon missions, but were training for the most part. He was a Petty officer Diver 2nd Class and would soon be eligible for the 1st Class exam. His second enlistment was for two more years. Options were in his future, but no decisions had yet been made. By October, 1955, Carol was pregnant with her second child, and Rex was eager to stick around close to home.

Therefore, it was bad news when his platoon was placed on alert for an imminent mission.

A platoon of eight warriors filed into the briefing complex.

A new Lieutenant introduced himself and started the briefing. "You men have been volunteered... or should I say, loaned out to the United Nations as observers. You will be parachuting into a foreign country with armed invasion forces of a friendly allied nation.

You have exactly four weeks to prepare. There will be one week of parachute review, a week of basic combat review, and two weeks of language and culture studies. You will move on-base for the last two weeks and be held without any outside communication. Your mission is confidential.

"What are the languages?" asked Rex.

"One is French and the other is secret. You won't know what it is until you begin your sequestered final two weeks. Eight of you will train, but only three will be chosen for the mission."

A few routine questions were answered.

"Your plane for Fort Benning will be departing this afternoon at 1330 hours. Dismissed!"

Rex had a bad feeling. The minute it was suggested they might be working with the French, his gut twisted into a knot. Homer Pickett was French, and he had to kill him. *No Frenchmen,* his soul pleaded.

Their week at the Georgia parachute training base passed quickly. Then they were hustled back to Camp Pendleton in California. Rex spent his eight hour pass with Carol, but the jet lag required some sleep catch-up.

At the Pendleton rifle ranges, they had to qualify on two new French weapons. The guns were totally foreign to anything they had ever used.

"What's wrong with our own armament?" was the chief question.

"If you get caught in a firefight," answered an instructor, "you have to use their supply, the same caliber ammunition as everyone else."

That made sense. The Americans would at least be able to carry their own side-arms with limited ammunition.

Their combat readiness review was just as grueling as their original training had been. After Camp Pendleton, they were moved into a special compound back at Coronado. No outside contact would be permitted, and no liberty was granted. They would be incommunicado until the mission was over.

It was *Parlez voix Francais* all morning and the answer to the most burning question every afternoon: Vietnamese and Laotian. Mission details were developing.

French Vietnam was currently one of the world's hot spots. The first Indochina War had been going on since 1946. Vietnam had been a French colony before the occupation by the Japanese in World War II.

After the Japanese surrender, Vietnam became an open target for whoever was strong enough to take it. The French, of course objected and sent thousands of troops to reclaim their lost property.

Communist China, with the Soviet Union's support, had other ideas. A third and very powerful force was the Vietnamese led by Ho Chi Minh.

For seven years the forces see-sawed back and forth with the entire world watching. In April, 1953, Communist forces massed to invade Laos, and shortly afterward, all French forces in and around Dien Bien Phu in Vietnam were tied down by the Viet Minh Communist supported forces.

Rex's Frogman platoon would have to be secreted into Hanoi, 90 miles up the Red River from the coast. Once at Hanoi, they were expected to meet up with the French 2nd Battalion of Light Riflemen parachutist under the command of a Major Brechignac. The battalion was scheduled to board C-119 aircraft for the 180 mile flight to Dien Bien Phu.

"How are we supposed to get to Hanoi?" someone asked.

The same new Lieutenant was there to brief them further, "A shallow water patrol boat will drop all eight of you about a mile off the mouth of the Red River. There's a Viet Minh garrison 300 yards inland. You will have to swim, partly underwater to get around them. You will be dragging two sand sleds on the river bottom, containing your inflatable boat, motors and weapons. The river is wide and the current slow, the water is shallow, less than ten feet deep, and the incoming tide will assist you.

"Once you get sufficient distance between you and the garrison, you will land, inflate your boat, mount the motors and proceed on up the river to Hanoi. You must arrive there by 0800 hours on the 21st.

"A French lorry will meet you at the Hanoi dock to transport three of you to the airport."

"Which three?" several Frogmen asked in unison.

"Petty Officer Rex Franklin will have a sealed envelope in his waterproof pouch. The envelope will be opened on the dock in Hanoi. The remaining men will return the boats to the Gulf of Tonkin where we will pick them up."

"Are you placing me in charge?" asked Rex. It was a fair question because special ops missions command often ignored rank.

The Lieutenant smiled, "Only until the group reaches Hanoi, so you still don't know if you were picked for the actual mission or not."

"Why all the secrecy?" one man asked.

"The French know we're coming, but the rest of the world must not know we are sending armed warriors into this area."

The language classes continued for ten more days, weekends included.

On November 18th, all eight Frogmen with full equipment were loaded into an old

Dakota aircraft for a 24 hour flight: North Island to Hawaii to Midway to Sasebo to Haikou.

In Sasebo, they were given 24 hours R and R, but still no outside contact allowed. Rex considered it to be another bad omen. He was not pleased returning to the place of his previous interment and trial. First, working with Frenchmen and now this!

He had little time to think about it though, because on the morning of the 20th, they were all loaded on another plane for a flight to Taipei then Haikou then aboard a fast patrol boat for the trip across the Gulf of Tonkin. At sunset, eight Frogmen slid quietly into the muddy waters just off the Red River Delta of Vietnam. They had until dawn to swim, paddle and cruise over 90 miles of hostile river.

It was child's play getting past the observation garrison. They simply mounted scuba tanks and walked submerged on the sandy bottom of the Red River right past the singing, drunken Viet Minh. Weapons, outboard motors, fuel and two inflatables followed on buoyant sledges, engineered with exactly the right weight so they barely dragged on the bottom. One Frogman swam 100 feet ahead, to make sure they avoided any sunken obstacles or deep holes.

At 400 yards, they surfaced on a muddy bar, hooked up Jato bottles and inflated two rafts, mounted the outboards and started upriver. There were not supposed to be any Viet Minh between there and Hanoi, so night fishermen would be assumed to be the cause of motor noise.

About 0330 the moon rose and bathed the river in soft light. They were more than three quarters of the way to Hanoi when they came under fire from the north shore. Quickly steering into the shadows of the opposite shore, Rex assessed damage. One raft damaged and taking water and one slightly wounded.

"It's barely a scratch," he said, while one of his buddies applied first aid.

"Who fired on us?"

"Probably Viet Minh."

The rafts in use were mostly unsinkable as they were divided into four separate air compartments. Rex asked, "Can you guys paddle straight with three compartments?"

"Aye."

"Then let's get outa here before they come looking," said Rex, "Stay in the shadows and in about a mile, we should be able to fire up the engines again."

Before that could happen, a French patrol boat spotted them and heaved to alongside.

"We heard gunfire," a man said in French, "Who are you?"

Rex knew a recognition password and repeated, "We are part of Operation Beaver."

"Beaver? What is Beaver?" asked the boat commander.

Rex realized his error and repeated the French word for beaver, "I meant to say Operation Castor."

"Ah," said the Frenchman, "We are expecting you.

Aboard the patrol boat, Rex decided they would let the French transport three of them to Hanoi and send the rest of the patrol back downriver from here. Opening the envelope in the presence of all, he read the names printed inside: "Seaman Al Kingston, DV2 Rex Franklin and DV3 Roger Emerson.

They sunk the damaged boat and mounted its engine on the other. The patrol boat escorted them past the place where they had been shot at, then turned around and headed full speed for Hanoi.

Al Kingston was from Kentucky. His family raised horses. He had this funny little piratical mustache that drooped over teeth like a fallen down picket fence. He was tall, broad shouldered with a stocky build. Al was fresh out of Frogman school and this was his first mission.

Roger Emerson had gone through training with Rex and they had been good buddies ever since. He looked the part of a hearty seaman with his broad, weathered face. His hair was secured in a tail at the nape, was black and thick. He was short but endowed with a stocky muscular build. He often answered to his nickname: Humpty-dumpty.

Hair grooming rules had always been relaxed in the military for men in Special Ops. Rex laughed when he considered what the French might think of either Roger or Al. Of the three, Rex was the only "properly groomed" sailor. All three faces, however, were smeared up with camo paint.

The patrol boat pulled into Hanoi at 0500, three hours early.

They were met by Major Biginac, a rotund, balding jolly little Frenchman. Major Big, as he was called, made them welcome by steering them first to a fabulous breakfast in an elegant provincial hall.

Major Big's Rifle Battalion were all assembled and enjoying their breakfast also. The Major called for attention and introduced the three Americans, who would be jumping with them.

Shortly after the three names were announced, one soldier near the back of the room rose up, leaving his breakfast uneaten and slipped quietly out of the room.

At 0845, the troops positioned on the two Hanoi airports to board 65 Dakota aircraft and 12 C-119 "flying boxcars" which, two hours later, poured them into the Muong Thanh valley on both sides of the village Dien Bien.

Operation Castor intended to establish a fortified airhead deep in the jungles of Vietnam. It was the largest airborne operation since WWII, dropping men and equipment steadily for three days, each aircraft making two or more trips from Hanoi.

Before this operation, Dien Bien was a tiny village, famous for its opium traffic. It had a small airfield built for moving the opium. Operation Castor included heavy construction equipment designed to extend one runway and build another.

Rex, Al & Roger were in the first wave preparing to jump.

"Why aren't we wearing some kind of arm band, as observers," asked Al.

"The world is not supposed to know we are here," said Rex.

"Yeah, we gotta blend in with the Frogs," added Roger, "and do everything they do."

"Just keep out of their way if it comes to any major offensive," said Rex.

A buzzer startled them. The jumpmaster called out in French, "On your feet, hook up guide wires. Drop zone 'Axe head' in sixty seconds." The jump light came on, the door opened, and 70 parachutes fluttered through the blue sky in perfect sequence, like huge snowflakes drifting lazily to earth.

Snowflakes, however, melt in hot jungles. This drop overshot its mark by half a mile and came down right in the midst of a Viet Minh company at drill.

A full scale firefight erupted. Fortunately three American warriors were able to hold the enemy at bay until the French platoons could regroup and organize.

The French company soon had the outnumbered Viet Minh on the rout. Rex and his companions gave first aid to several wounded and one man was killed.

Major Big quickly ordered them all to rejoin the main forces closer to Dien Bien. All day, the planes kept coming, dropping supplies, heavy artillery, construction equipment and many more men.

At 1400 hours the French commanding Generals declared the Dien Bien Phu airstrip secure.

"Our job here is complete," Rex told Major Big. The Major embraced him with cheek kisses, the way the French do. "We must thank you for your help when we overshot our drop zone. Without your extra firepower, I think we would have lost a few more good men. I will recommend you and your men for a medal."

Rex told his crew, "We rest up now and tomorrow a helicopter will ferry us back to Hanoi.

All day, Rex had an uneasy feeling that he was being watched by some unknown. True, there was much activity and many men milling around their temporary quarters. Twice, when the feeling was strongest, he would quickly glance over his shoulder. Was the movement he saw ducking behind a tree, real or only imagined?

That night, the three of them bunked with five Frenchmen in an eight man tent. Rex was bone weary as he spread his bedroll on a canvas cot, flopped down on top of it and was asleep the moment he stretched out.

Some time later he was jolted awake by a faint rustling noise, too near him to be normal. There was just enough light and it reflected off of a dagger, which was poised a mere inch from his breast ready to strike.

Rex's reaction was instant and automatic. While his left arm swiftly deflected the poised knife, he rolled his body rapidly into the attacker, rather than away as would be expected. His right hand held a .45 caliber automatic, firing into the attackers left hip, while his left foot crashed down on the back of the man's neck. The attacker's loud "ugh, the sound of the shot and the clatter of steel flying against a tent post brought the whole room instantly awake.

Roger was instantly at Rex's side, and Al had the strangers face smashed into the dirt floor. Lights flared on, bouncing around the camp like drunken fireflies. A sergeant barged in demanding to know what all the racket was about.

"This man tried to knife me while I slept," Rex told him.

"Let's have him up; let's see who he is. You'll both have to see the Major." The sergeant assumed the two had been fighting.

"Who is he?" asked Rex.

IIis attacker, facc now out of the dirt, glared at Rex and spat in his face.

"His name is Giles Pickens," said the Sergeant, "How did he get shot?"

"Ask him," said Rex, wondering about the surname. "Ask if he had a brother named Homer?"

Just then Major Big barked orders to the gathering crowd to let him pass in to the tent. The sergeants report to him was spoken too fast for the Americans to understand, but must have been fairly accurate because he smiled at Rex, growled at Giles and ordered him carried out.

In slower French, he explained, "I did not know that you were the same Rex Franklin from the Schoen Conspiracy. We followed the media very closely and were very ashamed when it was proven Homer was a traitor. We knew Giles vowed revenge, but had no idea Fate would send you here."

While waiting for their helicopter, Rex had much to think about, *Three strikes and you're out... First Frenchman Homer, Frenchmen then missed the Axe Head drop zone falling into a firefight, and third Frenchman, Giles also tried to kill. Enough!*

Rex had a favorite bible story about the Prophet Elisha: "...Elisha the man of God asked, "Where did the axe head fall in the river?", and the man showed him the place. Then Elisha cut down a stick, and threw it there, and the iron axe head rose up to the surface . *(2 Kings 6:6)*

And just as the axe head was wrought of heavy, hardened iron, so our heavy sinful natures are hardened and absolutely impervious to the grace of God.

Chapter Fifteen ~ Scuba Shop

All the French effort at Dien Bien Phu was wasted. Originally, the French tried to create an air-supplied base at Dien Bien Phu, deep in the hills of Vietnam. Its purpose was to cut off Viet Minh supply lines into the neighboring French protectorate of Laos, at the same time drawing the Viet Minh into a battle that would cripple them.

Later the next spring, the Viet Minh, under General Vo Nguyen Giap, surrounded and besieged the French, who were unaware of the Viet Minh's possession of heavy artillery (including anti-aircraft guns) and their ability to move such weapons to the mountain crests overlooking the French encampment. The Viet Minh occupied the highlands around Dien Bien Phu, and were able to fire down accurately onto French positions. This culminated in a massive French defeat that effectively ended the First Indochina War.

Rex Franklin's second contract with the U.S. Navy was up for renewal on June 25th, 1956. All his command and fellow Frogmen had no doubt that he would re-enlist and make a career out of the Navy.

Unknown to all except Rex, was the frustration and disappointment he felt about his present career. The French ouster in Vietnam was a big issue. The graft and greed in the Congress and the military was another.

Friendly Lt. Bill Ford walked in one evening on Rex, Al & Roger. The three were playing cutthroat pinochle in the recreation room of their barracks.

"Can I join you guys for a chat?" Bill asked.

"Sure," said Rex, "You know we Frogmen mix enlisted and officers at random."

"Have you Roger and Rex given any thought about your re-enlistment? You've got less than a month."

"How much time have you got to listen?" asked Rex with a smile.

"All night."

"Well, you know Carol and I have two young boys at home and she thinks she is pregnant again."

"Congratulations," said the Lt.

"I'd like to get real serious, Bill," Rex led off, "First let me ask you a question... The face of war is changing. Where are Special Ops & Frogmen going in the future?"

"You're so right, Rex," Bill Ford said, "The truth is, any government that thinks war is somehow fair and subject to rules like a basketball game probably should not get into a war in the first place, because nothing is fair in war and often the wrong people get killed or injured. It's been happening for about a million years.

"Future wars won't be fought on battlefields; they will be fought with weapons of stealth, infiltration and guerilla tactics. Our own Special Operations Forces are considering new names, names like Green Beret or Navy SEALS. You guys thought 'Hell week' was bad for you; it's going to be twice hell for future warriors."

"Faced with the murderous cutthoats of the Nazis, Charlie or Viet Minh we are not fighting anymore under the rules of Geneva. We are fighting under the rules of Article 223, the caliber of our M4 rifle.

"In the global war on terror, we have rules, and our opponents use them against us. We try to be reasonable; they will stop at nothing. They will stoop to any form of base warfare: torture, beheading, mutilation, hiding as innocent civilians, women and children. They're right up there with the monsters of history."

"Gee, Lieutenant," said Roger, "You're not making it easy for us to decide."

Al moved in to the discussion, "They don't have to follow the rules of engagement like we do, and if we slip up, we not only have our own navy judge advocate to rule against us, but the American media can be even more ruthless."

"Let me add to that," said Rex, "We all harbor fears about untrained, half-educated journalists who only want a good story to justify their salaries. The first minute an armed conflict turns into a media war, the news becomes someone's opinion, not hard truth."

"You're right, Rex," said Bill, "and two major problems come out of that situation: the media sensation is always good news for the enemy, and secondly poor reporting always has an effect on the decisions of our politicians in Washington."

"I just wish every media person had to spend an hour in the jungles of Vietnam or in 'Hell week', offered Al, "

"They probably wouldn't survive."

The session was very enlightening and the guys never completed their pinochle game. Rex made up his mind to leave the Navy, Al and Roger decided to sign up for another hitch. Rex knew he might someday regret the decision, but for the first time in months, he felt no mental burden.

* * *

Rex Franklin was up and out of his bunk early. Today was a special day. It was not yet daylight. This morning, he would not even stop at the mess hall for breakfast. His business was too urgent.

An hour later, he held more money in his hand than he had possessed since the Lmuma Mine adventure.. A six year Navy tour behind him and arms stinging from vaccinations, he was standing in the paymaster's office in San Diego. It was the last stop on his long list of required checking out chores. The paymaster's yeoman had thoroughly checked each signature by each item on the list, and, as expected, shook his head sadly, as if to imply some major person had been missed. But then, he shyly smiled and gave Rex seven-hundred and fifty dollars mustering out pay. Happiness flooded Rex and he turned to leave, seeking the elusive freedom just outside the base gate.

"Hold it, sailor," said the yeoman, "You're not done yet."

Rex felt a sinking feeling in his chest, "What now?"

"Down that hall, fourth door on the left," he motioned to his right, "Lieutenant Walker is waiting for you."

"Damned Navy bureaucracy," he thought, *"Hurry up and wait!"*

Rex had been dreaming of this separation day for four weeks, he was tired of Navy discipline anyway. It was a decision he might regret later, but for now all he wanted was to be a civilian again. He had great plans to open a scuba dive shop and had a financial partner lined up and waiting.

Rex joined the Navy in 1950, a few months out of high school. He figured the volunteer Navy would be better than being drafted into the Army. North and South Korea were in flames and he'd prefer not going there. By enlisting, he could have his choice of occupations: But Frogman was the only consideration. Now, his dreams had been shattered by national crooked politics and leaders of low moral standards.

He had no trouble finding Lt. Walker's office, but then had been ushered into a small anteroom to wait. *Please God! Let me get out of here so I can get back to my wife and new baby son.*

He glanced at his wristwatch and wondered why they were taking so long. The hands of the electric Ingersol wall clock crept past 10:45 and still he waited.

"Petty Officer Franklin!" called a yeoman, shrilly, "The Lieutenant will see you now." And under her breath she mumbled just loud enough for Rex to hear, "You lucky stiff." Rex thanked the good looking W.A.V.E. with a smile and a wink, then rapped softly on a door marked, 'Discharge Officer'. His knock was answered by a raspy, "Enter!"

This was Rex's last hurdle and he was anxious. He entered the office and stared unthinking at Lt. Walker, and Walker glared back. Pregnant seconds ticked by when finally the Lieutenant spoke, "Have you forgotten how to salute?"

Rex pulled out of his lethargy, remembering that he was still in uniform and rendered a snappy salute. "Sorry, Sir," he apologized, "I meant to be in civvies."

Motioning Rex to take a seat, Walker said, "So you want to leave us?" Without waiting for a reply, he continued, "Good Frogmen are scarce and in less than six years you've already become eligible for Chief Petty Officer. Another four-year tour, you could make Warrant Officer at the rate you've been advancing."

"I'm already mustered out, sir," Rex said, "You waste time trying to convince me to stay."

Walker shuffled some papers on his desk, "Yes, I suppose so. Here's your Honorable Discharge and your DD 914 papers." He shoved a large manila envelope across the desk.

"Good luck!" he added, "And your gate pass is attached. We are sorry to lose you."

Rex snapped a quick salute and a quicker about-face and was out of the building, headed for the front gate in a record thirty seconds.

In a parking lot just inside the gate he quickly located his new 1956 Chevrolet Hatchback sedan and slumped down into the back seat. Glancing around to be sure no one was watching, he stripped down to his skivvies. *What a relief to get out of this uniform and into some decent civilian clothes.*

As Rex pulled up to the gate, he nervously dropped his pass. Fumbling around on the floor of his car he retrieved the errant document and showed it to the guard. It was a friend and fellow Frogman who had gate duty that day. He also had a joker's sense of humor.

"Can't let you out, sailor, the pass isn't signed!" he said.

Dumbfounded, Rex sat staring out the window.

"Gotcha!" said the guard, "We'll miss ya, Rex."

It was barely 0800 and the sun was just breaking over the eastern Laguna mountains. Carol was there to meet him and they drove off into a beautiful sunrise.

* * *

Years later, Rex Franklin would look back at those six years as a Navy Frogman as delightful memories.

His father, Retired Captain John Franklin was dead now, but had financed Rex into starting the largest diving and scuba business on the west coast. There were store branches in every major city, including Honolulu.

Rex and his lovely Carol lived in a fancy mansion in Coronado with their seven children. Their oldest son, Nathan was 20.

"I want to be a Navy SEAL," he told his dad one day. The Vietnam situation was now full blown and there would be plenty of need for stealth warriors.

Over the years, close contact had been maintained with Ron Martin and Tim Caruthers, companions from school years at Christian Brothers.

Ron had written and published a young-adult novella about their earlier adventures in Forrest William's Nevada gold mine. It was his first attempt at fiction;

writing for the sheer joy of entertaining kids and early success generated many more novels.

All three frequently wrote, proposing the idea of a reunion at the old mine. That is, if they could ever find it again. They knew Forrest long since passed on, and the Nevada Mining records could find no record of a "Squaw" mine ever existing anywhere in Mineral or Esmeralda counties.

Another mystery? Or did they dream it all?

Al Allaway

Book Three

Tim

Chapter Sixteen ~ Tim's Revenge

Tim Caruthers excused himself from the others in the coach. It was too warm inside and he sought the cold air of Donner Pass. He settled on the vestibule between their coach and the Pullman behind.

After the adventure in the Lmuma Mine, the glory bubble burst, the train trip back to boarding school in Sacramento offered the boring ritual of Christian Brothers Catholic High School, which would start the following morning.

Cold mountain air slapped 14-year-old Tim in the face. It was sheer pleasure. He latched the Porter's upper Dutch door open to allow a view outside the train. Leaning out slightly, he looked forward, counting the Streamliner's cars right up past the baggage-mail cars to the two diesel engines, easily visible as the train curved up the winding mountain pass. He pulled his brown suede coat tightly around his neck.

Feeling in his coat pocket, Tim retrieved his one bad habit, a vice none of his friends yet knew about. It was a Kaywoodie pipe he had stolen from his drunken step-father. He tamped the pipe bowl full of sweet smelling Amphora tobacco and lit up. After ten or fifteen minutes, the cold forced him back inside the coach. He popped a couple of little black licorice like Sen-Sen into his mouth to cover up the evidence of smoking.

"What time does the train get in to Sacramento?" he asked.

"I think the conductor said around five," answered Rex Franklin.

It was already past 2 P.M.

A cloud of gloom settled over an already foreboding, cheerless future.

Tim's father had been killed during the first wave on Omaha Beach in France and his mother remarried three times since. Her current mate left ugly bruises on both mother and son; it was reason enough for a mother to protect her only child by sending him to a private boarding school.

Like Rex, Tim also was thinking about joining a fire department. But first he wanted to obtain a degree in Fire Science Engineering.

The past mine adventure resulted in three young men advancing toward maturity very fast during one short week and learning a lot about the rewards of being honest. And they learned another valuable lesson, that broken dysfunctional families can still produce winners, despite the odds. Considering all that had happened: the bottom line of their future lives was still basically the result of their own actions. A good prayer based faith in God reflected in much of what they did.

* * *

Tim Caruthers and Ron Martin filed out of the dressing room, joining a procession of forty other young men graduating from St. Mary's College near Oakland, CA. Above the podium a huge banner proclaimed the message: *Congratulations to the Class of 1953!*

Both scanned the audience for loved ones; Tim spotting his mother on an end seat in the fifth row. An ugly blue-green bruise was partially hidden under her bandana. Tim saw red.

After the ceremony, Tim had a chance to talk with his mother. He grew very serious, as she explained the most recent fight with her husband. It was the worst ever.

Shortly thereafter, it was time for friends to part. "Do you suppose the three of us will ever get back to Lmuma for some kind of a reunion?" The question had been bugging Ron for years.

"I'd like that," said Tim, "But only if I'm not still in jail. That bastard has hurt my mom for the last time."

Ron ignored the remark. "Has anybody heard from Rex?"

Rex joined the U.S. Navy right after high school, trained in underwater demolition, and was now part of an elite Frogmen team serving somewhere near Korea.

"Not a word since the peace talks started," said Tim.

"Well, turkey," continued Ron, "I've got the photo studios offer. What'r ya going to do?"

"Ha!" exclaimed Tim, "I decided against being a Christian Brother so I applied to a Portland area fire bureau. Next week, after I kill my step-dad I'll report for training." He winked.

Ron hugged his friend without any sign of embarrassment.

"Keep in touch, turkey butt! See 'ya someday at Lmuma."

* * *

Tim drove his mother up Highway 99-W to their home in Willows, about two hours north of St. Mary's College. She cried most of the way. She had once loved Billy Crispler, but after almost 7 years of his abusive behavior and drunkenness, she was ready to quit.

At home, there was no sign of Billy. Tim insisted on taking pictures of his mother, Helen's bruises. It was a repeat of events going on in millions of homes across the country. Battered women too afraid to tell; always filled with hope that the beatings and the abuse will end. But they never do because the perpetrator has a medical disease that can only get worse, until treated by professionals.

"These on my face are not the only ones," she confessed, "While you are at it, take pictures of my back and buttocks."

What he saw was shocking.

"I want you to hide out in the hotel down at Colusa," Tim said, "Pack for at least a week. Take a cab, so he can't trace the car. Register under a false name."

"But, Tim, isn't that a little extreme?"

"Do it, Mom! No questions. Just do it!"

After depositing the film for processing at the local drug store, Tim stopped at the main station of the Willows Fire Department, where he had many friends.

An hour later found him waiting for the local District Attorney. A plot was hatching.

The next day, the processed film and prints were shown to a judge, and a no-contact order was written.

Tim pleaded with his friend the DA, "Deputize me for one hour so I can serve him with the papers." Though not quite legal, it was done. Tim then gathered his firefighter friends and found Bully Billy Crispler, as he was now known, shooting pool in a local tavern.

Tim Caruthers did not have bulging muscles, did not weigh much above average, and never felt good about violence, but he did have a solid sense of justice.

Billy Crispler saw him enter the tavern and was instantly the aggressor, "What d'ya want, punk?" he slurred.

"You've been beating my mom."

"So, what's it to ya?"

"You're going to stop as of today!"

"Yeah? Sez who?"

"Judge Parker." Tim shoved the order at him, "Read it!"

Billy swatted the paper across the room and before Tim could duck he caught a vicious punch, bloodying his nose and landing him on the floor.

Unseen by Billy, three firefighters and two policemen witnessed this assault and he was instantly surrounded. The trap was sprung.

"Billy Crispler, you are under arrest for assaulting an officer of the Court in the performance of his official duty," intoned one of the officers. Billy's arms were pinned behind him and his hands cuffed.

As they hauled him out, Tim called after, "Be sure you get his house keys."

Back at the firehouse, Tim was given first aid for his probable broken nose. He'd have it checked at the hospital later.

"You knew he had a hot temper and would sock you," said one of the firefighters, "Why didn't you duck?"

Tim thought for a moment, "I guess I'm just stupid." His friends laughed at the obvious joke. "Seriously," he continued, "Assault is a whole lot easier to prove than attempted assault. And I've got the proof right here!"

Tim had an early supper, took a pain pill and turned in. Tomorrow would be soon enough to drive down to Colusa and pick up his mother. He drifted off into a restless sleep.

The girl in his dream was gorgeous, except she had two noses. They were having a picnic on the roof of the fire station, but a big thunderstorm was rolling in from the south, so they slid down the brass pole to the apparatus bay to finish their picnic, but then the firemen burst into the room with backpack hose tanks and started spraying everything down. One of the firemen was Bully Billy Crispler. It wasn't water they were shooting out the nozzles, it was gasoline and the nozzles were flame throwers. The girl melted because she was made of wax, and Tim woke up from the dream. He was soaked in sweat and could still smell the smoke of the conflagration.

He sat dazed on the edge of the bed, thinking he should get up and find some dry pajamas. *Why was the smoke still lingering?*

He could imagine orange flickering light coming through the bedroom curtains.

It was the pop, cracking and breaking of glass that brought him fully awake.

Jez, the house is on fire!

Tim sprang up out of bed and into a layer of thick poisonous and hot smoke that had been building down from the bedroom ceiling. Fully awake now, he realized that that was the wrong thing to do. Crawling on the floor, near better air was the only correct option. Too many people died in house fires by sucking in that first lungful of poisonous gasses in the smoke.

Feeling the door, he jerked his hand back; it was hot! That meant he would be toast if he opened the door. His next option was the window, but the jamb was stuck. It had been painted shut. He crashed a chair through the window with a loud clatter of breaking glass.

Air in the room responded immediately to the opening. It kind of sucked in, then blew out, and then sucked back in again. As Tim leaped from the window sill to a nearby dormer roof, there was a terrible whoosh-like sound and the whole bedroom ignited, blowing the top window out and peppering Tim with glass. This flash-over phenomenon was known as "back draft". Tim had learned as much from his fire fighter buddies.

From the dormer roof, he could see the whole outer front of the house was in flame, and flames were pouring out of all the windows on his side of the house, including his bedroom now. The asbestos roofing under his feet was hot and beginning to melt. He could hear sirens coming, but too far away to help. His bare feet were beginning to blister. Tim had no choice but to jump the ten feet to the ground and safety.

My God! That was close! Five seconds more and I'd be dead. "Thank you, Jesus for saving me. Praise your Holy Name!"

The shock over, Tim began to feel pain. His forehead was singed from when he jumped up out of bed, unthinking. His feet were blistered, and his left leg had fractured from the jump to the ground. Besides that he was peppered in a dozen places with hot flying glass.

The first engine stretched a 2-½ inch line from the hydrant on the corner and pulled up in front of the house. Lieutenant George Highland ordered two 1-½ inch pre-connects. The fire was too far advanced to allow any search and rescue.

Tim had been hollering, but due to the typical noise of an active fire scene, no one had yet heard him until the first responding team decided to make initial attack on his side of the house.

"Hey, an injured man over here!" shouted the Lieutenant, "It's Tim. Get an ambulance."

Tim spent two nights in the hospital while doctors watched his lungs for signs of blistering. The risk of pneumonia would be high for at least a week.

"Your house is badly gutted," firefighters told him, "It was definitely set by an arsonist. The State Fire Marshal has been called in and they know who set it. When caught they'll charge him with attempted murder."

"Who?"

"Billy Crispler left a gasoline can out front with full fingerprints."

"I thought he was in jail."

"He posted bail. He's on the lam and they've got a county-wide alert out for him."

Tim's over tired mind suddenly remembered his mother, "Get police down to the hotel in Colusa. My mom might need protection and I can't drive with this cast on my leg." He mentally kicked himself for not remembering her sooner, and experienced a great deal of stress and guilt until the word came back through the Sheriff's office that she was okay.

"Any word about Billy?" he asked.

"Nope, he seems to have vanished like a ghost. The search is spreading today from surrounding counties to statewide."

The crack in his leg bone was not compound so as soon as the cast came off, he would be able to meet his commitment to begin training in a Portland area Fire Dept.

Concern for his mother's safety was now a priority. It would be necessary to insure her safety before he could think of beginning a new career.

"Any chance of Billy sneaking back into town?" he asked his District Attorney friend, "You know how sick he is; revenge will be eating at him as long as he lives."

"Until we have him convicted and jailed for arson," the D.A. answered, "we can't guarantee anything."

"We can't leave her here with my family," said Tim, "Because that's the first place Billy would look."

"How about taking her with you to Oregon?" asked the D.A.

"No good," said Tim, "Billy knew I was joining a Portland area fire department." He paused for a moment in thought, "But I think I've got a better idea."

Chapter Seventeen ~ Over the Top

Later that night Tim phoned one of his life long friends, Rex Franklin in San Diego. Rex had gone straight into the Navy after high school, served six years as a U.S. Navy Frogman. Rex, his wife Carol and his dad now partnered in a rising scuba and diving business.

Rex and Carol had both met Tim's mom, Helen and when Tim explained the problem with her ex-husband Bully Billy, they insisted Tim put her on the next flight south. They had a spare room and would love to have her.

"Just be on the lookout for this bully named Billy," Tim warned.

"Not to worry, buddy boy," said Rex, Remember, I'm a fully trained warrior."

* * *

An aerial ladder truck was set up on the drill ground of East County Fire District #15. It had an 85 foot wooden ladder which had been extended straight up, 90 degrees from the ground. A slight breeze caused the ladder to sway a bit and look very unstable. Two rookies had been hired that day, and the crew of the ladder truck stood by waiting with glee to see if the new men had what it would take to become firefighters. They thought the whole object of the exercise was to scare these guys enough to find out if they really wanted to be firefighters.

Tim Caruthers and Pepper Ficek, the targets of this humbug, arrived like innocent lambs at the drill ground. They had already each been decked out in 45 pounds of boots, turnout bunkers and helmets.

"Welcome to Fire District #15," said a jovial rather tall man in the uniform of an Assistant Chief, "I'm Chief Virgil Haase. He had a thick black mustache that dominated his long pink face and a shock of salt-and-pepper hair he combed to one side. He looked to be about 50 under his equally thick black eyebrows.

"How do you feel about heights?" he asked with a swing of his arm pointing at the raised ladder.

Tim imagined he heard a light gulp from Pepper, so he spoke first, "No problem, Chief. I was a volunteer down in Willows, California."

"Good! You can be first," he said smiling, "Up eight stories on one side, over the top head first, swing around and back down the other side."

Tim said, "Piece of cake!" He jumped up on the aerial platform to begin the climb.

"By the way," added the Chief, "At the top you'll be tempted to go around the beam end of the ladder, keeping your head up. If you do, you fail."

Then one of the truck crew hollered up to him, "And if you puke going over the top, you'll wash the truck."

Thanks for the encouragement, turkey!

Now there is no way to get over the top head down, looking straight down, without feeling some degree of vertigo. In addition, the wind was picking up and the ladder swayed more and more. Tim knew that he had a problem, but he wanted this job. It was a matter of pride. Going over the top, he closed his eyes and trusted his instincts. Coming down the other side, he started to shake and his bad leg felt like it would break again. *Made it! Ha-ha, see! Haase!*

Next, it was Pepper's turn. He made it to the top just fine, but when he looked over the top and down the other side, he froze up. "I can't do it," he hollered down.

"Okay," said the chief, "Go around the side beam and come down that way."

One could see that Pepper was visibly shaking when he reached the blacktop.

"You get one more chance, tomorrow," said the Chief.

Their other test for the day was to climb to the roof of the training station, about 18 feet high, and jump off into a life net. That seemed easy looking up at the roof, but then looking down from the roof, the ground is much further away. *Nailed it too,* laughed Tim.

The second day on the job introduced them to life around the fire station, scrubbing, waxing, buffing, all manner of housework and equipment maintenance. These were the chores of everyday life in every fire station around the country, with one major exception: the rookies had to wear 30 pound Scott air paks, face mask and a 30 minute cylinder of compressed air to breathe. These were the same self-contained breathing apparatus they would learn to use later in search and rescue operations in smoky building fires.

Every 25 to 30 minutes a warning bell would clang, telling the wearer it was time to think about backing out to get a fresh full bottle of air. The only time the rookies could take off the face mask was while eating or changing air bottles.

Whenever this self-contained breathing apparatus exercise was conducted, there was always one joker among the regular crew, who watched the rookies from a distance. The minute one of them looked like he might be heading to the toilet; Johnny Utz was ready, waiting his chance.

Peripheral vision is somewhat restricted to those wearing a mask, so Johnny would wait until the recruit was sitting on the stool or standing at the urinal then would roll a lit M-80 firecracker in under the rookie's feet.

The reaction was usually hysterical, resulting in the poor recruit doing extra cleanup duty in the head.

Fifty years ago, training in small departments was nothing like today. Often paid men had to work with volunteers. Fire academies were known only to the largest cities. Fire District 15 had three stations, six engines, one ladder truck and one rescue car. The District's area of coverage was an unincorporated bedroom community on the outskirts of Portland.

Recruits like Tim and Pepper, were assigned from day one to a working engine or ladder company. Green as grass, they would begin with on-the-job training, getting their assignments at the beginning of each shift, depending on the mood of the station Captain.

Engines carried hose, couplings and nozzles and usually five hundred gallons of water. The motor served double duty and could run either the rear wheels or a built-in pump. At a fire the driver ran the pump and made the hose connections, while the officer and the nozzleman took a line into the building where they located the seat of the fire and put water on it.

Trucks carried ladders, including a hundred foot aerial, power saws, forcible entry equipment, hydraulic extrication tools, ropes and hardware. At fires, truck companies performed forced entry, searched for victims and ventilated the fire building, which was just as necessary as putting water on a fire. Ventilation was accomplished either by laddering the roof and cutting a hole with a chain saw, or by mechanical means with huge fans.

The first four months of training rotated new recruits to different jobs in different stations on different shifts, so they never worked together for long.

Tim Caruthers was assigned to Engine 52 on "B" Shift under Captain Charley Dunbar. Johnny Utz was the Engineer/driver and Bill Powers a fifteen-year veteran, was the Nozzleman. Tim was assigned a position called Hydrantman. He and Bill rode standing up on the back of the engine, called a tailboard. Going into a fire, the hydrantman would step off and anchor an end of a supply hose with an attached hydrant gate, while the engine drove off with hose flaking out behind it from the hose bed. After connecting the hose to the hydrant and opening valves, he would run to catch up and then assist the nozzleman.

One of Tim's first working fires happened during his second week. It was an old three story house. Tim was preparing to take the hydrant, but Capt. Dunbar told Utz to drive right on by it without stopping.

"We'll get the next rig in to lay us a supply line," he told his crew, "Powers come with me, Utz you and Tim take a second line around back."

Air cylinder on his back, Tim pulled out the first hundred and fifty feet of inch and a half hose load with the gated wye. By the time he got it on his shoulder, Utz had shouldered the second hundred and fifty feet. The smoke was thick and acrid, and they coughed as they moved through it. Even Utz, the hardened nicotine junkie had trouble. He followed Tim through the fog, dropping dry hose flakes onto the ground behind them as they proceeded. Tim, unable to see the house, followed the first line on the ground.

Utz hollered over his shoulder as he ran back to hookup hoses and engage his pump, "Don't waste any water. All I've got right now is that five hundred gallons in the tank."

The back door was half off its hinges, mute testimony to the rough passage of the first crew. Inside, Engine 51's hose stream was being directed into a sheet of orange without any seeming effect, and Tim could see the boots of two firefighters on their stomachs in front of him. He could hear the crackle of burning wood. Even in the doorway he was forced to tip his helmet so that the brim shielded his face from the heat.

Tim pulled his facepiece on, tightened the straps on the sides, opened the valve at his waist, and inhaled clean air; then he pulled his hood over the top of the facepiece, put his helmet back on, and knelt in the doorway waiting for his partner.

Utz reached the porch at the same time as the hose at their feet stiffened, the water knocking the kinks out with the sound of a cardboard box being kicked. They could hear the mellow, ripping sound of fire scratching at the structure. And they advanced their line into hell.

"The truck crew should be on the roof by now," Utz told Tim, "As soon as they cut a hole, most of this smoke will clear out of here so we can see the seat of the fire."

An hour later they were picking up and returning to quarters.

"Well, Tim, how'd you like your first fire?"

"Exhilarating!" he replied, "I feel like I'm helping out my fellow man."

Every time now that Tim heard an alarm, his adrenaline pumped and he was filled with the excitement of a new challenge.

A month later, duties were shifted around and Tim was checked out on driving and operating the pump. At the same time, Utz had alarm dispatch duty. The alarm room was part of Station 52. Tim had not forgotten the mean trick Utz had played on him with the M-80 firecracker while he was training with the Scott Air Pak.

Tim purchased half a flat of sweet seedless grapes and left them anonymously in the Alarm room. Utz loved to eat and Tim guessed right: Utz ate and ate and ate some more. Before the shift ended, he was groaning in pain as he sat in the john.

Tim asked him a shift later if he'd like to share some grapes. The cussing would have burned the ears off a truck driver.

Utz was in his late fifties, was a roly-poly man with an ingratiating smile and rumpled clothing. There was always a little something a little off about him besides his love of practical jokes. He was one of those who overflowed with elaborate government conspiracy theories and was a frequent caller to extreme-right-wing radio talk shows.

Alarms in a training company can be either serious or funny. One of the goofiest that Tim experienced occurred at 0330 one cold and foggy morning. Engine 52 was tapped out for a "public assist" to a homeless camp down by the river.

Pulling through the trees on a partially frozen mud road, Captain Dunbar told his crew, "Somebody is waving a flashlight up ahead," then to Tim, "Stop here, let's see what all the fuss is about."

A man ran up to the engine and told the Captain he had a friend down in the camp that was stuck and needed extrication.

"Stuck in what?" asked Charley.

"You gotta come see," said the man, smiling.

Charley Dunbar told Tim to stay with the engine and for Bill Powers and Pepper Ficek to follow him with the tool box.

After a moment, Tim heard laughing. Then his radio crackled, "Captain 52 to Engine 52, Tim, bring down your grease gun."

About that time, two police cruisers parked by the engine and a couple of officers walked down into the hobo jungle with Tim.

"What's up?" asked a female cop.

"Somebody's stuck," said Tim, "My Captain asked for engine lube."

A couple of bonfires flared up revealing a large plywood box, big enough for a man to sleep inside. Several flashlight beams were focused on a small hole that had been drilled into the box about three feet above the ground. There was a small trickle of blood oozing out of the hole, and something else.

On closer examination the lady officer gasped, "That looks like a penis!"

"Right on, lady," someone confirmed, "It's caught in the rough cut splinters. He was too cold or too lazy to go outside to relieve himself."

The officer's "Tee-hees" didn't help the victim at all because the object in question grew a bit larger.

Carefully cutting out the panel, Brave Engine 52's crew eased the problem out of the splinters.

"Cancel the ambulance," Captain Dunbar told the dispatcher, and everybody went home.

Tim advanced in firefighting skills and filled his memory with stories to tell his grandchildren.

After a year, he passed his probation with flying colors.

Four years later, Tim was over the top again, this time passing the Lieutenant's test.

The District was growing and opened two new stations. Tim was assigned to "A" shift at a brand new Engine 55.

He asked for and received Johnny Utz for Engineer, Pepper Ficek as Nozzleman and a trainee named Neal Murphy.

Firefighters have a sense of family and comradery. At the station that differs from their families at home. Neal Murphy fit in immediately. He was tall and lean, four inches taller than Tim with a dark complexion and jaws that stood out like walnuts when he chewed gum, which he did constantly. He spoke in a mellow baritone and was so deliberate in what he said and did that at times he gave the impression of being dim-witted.

Murphy earned instant respect with his tales of ancient fire heroes and martyrs, chief of which is the Patron Saint of firefighters everywhere: a Roman soldier named Florian. He had been assigned to gather up Christians but instead made a bold declaration that he too was a believer in Jesus the Christ. Embarrassed, his superiors decided to make an example of him and so they did in a most gruesome fashion. Florian was scourged, partially flayed (skinned) while alive, set on fire and then thrown into the river Enns with a stone tied to his neck.

Later a devout woman of faith recovered his body from the river and buried him nearby. As the story of his courage and professions of faith in Christ spread, Rome took note. More reports of miracles surrounding him were acknowledged especially from Poland where many of his relics were interred. He is now one of the patrons of those in danger from fire or water.

As soon as the opening of the new station 55 was announced by the news media, an unusual series of arson fires broke out in engine 55's first response area.

The State Fire Marshal was called in and could make no sense of it. The fires were all random with no apparent connection, except being in the same area. The only conclusion was, "Be watchful; You've got a serial arsonist on the loose."

* * *

The cab of the gasoline tanker had rolled up onto the back of the Toyota van, completely crunching the rear, before smashing through the wire barrier that lined the bridge. In the midst of the accident, the driver had locked the van wheel as she'd slammed on the brakes, and the truck had whipsawed across both lanes of the road, completely blocking both directions. The van, pinned beneath the front of the cab, hung off the bridge like a diving board, balancing precariously in a downward position. The roof had been torn open, like a partially opened can, as it ripped through the cable along the side of the bridge. The only thing that kept the van from falling into the river some eighty feet below was the weight of the tanker's cab, and the cab itself looked far from stable.

Its engine was smoking badly, and fluid was leaking steadily onto the Toyota beneath, spreading a shiny veneer over the hood.

Tim looked around, adrenaline coursing through his system. Finding a police officer, he hollered, "We gotta get these people out of here." He was referring to the gawkers and parked cars on both ends of the bridge.

Nearby, he saw the truck driver, unhurt but dazed. "What's in your tanks?"

"Gasoline, three quarters full."

Smoking engine . . . leaking over the car.

"If that cab explodes, will the tanks go with it?"

"They shouldn't, Lieutenant," said the driver, "unless the lining was damaged. I didn't see any leak, but I can't be sure."

Two additional units arrived, another engine and a ladder truck. The rest of Tim's crew ran up as the 2½ inch line they had stretched was charged.

The woman in the van was regaining consciousness and started moving about.

"Don't move, lady. Hold very still! We're trying to get you out," Tim hollered, "Any motion could make you fall." He could hear her sobs and feel her fear.

Tim would be incident commander until a chief officer arrived. He ordered the truck to extend its aerial horizontally and down about five degrees in order to attempt a rescue of the lady trapped in the van. Any contact with the van or cab of the truck could send the van plummeting to the river.

Ladders are not designed for horizontal weight bearing use so this maneuver was risky. The ladder would have to be extended almost to maximum and bear the weight of a firefighter and the victim on the end.

Flames could now be seen in the truck engine compartment, but a water stream, even a gentle fog could send the whole mess into the drink.

Because he weighed less than others on his crew, Tim opted to make the rescue himself. Tying himself to the top rung, he motioned for the truckman to start extending the ladder. Right away he could feel the aluminum bending and feel the instability. Slowly the ladder moved toward the torn open top of the van. About five feet away, the ladder buckled and dropped about a foot. It was obviously under mechanical stress.

"Just a couple more feet," said Tim. He could hear the groans of metal under stress as the van started to slip out from under the truck. It moved only two inches and stopped.

Tim had to stretch himself another foot off the end of the ladder to be able to see and talk to the victim. Fortunately she was slight in size and was coherent enough to follow his instructions.

"Very very slowly," he said, "Slip this looped rope under your arms, and then very slowly reach up and grasp my hand."

Activating his lapel mike, he told the truck to raise the ladder slowly, a foot at a time. Presently, Tim and one very frightened lady were suspended on the ladder end, eighty feet above the river below. Just then, there was a loud poof, igniting the leaking gasoline. The concussion released the van which then crashed into the river.

A loud screech like a banshee wail was emitted as the truck's undercarriage teetered and slipped ever so slowly over the concrete bridge abutment, no longer hitched to the gasoline tanker. Flames and black smoke now rolled out of the truck cab. One over anxious firefighter directed a straight stream of water into the open cab. That's all it took to send the cab over the brink. When it hit the rocky shallow stream below, it burst into a huge orange fire ball.

In the sudden heat, Tim almost dropped the panicking lady.

Fog streams hit both sides of the tanker trailer, while the ladder was slowly retracted to a safe position. Tim and the victim were soaking wet when helping hands finally reached out to them.

Tim's career was over the top, again.

Engine 55 barely backed into their station when they got another alarm.

Chapter Eighteen ~ Burn Baby, Burn!

From the quantity of the alert tones, they knew the alarm was major.

"Engine 55, Engine 51, Engine 52, Engine 72, Truck 52, Truck 5, Air 1, Rescue 15, Battalion 5, 3701 Pierce Marina, heavy smoke reported from a furniture warehouse."

"That's us," hollered Tim. A volunteer named Lew Adams was in the station at the time, so they roared out with a five man crew. Lew had been a member of AA for years, could give his sobriety time in months and days. As a drunk he'd been as cocksure as a man could be, and sobriety hadn't changed that. He was fifty-two years old, with a ruddy face and puffy tea bags of flesh under his green eyes. His head was so large it scared small children. He had a shock of pale brown hair he clipped himself and combed straight back, though by mid-day most of it stuck straight up.

Tim told Johnny Utz, "We just inspected that place last week, the day you were off sick. If there's any build up of fire, this one will be a greater alarm."

As they turned onto Pearce Marina from 28th Street, they could see clouds of black smoke boiling up hundreds of feet into the sky.

Tim radioed Dispatch, "Engine 55 arrived. This is a 3 story 300 by 90 foot warehouse. Smoke showing both east and west ends. Have Engine 51 lay a three inch supply line to Engine 55."

Tim glanced at the direction of the wind and planned an attack strategy. He would be the IC (Incident Commander) until relieved by higher rank. He sent two teams with 1½ inch pre-connects into the north-west door.

Back on the radio, he said, "This is Pearce Command. Have Truck 52 stage on Engine 55 and ventilate. I want Engines 52 and 72 and Truck 5 to attack the east end of the building. Give me a second alarm and have other incoming units stage at the front gate, 36th & Marine."

Tim regretted being the first officer on the scene because the IC must remain outside, commanding attack, directing traffic and observing conditions. He would much rather have been leading his own team in direct attack.

His own crew split into two pairs. No firefighter was ever allowed into a burning building without a partner. Partners worked together, advanced together, retreated together and sometimes died together. It was a time honored tradition to never abandon a partner.

Johnny Utz and Neil Murphy worked together while Pepper Ficek teamed up with the volunteer, Lew Adams.

Utz first directed a 100 foot stretch of 2½ inch hose into the loading dock. Two separate 1½inch lines were wyed off that. As soon as Utz engaged his pump to charge the lines, he was back on a nozzle with Murphy.

Truck 52 arrived, sending one crew to the roof, while another crew set up a huge fan, in order to remove smoke so they could search for trapped people.

According to common practice an exit is first found for the smoke, before firing up the fan, yet there was an easier – though frowned upon –method. Fire it up and watch the smoke. An experienced firefighter could tell within seconds if there was an outlet for the smoke elsewhere in the building. If there was no exit, the building didn't clear. But it was clearing.

The Battalion Chief arrived and Tim was relieved of command. "Good job," the Chief said, "You've got it set up just like I would have."

Free now to join his company, Tim was part of the attack team on the loading dock. The gasoline operated seven foot 'hurricane' fan cleared much of the smoke. Truck crews managed to search a series of offices adjoining the loading dock, when suddenly the smoke thickened. The hose crews, led by Tim located fire in a large side room, were instantly enveloped in a blinding envelope of smoke.

"What happened to the fan?" Utz muffled through his facemask.

"Check it out," commanded Tim, "I'll take your place here." They could no longer see if their hose streams were having any effect on the fire as only an orange glow was now visible through the dense smoke.

Utz followed the hose lines back into the building to inform Tim the fan had been shut off.

"Who's the idiot," demanded Tim. Before Utz could answer, fire flashed over their heads. Helmets began to scorch.

"Everybody out," yelled Tim, "She's flashing over!"

"Lew's vanished!" exclaimed Pepper, "he was here a second ago."

* * *

An intensive search found Lew Adams in the basement with a broken hip.

Somebody had cut a hole in the floor with a chainsaw. After incoming crews extinguished the fire, it was determined to be arson, set in three critical locations. The hole to the basement could not be explained. When the fan was examined, it was easy to see that someone had smashed the spark plugs with a blunt instrument. Conclusion, the building had been set and sabotaged with clear intent of injuring or killing firefighters.

A week later, the State Fire Marshal called for an inquiry. It was held in the Multnomah County Sheriff's office and Tim was subpoenaed to attend.

Three Detectives, State Fire Marshal Buck Smith and Battalion Chief Charley Dunbar were seated around a conference table when Tim walked in. He could feel accusatory stares from them all. Their silence overwhelmed him. No one asked him to sit down. The air was filled with static.

"What's going on?" Tim asked meekly.

"Sorry, Tim," started Chief Dunbar, "But these gentlemen think you are involved in all the arson fires."

"Of course, I'm involved," countered Tim, "Putting them out!"

"That's just the problem," said one of the Detectives, "All thirteen arson fires have occurred on your shift and in your first-response area. You could be setting or having them set for the glory of putting them out. Doctors sometimes call it the hero syndrome."

"My sentiments, exactly," added Buck Smith, "Will you take a polygraph?"

"This is ridiculous," said Tim, "Of course I'll take a lie detector test."

"Meanwhile," said Chief Dunbar, "I'll have to place you on administrative leave."

* * *

Tina Faith massaged the knots in Tim's neck. Though they were engaged, she knew better than to speak. She wished that she could help to absorb some of his anxiety and depression.

Kind and gentle by disposition, she didn't look twenty-seven. She enjoyed teasing Tim that the difference of two years in their ages looked more like fifteen. Her glowing olive skin and dark brown eyes added to her natural youthfulness. She looked more like sixteen. A little too plump for her own good, she was tall and carried herself confidently. The fussy quality about her elegant clothes betrayed her perfectionist and controlling tendencies. She always knew where she was going.

Her movements were like those of a little bird flitting from one branch to the next and Tim's buddies always admired her boundless energy.

The phone rang. It was Bill Powers from Engine 55. "Quick," he said, "Tune in to radio KXR! Johnny Utz is on Howard's right-wing radio talk show. And, he's spouting off about you."

Tina was quick to act and found the station right away.

The familiar voice of Utz flooded the room, "... and there's no way he could have started that warehouse blaze and the damned Chief knows it."

"You're talking about Lieutenant Caruthers?"

"You'd better believe it!"

"If you're calling Chief Virgil Haase a liar, do you think there will be repercussions?"

"I can take it," said Utz, "The whole damned department is about to go on strike."

"But Firemen can't strike. It's the law, said the radio host.

"Nuthin says we can't all take sick leave at the same time."

"Would you do that and leave the county unprotected?"

"Look," said Utz, "It's a bad situation, there's no evidence to justify suspension of one of our finest firefighters. Miscarriage of justice cannot be ignored. We need to get somebody's attention. That's why I'm talking to you."

Tim flipped the radio off.

It had only been two days since his suspension. Today would have been his regular day to work

"Now the whole county knows about my suspension," complained Tim, "Why did he have to open his big mouth?"

"He's only trying to help you," purred Tina.

They were in Tim's condominium, perched high on the Corbett Bluff, overlooking the juncture of the Sandy River where it joined the mighty Columbia.

Tina strolled to the window that overlooked the front parking. "They're still there," she told Tim. County Detectives had kept him under surveillance for the past 48 hours

The phone rang again. It was Pepper Ficek, acting officer of Engine 55.

"Guess what we just found?" he said, "On a routine building inspection, we checked a vacant three-story house and it's all primed and ready to be fired. And it's booby-trapped. Some sick-o wants to kill firefighters. I've called the cops and the Fire Marshal."

Police kept Tim under close observation for at least two more weeks. He passed his polygraph with flying colors, but still was not released to return to work. However, public outcry did result in his pay being reinstated.

The bad (or good) thing was that no more arson fires occurred during this time.

Tim knew that he was innocent, so with that truth factored into the formula, the only conclusion he could reach was that the arsonist was aiming his venom at Tim personally! It was a scary thought.

About this time, District 15 and the City of Portland ended a long series of consolidation talks. The unions and all concerned agreed to a merger. District 15's dispatch center would be integrated with the county's 911 center, just being developed in an old bomb shelter under Kelly Butte.

District 15's 65 firefighters would join the 600 already working in the city. Apparatus would eventually get moved around.

The new fire chief, David Pickett released Tim back to active duty. There just was not sufficient evidence against him. Tim had requested a change of shift as well as a change of station, but did not share his reasons; still believing the arsonist was targeting him directly. Any mention of that fact to authorities would bring instant thoughts of paranoid behavior and appointments with a shrink.

Chief Pickett also recognized that Tim had been running a finely knit crew who worked most efficiently together.

Keeping them together made sense, and together they stayed, at a newer uptown Station 11. Their first "C" shift passed without serious or unusual incident. Elevens housed Engine 11 and Ladder 3

* * *

Two blocks from Station 11, a middle aged man sat in a tavern sipping a beer. It was no ordinary beer, but a special order item called Full Sail Amber Ale. It was manufactured by a new kind of micro-brewery in Hood River.

The man had a ring of dark brown hair, turning gray, but was mostly bald. He had a relatively square ruddy face interrupted by two long scars, but only a few telltale wrinkles to suggest his fifty-seven years. His coal black eyes seemed to spark devil's fire in full contrast to the puffy tea bags under each eye.

The barkeep looked at the man with suspicion, "You're the first customer I've ever had who brings in his own beer."

The customer glared at the tavern owner, and said, "Keep yur pants on.

Charley! Sell me a Heineken and keep this empty bottle of Full Sail. Order a minimum of two cases of it and keep it in stock. I'll be here every three days."

"That beer is over three dollars a bottle, wholesale!" the barkeep said.

"Two cases, no less," barked the man, then retreating to the back to shoot some pool.

Three or four other patrons drifted in and out of the tavern during the next two hours. Some wanted to shoot pool on the only table, but the man growled that he was practicing for a tournament and "No, I don't want any damned company!"

Later in the afternoon, the siren and air horn for the engine down the street could be heard as they left the station for an alarm. Only then, did the man leave the pool table and walk out of the tavern.

Chapter Nineteen ~ Arson and Old Lace

Three "C" shifts passed at Station 11 with no appreciable evidence of arson, and Tim began to relax, thinking he might have imagined the previous patterns. True, there were routine dumpster fires, usually arson. But, uptown always had those.

Tim enjoyed working at Station 11 because their average alarm runs almost doubled that of Engine 55.

One of the big downtown department stores named Corder's had an electrical fire that filled the store with thick smoke one morning right after the store opened during the holiday shopping season.

Firefighters had to block the doors to keep customers from coming in. No one was injured in the fire, but some bargain hunters were inconvenienced.

Battalion Chief Charley Dunbar was quoted in the evening news, "Even though there was heavy smoke in there, they all wanted to stay and shop. We even had to put people at the door to keep people from coming in. The fire burned circuits of a high-voltage electrical panel near a women's dressing room," he said, "It took Engine 11 eight minutes to put it out." Dunbar estimated fire damage of about $30,000 and about $100,000 in smoke damage to merchandise.

It was the laugh of the day around the kitchen table of Engine and Truck 11.

Later that afternoon, nobody was laughing. A vacant tenement a block from the station that had been earmarked for demolition, was torched in three places by an arsonist.

Again, Lt. Caruthers was the initial IC. Flames were visible on the second and third floors, with smoke fully ventilating through the fourth through seventh. It was obvious any fire doors or fire walls were either inoperable or had already been removed.

Tim arranged incoming units to fight the fire from the outside with deck guns and aerial nozzles. The building had already been condemned and all occupants moved out.

It would be a simple uncomplicated working fire, that is until a man of about sixty ran up to Tim and said, "I thought I saw somebody up there on the sixth floor."

Tactics had to instantly change.

"Get a search and rescue crew in the bucket up to six," he ordered Truck 11.

Before the truck crew could don their Scott Air paks, there was a sound of glass shattering, and a window on the sixth floor blew out.

Forty firefighters watched in helpless horror as a slight figure dressed in white lace plummeted 55 feet to a deadly impact on the sidewalk. A ball of flame followed the body out the window.

Six engines were each pumping 1250 gallons a minute through a dozen hose lines. With the lack of furniture and other fuel loads, the fire was quickly drowned out.

Tim supervised the loading of the body into the Medical Examiner's wagon. The victim was female, appeared to be about 80 years old, small and frail, hands, neck and hair badly burned. She was dressed completely in very old lace. It later turned out that the elderly lady was homeless and had stolen the lace during the confusion at the Corder's Department store fire earlier that day. A police officer recognized her.

"We wondered where she was holed up," he said, "We should have guessed she was here. Her street name was 'Old Lucy' and she lived out of a shopping cart."

Tim had regrets also and told the officer, "I shouldn't have assumed the building was empty just because it was supposed to be. If I'd sent search and rescue in there from the beginning, we would have found her."

Tim radioed the City Dispatcher, requesting a Fire Investigator, and then he entered the downstairs lobby to look around. First, he noticed the elevator had been removed as well as the outer doors. Doors removed on all floors would explain the rapid spread of the fire. Peering down into the elevator machine well, it had obviously been filled with combustible materials. The smell of gasoline was still evident.

At the base of the stairwell, he found another deep char pattern, indicating a second set and it also reeked of gas. Stair supports had been cut deeply with a large saw. If firefighters had entered in the smoke, they would never have known about it until the stairs collapsed under the weight of the men. It was another booby trapped attempt to kill firefighters. He was about to pick up a couple of beer bottles when Investigator Johnson announced his presence.

Johnson was at first skeptical about Tim's assessment of the fire's start, but the more he looked, the more he agreed.

"I think you'll probably find additional sets on the second or third floors," Tim told him, "because the hottest fire was at the other end when we arrived." Tim warned him about the sawed stair supports and left.

Back on the street, companies were overhauling or picking up in order to return to quarters.

One thing firefighters take pride in is to present a calm demeanor at emergency situations no matter what was happening in front of them. Anxiety on the fire ground and particularly over the airwaves was fodder for long-running jokes and cruel parodies.

Because there had been a death here, the place was crawling with media. Tim was thankful that a Battalion Chief finally showed up, sparing him from a media inquisition.

Tim and company quietly picked up their hose and equipment. Like a wraith they slipped through the cordon of reporters. Back in quarters, Tim separated himself. He had a lot on his mind; things that had to be thought through and through, searching for answers.

The crew called him for dinner, but he said, "Chow down without me."

And they wondered. What is going on with the Lieutenant? This is not like him. Depression was one of the biggest enemies of firefighters.

* * *

Sitting around the kitchen table, the crew of Station 11 was concerned about their friend and leader. Lt. Tim Caruthers was a hero icon for many.

Utz said, "His birthday is next week. Let's get hold of Tina, and see if we can't set up a surprise party."

Before they could make further plans, the bell clanged again, "Fire reported in a vacant house at NE 12th and Tillamook. Engine 8, Engine 11, Truck 3..."

Utz always drove too fast and Tim cautioned him to slow down to keep an eye out for other rigs responding. Suddenly, the fog lifted and Utz ended up skidding the 33,000 pound rig to a halt only two feet shy of Engine 8's tailboard.

Tim had been smelling smoke for blocks, and now it mingled with the odor of hot brakes and the back-of-the-throat tang of a week's worth of pollution suspended in the fog. Between the smoke and the fog they would be working blind.

For a split second, Tim glimpsed the roofline and a wind blown chimney, dense black smoke pumping from a dormer at one end. Then the smoke and the fog damped out his view.

After a quick word with the driver of Engine 8, Tim spoke to Pepper, "He thinks there's a hydrant about a hundred yards back. I'm going to send Utz to find it. You and me are going to take a second line off Engine 8 and back them up.

The smoke was thick and acrid, and they coughed as they moved through it. Inside the front door, they were forced to their knees. Tim crawled twenty feet inside before his helmet rapped against the yellow air bottle on another man's back. Even with every bit of skin covered by think protective clothing, the heat had pinned Engine 8's crew to the floor. Tim and Pepper were still on their hands and knees, but they would get lower as their clothing and equipment began to heat up.

The hiss of water rushing through two nozzles mixed with the ripping roar of fire blended into a cacophony of sound. The five minute warning bells on Engine 8's crew was barely heard above the clamor. Presently, they backed out; Tim and Pepper were alone. A pillow of steam from their nozzle bursts came down and forced them flat again. The next time Pepper opened his line, it went slack. It took them a few seconds to figure out that Engine 8's five-hundred gallon tank outside had run dry. Now everything would depend on Utz finding and opening a hydrant.

It was hard to believe five hundred gallons hadn't made a dent in this fire.

The rubber facepiece against Tim's cheeks was slick with sweat. A pulse pounded in his temple.

"Okay. Let's get out." Tim began pulling the dead hose line toward the door.

Outside now, "We've lost it," he said sadly to the Engineer of Engine 8. Where in the blazes is Utz with the hydrant supply?"

Battalion Chief Dunbar pulled up just then. He had an answer; they had trouble believing. Some perp had jumped out of the bushes down by the hydrant and swung a well placed axe into the lay-in line Utz had just tried to stretch to Engine 8. It took many minutes to remove the fifty foot length of damaged hose and replace it with a fresh length. Utz did not have time to call for police because he knew the fire crews would by then be desperate for water. But the second time the line was cut, Utz had no choice but to call for police protection. Meanwhile, Engine 8's tank water was all used up and the building was lost to advancing fire.

It was an obvious attempt at sabotage; it was a continuation of Tim's nightmare.

Why are these arson attempts only occurring on my shift and in my first response area? Who is trying to kill me or my fellow firefighters?

Tim asked Chief Dunbar to request a Marshal 3 response. This whole situation was getting out of hand. "I can't continue to function under these circumstances," he told the Chief.

"Maybe you should take some time off," Charley Dunbar suggested.

Tim was beginning to think the Chief might be right.

* * *

Tim was 32 years old and he had a world full of friends and support. It was a great party and a total surprise.

"Happy Birthday!' they sang. "We love you," they said.

After everyone left, Tim and Tina went out onto the lower deck. The sun was sinking over the hills to the west, and a great shadow was quickly sweeping across the choppy waters of the wide river below. On the far shore, cars on the highway sent the occasional sliver of reflected orange light across the water.

"I think it must all relate," Tina said, "Why do these obvious attempts at arson plus sabotage always happen when you are on duty?"

"Honey," he answered, "I wish I could answer. I've searched my past, looking for enemies or obvious answers and have found nothing."

After a while Tina touched Tim on the cheek with the back of her hand. "Is there any thing else bothering you?"

"A lot of things."

"Me, too," she said, "But the farther we travel away from it, the smaller it gets."

"What philosopher said that?"

"Me."

When he sat down, she straddled his lap, facing him. They kissed. After a few moments she said, "Are you going back to the department?"

"I don't know what else I'm good for. Somehow, I've got to have an answer."

She looked into his eyes and said, "Answers can wait. Right now you need to relax." She kissed him again. "I can think of a couple of things you'd be good for about now."

"Yeah? Are you going to show me?"

Kissing the tip of his nose, she said, "I think I just might."

Chapter Twenty ~ Marshal Three

Earlier in his career, Tim had turned down a promotion to District 15's first Fire Prevention Inspector. The Inspector job also included training in determining fire source and arson investigation.

Now the same opportunity presented itself again, in the form of a recommendation from Portland Fire Investigator Johnson, who told his superiors that Lt. Tim Carothers had a natural ingrained ability to determine fire causes. He added that Tim had a super sleuth's nose and he could smell hydrocarbons at a fire scene long before anyone else could sense them. This was about the time electronic "sniffers" were marketed to assist in the detection of hydrocarbons, later replaced by a more efficient detection system: arson dogs later employed in the fire service for their sensitive smelling abilities.

He couldn't wait to begin work and to stop the serial arsonist.

And the strange thing was that it was apparent to all, that as soon as Tim was transferred out of an engine company, the suspicious fires stopped. There were still those in the Portland Fire Bureau who talked about him behind his back. Not every chief in the administration trusted him. The rumor mill was active and vicious.

Marshal Three was the department's fire investigation unit and was comprised of eight firefighters or officers of the line cross-trained as law enforcement officers, along with two officers from PPD, the unit overseen by Captain Jason Mulhair.

Mulhair was a friendly supervisor. He accepted Tim like a long lost brother.

"Tim," he said, "The Pacific Northwest is organizing a Fire Arson Seminar and I want you to represent the City of Portland. These guys here have been with me for years and they are kinda stuck in a rut. There's a lot of new information and training methods available, and the old school guys are going to resist change. I want you to be involved and bring some fresh new ideas into the City.

It was the challenge that Tim needed.

"Sir, if you like," he said, "I'd be happy to learn new fire investigation techniques and teach anyone whatever we learn."

"You are my man, Lt. Caruthers."

At the Arson Seminar pre-plan, Tim met up with Bryce Spencer, the new Fire Marshal of his old District 15.

"I want you to make up a scenario," Spencer said, "To explain why 'suspect A' burns down this two story house." He took Tim to a structure out in the next county. It was a condemned vacant house that volunteers from a local fire district would be called upon to extinguish. It was up to Tim to develop a reasonable and believable story for the arson school attendees who would later sift through the ashes to try to determine the cause of the fire. Tim would set the fire up to make it appear as real as possible, then set it off. What a challenge! He would learn more about fire causes then the students. In the final day of the seminar, Tim would have to stand before the class and prove to them how the fire started and then judge each class member on his/her analysis of how the fire really started.

The fun part of all this, of course, was the imagination Tim could generate about the characters the class "investigators" would interview while attempting to solve the cause of the fire.

Would it be accidental? Or would it be suspicious? Only the students of the seminar could determine, and then be graded on their final answer.

What fun, Tim decided. He didn't even share his results with Bryce Spencer! Only he knew the correct answer!

Spencer was of average height, he was in his mid fifties, stocky, and hirsute everywhere except for the head, which was shiny on top but for a few long gray strands crossing from right to left. As always, he was as playful and friendly as a Christmas puppy.. He displayed teeth the size of baby corn and his glasses looked like they were made for a woman. His voice was deep and loud and cracked.

Many of these students were professionals, and, by golly, Tim better be right, or he would be laughed out of the auditorium.

He set his burn methodically, checking air currents, and draft conditions. Fuel load was a major consideration. His scenario was about a divorce situation involving a fortune. He dressed the victim (a sexy mannequin) named Cindy and put her to bed in the upstairs bedroom. Then he lit the fire, supposed to be accidentally ignited from excess lint in the furnace.

Hee hee hee, Let these guys figure this one out!

When the fire was well advanced, he called the local volunteer fire department drill team to put it out.

Next day, the students arrived to figure out what happened. Tim watched each student as the ashes were probed.

On the last day of the week-long seminar, he showed slides of his set and listened patiently as each student explained his theory about the set. Tim was in his glory. Not one student got the right answer, and Tim wasn't sure who learned more: the students or the guy who set it all up. *Ain't no arsonist gonna fool me,* he was convinced.

A week after the seminar, Tim was hidden in a field of brush and grass, waiting for some kid arsonist to strike.

The field had been set on fire three or four times a day for three days. As soon as Engine 55 extinguished a brush-grass fire, it would take off again an hour later in a slightly different place.

Tim and a volunteer from District 15 staked themselves out in the middle of a huge brush field. They had walkie-talkies and figured it would be a snap to catch this serial presumed juvenile arsonist.

The brush was over eight feet high and thick. No one could see more than ten feet in any direction.

Tim set himself and the volunteer about 150 feet apart in the most logical places and settled down to wait.

The heat and the insects became the enemy. Tim suffered through hours of waiting, wondering if the arsonist had out guessed them.

"Frank," he called out to the walkie-talkie volunteer, "See anything?"

"No"

"Think we better call this off?"

"No," answered the radio, "I wanna get this guy."

"Okay," said Tim. "One half hour more."

Twenty minutes passed. The heat grew more intense and the biting flies and midges were unbearable.

Tim reached for his walkie-talkie to tell Frank that it was time to retreat. *But what was that crackling sound? And the heat? And the smoke?*

"Marshal Five to Frank, move in to me! I've got fire!"

"Uff!"

"What's happening?"

"Got 'im", said Frank. "The little s.o.b. set a fire between us!"

Frank and his captive broke out of the brush into Tim's view. "Get an engine down here," Frank said, "And if we don't move, we're gonna cook!"

The captive was a 13 year old kid, and Tim felt sick at what society was becoming.

As soon as the three vacated the area, flames burst through the gorse and oils of Scotch broom where Tim Caruthers had lain for the past four hours.

"Are you embarrassed?" I am!

* * *

Slowly the room filled with body heat, music and chit-chat. Now it was Tina Faith's turn at being the birthday girl and over one hundred friends had surprised her. Waiters waded through the assemblage, balancing trays of hors d'oeuvres. Tim was pleased the whole affair was in her honor. His birthday was the month before and now it was time to celebrate for someone he cared deeply for. It was just the sort of well-meaning diversion his life lacked.

Tina Faith was only a few inches shy of Tim Caruthers's six feet, and when they danced he couldn't help noticing they fit together like a hand and a glove. He'd had a lot of surprises recently, few as pleasant as the kiss she'd given him earlier. There was something vaguely adolescent in the way he couldn't stop thinking about her.

She rubbed her nose against his cheek. "I broke this playing football when I was twelve. I broke it again when I was thirteen. My parents refused any cosmetic surgery."

"Ever regret it?"

"No."

"It's cold."

"That's why I'm warming it up on you."

"Oh, Tina, I feel so relaxed when I am around you. Why is that?"

"Figure it out for yourself, silly."

The room full of dancing, laughing and talking guests seemed suddenly withdrawn into the hazy background. They could only see and hear each other.

They talked on about the strange sequence of arson fires that always seemed to occur when Tim was commanding a responding fire engine.

"Some people think that I am setting the fires," Tim probed, "What do you think?"

"I know you well enough, darling," Tina replied, "There is no way you could do that."

Darling? Tim thought. *That's a first! Will it become a future memory?*

They shared much about their school and past secrets.

"I love the way little kids go crazy when we drive by in an engine," Said Tim.

"Do you want kids?"

"I love kids. Whenever I get married. You?"

"Absolutely," she replied, "I want to have at least four. My mom and dad have already placed their orders."

Tina had a BS with a major in horticulture. Her family grew wine grapes on forty acres in the Napa Valley.

"I'd like to meet your folks," Tim said.

"And I yours," she was quick to respond.

"My father died in the Normandy invasion, and Mom is living with some friends of the family in San Diego. She'd love to meet you."

"How many girls have you taken home to meet Mom?" Tina teased.

"Oh, only twenty or thirty."

"Liar!"

"Yeah."

* * *

Firefighters in Portland have always been expected to work "Call-shifts." A call shift is like extra pay for extra duty when vacancies occur due to vacation or use of sick leave. Men assigned to 8-hour, 5 day work weeks (Inspectors, etc.) are required to keep current on their fire fighting skills. One way to do this is to work full 24-hour call shifts on their regular days off.

Lt. Tim Caruthers worked a normal 24-hour shift just like line firefighters. Marshal Three units were housed in the headquarters station to be on call 24-hours every day.

At every opportunity, Tim would work extra call-shifts on either truck or engine companies anywhere a vacancy occurred.

The extra pay was great and he could keep his skills finely honed.

One spring Saturday, he took a shift in his old station, on Ladder Truck 3.

Truck 3 carried a fifty-five foot ladder that weighs 250 pounds and takes four people to handle. Drill time that day was putting that up and then climbing it with a roofer slung over the shoulder.

As truck officer, Tim was also drill instructor. "This is how you do it, guys." And he demonstrated the whole procedure.

Roof ladders can get heavy, and if taken all the way to the top of the fifty-five, the trainee would be four stories above the ground and all by himself. The drill didn't finish until every man raised it hand over hand and lay it down on the roof, hooked over the peak. It was the worst thing in drill school.

That afternoon, they had another chance to raise the fifty-five foot ladder, but not for drill. It was at a fire in an old three story apartment hotel on Lovejoy Street. The building covered a whole city block, except for an adjoining theatre. Both were scheduled for the wrecking ball. On Truck 3, Tim was thinking: *How easily we jump to a premature conclusion of arson in situations like this, even before arriving at the fire.*

The first arriving engine announced, "Thick yellow smoke showing at three third story windows on the west side. Have the next engine lay a supply line to us. Have the first truck company ventilate the roof. I will be Lovejoy Command."

"That's us," said Tim, checking to see if all his crew were ready. "We'll extend the fifty-five." Then to his driver, "Park across the street on the north side."

As soon as they got the big ladder raised and secure, Tim sent two truckmen into the building to make sure no one was trapped.

The roof peaked at a forty-five degree angle, too steep for a man to safely stand. Tim and three others carried two roofer ladders to the top, working in teams of two. Once the roofers were hooked over the peak, they had a platform for safe footing.

Smoke was already seeping through nail holes in the composition asphalt roofing. It looked like tiny miniature jets, being pushed outwards by the built up pressure from the attic and the floors below. There was the distinct smell of sulfur, unusual in such high concentrations.

With full protective bunkers, air-pak and chain saw, Tim could feel his total weight straining the already spongy roof beneath his feet. Some of the asphalt tar was beginning to soften. Apparently, there was more heat built-up immediately below them than first thought.

Originally, Tim planned to cut two holes, roughly six by four feet each, but now the situation changed. For safety, he ordered half the crew, the other team off the roof, to assist in setting up fans. He and Neil Murphy were left alone on the roof when Tim started to cut the first hole between the two roofers. As the pieces fell into the attic, a shower of heat and sparks rose into the sky above them.

At that moment there was a muffled "whoomp" sound from somewhere inside the building and the hole next to them suddenly erupted like a volcano. The escaping hot gasses ignited on contact with fresh air and cycled into the sky like a miniature tornado. Pieces of the edge of the hole were torn loose by the blowtorch from below.

The heat was unbearable, almost knocking Tim and Neil from the roof. They slid down to the fifty-five, their only escape route.

Another "rrump" like an explosion rocked them as they descended.

Tim took immediate action, "It's another booby-trapped building," he radioed to Lovejoy command, "I suggest you order everyone out, asap."

Lovejoy command answered with three blasts on an air-horn, the pre-arranged signal to vacate. Not every firefighter was yet equipped with portable chest radios.

Firefighters swarmed out of three sides of the building just as another explosion blew out top floor windows. Fire by then was extending into the theatre. Apparently the fire wall between the two had been breached.

Lovejoy Command had by now three alarms representing 5 trucks, 12 engines and over 79 firefighters. All they could do was pour water into the shell from aerial and monitor nozzles.

Marshal 3 on-duty Investigators were already tied up elsewhere, so the Assistant Chief in charge of this fire, relieved Tim from Truck 3, promoting Neil Murphy to acting officer.

The building began to cool and units were gradually released back into service. As soon as he could, Tim began a cursory investigative size-up. One of the first things to attract his attention was a cluster of three beer bottles in the hotel lobby. The brand had been collected at previous suspicious fires; it was Full Sail Amber Ale. Tim remembered it from the vacant tenement where the lace clad lady died.

Later investigation showed this building had been set up, waiting to burn, for several days. Contractors remembered a sixty-ish man with two scars and a nearly bald head hiring them to place effective nitro charges almost two weeks earlier. They were told he was the agent responsible for the demolition.

To Tim, this sounded too much like the perp had everything set up, waiting for Tim to be on duty in that part of town. Scary! But why did he wait to torch it until Tim Caruthers was on duty? The old fears returned. *There was still someone out there trying to target him personally.*

One thing was certain, his enemy had to be a member of the fire department or have close ties to someone who was. How else could he know when Tim was or was not on duty?

Chapter Twenty One ~ Time Out

Driving south on Interstate 5 from Portland, Tim and Tina were testing out Tim's brand new 1965 Suburban.

There had been talks of possible marriage. After the last arson fire, the City's psychiatrist had suggested Tim take some time off. There was no argument that these two issues together made an excellent time for Tim and Tina to travel south to meet each other's parents.

There was freshness to the air the further south they traveled. Cottonwoods, alders and some willows release a resin as the buds burst in early spring. Sensitive noses produce memories of good times past, often relaxing tensions. The pollen from the fresh pea-green trees reminded Tim of Dorothy's adventure in the flower field in Wizard of Oz. He glanced over and believed, as Tina was sound asleep. He eased the car slowly into a rest area parking lot and reached over to kiss her.

Tina stirred in the warm cocoon of her blanket, breathing deeply of the fragrance she'd come to savor, an earthy scent that triggered a basic need deep within her.

Consciousness slowly returned; she wasn't in bed. This wasn't her blanket she'd just curled her fingers into, a button poking into her palm. The heat encompassing her came from the body invading her space. And the earthy scent she breathed was Tim.

Tina closed her eyes as he settled his mouth over hers, a soft touch that reached deep. With the rasp of his whiskery jaw and the warmth of his breath on her skin, longing rose within her, had her pressing her lips against his. A kaleidoscope of color wheeled behind her closed lids, his kiss stealing her breath. Helpless, she felt her heart race as he blew her away.

"You looked so peaceful, I just couldn't resist," he apologized

"Don't make excuses," she chided, "I loved it. How long have I been sleeping?"

"Only an hour," he replied, "We'll stop soon at a Redding motel."

As they pulled out of the rest area, an old white Pontiac station wagon pulled in behind them. The Pontiac had trouble keeping up with Tim's new Suburban, but it tried. Tim, like many firefighters, drove as much over the posted speed limit as he thought he could get away with. The old Pontiac was driven by a balding sixty year old with two ugly scars on his face. He was sipping beer from a bottle whenever it was safe to be unseen by the CHP. Four or five bottles rolled around, clinking together on the floor. They were. Full Sail Amber Ale.

After dinner, they checked in to a Best Western motel in Redding. Their room, on a second floor balcony, overlooked the parking lot. While hauling up luggage, Tim caught a view of the old Pontiac as it cruised through the parking lot. He had the impression that he had seen it several other times, but could not be sure. He and Tina were tired, having driven all day. They retired early, hoping to get an early start in the morning.

About 0330 hours, they were awakened by a loud pounding on their door, then a bell clanging somewhere nearby.

"Fire Department," yelled a voice, "We need to evacuate!"

Tim, used to sudden wake up calls, was instantly awake and alert. Tina was a little slower. "No time to dress," he coached, "Bathrobe and slippers and we're outa here."

When he opened the door to the balcony, there was heat and smoke. An engine company was parked in the lot, with booster lines extinguishing a dumpster fire.

The trouble was, the dumpster was immediately below their room.

The fire was quickly extinguished, the dumpster rolled away with no damage, except the cloying odor of smoke in their room and belongings.

Tim identified himself to the local fire officer. Glancing around, he spotted the old Pontiac parked with engine running across the street. When he mentioned it, the officer turned to look, causing the occupant to speed away.

"I'm pretty sure he's a serial arsonist and has followed me all the way from Portland. "Also," he added, "I saw a beer bottle on the cement next to the dumpster. You'd be wise to check it for fingerprints."

"I'll get the police on it," the firefighter said.

"So much for a good night's sleep." He complained to Tina, as they tried to air out their stuff. "We can have an early breakfast in Willows, my home town."

After they packed up, the motel refunded their lodging fee, as the room would have to be purged of all smoke odors before anyone could rent it again.

Tim had to spend another hour at the local police station, while the officer filled out his reports.

Dawn was streaking the eastern sky as they finally got away.

"I'm tempted to stay and work the clues, Tim said, "This guy is out to get me, and I don't trust these small hick town investigators."

"My folks are expecting us today," Tina reminded him.

"Yeah, I know honey."

An hour and a half later, Tim was giving Tina the five dollar tour of Willows, California, a sleepy quaint town, the county seat of Glenn County. As of the 1960 census, the city had a total population of 3,220.

His old house was gone, now marked by a vacant lot full of wildflowers.

A degree of nostalgia overwhelmed Tim, as he tapped on the back door of the fire hall. Some of his old buddies were still working, including George Highland, now a Captain. He introduced Tina around and they insisted on serving a gigantic breakfast to their guests.

Out of Tina's hearing, Tim told George how he felt he was a pariah. Disaster and fire seemed to follow him wherever he went.

"Who could be so angry they were willing to risk hundreds of other lives just to spike me?"

"You had an enemy here," George said.

"I haven't thought about Bully Billy Crispler for years," Tim admitted.

"Well, it couldn't be him," George said, "He hung himself three years ago in Mexico."

"Really? How come nobody told me?"

"We all thought you knew."

Tim informed them about his shadow. "If you get a chance, get a license plate." He left a cell phone number and detail about where they were heading and why.

Tim thought it odd when George wrote down every detail and pumped him with more questions, but soon there was nothing on his mind except the pleasure of the trip ahead.

Near the town of Williams, they turned west on State Route 20 to Clearlake and then south on State Route 29 through Boggs Mountain State Forest, then down into the Napa Valley near Calistoga.

South of the small town about a mile, Tina instructed Tim, "Turn right on Diamond Mountain Road."

They drove more than a mile through perfectly pruned vineyards until they reached a beautifully stone carved and wrought iron gate. Water falls decorated both portals. An arch over the top told the world in large polished bronze letters, 'FAITH VINEYARDS.'

Tim pulled up to the closed iron gate, and started to reach for an intercom button.

"No, no!" said Tina, "I want to surprise them." She instructed him to lift a little steel door and enter a series of numbers. As he punched in the last number, the gate slowly started to open, and Tim drove through.

Howard and Kathleen Faith were a couple of the most gracious people Tim ever had the pleasure of meeting.

Their 400 acres off Diamond Mountain Road, south of Calistoga, produced some of the best wine grapes in the valley. Howard was president of the local vintners association, well known and liked by everybody.

Their home was in the style of the Southern California early Spanish missions, ornate in every way. Tim sighed as he looked around, *I had no idea Tina was from such a wealthy family.* And it never occurred to him that someday she might inherit all of this wealth.

"Why didn't you tell me your folks were so well off?" Tim asked Tina when they were alone.

"I didn't want you marrying me for my money, silly."

They stayed at the Faith Vineyards for five glorious days, soaking in the spring sunshine, a rare treat from the dampness of Portland.

The Faith's had stables and Tim and Tina rode about the countryside on magnificent and well trained horses. Several times, Tim directed their rides to a hill overlooking the approach road, the entrance gate and the distant town. Like many of the old Spanish vineyards, there was a beautiful little chapel on this hill.

On special occasions like planting and harvest, Lent and Holy days, a priest would come out from the local parish, gathering all the vineyard's workers and family to hear Mass in the little chapel.

Today, Tim used high powered binoculars to carefully scan the countryside, looking for any sign of the beat-up old Pontiac.

"We may have given him the slip," Tim said.

"I certainly hope so," replied Tina, "C'mon, I want to show you the creek and my favorite swimming hole."

"My swim suit is back at the hacienda," he complained.

"So?" she asked with a twinkle in her eye.

"You have our blessings," Howard told Tim, when it was time to leave, "But only if you name the first baby boy after me."

Tim knew Howard was joking and he had no doubts that he would forever love these future in-laws. It was difficult to say good-bye to sweet Kathleen.

"You can figure on a wedding about this time next year," Tina told her mom.

* * *

"We need to go east to pick up Highway 99," Tina told Tim after they left Faith Vineyards.

"Have we time for me to show you around Sacramento?" Tim asked.

"We've all the time you want, honey," she said, "What's so special about Sacramento?"

"I've mentioned my friends, Ron Martin and Rex Franklin many times. We lived at Christian Brothers School for four years and I have lots of memories. I thought I might share some with you as long as we are in the area.

The first place he stopped was the eight square block park surrounding the California State Capitol. It was a beautifully maintained park. Tim wanted Tina to see the giant koi in the reflection pond.

"They look like huge goldfish," Tina observed, "There's one that must be three feet long!"

"I thought you would enjoy these," said Tim, "But you know they are related to carp?"

"Really?"

"Did I ever tell you that all three of us kids walked right in to the Governor's office?

That was in 1946 or '47. We sat right down and chatted with Earl Warren, the Governor of California. We spent almost an hour with him. No secretary, no staff, no appointment, and no security guards! Not like today, for sure."

"He's Chief Justice of the Supreme Court, now, isn't he?" asked Tina.

"Yes, and what a fine person he is."

From the Capitol grounds it was a short drive to 21st and Broadway where Tim received a brutal shock. There stood the old school with crumbling walls and broken out windows. They drove into the back play courts where a man was salvaging window frames.

"What's happening to the school?" asked Tim.

"They've build a new campus out on Martin Luther King Junior Blvd., about 43rd. The new Interstate freeway is planned to go through here next year."

Tim was devastated.

He showed Tina where his old dorm room had been and the Spanish tile roof that housed thousands of little bats. "We used to come out here right after supper and watch the swarm. They all seemed to emerge at the same time and the sky was almost black with them."

Returning to U.S. Hwy. 99 southbound, Tim watched every car in his rearview mirror until he felt confident they were not being followed by the mystery man in the old Pontiac.

"San Diego, here we come!"

Several years earlier, Tim sent his mother, Helen Crispler to live with his friends Rex and Carol Franklin in San Diego.

The move was made to hide her from her crazed ex-husband Billy the Bully. Rex and his father, retired Navy Captain John Franklin were in the largest scuba sales and service business on the west coast. There were store branches in every major city, including Honolulu.

Helen Crispler took a shine to Captain Franklin and decided to stay on with Rex and Carol. They too had developed a relationship with Helen, loved her dearly and accepted her as a family member. She would probably never return to her home in Willows, CA.

The main office for the scuba and diving business was in a mini-mall storefront Rex owned with a comfortable four bedroom apartment over the store. Helen occupied one bedroom, John a second, another for Rex and Carol's baby son, Nathan.

When Tim and Tina arrived, they checked in to a hotel next door in the same block. Tim had not seen his mother personally for over a year.

After hugs all around, Helen asked the first question, "Why did you bring this lovely person to meet me?"

Tim evaded the question.

"Why are you still here, mom?" was his first question, "You know that Billy is dead?"

"Billy dead?" she said, "I don't think so. The Glenn County DA just recently sent me some papers to sign to finalize the divorce. He said Billy was working somewhere in Nevada."

"Well, that's really strange," said Tim, "Captain Highland in Willows told me Billy hung himself in Mexico three years ago."

"I never did trust George Highland," Helen said, "Anyway, to answer your question, I love it here, they love me and I've got a lifetime job."

"Job?"

"Yes, didn't I tell you? I'm head accountant for all of Rex and John's diving stores."

"She's a whiz, too," said Rex, "We'd be lost if she left us."

After a wonderful dinner, prepared by Carol and Helen, they sat around reminiscing old times.

"What have you heard from Ron?" Rex asked.

"Nothing for a year," said Tim, "but did you know they're tearing down CBS?"

"Our old alma mater?"

"Yeah, making room for a new freeway. A man told me they've built a new school further ...."

A startling crash interrupted before he could finish the sentence. It was followed by the sound of breaking glass.

A burst of flickering light brought Tim instantly to his feet. He darted down the stairs, grabbing a fire extinguisher on the way. The stairs led into the back of the scuba shop, which was now starting to fill with smoke.

An old fashioned Molotov cocktail had been attached to a brick and heaved through the front plate glass window, breaking on the floor and ignited some rubber wet suits. Tim effectively and efficiently extinguished the small blaze with minimum damage.

"Do you have any enemies?" he asked Rex who was right behind him.

"Every business man has enemies," Rex replied.

"This was not caused by your enemy," Tim said as he examined the area closer, "But by mine."

He showed Rex a piece of the broken bottle: It was a Full-Sail Ale and reeked of gasoline.

Chapter Twenty Two ~ Doubly Dead

After more police reports were filed with the San Diego PD, Tim requested a special investigator from the fire department.

"I'm afraid I've brought you a serious problem," Tim explained to Inspector Ralph Damien, "This nut has been following us all the way from Portland. Up there we first thought he wanted to kill firefighters, any firefighters, but it turns out he's after me and will kill anybody who gets in the way."

"How long will you be staying?" Damien asked.

"We planned to be here a week," Tim replied "but under the circumstances, we'll leave tomorrow, unless he's caught."

Rex cleaned up, boarded up the window and hired a full-time "Rent-a-cop" to park all night in front of the store.

San Diego arranged for extra patrols in the area and posted a full-time officer in the lobby of Tim's hotel. They got to bed sometime after midnight. Both were steamed about having to leave six days early.

"How do you suppose he found us?" asked Tina, "Nobody knew where we were going, except your family.

"There was one other," said Tim, "I just thought about. And that's the fire Captain back in Willows. I told him our exact itinerary."

"That suggests a conspiracy, but would certainly explain why the bad guy didn't have to follow us from the Napa Valley. He could have been told and knew in advance where we were going."

"Are you sure you want to marry a fire investigator?" Tim teased, "I'll have to put you to work on all my cases."

In his mind he was going over all the construction features of the hotel, wishing that it had fire sprinklers and a few other things.

"Go to sleep, darling," she cooed, "We're safe here. The whole place is swarming with cops. We're clear up on the fourth floor."

"That's what worries me," said Tim, drifting off to sleep.

* * *

The police officer stationed on the main floor was very conscientious, watching everybody in and out of the hotel lobby. After 2 A.M., things were pretty quiet and he struck up a conversation with the hotel desk clerk and shared coffee. A few hotel guests staggered in from time to time, but nothing unusual occurred to attract his attention until 0330 hours.

Three people in bathrobes exited the elevator, screaming, "FIRE on the 4th floor!" Some smoke rode down the elevator with them.

"We pulled the fire alarm station up there, but nothing happened."

The clerk pushed a button, sounding bells, then said, "My annunciator panel indicates the bells are ringing everywhere except the fourth floor. The fire department is on the way, but somebody has to get up to four and wake people up! More people were streaming down the stairs and exiting three other elevators.

Tim smelled smoke before the muffled sound of the bells from the floors above and below reached him. *Déjà vu Willows all over again!* He checked the door. It was cool. A quick look outside revealed a relatively smoke free corridor. *Why aren't the alarm bells working on this floor? Somebody has to rouse these other people!*

He dispatched Tina down the stairs then stopped long enough to pull on a pair of pants. He rapidly, but calmly made his way down the corridor, knocking on doors. "Fire!

Everybody out!" he repeated. He could sense fire was in both ends of the corridor, apparently in maid's storage. The smoke grew thicker.

Feeling sure the floor was cleared of people, Tim headed for the stairway in the center, intending to go down.

There are times in a man's life when he cannot believe what the eyes tell, and this was one of those times. At the up staircase to the fifth floor, he saw a man beckoning to him through the smoke. Unsure what he was seeing, he hesitated. The man climbed three steps and stopped. Tim could see now that the man carried a lit blowtorch. *The arsonist? A trap?*

The man with the torch turned and bounded up the remaining stairs, through the fire door, and up the next flight to the roof.

Tim had no choice but to follow. He had no shoes, no shirt and no weapon.

The door to the roof stood open, sucking some of the smoke into the warm night sky. Tim cautiously peered around the corner of the roof house. Suddenly without warning, hands were around his neck in a choke hold. He could hear sirens and see stars at the same time. But the vigor of youth prevailed. His assailant was small, but strong. A quick backward kick to the man's groin loosened the grip. Tim turned around to face his attacker. He was at least 60. The blow torch was set upright on the roof.

"Who are you?" demanded Tim, advancing closer. The man had a familiar look to him, but he was not Billy.

"I'm Jack, and I'm going to kill you!" he said as he pulled a large switch-blade.

Tim backed off, "Let's talk. Jack who?"

"Jack Crispler, you caused my brother's death, and now it's your turn. He lunged and Tim parried with a length of two by four he picked up earlier.

"How'd you know where to find me?"

Jack sneered, "You've more enemies than you know!" Capt. Highland in Willows is my son and nephew of Billy."

Tim was watching the blow torch behind Jack. He started a wild furious swing with the two by four, forcing Jack a couple of steps back. The blow torch had been burning into the light aluminum support of a television antenna, melted just enough to collapse on Jack. Tangled in the numerous rods, Jack was vulnerable to Tim's swift attack. Before he could recover the weapon, Tim received a nasty cut on his arm. The sight of blood and flowing adrenaline spurred Tim to a super human effort. He wrenched the knife from Jack and sent it flying over the parapet.

"Hey," hollered a firefighter, "What's going on up there?" Men were apparently raising a ladder.

Tim landed a couple of bone cracking blows to Jack's face.

"I've got you an arsonist," Tim yelled back. A San Diego firefighter peered over the parapet as the aerial stopped rising.

Jack broke loose from Tim's hold and bolted to the opposite end of the hotel roof. For the first time, Tim noticed the top end of an extension ladder. Jack lunged for it just as his shoe caught on a chunk of blistered roofing. He tripped and went flying over the edge of the building. Tim heard his scream followed by a crash and glass breaking.

Jack fell twenty feet headfirst into the roof skylight of Rex and Carol's apartment. The coroner later pronounced him dead.

They found his old Pontiac parked in the alley behind the hotel. It was filled with sophisticated fire starters, incendiary devices and many empty beer bottles. Full-Sail Ale, of course. The extension ladder was for his planned escape. He must have had this escapade planned out hours in advance, but his luck just ran out.

Tim was filled with a conflict of emotions as the San Diego Fire Department guiding him down the aerial ladder to the waiting aid car.

Tina was waiting there for him, as were Rex, Carol and Helen, Tim's mother. Tim's nostrils had a black ring of carbon from smoke and they insisted he be checked at a local hospital for lung damage.

"I never really got into any heat," he complained. They compressed the bleeding on his arm and Tina rode with him in the ambulance to the hospital.

Fire investigators located three fire starts, all in maid's storage rooms on the 2nd and 4th floors, and the fire damage was confined to those areas. The smoke-damage throughout the whole hotel would cost much more to remove. The off-brand of beer in bottles was also found in the maid's rooms. Jack had disabled fire alarm wires on the 4th floor, hoping to catch Tim unawares.

When the City nominated Tim for a hero award for braving the smoke to warn others on his floor, Tim declined with a simple, "I'm a professional firefighter...it's my job!"

"Well then," wise-cracked a local fire chief, "Next time you come visit us, leave your crazy arsonists up north!"

Later, back in Rex's apartment, Tim explained, "We have two unanswered questions: First, is Bully Billy Crispler really dead? And, second, how do we approach the

Willows Fire Dept. about George Highland's conspiracy?"

"I was married to that creep's family for almost twenty years," Helen said, "And there was never a mention of Billy having a brother. George Highland was never mentioned and never visited."

Rex commented, "There must have been a reason to keep that secret all these years, for shame or what?"

"Sounds to me like there might be more to this conspiracy than meets the eye," said Tim.

"But if Billy and Jack are both dead," said Tina, "and if George gets tried and put away, won't that be the end of it?"

"I sure hope so," said Tim, "I'm getting tired of having a mystery arsonist stuck on my backside wherever I go."

There was a Scripture Tim recalled about the depression he felt before Jack was caught, but now applied to Jack alone: Feeling "... like clouds without water, carried along by winds; autumn trees without fruit, doubly dead, uprooted; wild waves of the sea, casting up their own shame like foam; wandering stars, for whom the black darkness has been reserved forever." Jude 12-13 (NAS).

Chapter Twenty Three ~ Un-Plugged

It took Tim and Rex a few days to learn how to relax after the stress of the fire incidents.

With Jack dead, the string of arsons and attempts on Tim's life should have been over. Tim felt in no rush to report George Highland's involvement to the Willows officials. There would be time enough for that on the way back to Portland. Tim and Tina still had two weeks of vacation left.

John Franklin convinced Rex and Carol to take a few days and show Tim and Tina the sights and sounds of San Diego. He and Helen could manage the store.

In 1964, the idea of computer aided police and fire dispatch was still in its infancy. Always a firefighter at heart, Tim asked if they couldn't first visit the SDFD dispatch center. His chief back in Portland heard that San Diego was in the forefront of developing what would later be known as the 9-1-1 system. Tim was prepared to take many photo slides.

In the afternoon, they started in world famous Balboa Park and the equally renowned San Diego Zoo, home to more than 4,000 rare and endangered animals representing more than 800 species and subspecies. Tina fell in love with their cuddly little koalas.

When it was determined the many attractions in Balboa would take almost a week to do justice, Rex and Carol left them on their own. Tim & Tina rode the Miniature Railroad to other features such as a Spanish Village Art Center, a Japanese Friendship Garden, and lots of museums. Many of these attractions were built during the 1915–16 Panama-California Exposition or the 1935-36 California-Pacific International Exposition

John Franklin told Tim to be sure and drive around the bay over to the Coronado Strip, where all the high ranking Naval Officers lived. When the Fleet was in, these Captains and Admirals had their own docks. Otherwise, it was a 20-mile drive around the south end of the bay. There was talk of someday building a bridge.

Every Saturday, there would be a new class of recruits graduating from the Navy Training Center (Boot camp) at Ft. Rosecrans, and they generally paraded down Coronado's main street.

Tim and Tina were allowed back into the hotel three days after the fire. It took that long for professional cleaners to eliminate the sour smell of smoke.

Tim wasn't one usually prone to nightmares, but he did have a bit of sleeplessness the first night back in the hotel.

One night at dinner, Rex told Tim. "There's one more major attraction you want to see, before you head back."

Carol cut in, "Have you heard about the new concept in aquariums that just opened this year? It's a huge new theme park called Sea World."

"We'll give it a try in the morning," said Tim.

It was a venture beyond the ocean's door at Sea World. They could get close enough to touch a dolphin's fin, stare down a shark; encounter polar bears eye to eye, keep ears open for a squawking bickering noise coming from the hatching members of the Pink Flamingo, and connect with all the sea's creatures in their own world.

Everywhere one would look, the energy and wonder of the world's water surrounded the visitors in the sights and sounds of Sea World.

After a most joyous day, Tim and Tina were worn to a frazzle. Carol and Helen put on a most sumptuous goodbye dinner.

"How are you going to broach the subject of George Highland to the Willows authorities?" asked Rex.

Tim pondered the question, slowly answering, "We all know he was involved in a conspiracy with Jack and maybe Billy. Conspiracies are never limited to only a few people. I'm going to fish around a bit before I say anything to anybody. Highland was pretty high up in the fire department and for all I know, the whole department could have been involved."

"Do you have to leave so early in the morning?" Tim's mother Helen was crying.

"Sorry, mom," replied Tim, "I've got to report back on duty the day after tomorrow, and It will take a full day to drive from here to Willows."

Changing the subject, Rex broke the sad moment, "I could get away for a trip to the Lmuma mine in Nevada almost anytime with a little notice."

Tim said, "Amen bro! I'd sure like to do that, but nobody's heard from Ron for over three months, and I'm not going without him."

* * *

By 0730 hours, they were well north of San Diego on the coast highway SR 1. In Los Angeles, they picked up US 99 and drove north to Tejon Pass, often called "The Grapevine." It was an unusually pretty day. They made good time by switching off each two hours, while one drove and the other napped.

Parts of US 99 had been converted to the new Interstate Hwy System and now became known as Interstate 5. The Interstate system was authorized and begun by Congress in 1956.

It was a long, hard drive to Willows, even with the new faster stretches of Interstate freeways. They arrived about 7:30 P.M. and checked quietly into a motel.

Tim made a few discrete phone calls. He planned to see his old friend, Judge Parker, in the morning.

Sometime after midnight, Tim woke briefly, thinking he heard distant gunfire, and then he drifted back to a deep sleep, remembering that it was July and somebody was probably finishing up the last of their fireworks.

Four hours later, they were jerked out of a sound sleep. Pounding on the door was so severe; Tim could feel vibrations of it while still in bed.

"Police!" screamed a voice, "Open this door, NOW!"

"Wha..?" murmured Tina as Tim jumped out of bed to the door.

Before Tim could get the night latch off, the door splintered off its hinges from a violent force behind it. The door crashed into Tim and flung him bruised, back onto the bed.

Three police officers in full battle gear, crowded into the room; Tim and Tina were instantly overcome and handcuffed.

"What's the meaning of this?" demanded Tim, "This is a mistake!"

"No mistake, cop killer," growled an officer, "You're going down!"

Placed in separate police cruisers, Tim and Tina were hustled downtown. Tina was shivering in a flimsy nightgown, knowing the officers were getting an eyeful. At the county courthouse jail, she was given a blanket to cover her nakedness. They were both thrown into separate cells, with not a word of explanation.

These people are acting like Nazi Storm troopers, Tim thought.

* * *

At 0900, Judge Amos Parker robed up and entered his courtroom. He had been informed of a serious drug deal that had gone bad, wherein an officer had been shot and killed.

The local District Attorney arrived in the courtroom, while the clerk and stenographer were still setting up.

"Good morning, Amos," he addressed the Judge. In small towns like Willows, most folks kept things on an informal first-name basis.

"Good morning to you LeRoy," said the Judge, "How did you manage to catch these people so fast?"

"An anonymous tip led us to their motel, where we found drugs, and the murder weapon in their car. They were so stupid they didn't even lock it."

"And you searched the car without a warrant?"

"Yes, your honor."

"Tsk, tsk! Well, let's have them in here and see who they are."

Tim and Tina, barefoot and in leg irons, were ushered into the courtroom.

Judge Parker and D.A. LeRoy Maxim both registered surprise.

"Tim Caruthers!" exclaimed LeRoy, "And Tina Faith! I don't believe it." He once had a crush on Tina.

"This has got to be an error," said the Judge, "I want the prisoners in my chambers for a private conference."

"But..." said the arresting officers, "They're murderers!"

"And you are both idiots!" said the Judge, slamming his gavel.

The few others who drifted into the courtroom were left alone with the clerk and stenographer. The judge allowed one officer to accompany Tim and Tina into his chambers along with the D.A. The door slammed shut and all was quiet for the better part of an hour.

The local media began hounding the court clerk, but he could provide no answers.

At about 1000 the door opened and one lone police officer and the D.A. exited the judge's chambers.

"What's going on?" shouted a reporter.

"Stick around," said LeRoy, "You'll have a story."

At noon, they were back, with George Highland and three others in tow. Highland was bruised about the face. No one dared ask why. The Miranda decision requiring the reading of rights, had just been passed, but many smaller departments were slower to comply with the new regulations.

In front of a full courtroom, Highland confessed to conspiracy to commit murder, and many lesser crimes. He told the Court that someone tipped him off that Tim was back in town so he set up a frame. The drug deal and the murder were part of his operation, but happened at just the most convenient time to be used to frame Tim.

Highland's crime syndicate involved arson for profit, drugs and gambling. As his empire crumbled during the next few months, more than sixty people, many in the government, fell with him.

"They were vultures circling with clawed feet, sharp and bloody teeth and hungry eyes, giddy with the anticipation of unlimited wealth," Judge Parker told the media.

* * *

Freed that same day on temporary bond, Tim and Tina had much to be thankful for.

"Well, at least you didn't have to confront Highland in person," Tina said, "He sorta did that for you."

Tim sighed a big sigh, "We'll head for home in the morning."

They sat quietly, and the setting sun enthralled her, gold rays shooting between clouds to cast a distant grain elevator in a violet silhouette. As the sky darkened, diamond stars winked between the clouds. "This is beautiful," she murmured.

"Yeah, it is." His husky voice drew her, holding more wonder than the horizon. He was looking at her...

...But he could also see that soft spot she had for children, developing naturally into a need for a child of her own. Though she hadn't yet realized it, she'd already learned the real riches in life weren't material, but rather the people you shared life with.

Tim served fifteen more years with the Portland Fire Bureau, the last five as a Battalion Chief.

Tina bore him four wonderful children.

Over the years, close contact had been maintained between Tim Caruthers, Rex Franklin and Ron Martin, companions from school years at Christian Brothers.

Tim would be retiring from the fire service in a couple of years and Rex, as we know, after action as a Navy 'Frogman' in Korea, now ran a diving and scuba chain of stores headquartered in San Diego.

After hanging up his wildlife camera, Ron perceived the idea of writing a young-adult novella about their earlier adventures in the 'Lmuma' Nevada gold mine. It would be his first attempt at fiction; writing for the sheer joy of entertaining kids.

He wrote Rex and Tim, proposing the idea of a reunion at the old mine. That is, if they could ever find it again. They already knew that Forrest Williams had long since passed on, and the Nevada Mining records could find no record of a "Squaw" mine ever existing anywhere in Mineral or Esmeralda counties.

Another mystery? Or did they dream it all?

Book Four

Together Again

Chapter Twenty-Four ~ The Lost Mindoro

Thirty-nine years after the amazing adventure in the Lmuma Mine, Ron Martin, Rex Franklin and Tim Caruthers planned a big reunion in Hawthorne, Nevada.

Ron, raised in Hawthorne would be their host. He would rent a whole floor of rooms in the El Capitan Lodge. Two rooms were for Rex and Carol, their oldest son, Nathan and wife, plus two rooms for Tim and Tina, and two of their four children, Steve and David. Possibly more would be needed if Steve and David brought families.

Ron never married. Another room was for a Reno attorney who was an avid four-wheeler and amateur prospector. His name was Paul Pinnacle. After Paul read Ron's published book, *Mystery of the Lmuma Mine,* he was so taken by the story that he called Ron for more information. They had been in contact for several years, exchanging thousands of words.

His first e-mail was lengthy:

"Hi Ron Martin, A couple of weeks ago, I finished reading your book, *Mystery of the Lmuma Mine.* The attraction was twofold. I somewhat specialize in young adult literature, having aspirations to write in that area myself. More important, the location of the story caught my attention.

"In 1947, I was in the first grade, living in Babbitt, NV. I now live in Sparks, but visit Hawthorne four or five times a year. So I am eager to read a story set in Mineral County.

"Your first novel is impressive. The presence of the coyote unifies the story. You employ the famous "red-herring" device common to most mysteries in a skilled manner. Everyone is suspect except the three boys. And there is the surprise twist at the end when we learn the identity of the spy.

"You have left us with one puzzle. By "us," I mean me and a couple of friends. We have spent considerable time in Mineral County tramping the hills, visiting Lapon Meadows, Lapon Canyon, the Aurora Crater (new promising gold deposits have been found recently near Fletcher!), and some claims around the rock cabin in Long Valley.

"Our efforts recently have been aimed toward finding the Squaw mine you describe in your book. Piecing together the clues of distances driven, and walked by Burt, we suspect that the Lmuma mine is located in New York Canyon. However, we cannot find the Squaw mine name on any of our maps, and we can't seem to locate anyone who knows a mine by that name.

"Although my friends suggest you have taken poetic license with the location, I believe the location of the volcanic cone to be, in fact, Volcano Peak. My suggestion is that you changed the copper found in that region to gold for reader appeal. By the way, a promising copper deposit has recently been located in New York Canyon.

"We would appreciate it if you would be willing to tell us the location of the Squaw mine. Our purpose is mainly to have a destination when we get outdoors for exercise and fresh air.

Sincerely, Paul Pinnacle."

Ron also visited Hawthorne on several occasions, but had not attempted the arduous journey to the mine location. He wrote back to Paul with limited information.

Old Burt stayed with Forrest Williams for another two years, until Forrest sold his failing mine to an eastern conglomerate. The last anyone heard, Forrest was working as a bouncer in the main casino of Hawthorne, the El Capitan Club. Poor Burt, after he was paid off, turned back to the bottle, which eventually consumed him. Sometime in late 1949, Ron, then attending Mineral County High School, bumped in to Burt in an alley behind one of the casinos. Burt was filthy and homeless (and quite drunk). Ron took pity on him, took him home, fed him, provided a hot bath and some clean clothes, and for his effort got thoroughly chewed out by his mother. A month later Burt passed on.

The next time Ron visited Hawthorne, he found Forrest deceased almost ten years earlier. Later, when Ron published his book, he tried to contact Forrest's wife and daughter, living somewhere in California, thinking they might enjoy the book. But his efforts failed. Through their church he managed to locate a distant relative to which he sent a letter, but got no answer --- that is, until five more years had passed.

Then, in 1984, an anonymous note arrived from a California postmark with a brief and mysterious message: *"F. Williams left something for you in the News office."* Ron's curiosity was piqued. If the note was from Forrest's family, why the long delay? He figured the note referred to the weekly newspaper in Hawthorne. What could it be?

At the time, Ron was pressed with publisher's deadlines for two more books and the unusual note was misplaced, then eventually forgotten.

Paul Pinnacle's first e-mail arrived that year and Ron opened up a lengthy discussion with him and his friends, trying to help them pinpoint the exact location of the mine. These communications lasted for more than a year.

Paul was doubly good at baiting Ron into prompt answers. In his next missal, he said:

"Recently my two friends have visited a mine site I told them about. It's located in Little Powell Creek Canyon, adjacent to Squaw Creek Canyon which we locals call Ice Canyon. It is an unnamed mine, and for a while my two friends thought this must be your mine, but I called them to a closer reading of the text of your novel, and we all now agree that it must be closer to Luning.

"I enjoyed the details about carbide lanterns. The description of the interior of the mine reminded me of the tunnels found in Candelaria before it became an open pit mine.

"We thank you for writing your book. It has stimulated extensive conversations and some exploration. It would be a thrill for us to visit the location someday, with you as our guide. Sincerely, Paul."

In October, Ron penned a detailed answer: "Good Day to you Paul Pinnacle, Thank you for your kind words about *"Mystery of the Lmuma Mine"* which now appears to be turning into another 'mystery.' I'll try to help you locate the specific area, understanding that I too have tried, and failed! Oh, I can lead you to the faded road a couple of miles west of Luning and I can still see the cinder cone. Past the cone, the road left the canyon and ended up climbing for a few miles, ending up on a high north facing slope.

"In April, there were still a few patches of corn snow in the juniper shadows. (The steppe was primarily still sage). But the road ends there. I've searched through Mineral County mining claims record (at Hawthorne Library) but found nothing even close. None of the canyon names you mention sound at all familiar. I'd love to join you, rent a horse or a Jeep and go looking for it!

"Yes, the mine really existed, south of the highway, probably under some other name. It was worked by Forrest Williams and Burt (?) who were real people. That was in the middle 40s and I was there on at least two occasions (maybe three). I assumed that Forrest owned the claim, but what would a fourteen year old kid know or care about such things at the time?

"The 100 foot shaft was exactly as described in my book, with a side tunnel at the 50 foot level and an opposite drift at the bottom (100 foot level). There may have been a couple of short exploratory branches off the main (and only) drift, but nothing as elaborate as suggested in the book (Lot's of poetic license there).

"I would guess that the main tunnel did not exceed 350 feet, and ended with a sharp stope upward for maybe 60 feet. If there was anything above that, I was not aware of it. The 50 foot level did not contain any tunneling much beyond the shaft, and was primarily used as an emergency escape route and air vent.

"The tracks, ore cars, interior loading chute and hoist were much as described, I think that I invented any track "switching" like that required where two major tunnels converge. If anything remains of the cabin, it would be uphill from the hoist house about 150 feet.

"In 1946 and 1947, Forrest was hauling ore to the Virginia City area in a five-ton dump truck, and I rode with him at least once. A little detective work there might turn up some clues about the real name of the mine or its' owner.

"It was definitely a shirt sleeve operation, as they paid $32 an ounce for gold in those days and Forrest told me that his yield was about two ounces per ton. I remember his wife complaining that he was just a little boy with his toys, wasting his time and money for a myth.

"I graduated from Mineral County Grammar School (Class of '46) and spent the next two years at Christian Brothers School in Sacramento, returning to Hawthorne for my junior year of high school, before leaving the state.

"I appreciate your comments about the coyote and red-herring. I would like to quote them, using your name, with permission, of course.

"I don't get to travel as much as I'd like. We were in Hawthorne for two days this past spring on a book signing tour, but didn't get much response. Hadley in Round Mountain was much more interested in my books, treating us like royalty! We now live in Yakima, WA and I hope to hear more from you and your friends.   Sincerely, Ron Martin (a.k.a. Al Allaway)."

Ron read and reread Paul's previous letters and pondered the landmarks. There may have been a road extending from one of the existing roads that would have provided easier egress. But, after 40 years, some of those roads wash out and totally disappear.

Another problem they had was the location of the cinder cone.

The elusive cinder cone and track to the Mindoro mine.

Ron could stand it no more. He was truly interested in helping them locate the mine, but the constant e-mail traffic kept interrupting his pressing book publisher deadlines.

Finally, he ordered two 7.5 minute USGS topographic maps of the suspect area. He wrote Paul, "I have ordered maps for Indian Head Peak and Mable Mountain to see what I can see."

When the maps finally arrived, Ron sat down and wrote a newspaper article for donation to all central Nevada weeklies:

Whatever Happened to Squaw Mine?
(Digging Up a Deep Mystery)
By Al Allaway

"Where is it?" As people searched through Mineral County mining records and found no trace of a "lost" gold mine I'd written about, this became a question that went on to create a new mystery, all its' own!

For my part, I found myself adamantly repeating that the "missing" mine really did exist. And, if my memory served me correctly after 60 years, it was located near Luning, Nevada.

Throughout this challenge, I held to the rationale that, even if the name might be wrong, the mine certainly was a reality – somewhere! I knew that I'd worked there in 1946-47. And over the years I'd retained vivid recall of its details. My memories remained so clearly defined that I wrote a novel for young adults about Cold War espionage – using the mine and the Hawthorne Naval Ammunition Depot for the background.

Published in 2004, I titled the book, *"Mystery of the Lmuma Mine."*

An early complaint I kept bumping into was: "LMUMA...? I can't pronounce it, let alone know what it means!"

As it happens, Lmuma is a Native American word that is generally translated as "mature woman." Not wanting to offend the political correctness crowd as I sat down to write the book, I chose to use Lmuma within the text, instead of "Squaw."

So, where was this mine actually located? Three local prospectors – those who now prefer to avoid any notoriety by being named here -- ended

---

313

up exchanging over 5,000 e-mail words with me, committed to looking for clues beyond those in the book.

Then, as the mystery continued to ensnare our small search party, these determined three went on – traipsing over many miles of Mineral County back trails. Ultimately, their search went to a USGS quad map, "Mable Mountain, NV," Section 10, R33, T7 – which ended up showing an unnamed mine containing three shafts and two structures. (Viola! That had to be it!) Following up on this very optimistic clue, my three prospector friends personally visited the mine on November 12, 2005, and were finally able to confirm that my memory was indeed still intact—except, that is, for the name I'd ascribed to it. For which I must certainly apologize to *"Mystery of Lmuma Mine"* readers.

However, I may perhaps be forgiven this pitiful memory lapse if I ask you: "Can many among us remember a name we may have heard rarely – and then, some sixty years ago?" So hopefully I will be able to rest my case.

The mine I have over the years remained so enamored with (the essence of which I went on to capture in a small adventure novella) is today staked by Nevada Sunrise – under the name "Mindoro Mine." Which happens to be the same name used by its Hawthorne locators, Forrest Williams and Chris Smith, back in 1935.

Mindoro is *"Mina de oro,"* in Spanish and translates into English as "gold mine."

The final postscript, therefore, would seem to be, thanks to my indomitable prospector friends, the state of Nevada now contains one less mystery!

Paul's two friends also sent e-mails, one of the latest said: "If you decide to come to Hawthorne this summer, either Paul or I can give you a tour of the Mindoro aka

Lmuma aka Squaw Mine. If you have any interest in doing so, I can also take you to the Mineral County Recorder's office and show you the various record that are kept on mining claims, in case you want to see what you can find.

When Paul, Ned and I were at the mine, Paul took some pictures for you, but he said they didn't turn out too well. He was going to have them scanned and sent to you by e-mail, but he may have decided to send then to you by Pony Express (US Main in Nevada) instead. Paul did take some pictures of the "cone" or "lava outcropping" that you mentioned in your book.

As soon as Ron could break free from his publishing obligations, he wrote extensive letters to his high school buddies, Rex Franklin and Tim Caruthers.

"We've talked about it for years," he began, "Now it's time we meet in Hawthorne for a week or two of summer vacation." He wrote lengthy details offering to host the reunion. Families were to be included. People could be assigned to create games to manage the kids. Lots of hiking, fishing and exploration would be available. If they all stayed in the El Capitan Lodge, there would be a great swimming pool, and of course, access to casino type shows. Ron suggested the first two weeks of June, before the weather got too hot.

"I've already confirmed that we can rent horses or Jeeps for travel in the back country," he told them, "And there are other people besides us who want to go along to the mine."

Rex Franklin, a retired Navy Frogman and scuba store owner replied right away that he would be bringing his wife Carol, plus three adults and three children.

Tim Caruthers retired in 1983 as a Battalion Chief from the Portland Fire Bureau. He and Tina purchased a big diesel motorhome that year and were "snowbirds" yo-yoing between Portland and Arizona.

When Tim called to confirm, he said he and Tina would bring the motorhome and stay in it. His two sons, Steve and David and their families would join them by car.

When Ron called Paul Pinnacle with the plans, Paul said that he and his friend Ned would meet them alternately, as they couldn't both be gone from the law office at the same time.

The date was set, the reservations made for the motel and conference room and the excitement mounted. Ron almost felt the same anticipation as he did 40 years earlier at Christian Brothers School. It was all coming together.

A couple of days before the others were scheduled to arrive, Ron Martin and his lady friend; Ronda Fletcher arrived in Hawthorne and checked in to the El Capitan Inn.

While Ronda entertained herself at the El Capitan Casino, Ron visited the office of the local weekly, *The Mineral County Independent Gazette.*

As a boy, Ron delivered papers for the *Gazette* and knew most of the staff. When he entered the office, he felt right at home. There is something in the odor of printer's ink that stays with a person forever. The shop looked much as it had 40 years earlier; trays of lead typeset still cluttered the side benches. While the old linotype machine was now silent and cold, Ron wondered why it was still there. Modern printing methods had made it obsolete.

He rang a bell on the front counter which was answered by a tiny grey-haired lady.

Ron asked for Jack.

"Jack died seven years ago," she said, "I'm his widow. How may I help you?"

Ron introduced himself.

She said, "I've been waiting for you to show up. Don't you remember me? I used to be your next door neighbor when Jack first bought the paper."

"Mary! Of Course!" exclaimed Ron, as he took her cold hand. He felt a momentary shudder.

After a moment, she pulled away, "I've got something of yours."

Ron could hear her shuffling around in the back room. When she finally returned, she carried an old yellowed manila envelope.

Her wrinkled features and sagging eyes made her look older than her seventies. She wore a faded black scarf and a heavy black dress. Most of her teeth were gone. When she reached out, her fingers bent beneath large, distorted arthritic knuckles and tears stained her rough weathered face.

"Forrest Williams left this for you fifteen years ago before he died, with instructions to deliver to no one else."

Ron opened the envelope. Two odd shaped keys clinked onto the counter. One looked very much like a bank safe-deposit box key, but the other was much older, cast in iron, suggesting some type of an old trunk or chest.

"Whatever do you suppose?" queried Ron.

"That's an oddity! I've not a clue," said the old lady.

He shook the envelope, hoping there was something else. He examined the envelope closely inside and out. Perhaps there was something written?

There were only the two keys. Nothing else!

Chapter Twenty-Five ~ Reunion

Rex and family were the first to arrive. Ron greeted his old friend with a huge bear hug.

"Easy, old man," complained Rex, "I've a herniated disc back there."

"Who are you calling an old man?" Ron said.

"The turkey standing in front of me who has turned into a white headed old buzzard," joked Rex.

Ron motioned to Ronda standing politely off to one side, "I want you to meet my special lady, Ronda Fletcher."

Rex took her hand and said, "Any relation to my favorite mystery writer, the Fletcher of *"Murder She Wrote?"*

"My step-sister," declared Ronda, proudly.

Carol Franklin introduced her son Nathan and his wife Ann. Then, she, Ann and Ronda took off somewhere for girl talk.

Nathan proudly showed off his 9-year old son, Mark.

"Is there really gold around here?" Mark asked.

"Yep," answered Ron, "and lots of other good stuff, like silver, turquoise, copper, uranium and boxite.

"Uranium, really? The stuff they make atomic bombs out of?"

Ron told Mark, "Absolutely!"

"Did you see all the ammunition bunkers when you drove in? Are there bombs stored in them?" Mark was full of questions.

A fire engine airhorn and siren startled them. It was Tim Caruthers arriving in his huge diesel motorhome. Many retired people paint beautiful scenes of nature on the sides of their recreational vehicles, but not Tim. Someone had artfully painted a fire engine pump panel and intake ports on the side of this all red coach. On the back was painted, "TFD, Eng. 69"

"Here's the other turkey," said Ron, "Welcome!"

Tim introduced his wife, Tina, who then went off the join the other ladies.

"Ain't that siren illegal?" Ron asked.

"Yeah," said Tim, "But don't tell anybody."

"This little berg in the middle of the desert probably never heard one. Ha!" Rex laughed.

Tim said, "My two boys and their families should be arriving at any time. Are your attorney friends here yet, Ron?"

"Not yet," said Ron, "And before anybody else gets here, we three need to have a private talk."

"You sound serious, buddy, What's up?"

Ron told them about his failed attempt to reach Forrest Williams's family, thinking they might be interested in his book about the 1947 mine adventure.

He expressed his surprise when the anonymous note arrived after five years delay. It said that Forrest left something for him at the News office. Ron said he forgot about it for a few more years until yesterday when he went to see Jack's widow and received the two keys.

"Have you tried them anywhere, yet?" asked Rex

"Nope! Even though the note was addressed to me, I wanted to wait until all three of us got together." What do you want to do?" said Tim.

"There is only one bank here in Hawthorne and we need to try the safety deposit box key there." Ron hesitated, speaking softly, "I have this weird premonition that we need to do this in secret."

"Are you implying a mystery?"

"You might say that!"

"Is there a number on the key?"

"Yes," said Ron, "it's number 50."

"What time does the bank close?"

"An hour from now at 3:00 P.M.," said Ron. "Here's what I want you to do. Get everybody in the pool; organize a pool party. I'll duck into the bank right at closing time to see if the key fits box 50, then I'll join you at poolside. That should allay any suspicions."

Entering the bank at 2:56, Ron was pleased to see the lobby was almost empty. Feeling like a criminal casing a heist, he approached the only teller.

She was first to spot his shifting eyes as they darted all around the room and her hand inched closer to her panic alarm button.

"I inherited a safety deposit box key," he told the young lady who began to relax. "Can you admit me?"

She checked her deck of signature cards and frowned. "This is most irregular," she said, "The card for that box says that no signature is required, but the key holder must show identification proving that he is Ron Martin. Can you do that?"

"No problem," said Ron, producing his driver's license and photograph.

"One more thing," she said, "The card also says that you must pay back rent on the box before I can let you in."

"And that is?"

She went to a nearby calculator and started adding up a long list of numbers. Ron panicked. *That dang Forrest always did have a sense of humor,* he thought, *and it looks like he's going to have the last word.*

The teller came back to the counter and said, "That was five years at $16, four years at $18, and four more at $25. Rates went up every few years. Your grand total is $252.00."

"Ouch! Will you take a check?"

In the box he found a large lonely yellowed envelope, just like the one at the newspaper office. He unceremoniously slipped it still sealed into his pocked and headed for the door.

"Do you want to continue the box rent?" asked the lady.

"No way!"

The teller locked the door and pulled the shades as he went out.

Ron glanced around and ducked into his car. Curiosity overcame him and he carefully opened the envelope, wondering what could be worth so much cash.

It contained a single card with two words hand printed in ink:

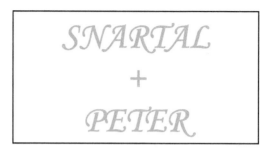

SNARTAL + PETER? A code? A riddle? *What could it possibly mean?* Ron searched his memory for anyone named Peter and drew a blank. Was this a coded location for where the other key might be used?

He felt like a kid again, trying to solve some silly riddle in grammar school.

Of course, he had to share the coded card with Rex and Tim, who instantly sought him out at the pool. "Did the key fit a box at the bank?" and "was there anything in the box?'" they asked.

"One question at a time, fellas," said Ron. "No one but us three can know about this," he cautioned, then adding, "It cost be a bundle in back rent and your share is $84 bucks each."

He showed them the card.

"I'm too old to be solving riddles," said Tim, "My brain died when I retired."

"That's a load of bull," said Rex, "You were the top dog fire investigator."

"That was then, this is now."

"Tuck it away and sleep on it," said Ron, "Here comes some more of our party."

As he finished speaking, two more cars pulled up. It was Steve and David Caruthers with wives and kids. As the doors flew open, four children of varying ages rushed poor Tim, hollering "Grandpa!" They about bowled him over with hugs.

There was a fleeting moment, when Ron Martin regretted never marrying and having children, but the moment passed.

"Welcome," said Ron, "Everybody else is in the swimming pool. You folks are in rooms 208 and 209, and I'm Ron Martin."

Steve introduced his wife, April and two daughters, Susan and Sarah. David's wife was Darlene with sons, Dan and Darrel. The kids all ranged in ages from eight to twelve.

As the newcomers hauled luggage to their rooms with intentions of changing for the pool, Ron Rex and Tim were left alone to finish their conversation.

"If Forrest wrote that as a clue to something, we have to let our minds drift back forty years and try to place things in perspective," Ron advised.

"I'm going to have trouble getting beyond my third of $252.00," said Rex.

"Like maybe check your notes for writing the book?" Tim was teasing.

"Let's be sure to keep this among us three," Ron concluded. "We need to join the rest of the folks."

Snartal + Peter..? Dang!

* * *

"This is turning into quite a shindig," Ronda Fletcher said, nudging Ron. "I love your friends and their families."

"Yeah," answered Ron, "Counting us, there are seventeen people so far, and more coming."

It was evening and they were all eating banquet style in one of the El Capitan's meeting rooms.

Ron clinked his glass with a spoon, as a signal for silence. He stood up to make an announcement.

"Most of you have met already. All I need to say is welcome. We still have some Reno prospectors coming to join us within a day or two.

"Tomorrow, Rex, Tim and I will drive out to the road that used to lead to the mine, just west of Luning. We'll take a four-wheel drive Jeep and see how far up the slope we can drive. We'll try to go past the cinder cone and maybe a mile into the canyon, but no further, because we are waiting for Paul Pinnacle to guide us the rest of the way. It's only a short exploratory and planning trip.

"Some of you youngsters have asked to be included. You'll have to wait until we check things out a bit more, but you can be sure that anybody who wants to will probably be able to see what's left of the mine, by next week. You've been hearing us talk about it for years, I hope it doesn't burst your bubble!

"On Tuesday, I'm expecting Paul Pinnacle or one of his friends. They've been to the mine within the past couple of years and will give us some advice. Meanwhile, Ann and April will be organizing events and things for the youngsters to do. Ronda knows all about the casinos in town and will share whatever she can with whoever wants to know.

"I've already been informed that David, Steve and Nathan have rented a boat and will be spending all day Tuesday out on Walker Lake, fishing for those huge cutthroat trout.

"So, everybody get a good night's sleep as we have a busy and fun day planned for tomorrow. You'll be on your own for breakfast. We'll meet back here at 6:00 P.M. for dinner."

Ron, Tim and Rex met later that evening in the lounge at the El Capitan. They chose a secluded booth in a back corner, expecting to talk in private.

Except for cocktail waitresses and a Keno girl they were basically alone. Tim and Rex were both wagering on the Keno games that were played every ten minutes, which made Ron a little nervous because the Keno runners kept interrupting their private conversations.

"We have to approach this riddle with intelligence," Tim started. "When I had a really mixed up fire investigation, we often had to take clues one at a time, think about them separate from all the others. That way we could maybe fit two small pieces together in order to have something on which to start to build. What I'm saying is that we need to assign each clue to a single person and have him think of nothing else except that word or clue."

"That makes a lot of sense," said Rex, "Take one word and play with it upside down, inside out, backward, forward and concentrate only on all possible variations, even foreign language interpretations and maybe synonyms too."

Ron said, "There's a pretty good library here in Hawthorne. Those new computers are still too expensive for individuals to own, but I think the library has one."

"Hold that thought, here comes the Keno runner."

After the young lady passed, Ron continued, "I think I should search for any clues in the notes or manuscript for the book."

"Agreed," said Rex, "And I'll take that goofy word... What was it? SNARTAL!"

"I'm happy with the Peter clue," agreed Tim, "I just wonder though, how important is the plus sign?"

"If it's a math formula, it could be vitally important."

"Yeah!"

"One word of caution," said Ron, Too much time spent at the library might raise suspicions."

Monday dawned clear and warm, promising a hot but calm day. As planned, Ron, Tim and Rex, with lunch and drinks iced down in a cooler and breakfast in their bellies, we in a rented Jeep ready to depart at 7:00 A.M. Everybody else was still sleeping. The anticipation of the coming trip was running high. They felt like kids let out of school on the last day before summer began.

What they could not know was that a moist, fast moving mini cell was caught in the jet stream off the Pacific, just about to collide with hot dry air moving up the San Joaquin Valley. The collision happened in

Tulare County, California; it was a total surprise to all local meteorologists.

Suddenly ablaze with lightning, the piled-up thundercloud swept north-eastward at a high rate of speed. When it struck the Sierra Nevada Range near Sequoia, the sudden updraft towered the cumulonimbus clouds even higher, producing baseball sized hail.

With celestial unconcern, the blasting strokes of lightning fell here or there—to splinter a half a dozen snag-top firs on the flanks of Mt. Whitney.

About 8:00 A.M., Ron turned the Jeep off US Highway 95 onto a barely visible dirt track, not much more than a line lacking vegetation with sagebrush and rabbit brush on both sides.

"That sand looks awfully soft," said Tim.

It's deceptive," Ron said, stopping the Jeep. "Here, let me show you." He stuck a small shovel into the sand only about four inches deep. Scraping the sand away, he said, "This is hard packed caliche drifted over with soft sand. Most of this desert is like that."

Caliche is a hardened deposit of calcium carbonate that cements together other materials, including gravel, sand, clay, and silt, occurring worldwide, generally in arid or semi-arid regions, including High Plains of the western USA. Caliche is also known as hardpan. The term *caliche* is Spanish and is originally from the Latin *calx*, meaning lime.

"I remember that it was Easter Sunday when we drove this road last time," offered Rex, "and there was a violent wind storm."

"That's right and we were in a big dump truck," said Ron, "Do you recognize the old cinder cone or lava outcrop ahead on the left? Remember Forrest giving us our first lesson in geology; he said that gold is almost always found somewhere near volcanic activity."

Looking south, they were all surprised to see the white top of the approaching thunderheads, reaching almost 30,000 feet, in stark contrast with the azure blue sky rapidly being replaced.

As if on signal, the wind picked up and the small grains of sand began to stir.

By the time they drove another thousand yards up the saltbush steppe, the sand was blowing horizontally, totally blinding them from any further progress.

"*Déjà vu,*" said Tim, "Just like forty years ago."

"I think that we'd better turn back," said Ron, "There's lots of rain in that thunderhead, and we could get caught in a cloudburst, especially where the canyon gets so narrow."

Cloudbursts in desert areas occur on occasion, creating flashfloods which when channeled into narrow canyons will create a fast moving wall of water, sometimes reported eight to ten feet high. These can sweep down dry canyons, arroyos or gulches with such force that any person or animal caught unsuspecting could be torn limb from limb and washed for miles.

The clouds now gray, then roiling and black were very threatening and it was a wise decision. By the time they returned to the paved highway, it was pouring rain. A half an hour later, they pulled into the outskirts of Hawthorne. The sun returned and was again shining as the fast moving storm was disappearing over the north-eastern mountains.

Thinking that they might be able to go back, Rex asked, "How long does the flash flood threat last after the rain stops?"

"In those deep and winding canyons, they could be delayed up to four hours," answered Ron, "So we won't be going back today."

"It might be a good time to invent some legitimate reasons for visiting the library," suggested Tim.

"Good idea. Let's do it before those Reno attorneys show up."

Chapter Twenty-Six ~ The Key

On Tuesday Ron decided to postpone another attempt on the old mine road until Paul Pinnacle of friends arrived. Instead, he called all those interested to a planning session and spread out copies of the topographic map, "Mable Mountain, Nevada, Section 10, Range 33-East, Township 7-North

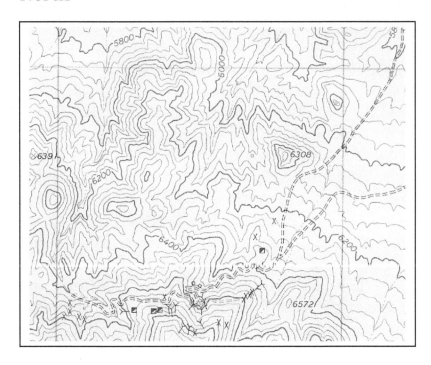

Ron also had a copy of the grid map just to the north, so they could see every twist and turn of the old road. The junction with US 95 was estimated to be exactly 4.3 miles west of the Gabbs Valley State Highway 361 and exactly 19.8 miles east of Hawthorne. The current map showed two different roads up to Mindoro, but everyone agreed one was not there in 1947.

If all the twists and turns of the older road were straightened out, it appeared to be just a little under 5 miles total, a much easier walk for old Burt to find his watering hole in Luning, than was earlier suspected.

"I imagined it to be twice that distance," said Rex, "Are you sure that's the right road?"

"It has to be," remarked Tim, "Remember, we were only 14 and everything appeared larger then than it is now. The contours show how rough it was. Remember? It took Forrest over an hour to drive his old dump truck through that short mile-long canyon, and we were all car-sick from the rolling motion."

"It's all coming back now," said Rex, "What was the name of Forrest's trusty old truck?"

"He called her Eleanor, after the President's wife," replied Ron, "That's still the only apparent way in there; unless Paul

Pinnacle indicates that he and his buddies went in some other way."

"We could always hire a helicopter," said Tim.

"Sure! And who's going to pay for that?" countered Ron, "We're already out *mucho dinero* for these ... He caught himself in time to keep from completing the sentence ("stupid clues!"). All we can do now is to wait for Paul to show up."

Nathan asked, "What about these new four-wheelers that he talks about?" It was a legitimate question, as in 1986, ATV's and Off-road vehicles were still in the twilight of developmental stages.

"I guess they can be pretty powerful over hills and rocks," Ron said, "I think he and his friends each have one, but it's not likely they'll all be here at the same time. We are going to have to rely on more conventional means of transportation like our Jeep or horseback."

One by one, people got bored and drifted off to more attractive activities, until only Rex, Ron and Tim remained.

"Any luck at the library last night?" Ron queried Rex.

"Well, the librarian helped me find a dictionary of common abbreviations, you know, like UNESCO and stuff like that, but there wasn't anything even close to Snartal.

We also checked language dictionaries for Spanish, French, German, Portuguese and Russian. No luck there. She did observe that if you spell it backwards, it resembles Latin. The bad news is that someone has snitched the Latin dictionary out of the reference department."

"Wouldn't they have one in the High School?" asked Tim.

"Sure they would, except school is closed for the summer," replied Ron.

"Funny," observed Rex, "we all attended a Catholic school and were forced to learn Latin. Why can't we solve this without help?"

"All the word *latrans* suggests to me is latitude or length or transit," put in Ron, "and that gets me nowhere!"

"What about the Peter clue?" Rex addressed Tim.

"A total blank! I've listed every Peter I can think of: Peter Ustinov, Peter the Wolf, Peter Rabbit, St. Peter the Apostle, Peter Paul and Mary, and even (Tee-hee) peter penis."

"Nah," said Ron, "Forrest would never use THAT for a clue. I'm thinking it might be something Native American. If you remember, he was part Indian."

Tim said, "I'm thinking maybe the Apostle Peter might be our best choice."

"Okay," said Rex, "So what does it mean?"

"I guess we just have to keep thinking outside the box."

* * *

Paul Pinnacle didn't arrive until almost 2:30, too late in the day for any attempt to penetrate the rough hills or the mystery. He towed a flatbed trailer with two ORV's (Off-road vehicles). They looked like enlarged little kid's tricycles with big balloon tires, definitely designed for only one person.

Paul greeted those present and introduced himself. He appeared to be in his late thirties, wore light blue coveralls over a starched white shirt and red bow tie. He had a hard, rawboned face, close cropped hair, black stabbing attorney's eyes, and ears that stuck out like a judge's gavel.

About the vehicles, Paul said, "They are working on a four wheel design that will be much more stable. These three-wheelers can flip over and crush the rider if you are not careful. Every rider has to wear a helmet, and then, only after I approve his/her driving skill. That's for liability, you know."

"Well, come on in and get settled," Ron said. "Yours is room 213. You'll meet the rest of the gals and kids at dinner, 6:00 PM." Ron held out his hand. Paul took it—rather like a crustacean claw than a hand—gave Ron a painful nip. His forehead was scoured with deep furrows. Ron stared with amazement at the see-saw motion of his jaw.

"I've got a friend out at the Hawthorne Army Ammunition Base," Paul said, "Do you mind if he comes along out to the mine?"

"The more the merrier," answered Ron, "as long as there's no liability. What's his name?"

"He's Sonny Crispler, a nice kid. He's about 40 and from Oregon, but now works at the base."

That evening, Ron had a surprise visitor. Opening his motel room door, Ron saw a large man about his own age, who said, "Hi Ronnie, remember me?"

Ron thought there was an old familiarity, but was embarrassed when he couldn't place the guy.

"I'm Danny Del Purto. We were buddies here in grammar school."

"Of course, Danny, how are you?"

"I heard you were in town looking for treasure out at Forrest's old mine." He said.

Ron was taken aback and thought, *This guy was never very friendly; what's he want now and who said anything about any treasure?*

"I guess Hawthorne's famous rumor mill is working full speed," said Ron, "What is it you think we are here for?"

"Well," stammered Del Purto, "Some Reno attorneys have been out to the mine a couple of times, and now you are here and today the attorney shows up again with his new fangled tricycles. It's all over town that you borrowed a Jeep and tried to get up there the day of the big thunderstorm."

Ron laughed a big guffaw, "So the whole town thinks we are here for treasure? Ha! That's a laugh."

"Yeah?" countered Del Purto, "Then what about the secret keys and the big envelope full of clues?"

Damn! Jacks' widow and the bank teller must have both talked.

Ron gently narrowed the space between the door and the frame, "Well you've got it all wrong, Danny. Now if you'll excuse me, I've got to get ready for dinner." He snapped the door shut before Danny could get a foot inside.

Tuesday night's banquet was attended by eighteen people and Ron noticed they had extra waiters and other hotel staff inventing 'make-work' in the area. It was obvious that the whole town had by now developed a bad case of 'the flapping ear syndrome.' If there was any treasure to be found, they would be ensured of lots of company.

Up until now, the rumor mill avoided the specific words in the clue, so at least perhaps the librarian had sense enough to keep her mouth shut, but how long would that last? Time would tell.

They were seated at a long banquet table, eight to a side, Ron at one end and their guest, Paul at the other.

Ron's spoon clinked his water glass for attention.

"Tomorrow morning at 0900 hours, we will drive to Luning and attempt to reach the mine. We will take the Jeep and Paul's two ATV's which will limit us to six people, unless others want to walk.

A few laughed at his feeble attempt to joke.

"Obviously, Tim, Rex, Paul and I will fill four seats. What is the fairest way to decide who else gets to go?"

Rex said, "We've already promised my son Nathan. Remember?"

"Right," said Ron, "Who else?" Several hands were raised.

Paul spoke up, "None of you are checked out on the safety rules to drive the ATV, so we either leave one here, or take my friend from the army base."

"Right, again," said Ron, "We old farts have frequent memory problems."

There were more chuckles.

"What did you say his name was?"

Paul said, "Sonny. Sonny Crispler."

Tim Caruthers, who had been daydreaming, came to immediate attention. He had not been present when Paul first mentioned his friend. At the sound of the name, Tim turned pale, visibly shaken.

"Who?" he blurted out.

"Sonny Crispler, a guy from the base."

Tim looked at Rex and Carol. "Don't you recognize the name of the guy that tried to burn you out and tried to kill me? Billy Crispler used to be my abusive step-father, until I had him arrested. He and his brother Jack followed me through most of my fire department career, killing innocent firefighters. There can't be very many people around with that surname."

"Yeah, and he's from Oregon," added Rex. "Before she died, Tim's mother, Helen told us that Billy had kids by other wives and if this guy is in his forties, he could easily be one of them.

Paul Pinacle said, "This beats me and I don't want to add any stress here, so I guess the simplest answer is to rule Sonny out."

Everybody agreed.

"Well then," Paul continued, "Who are we going to train to drive my other little machine, or do we not use it?"

"I've got a motorcycle," Nathan said, "and this should be easy to learn."

"You're on," said Paul, "We have two hours of daylight left and lessons will begin in fifteen minutes."

Tim was still shaking with the thought of the Crispler brothers and any possible relations anywhere in the area.

Dinner over, folks drifted off until only Tim, Rex and Ron were left in the room.

"Seems like there has been a myth around here for years about a lot of treasure or lost gold from Forrest's mine, the Mindoro," said Ron, "What do you guys think?"

"Everybody loves the lure of a lost gold mine. Consider the Lost Dutchman down in Arizona," replied Tim, "And everybody wants to enjoy the fame of having one in their home town or home state, so why not here? Chambers of Commerce thrive on such attractions."

Rex said, "I think it's a bunch of hogwash. We saw the high-yield gold Forrest found in that "glory-hole" and he convinced me that it was only a rare pocket. The gold should be all gone, sold to the smelters up in Virginia City."

"He would never have abandoned it," said Ron, "if there was any gold left."

"Maybe he got tired or sick and couldn't work it anymore," said Tim. "We know he sold to a mining company back east. Is it possible that he got a great price because there WAS still some gold?"

"Yeah, but remember, it is still abandoned, so if there was any, it would be gone by now," said Ron, "I agree with Rex; too many people have looked since. I say, there's no gold left. Paul told me that the tailing piles have been sifted through and moved at least twenty times."

"We're here with our families enjoying the warm desert sunshine and for us three to reminisce by going back to a childhood adventure, nothing more," said Rex, "And if I'm any judge of human character, there's going to be a lot of disappointed people."

"But," broke in Tim, "What did Forrest leave for us, if anything? What's the funny key for? What's the code mean?"

"Oh, yes," said Ron, "I forgot to tell you guys... I've got that code all figured out! It was so simple, you wouldn't believe it."

Chapter Twenty-Seven ~ Wiley Coyote

Wednesday dawned with a light layer of haze under a ceiling of high cirrus. Fires fed by Santa Ana winds in Southern California were the source of the haze.

Life on the high steppe around the old Mindoro mine was good. There had been sufficient precipitation the past three years to allow the desert a continuation of bloom. Blades of green and occasional orange globe mallow usually never lasted so late into the summer.

The permanent animal residents of the steppe ballooned in population due to increased food supplies. They also could appreciate an abundant bloom of flowers. The ground squirrels, feasting on fiddle neck leaves could anticipate a bountiful fall harvest of seeds and fruits.

The desert tortoise, lumbering from plant to plant, munched a fresh dandelion salad. And the horned toad eyed, with greed, the spring crop of globe mallow, a welcome change from his winter diet of tough creosote or sage leaves.

Most coyotes might choose to ignore the beauty of the delicate flowers; they nevertheless enjoy a meal of jackrabbit that was fattened on the plant leaves.

The resident coyote was an opportunist. Even though her belly was full, she still stalked anything and everything that moved. She was driven by instinct, as opposed to raw hunger, like the many generations before her.

Her curiosity was attracted to a nearby horned toad busy stalking a large horsefly. The coyote was languidly spread out in the cool sand, reclining to catch the first heat of the rising sun.

Suddenly, her ears shot up to a point. Ground vibrations caused the horned toad to scurry off, surrendering the horsefly. The coyote was instantly on the alert. Something sinister was approaching! She emitted a low growl before loping off to her den.

Under the rotting supports of an old ore chute, she had chosen a manmade prospect hole for her den. From the shadows therein she watched as two men on horseback rode up, shattering the peace and tranquility that had been.

* * *

Tim and Rex were still upset with Ron. The night before, he told them that he had figured out the clue Forrest had left for him, but now he still refused to share it with them.

"After all," he said, "Forrest's family or whoever sent the clue to me only." It was difficult for them to figure out if Ron was joking, or if he was serious.

So it was that some gloom was present on Wednesday morning while they were loading up to make their way at last, up to the mine. It was difficult for everybody to erase "Squaw" in their thinking and their speech, to be replaced with "Mindoro."

Paul loaded the ATV's back onto the trailer, intending to unload them at the juncture with the mine road, then leave his pickup and trailer parked there. He was satisfied with Nathan's newly learned skill at handling one of them.

Steve and David Caruthers youngsters, Dan and Darrel and young Mark Franklin had previously drawn straws to see who got to fill the fourth seat in the Jeep, and 9-year old Mark won the draw.

"After we make sure the way is clear, and the mine is safe," Ron told everybody, "Later this week, we'll take any and all who want to go in as many trips as it takes."

Paul advised certain tools and supplies to be included. About 10:00 A.M. a small caravan left Hawthorne for the twenty mile drive to the mine road. Paul's truck and trailer were in the lead, followed by the Jeep. Bringing up the rear was Ronda Fletcher in Ron's pickup accompanied by David and Dan Caruthers. Their job would be to provide security. They would park by the trailer and guard the road to be sure Crispler or Del Purto or others did not sneak up behind the Jeep and the ATV's.

The road east out of Hawthorne was a smoothly paved highway with a gentle climb.

Looking back, they could see the entire Hawthorne valley with its saline lake and row after row of cement ammunition bunkers. Other storm-cellar like structures, remnants from World War II could also be seen. They were abandoned bunkers, covered with sand and desert growth to be camouflaged from enemy aircraft.

The town of Hawthorne appeared as a tiny island of green trees in the middle of shimmering tawny buffs and whites. Mt. Grant and Cory Peak rose majestically in the backdrop, still sporting patches of snow.

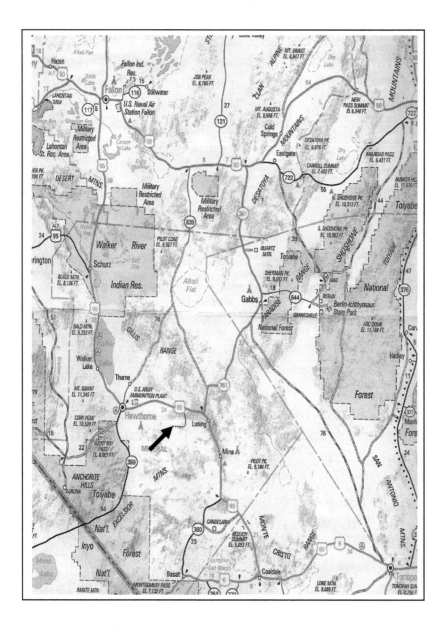

The five mile road to the Mindoro Mine was rough and steep, strewn with many boulders

Reaching the mine junction, vehicles were parked and everybody wondered around, stretching, while Paul and Nathan unloaded the ATV's, driving them down a portable ramp, one at a time.

"Great day with hardly any breeze," commented Ronda Fletcher, "Sure wish I could go on up the hill with you guys."

The faint trail ahead was fairly straight until it reached a brown topped hill a mile or two up the steppe.

"That's what I learned to be a cinder cone," Ron explained to Paul, "It sticks out like a sore thumb, marking the entrance canyon, separating it from all the other look-alike canyons."

"We call it a volcanic cap," said Paul, "There are some real big cinder cones around this county, and that's why your early clues led us astray."

"Cone or cap or whatever," growled Rex, still glaring at Ron, "Let's get going."

Ron felt Rex and Tim's anger building and decided it was time to end his mean little joke. Motioning them aside from the others, he whispered, "Forgive me guys, but I felt we could be bugged in town, and wanted to wait until we got out here. Of course, I'll share the secret clue with you..."

Tim nudged Rex and said, "I told you he'd tell."

Ron continued, 'SNARTAL spelled backwards is 'latrans,' as we already know. Latrans is the sub species of the coyote that lives in this area; *Canis latrans*, from the Latin.

"Okay, how does Peter fit the puzzle?"

"I remembered my Scripture. In Matthew 16:18, Jesus told Peter, *"...thou art Peter, and upon this rock I will build my church..."* Peter, of course, was the first Pope and church leader, often called "the rock." So, putting the two words together makes Coyote Rock. That can only mean one place, under the rock slab where the Russians stashed Soo Ling's money in 1947."

"Keep cool! Let's ride!"

Paul took the lead with his ATV, the Jeep followed and Nathan followed the Jeep on the other ATV. They looked like space explorers in their snug little helmets. The first mile was easy and the vehicles maneuvered the soft sand like they were designed to do. Before they entered the canyon, Paul stopped, got off and looked at the sand in front of him.

"Two horses have entered the canyon within the past few hours," he told the others, "Any ideas?"

"Not a clue. Let's just keep going and find out."

They started out again, only much slower now. The floor of the canyon was pure rock; a chute that had been carved out by eons of cloudbursts. While somewhat smooth, it was like a roller coaster and before long, little Mark was complaining of nausea.

"But it's going to get a lot rougher," Ron told him, "So keep your seat belt tightly buckled."

The Jeep interior was enclosed with a collapsible metal frame holding plastic sheeting and canvas. Indeed, it got so rough, the guys in the back seat were getting bruised. Not even their whitening knuckles could hold them from being flailed around inside the small space.

"Slow down!" hollered Tim, "I'm too old and tender for this."

"It's only a couple more miles to the mine," offered Ron who was driving, "Who wants to walk up the rest of the way?"

Rex said, "Aren't you borrowing words right out of Forrest's mouth forty years ago?"

Ron slammed on the brakes, as Paul had stopped just ahead of the Jeep. "Everybody out," he hollered.

There was a boulder almost the size of a small truck, blocking the road. There was no way to get vehicles around it as they were now on the side of a steep cliff, the wall of which went straight up on the left and straight down on the right.

One of the tools Paul had earlier insisted on them bringing along was lashed to the side of the Jeep. The need for a nine foot long steel pry bar now became apparent to all. They fitted some wooden blocks under one end of the boulder and inserted the pry bar for best possible leverage.

With five men and a boy working the fulcrum, the boulder was soon bouncing down into the chasm below. It made a horrible crunch sound when it hit bottom and shattered.

"I hope that killed a few rattlesnakes," joked Tim.

They stopped several more times to remove rock-fall. "These rocks look pretty fresh," observed Paul, "They were probably washed down by the last storm."

The odometer on the Jeep showed 4.7 miles from Highway 95, when they pulled up and parked next to where the old cabin had once been. The only evidence of it now remaining was a few rusty nails, a hinge or two and a couple of pieces of corrugated tin roofing. Some of the rusty cans had to have once held old Burt's trusty beans.

"I sense something is wrong, here," complained Ron, "There should be more wood remaining from the cabin. In this dry climate, these weathered old boards can last for a century or more. But there's not a scrap here anywhere."

Paul asked, "Is this where the cabin was in 1947?"

"Yes."

"I think I can help you, then," said Paul, "Somebody used all the good boards to build another bunkhouse and kitchen just over the hill."

Tim's first action was to wander up to where the old outhouse (without a door) once stood. It was the place where he first found $50 bills blowing by during a sand storm.

"I wonder if there might be any more?" he asked.

"If there were," chided Ron, "They'd be nothing larger than molecular dust."

"Hey! Here's a piece of chain," hollered Rex, "It was right about here where Burt kept those two fierce watch dogs chained up. What were their names?"

"Uh? Oscar and Ernie, wasn't it?"

"Yep."

"You know," said Ron, "This is kind of a disappointment. We knew it couldn't be the same, but somehow we wanted to relive the past, anyway."

"I'm glad we came," said Tim, "It's very educational to see what the environment can do to a place like this in just 40 short years. I can't even find the hole in the ground where the outhouse used to be."

Rex said, "Let's go see what other changes there are."

Paul Pinnacle was already down to where the hoist house and shaft had been and hollered for them to join him.

One scarred badly weathered 8 x 8 timber stood like a lone sentinel. It was broken off, possibly shattered by lightning, about nine feet above the ground; it was the only remains of a once proud 50 foot high head-frame. Other evidence of human habitation was the splintered skeleton remains of an ore chute where the good stuff was dumped from ore cars, to slide downhill into a waiting dump truck.

"There's where all your old boards ended up," said Paul, pointing to two more fallen down shacks. "They must have been built after you guys left here."

Young Mark stood nearby, pitching rocks as most 9-year olds will do.

"Are you looking at those rocks before you throw them?" asked his grandpa Rex, "You might throw away a gold nugget."

One of Mark's flying missiles bounced off the chute support and ricocheted back into an opening under the chute.

They were all startled to see a young coyote sprint out of the hole and down the hill. A couple of hundred yards out, she stopped and looked back at the collection of humans with what could be considered a disgusting look. She then loped off over the edge of the hill and was gone.

Ron, Rex and Tim all looked at each other, reminded that they had a secret mission to achieve. Rex felt his pocket for the reassurance the lump of the strange key was still there.

Paul interrupted, "I called you down here to examine these horse tracks. They're fresh, just like the ones we saw earlier. Some body's snooping around up here besides us."

Mark, like most curious kids, was climbing down the ore chute in order to poke around in the coyote's den. He suddenly let out a loud, "Whoop!"

"What is it, son," called down Nathan.

"I found some gold!" Mark hollered.

"Let's see, kid," said Paul who was closest. "I hate to disappoint you," he said after a quick look, "It is iron crystal, usually called pyrites."

"It looks like gold," protested Mark.

"Don't feel bad son," Nathan put in, "Fools' gold has been beguiling men for hundreds of years. Take it back home to show your class next fall."

Ron and Rex were still up by the remains of the head-frame. Nevada law required mine shafts to be sealed or fenced off. The present owners had not capped the top of the shaft. The only protection against humans or animals falling into the hole was a sturdy metal fence. Rex noted another nearby shaft that had not been there in 1947.

"I'd say somebody did a lot of work here after we left," said Ron.

"Do you think we should be concerned about the horse tracks?" Rex asked.

"It's basically public land, so unless they try to remove minerals or steal equipment, they've as much right to be here as we do," answered Ron. "Right now, I'm more interested in seeing if the 50 foot level is still open."

He called everyone together and announced they might see how far they could get into the drift tunnel at the fifty. "We have powerful electric torches for four."

"I don't think that's such a good idea," warned Paul, "My friends and I didn't chance it the last time we were up here because the support timbers in there would be pretty rotten by now."

Ron was trying to remember, *I don't recall any timbers in there, except maybe one or two. The walls and ceiling was of virgin rock. The main timbered support was at the entrance.* "I've been in there a bunch of times," he told Paul, "and I'm willing to try a few feet, anyway."

Borrowing a helmet and a light, he entered the cave. Tapping the overhead support timber with a hammer, gave him confidence because the reverberation indicated sound wood.

The fifty-foot level exit tunnel cut through the shaft at the halfway point. It had been cut into the side of the mountain prospecting a weak vein, but was not used prior to 1947, except for ventilation for the level below, and by Soo Ling for sleeping. Now, it was apparent that much more work had been done, as several new tunnels branched off in different directions. New support timbers had been installed at various intervals.

About fifty feet inside, he stopped and looked back. He could see a hint of daylight in one direction, but worked his way around the shaft and started in the opposite direction, going deeper into the mountain. He had to be very careful, as large boulders lay strewn about, and some deep, possibly bottomless holes broke through the floor. His passage would have been impossible without the benefit of the powerful lantern to see where he was going. *These lights are a far cry from the old carbide gas light we once had to use,* he thought.

A rattlesnake challenged his progress, but the passage was wide enough for him to bypass it. A few bats fluttered by his ear. He could see evidence of coyote scat. The drift continued on deeper than ever before, but Ron turned back, satisfied the tunnel was otherwise empty.

The fifty foot escape tunnel exited at the outside ore chute where the dump trucks had once been filled. It was one of the few places that was level, and everybody was standing there waiting for him.

"It appears perfectly safe," Ron said, "There used to be an iron mesh cap over the entrance to the shaft, but vandals or someone have removed it. I shone my light down to the bottom and it reflected water. The escape ladder looked like it had been repaired with new wood and has recently been used."

"I wanna go down, dad, pul-e-e-ease?" pleaded Mark.

"No way," said Nathan, "If anybody goes in there, they'll be grownups."

Ron called them all together and said, "Let's talk about this... We didn't come up here for spelunking, but, I've been in there to get a taste of the forbidden, and I would love to see more."

"What about the water; is the bottom flooded?" asked Paul.

"I couldn't tell how deep it was from fifty feet up," said Ron, "But it didn't look deep. And, if I remember correctly, the 100-foot tunnel goes up hill several feet after leaving the shaft."

"That's right," said Tim, "When I was pushing cars full of ore back then, I remember the last fifty feet to the hoist was slightly downhill and the cars were a lot easier to push."

"Well then," said Rex, "if there's water at the bottom of the shaft, it's probably only a rain puddle from Monday's cloudburst."

"I don't mean to be a spoil-sport," said Nathan, "but how could we trust the ladder?"

"If we can anchor it, I've got a seventy-five foot nylon rope," Paul advised, "We could use that for a safety line."

"But, we've only got two safety helmets, mine and Paul's back on the ATV's.

"Okay," said Tim, "This is Ron's party. I say he's in charge, so let him decide who goes in first."

Ron nudged Tim and said, "That's a real cop-out, turkey!" They were all standing at the mouth of the escape tunnel, looking inward and speculating.

"Well, what's it going to be?" growled Paul.

Ron studied the faces that were staring at him. He felt that nobody should go down, but that wouldn't seem to be very fair seeing as how he'd already been inside the upper tunnel. Now, he was faced with a decision that could be critical. Making matters worse, people like Paul were becoming angry.

He cleared his throat to speak...

"Ain't nobody going in there," barked a deep voice behind them. Startled, they turned to see two men sitting on horseback, both holding unsheathed rifles, pointed to the sky.

The speaker was instantly recognized.

"Danny Del Purto!" exclaimed Ron, "What are you doing here?"

"I should ask you the same question," Del Purto said, "And the answer would be that you are trespassing."

"Sez who?" demanded Paul.

"This hombre riding with me," said Danny, "Meet Jake Clark, the West coast representative of the company who happens to be the owner of this claim."

"Paul raised his brow, very skeptical, "And I suppose he just happened to be in Hawthorne today?"

"What's that supposed to mean?" growled Del Purto.

"That means, I'm familiar with Nevada mining law, and I don't believe you!"

"I don't give a damn what you believe," said Del Purto, "My 303 Enfield says you boys are leaving." The rifle was lowered a bit to point just over their heads."

Ron looked at Paul, questioning.

A change of attitude in Paul was immediately apparent, "You're right, of course," he said meekly, "We're leaving." He motioned with his eyes for the others to start moving back toward the vehicles.

A few minutes later, they were all assembled back at the Jeep, filled with questions.

"They're still watching us," cautioned Paul, "Let's drive on over the hill, out of sight."

A bit later, Paul said, "We are off the mine property now. Those guys are liars. I know the representative of the owning company and that's not him, although they used the correct name."

Ron said, "Yeah, and I noticed that so-called Jake Clark never said a word. Danny did all the talking. Clark is a stooge."

"What d'ya suppose they're hiding?" asked Tim.

"Who says they're hiding anything?" said Rex.

"Whatever they are hiding, is down the shaft," said Ron.

"How'd you know that?"

"I haven't had time to tell you about everything I saw inside the drift tunnel;" Ron replied, "A horizontal steel bar was wedged into the rock sides of the shaft just above the fifty foot level, and welded into it was a very large pulley that can be reached by a tall man. It had fresh oil dripping from the bearings. If it were to be rigged with a good long rope with block and tackle, one man could lift or lower up to 200 pounds at a time."

"200 pounds of what?"

"Maybe we need to sneak back some other time and find out," suggested Ron.

"What about the other thing we came up here for?" asked Tim.

"That can wait, too."

* * *

Thursday came and the team stayed in Hawthorne. Some of the boys tried fishing again on Walker Lake. Paul returned to his Reno law firm, but he left the trailer and the ATVs. He said he would be back on Saturday.

"Why didn't we check out the coyote rock?" complained Tim.

"Hey, turkey," answered Ron, "That's our secret, remember? What chance did any of us have to sneak away, unseen by Paul and others in order to check it out?"

Ever since high school, Ron, Rex and Tim had somehow adopted the slang, "Turkey" as a term of brotherhood or acceptance. This was hard for some folks to understand, especially when one called another, "turkey-butt!"

The place the money had been stashed forty years earlier, was off the mine property more than half a mile and was hidden up on top of the plateau, carefully tucked in a cavity under a large flat rock. They were sure, today that was the place Forrest's note referred to as 'coyote rock.'

Several times during the day, Danny Del Purto was observed driving by the motel. It was assumed he was watching for any departure activity.

Ron had a plan, "As long as we appear to be inactive, they will seem to feel safe. I've a shopping list of a few things we are going to need when we sneak back up to the mine."

This last statement caught everyone's attention.

Ron continued, "Tomorrow, before dawn, Ronda will drive the three of us to the mine road junction, drop us off unseen, and return to town before sunup. It's a little over four miles to the mine, we should be able to hike up in two and a half hours."

"Why don't you take the ATV's? asked Mark.

That would tip them off, the minute the ATV's leave town," answered Ron.

"What happens if we run into trouble or opposition?" asked Rex.

Tim said, "You were trained as a Navy Frogman and in physical hand-to-hand combat. From my Fire Investigator days, I'm still considered to be an officer of the law and licensed to carry a weapon. Between us, we should be able to handle anything."

"I've purchased three high powered walkie-talkies," continued Ron, "so we can keep in touch with Ronda and the outside."

"And I've got lots of mountaineering ropes and tackle in my motorhome," added Tim.

"Okay, gentlemen," said Ron, "set your alarms for 0330, but don't involve the night clerk of the motel. Ronda and I will be waiting in my Suburban, parked out behind the post office. You'll have to drift down there one at a time. Keep out of the street lights. Avoid being seen by anyone. It's a two block walk."

* * *

Friday morning at 0335, Rex Franklin, ex-Navy Frogman, slipped unseen down the back stairs from the second floor balcony of the El Capitan Lodge. He was wearing full camouflage and black face paint, a truly frightening specter.

The only thing missing, he thought, *is my trusty old M4 rifle.* He did carry a Glock 40 caliber hand gun in a hip holster, and a ten inch Navy-issued diver's stiletto in a special leg pocket.

The streets and alleys were deserted except for a homeless drunk who was foraging through a dumpster. Rex was trained to be able to pass anybody without being seen, but his fun nature decided to show himself to the old drunk. Rex chuckled when the guy's eyes bugged out in fright at the sight of his camo. The drunk was so startled that he dove head first into the dumpster and slammed the lid shut after him.

Still feeling feisty, a block further on, Rex snuck up on Ron's Suburban and rose up just inches outside Ronda's window, scaring her half to death. Her reflex action caused hot coffee to spill into her lap.

"Always the jokester!" scolded Ron, "Tim is already in the back seat. Hop in and we'll be off."

It was moonless and very dark. Ron had doughnuts and coffee available, as they sped east and south on Highway 95. A few eighteen-wheelers were the only other traffic.

Every once in a while, they would catch a brief glimpse of a white desert owl in the beam of their headlights. The owls were attracted to the only lights on the night desert, as were the moths and other insects the owls were stalking.

As they approached the twenty mile mark, Ron told Ronda to just drive right on past the junction to the mine road. "Don't slow down," he said. He wanted to make sure no one was parked there, waiting.

"Drive on a couple of miles to the junction with the Gabbs road, Highway 361, stop there and kill your lights," he told her.

When they were stopped and turned around, Ron said, "I can see a few lights of Luning a few miles south. We can see back the way we came for over ten miles, and there are no vehicle lights anywhere.

"When we get to the mine road, Ronda will slow down just enough so we can hit the road running. If somebody is watching the road, I don't want the car sitting there any longer than is absolutely necessary. You've each got a pack on the seat next to you. Be sure you grab it and take it with you."

Checking once more to be sure no other headlights could be seen, Ron told Ronda to start the short sprint back. At a predetermined odometer number, he told her to slow, but not use brakes.

At a precise speed, he told the guys to "Bail out."

As soon as they did, Ronda accelerated and was soon out of sight. They were within twenty feet of the road and immediately started the long hike.

"We want to get into the canyon and out of sight from the highway before it gets light," Ron said. The faint light of pre-dawn was already showing over the eastern hills.

A dim red penlight was needed to keep them in the track.

"It's warm enough for rattlesnakes," said Ron, "and they move around a lot at night."

"Look here," said Rex, focusing his light on a large orange desert scorpion, "This desert comes alive in the night." They could hear coyotes or desert foxes yipping from three different directions.

About then, Ron's radio squawked. He pulled it out of his pack and made a few adjustments. It was Ronda, already back at the motel, reporting no sign of any opposing activity.

In another thirty minutes, there was enough light for them to safely walk, and they picked up speed.

"Are we going to check out the mine first or the coyote rock?" asked Tim.

"Take a vote," said Ron, "We can climb to the plateau from that last curve before the road reaches the cabin site, or we can do the mine first and then go up the plateau. The first option is a pretty steep climb."

"I vote to save the best for last," said Rex.

"Second that," Tim said, "We go to the mine first."

They reached the rock canyon about fifteen minutes later, and the climbing became more strenuous. After another hour, Ron called for a rest on the road about where they pried the big boulder loose.

"I thought I was in better shape," he complained, sounding a little winded.

"Hey, turkey, shape up!" Tim barked, "We should all be winded, and we are. It's normal, considering we're all pushing sixty and we're almost a mile high in elevation."

"What makes you such an expert?" kidded Rex.

Drinking water and eating an energy bar each, they were on the way again. By then, the sun was reaching into the canyon and backsides started heating up.

"The worst of the climb is over," said Ron, cheering them on, "We've less than a mile to go."

Rex was the first to hear it... "Listen!"

"What?"

"Sh-h!"

The whump-thump-whump-thump of a helicopter soon became audible to all.

Ron glanced around and hollered, "Hide! Duck in here, in this prospect drift. The hole was only four feet in diameter and about five feet deep, and barely held them, scrunched down together.

The chopper flew right over them, headed for the plateau. It was the small variety like the ones used by big city traffic reporters. The plexiglass dome wrapped all the way around the front end, revealing a pilot and one male passenger.

"Did they see us?" asked Rex.

"Get off me; I can't breathe," complained Tim.

"I don't see how they could have seen us," said Ron, "They've landed below the ore chute at the fifty foot level."

"Let's creep up a little closer and see what they're doing."

Two men exited the chopper, whose rotors still churned slowly. They carried four huge bales from the chopper into the fifty foot level, returning empty handed. After the fourth trip, they stayed inside the mine out of sight, for about twenty minutes. Presently, they returned to the helicopter, and took off, flying to the south.

"I can't wait to get in there and have a look-see!" said Ron.

"Let's go!"

Chapter Twenty-Eight ~ Lmuma Dust

"Careful and slow," cautioned Tim, "If these guys are up to something illegal, they could have booby-trapped the entrance."

"I think maybe I'd better update Ronda on the radio, before we go in, said Ron. "The radio probably won't work inside the mine."

Contact established, he brought her up to date and asked her to stay tuned in. He activated the third radio and said, "One of us will have to keep watch at the mouth of the tunnel. That will be Tim. Rex and I together will do a quick inspection of the 50 foot level, and then I'm going down to the 100. Rex will stay at the entrance to the shaft by the ladder. You be sure to stay by the radio in case we need the sheriff."

"Ron?"

"Yes, Ronda?"

"I love you! Keep safe and come back to me..."

"Ten-four."

Tim was instantly unhappy with the arrangement, "Awr, but..."

"No buts! That's an order!" Even when they were boys, Ron was always the unofficial but accepted leader of the three.

The entrance to the mine appeared exactly as they had left it two days earlier. They started with caution and carefully observed as much as possible. In a cavity above the two horizontal supports at the entrance, they found a large coil of nylon rope not seen earlier. There was also a can of machine oil which they assumed was used on the pulley.

"That could have been there before," said Rex, "and we probably just missed it."

Ron asked Tim to test his radio one more time with Ronda and then move inside the tunnel as far as he could while still maintaining a radio connection.

Ron then moved slowly on into the tunnel to the intersection with the shaft. Easing past the shaft, they continued on exploring each of three side tunnels Ron avoided earlier. Whenever the encountered overhead support timbers, Ron would tap them lightly with a geologist's light hammer, listening to the resonance of the wood.

Satisfied that the new tunnels contained nothing unusual, they returned to the shaft opening. Everything looked the same as on the previous visit. Ron dug a hundred foot length of mountain climber's light nylon rope out of his pack and threaded it through the pulley. With the end

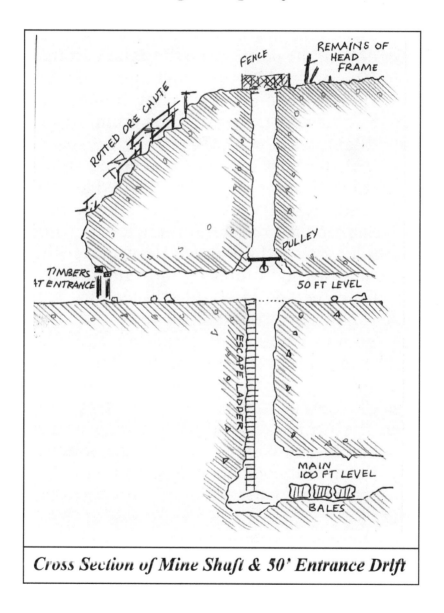

Cross Section of Mine Shaft & 50' Entrance Drift

he made a fireman's lift knot, stepped into the two loops and secured it around his chest with a bowline on a bight.

"I'm going to start down the ladder. You hang on the other end; maybe take a couple of bights around your waist; you are my safety line in case a ladder rung breaks," he told Rex. "If you hear anything from Tim or Ronda, let me know ASAP!"

With lantern and radio secured in his jump-suit, Ron was over the edge and swallowed up by the blackness of the shaft.

Rex paid out the slack as Ron descended down the ladder. He was working in the faint twilight filtering in from outside.

Time seemed to stand still for Rex, who felt caught up in something he couldn't be sure about. Occasional jerks on the line, kept him alert until finally his radio crackled, "I'm at the bottom." It was Ron. "There's been a huge cave-in forty feet or so down the tunnel, so the old working part of the mine is completely cut off. The water is only a couple inches deep. The tunnel before the cave-in has been widened into a storage room."

There was a long pause and then Ron radioed back, in a panic, "We need to get out of here, and fast! I'm coming up!"

Ron gave a yank on his safety line, thinking it would signal Rex to pull up the slack. Instead, he jerked the line right out of Rex's hand. Before Rex could capture the wayward end, it was through the pulley and falling down the shaft to land in a nice coil right at Ron's feet.

"Sorry about that," radioed Rex, apologetically.

Now Ron was faced with a dangerous assent without the safety line.

He started slowly up the ladder, straight up the shaft, fifty feet to the next level. He'd made the same climb, years before and it still scared him. He tried to remain calm and fight off his rising panic. It was like being on the outside of a six story building with no safety line, climbing in total darkness. There had been a couple of loose rungs he noticed on the way down. Now he racked his brain trying to remember exactly where they were.

Also, he had pulled his gloves off at the bottom and forget to get them before he started back up the ladder. Now, feeling thick cob webs with his bare hands, he regretted this oversight. The desert was filled with violin, brown recluse and black-widow spiders, and a dank, dark place like this was perfect habitat for them. To make matters worse, Ron had always had a deathly fear of spiders, call arachnophobia.

Right then, it took a great deal of courage for him to reach upward and grasp each new rung of the ladder, feeling more webs with each step. Twice, his foot broke through rotted wood. He was terrified. This was worse than the jungles of the Yucatan.

"Rex," he hollered, "If you have any more rope, drop an end down the ladder. I'm about twenty feet from you and need help."

He was imagining spiders on his ears and the back of his neck. Only his faith in God kept him from pure panic.

Tim overheard the cry for help and grabbed a length of rope from the horizontal timbers and rushed it to Rex. Together they threaded it down to Ron, who used it to relieve just enough weight so he could recover his balance and get purchase on good wood.

As they helped him over the edge, he emitted a huge sigh.

Shine a light on my head and neck," he demanded, "I feel something crawling."

They did and found nothing.

"What did you find down there?" asked Tim.

"Sixteen huge bales of marijuana," said Ron, "Let's get out of here!"

"What about our Coyote Rock?" said Rex.

"It's going to have to wait," said Ron, feeling their disappointment, "If we get caught up here, we're dead meat! Now, move!"

"Can't we get Ronda to call the cops and meet us up here?' Tim was in no hurry to leave.

Ron answered, "Knowing the people of Hawthorne, I don't know who we can trust. I'll have her get hold of Paul and the Federal Drug and Alcohol people in Reno. But, right now, we've got to get off this mountain."

"Well, at least we'll get downhill to the highway easier and faster."

Ron radioed Ronda with detailed instructions to call the authorities and then pick them up at the highway in an hour and a half.

* * *

It didn't take Federal Agents very long to jump on Ronda's phone call. They had been following many tips about a huge drug cartel operation in central Nevada, and Ronda's phone call seemed to be just the link they needed. Agents were already waiting at the El Capitan when Ronda brought the guys in from the highway. More agents arrived hourly from both Reno and Las Vegas.

Ron, Tim and Rex were interrogated over and over mercilessly. A major raid was scheduled for Saturday morning, based on information agents gathered from Ron and company. Ron made sure that agents realized that if the bad guys came back, they would be tipped off that someone had been snooping around in their hidey-hole.

"How's that?" asked the lead agent, a big fellow named Stanley Morris.

"I left my gloves on top of a bale of pot. I'd taken them off in order to dig a pocket knife out of my pocket in order to probe into the bale with my fingers, haul some out and sniff it. Then, my safety line, a hundred feet of mountaineering nylon is laying there where we dropped it at the bottom of the shaft.

"And don't forget their piece of rope," added Rex, "It's still looped through the pulley."

"Yeah, I guess any one of those three items would tip them off, we'll just hope it doesn't," said the agent, "Be ready to leave at 0800."

"All of us, or just me?" Ron asked.

"There's no reason you can't all three go. Maybe you can help. We've plenty of room in two military choppers."

* * *

The coyote was on the prowl again, after all the disturbing activity of the day. She did not like the whine of that flying machine. It hurt her ears, and she was grateful that all the man creatures and noisy machines were gone.

She sniffed around her old den under the ore chute, but caught only the disgusting odors of the men. The sun had been set for about two hours, and the moon was due to follow soon.

Her nose suddenly twitched and her ears went up. Opportunity was there, a few feet distant. It was in the form of a young jackrabbit grazing in some fresh dandelions. The survival of species has always been dependant upon alertness and caution. This young rabbit had neither and was totally oblivious to the nearness of the coyote and the imminent danger.

A brief stalk and a quick pounce was all that was needed and the coyote settled down to enjoy her dinner.

Her joy was soon interrupted. That hated machine noise was coming back. The flying object appeared over the ridge so suddenly, the coyote startled and abandoned her meal.

Three times that night, after waiting for quiet, she sought her quarry, and three times the dreaded flying machine returned. Have you ever seen a frustrated coyote?

Canis latrans

* * *

On Saturday morning, the R.V. parking lot behind the El Capitan Lodge and Casino looked like a war zone triage area. There was an army ambulance, three army staff cars, vehicles for the FBI, Nevada State Police units, police cars from the Mineral County Sheriff, Federal D.E.A. vans, and Tim

Caruther's bright red motorhome made to look like a pseudo fire engine.

The parking lot, a full block in size, was usually filled with eighteen-wheelers and recreational vehicles taking advantage of free overnight parking provide by the casino.

Sometime around midnight, the sheriff had ordered complete evacuation of the lot, and cordoned it off with bright yellow warning ribbons.

At precisely 0800, two Black Hawk UH-60 army helicopters landed on the north end of the parking lot, causing a whirlwind of dust.

All Hawthorne town folks by this time, whether friends or enemies knew something serious was happening and that it related to Forrest's old gold mine.

In all, eighteen people were seen loading into the two choppers, 4 crewmen, 1 Army Colonel, 4 DEA agents, 2 FBI agents, 1 Attorney (Paul), 3 Sheriff's deputies, and Ron, Rex & Tim.

The flight to the mine took less than ten minutes. The coyote was first to hear them coming, and this time, had presence of mind enough to grab her half eaten jackrabbit and carry it off with her as she fled the noise, the dust and the chaos that was to follow.

One of the Black Hawk gun ships buzzed the landing site, the only flat space at the 50-foot entrance. It raised clouds of dust and grit. The other chopper hovered considerably higher, scanning the road and surrounding landscape.

After the third pass, the first Black Hawk settled gently to the earth. Two sheriff's deputies in full body armor were the first to embark.

The second Black Hawk then landed, creating more dust for those already on the ground. Its downdraft was so severe that remaining parts of the newer two shacks were sent flying into a nearby gully.

Sheriff Tom Jefferson and his two deputies entered the drift tunnel first, followed by some of the agents. Lead Agent Stanley Morris established his command post outside by the helicopters and ordered Ron and company to stay with him.

"This is just like one of my Frogman assaults," observed Rex, "At least we didn't have to parachute in, this time."

"Did I ever tell you, I had to jump a couple of times when I worked for Geographica?" said Ron.

"No, and I don't think I could ever jump in a parachute," said Tim. "Going over the top of a 100 foot aerial ladder was scary enough."

Agent Morris was giving his attention to voices in a headset, when he suddenly turned and glared at Ron.

"They're telling me you made all this up," he shouted, "There's no bales and no evidence of any drug storage."

The deputies and agents presently emerged from the mine.

"What's going on?" Agent Morris demanded of Ron, "What are you trying to pull?"

"But-t-t," stammered Ron, "It was there yesterday!"

The other agents walked up to Morris, also glaring at Ron. "We rappelled three men down to the bottom," one said, "The only thing we found were these gloves and a rope."

"Even if there were sixteen bales of pot in there yesterday, there's no way they could be extricated in such a short time," said another agent.

Rex and Tim were also having doubts about the sanity of their friend Ron. Neither had been down the shaft or actually seen any marijuana. The whole operation was based solely on Ron's word.

"Were you drunk, or dreaming?" demanded a third agent.

The army colonel, Adrian Foster up to this point, had been simply observing. Now he entered the conversation, "Let's not jump to conclusions," he said. "I think there's more here than meets the eye."

"Explain," said Morris.

"Our radar down at the base was swamped with unexplained blips last night somewhere out this direction. The distance was too far to get any positive data," Colonel Foster said, "As it posed no threat to our security, they were ignored. Let me radio the base and see if we can get better coordinates."

"Go for it," said Agent Morris. "Meanwhile, I want this Ron Martin in irons."

Sheriff Jefferson clamped handcuffs on Ron, who couldn't believe what was happening. "I'm telling the truth," he sputtered.

"Sure you are!" growled the Sheriff, "That's what they all say."

Colonel Foster was on the radio in the cockpit of one of the helicopters. For Ron, Tim and Rex time seemed to stand still. Except for the slow churn of the rotors, it was deathly quiet. The sun was becoming unbearably hot. Ron wished that he'd remembered to bring a hat, but the sun was not the only reason he was sweating.

After what seemed an unbearable length of time, Colonel Foster finally appeared at the chopper door.

"Radar analysis reports that at least six moving objects were at this location during the night, returning at intervals of about one hour each."

Rex and Tim let out a cheer.

The Colonel continued, "Plot indicates the blips were probably a small helicopter that flew northeast towards Luning and returning here every hour."

"I told you it was here!" shouted Ron, "There are people in town who knew we were coming out here, and they must have tipped someone off."

Colonel Foster spoke again, "Let me call back and see it we can get better coordinates about where the chopper went after leaving here." He disappeared again, back into the cockpit.

One of the agents addressed Morris, "If you had to move sixteen big bales in less than eight hours and hide it, what would you do?"

"The desert is a huge hiding place," said another, "I'd consider burying it if I had access to equipment."

"That's it!" exclaimed Ron, "There's a borrow pit just outside Luning. A backhoe and grader were working there a couple days ago for no logical reason."

Colonel Foster stood at the chopper door and overheard, "That sounds about right, according to these fresh coordinates."

"Everybody back on board," exclaimed Agent Morris, "Let's go!"

But, poor Ron was still in handcuffs.

* * *

Sonny Crispler and Danny Del Purto gazed around the horizon and cast a big sigh of relief. Danny cut the ignition on the big D-8 Cat, and said, "That ought to do it! Let's split."

"Shouldn't we pick up some of these beer cans, first?" asked Sonny.

"Nah, let's get outa here."

While they were walking toward the pickup, Sonny suddenly cried out, "Uh-Oh! There's a sheriff's deputy turning in here from the highway."

"I see him," said Danny, "Keep cool and let me do the talking." When they reached Danny's pickup truck, the deputy was waiting.

"Howdy," he called, friendly like, "What are you boys doing?"

"Just getting ready to haul some sand,' said Danny.

"Yeah?" said the deputy, "Have you a permit to excavate here?"

"I didn't know we needed one, sir."

"You boys hang on a minute," the deputy smiled still friendly; "I got interrupted." He rolled up his window and they could see he was busy on his radio.

Minutes passed; Sonny and Danny began to get nervous. The deputy was still yakking on his radio.

Shortly, their nervousness was justified as two Army Black Hawk helicopters appeared over the horizon and circled their location for a landing.

Danny thought about fleeing, but the deputy's patrol car blocked the way. They were trapped.

When the whorls of dust caused by the landing subsided, the deputy was out of his car, pistol in hand. Other deputies and agents placed themselves in a circle on all sides of the two men.

"I'm Drug and Alcohol Enforcement Agent Stanley Morris," said the tall man, "Who are you?" Not giving them a chance to answer, he continued, "What were you burying here?"

"Burying? We weren't burying anything. We came to pick up some sand," Danny said.

"Then why does army radar have you out here working that big cat all night long?" demanded Morris, "And what was the helicopter ferrying down here from the mine in six different trips?"

Danny was speechless. Then he spotted Ron Martin standing in the door of one of the big choppers, and he knew the jig was up.

"Are you going to dig it up for us, or do we have to take the keys for the Cat and do it ourselves?" Agent Morris flushed red around the neck.

"Told ya not to drink all that beer," growled Sonny to Danny.

Surrounded on all sides by armed officers, Danny Del Purto and Sonny Crispler dropped hidden handguns into the sand and raised their arms in surrender.

"Cuff em!" said Morris. Agents had already unearthed the first two bales of marijuana.

"What about me?" pleaded Ron.

"I kinda like to see turkeys all trussed up," kidded Tim.

"Do you suppose we should get him set free?" joked Rex, "He's been awful bossy lately."

Sheriff Jefferson sauntered by, joining the fun, "He's forgotten her, but he almost married my Aunt Dottie."

Ron did a double take, "Dorothy Jefferson, of course!"

"But she wouldn't have him!" How much is this key worth to you, 'almost uncle?' He dangled the cuff key in front of Ron.

"Quit horsing around," said Morris, "I made a mistake; let him go!"

Ron rubbed his wrists and said, "Thanks! Now can we go back to the mine?"

"We'll drop you off in Hawthorne and book these birds," said the agent, "Then we've got the rest of the cartel to bust up.

He left all the agents and deputies there to manage the removal of the marijuana. Trucks had been ordered for hauling. One helicopter ferried Ron, Rex, Tim, and Paul back to town.

"Did you ever get a chance to ask Sonny Crispler if he was related to Billy and Jack?" Ron asked Tim.

"Nope, but I'll bet he was," replied Tim, "Bad blood is usually inherited, and he looked just like Billy."

"Forget that!" exclaimed Rex, "We still need to check out Coyote Rock."

Al Allaway

Chapter Twenty-Nine ~ Coyote Rock

Is there a chest under the Coyote Rock? If there's a chest, will the key fit? If the key fits, what is in the chest? Will it be something of value (treasure?) or will it be another clue?

Forrest was always a jokester, so what can we expect? What do you expect? Will it make people happy, or will they be disappointed?

Here's the key, now open the chest! Look out for that huge rattlesnake. It's chasing me, faster than I can run. My feet are like lead. It's going to strike! Look out! A marijuana plant is growing out of the snake's gullet and the fangs looked like helicopter rotors...

...."Wake up, Ron; your sweat has soaked the entire bed!" It was Ronda Fletcher. She had to shake him three times, "You're having nightmares. Honey...wake up!"

Ron Martin stirred from his stupor. After the Black Hawk brought them back from the Luning borrow pit, Rex and Tim had helped him dull the trauma of the day with too much alcohol.

"Do you have you any ice for my head?" pleaded Ron.

A little disgusted, Ronda said, "It is 6:30 in the morning! Are you going to try to go back to the mine this morning at eight? I'll get some ice."

Ron groaned, remembering that he had promised Rex and Tim a Jeep ride this morning. He said, "I'm not up to driving that bumpy road today. Call Tim and Rex. Tell them it's Sunday, a day of rest. I'm going back to bed."

* * *

Paul came by at noon to tell Ron goodbye, but was detoured by Ronda. "He's out like a light," she said.

"I've enjoyed the adventure," he said, "Tell him I'm returning to Reno with my trailer and ATV's. Sheriff Jefferson told me the pot recovered has a street value over 24 million dollars."

Rex and Tim, when they learned Ron wasn't going anywhere, first tried to talk Ronda into snagging the Jeep keys from Ron's trousers. They would have gone mining, but she refused.

"So when are we going?" demanded Tim.

"How about first thing Monday morning?" replied Ron, "We still have the Jeep, and it will be just us three. After we check out the rock, then we can escort some of the kids and grandkids back up there."

"After all the bad stuff that's happened, they may not want to go," said Tim.

Plan "B" for the balance of Sunday, worked up a fishing trip with their grandkids, Mark, Dan and Darrel.

Coyote Rock was a huge slab, under which lived a sundry collection of weird things.

On Monday, the three families had been in Hawthorne for a whole week and those who knew about the secret clues, still had no idea what might be hidden under the Coyote Rock, if anything. Those family members, who had not shared in the knowledge about a clue or riddle, were beginning to wonder why their elders (Ron, Tim and Rex) were showing such deep signs of frustration.

This was a new day. Perhaps the mood would change. "Snartal + Peter" had to mean Coyote Rock! There was no other explanation.

They loaded the Jeep in front of protesting grandchildren, each one feeling left out because The *Grandpas refused to allow any kids to go along.*

"Why?" was one loud protest.

"You took Mark last week!" was another complaint

"We have a secret mission," announced Tim.

"Something special that only we three can do," added Rex.

"If we get back in time today, I'll give the Jeep keys to you grandpas and everybody will get a turn to see the mine, okay?" said Ron, who had no grandchildren to pester him.

As the protests died, Ron slipped the Jeep in gear and they were off again, finally free and clear to check the Coyote Rock.

On the way to the mine, each landmark they passed imparted its' own special memory; something like a diary of the past week.

"At night, this sand was crawling with wildlife," said Tim, "and there's not a sign of it anywhere during the day."

"Here's where we muscled a three ton boulder into the canyon, Just to kill rattlesnakes," joked Rex.

"How in the world did all three of us fit into this little hole,' said Ron, "just to hide from a helicopter?"

When they reached the cabin site, they turned left and followed a faint track part way up the hill. When the terrain became too rough for the little Jeep, Ron parked it so they could walk the remaining quarter mile to the strange outcropping of sedimentary rock protruding from a mountain of igneous material. Geologically, it was a mystery in its own right, but that was not the reason three retired men sought out what was also known as Coyote Rock.

Tim carried two fire department style electric torches.

Rex had a leaf rake with a special extendable handle.

Ron had two small shovels, something like the ones used to dig clams at the beach. He also carried the mysterious key.

The quarter mile hike took about ten minutes up a gentle climb. At the top of the plateau there was a grand view of the entire Hawthorne valley, including most of the old Navy, now Army ammunition depot.

"It looks a lot different," observed Rex, as they lined up in front of the opening.

"There was a lot more head room," said Tim.

"I could crawl in there on my hands and knees for at least six feet in," said Ron. "Now the head room is less than two feet high."

"It's just like ocean tides," said Rex, "Except the wind scours out the sand one year and fills it back in another year."

"I ain't gonna crawl in there unless we dig a lot of that sand out first," said Tim. He knelt down at the crack and aimed in a powerful beam of light.

"See anything?" asked Ron.

"Yeah, it's full of rattlesnakes."

"How many?"

"At least three."

"Can we rake 'em out?"

"Hand me the rake," said Tim.

"Do you see anything else, turkey?"

"Not yet."

Rattlesnakes are generally docile in nature, and would rather run than fight. They are probably more fearful of humans than people know. Even when trapped, a rattler will not show aggression by chasing or charging. They will coil up and strike like lightning. A general rule of thumb is that no pit viper can strike further than two-thirds its total body length. So, a three foot long snake has a striking distance of approximately two feet.

Tim's rake handle with extension was almost nine feet long. He extracted five snakes total, three about eighteen inches, one two feet and one three feet long.

The process took a few minutes, as each snake was raked out from under the rock into daylight, it would coil and buzz for thirty seconds or so, and then crawl away.

"The rock slab looks to be twenty feet wide, and the opening might go back in about ten feet," he announced.

"The first five are Pacific Rattlesnakes," observed Ron. "But we also have little Horned Rattlesnakes. Many people call them Sidewinders. They're usually smaller, but often burrow into the sand. I'm telling you this because there may be more in there, hidden."

It took the better part of an hour for them to remove enough sand around the entrance so that a man could squiggle inside far enough on his belly to examine the back wall. Part of the enclosure was hidden from view because it took a slight bend around a large boulder.

Several scorpions were included in the sand they removed. A couple of Long-nosed bats were also using the little cave for a residence. They found no more rattlesnakes, but did unearth a large fat black lizard which was first mistaken for a Gila monster.

"It's only a Chuckwalla," said Ron, "I ran into a lot of those down in the Yucatan and chuckled at his Latin name. It's *Sauromalus obesus*. See how fat his beer gut is!"

"How deep do you think the sand is in the back?" asked Rex.

"Who's going to crawl in and find out?" said Tim.

"I guess I'll have to do it," said Ron. "I know a couple of turkeys that have turned chicken."

Ron squirmed into the cavity far enough so he could probe the sand at the back of the hole. Probing with Rex's long knife, he hit something and hollered back, "There's something metallic and hollow sounding buried about six more inches. Send in the little spade."

Ron started moving sand from the cramped space, flinging it off to the sides when he was startled by a heart stopping sound, a cross between a screech and a hiss.

He turned his light and attention into the space behind the boulder and came face to face with one nasty and very angry badger.

"Pull me out," screamed Ron. Tim and Rex each grabbed a foot and slid Ron back out into daylight. "There's a big old mean badger in there," he said, "I thought he was going to take my nose off."

"Dang it!" exclaimed Tim. "If there is a chest buried in there, these critters are sure guarding it well."

"Yeah," added Rex. "It reminds me of the fabulous treasure Mowgli found that was guarded by that big cobra. It was in Rudyard Kiplings *"Jungle Book."*

"Whatever!" said Ron. "How are we going to get rid of the badger?"

"Easy," said Tim. "Wedge this rake in so as to block him in his hole, and he can scream and spit at you all he wants. We gotta dig that box or chest out of there."

"That's good," said Ron. "It's your idea, your turn to crawl in there to dig!"

"You thought I'd complain, didn't you, turkey!" said Tim. "Gimme the rake and the shovel." And he dove headfirst into the hole.

Rex spelled Tim a half hour later and within another hour, they were dragging an iron chest out into the sunshine.

The badger gave them one final snarl.

"I guess he got the last word," said Ron.

"Try the danged key!"

"It's too badly rusted," said Ron, "I'm afraid the key will break off. Let's take the chest to town and open it there."

Back in Hawthorne, they purchased some liquid wrench at the local hardware and worked over the old chest. The chest itself was about one foot high by one foot deep and eighteen inches long, weighing less than twenty pounds.

In the alley behind the hardware store, the drama continued, eventually resulting in the rusty hinges being compromised. The key never did open the lock.

With the lid pried off, the rusty old chest revealed contents of three beautiful gold nuggets of about two pounds each, an old yellowed letter, wrapped in plastic, three 1940s $50 silver certificates and a cremation urn.

Ron carefully opened the letter and read:

Dear Ron; I've saved a few mementos for you and your friends. I know that I'm destined to die of alcoholism as did old Burt. I so enjoyed the week with you and Tim and Rex back in 1947, that I'm stashing some stuff here for you because I know that as my disease progresses, I will not have the ability to continue thinking straight. There will be a time when I will need a drink so badly that I would use up the value of these gifts, but by stashing it away out here, I think it will be safe from predators, even such as me myself.

Enjoy the nuggets. They are hold-outs from the "glory hole" you and your friends helped me find in 1947. Three more $50 bills showed up in the next windstorm. My estate and ex-wife must not know about this secret gift. The urn contains the ashes of old Burt. I didn't know what else to do with them. You should probably leave them here. Burt would like that. Have a wonderful life, you deserve it.

Love, Forrest Williams

"Holy Toledo!" exclaimed Tim, "Those nuggets look pure and must be almost two pounds apiece. Back in 1947 they were worth maybe $38 per ounce."

"Gold has gone up," said Rex, "I think the last I heard was $380 to $400 an ounce."

"Figure it out," said Ron, "They come out to about $12,000 each!"

"One for each of us, right?"

"Right!"

" The bills are 40 years old," said Ron, "They're probably worth up to $200 each to collectors. Remember Forrest was like Peter Pan, always a kid who never grew up."

The newspaper office called and asked Ron about the reward.

"What reward?" he said.

"It's rumored that there was a $10,000 reward for any major break in the drug cartel case. We heard from the Army that you've earned it!"

* * *

"Tomorrow, you can each make trips up to the mine with your kids and grandkids," said Ron. Make as many trips with the Jeep as you need. One of you will have to return Burt's urn to Coyote Rock. It would probably be wise of you to avoid any mention of the nuggets until after we leave the state. I think Ronda and I will start packing up by Wednesday.

That evening, Ron answered a knock on his motel room door. "Dorothy Jefferson," said Ron, "What brings you here?"

A stately gray-haired woman of 60, but with the figure of a model of 18 stood at the door. "Can I come in?" she asked.

Ron introduced Dorothy to Ronda, "We were engaged at one time, but circumstances changed and I never married," he explained to Ronda.

"Did you know the Feds arrested our Sheriff?" she asked.

"Why?" queried Ron.

He and some of his deputies, along with Del Purto, Crispler and three or four others were up to their necks in this drug cartel. I don't know whether to hate you or thank you, for bringing all this down on our town. What really happened up there at the mine?"

"Buy the book, said Ron, "I think I'm going to write another one!"

One of the Shafts Remaining Open in 1986

Book Five

The Origanal Lmuma Story, 1947

A Young-Adult Novella originally published
in 2004

I wish to dedicate this book to my wife and my best friend, Del Allaway, who pushed and cajoled and inspired me frequently, until the work was finally begun.

For over ten years we traveled south from the Pacific Northwest to a winter escape in Yuma, Arizona, frequently driving through western Nevada and past the now fading dirt track entrance to the old Squaw Mine.

She got so tired of hearing me reminisce about my teenage years there, that I finally had to put the tale into written words.

PROLOGUE

Far out in the deserted Nevada hills, just before daylight, a lone coyote was making her regular rounds, hoping for a lizard, squirrel or a small bird. Her hunger was so intense that she would have even settled for a crunchy scorpion.

A sudden breeze brought an interesting and tantalizing odor to her sensitive nostrils; a smell of gastronomical remembrance and juices began to flow inside her tortured gut. The maddening odor reminded her of a deer, cow, horse or some other large mammal's leathery skin.

Sensing something wonderful to eat, she persisted in her search and was rewarded at last, when she located a brown leather briefcase, which had been carefully hidden in a cavity under a large flat rock. Cautiously, at first, she nuzzled the handle of the case. A disgusting smell of the man creature pervaded the space under the rock and temporarily horrified her. Then she discovered that by dragging this "prey" out from under the rock and into the open air only the good smells remained. When it had been dragged to a more favorable place, she then "attacked" the "creature".

The outer skin surrendered easily to her sharp fangs, and was interesting to chew, but difficult to swallow. The coyote shook this tough prey while moving it several more feet. One side and part of an end had been chewed away, before she tired and slunk off in search of more edible choices.

A new rising wind ruffled some small stacked green cloth-like papers inside the case, and a few of them went fluttering away on the breeze...

If the coyote had been able to read, she could have seen something like: "The United States of America, Fifty Dollars, Silver Certificate" printed on some of the papers.

Chapter 30 ~ A Day of Freedom

Rex Franklin heard a distant pounding noise, vaguely penetrating the cobwebs of his state of sound sleep. He turned slightly, starting a waking stretch, until his inner self vetoed that idea in place of another, which was to drift back into a deep, warm slumber. The teenage girl in his dream had been interesting and beautiful and he wanted to learn how to get to know her. But, the irritating noise persisted, growing louder, like annoying radio static. It was invading his consciousness like a devil.

After considerable resistance to waking, his foggy brain began to identify the rhythmic sound. It was hot water beginning to surge through the cold pipes of the steam radiator, causing the metal to expand with reverberating clicks, as it warmed. This was a familiar sound now, one heard before daylight every morning in the boarding dormitories of Christian Brothers School (CBS) in Sacramento California. Residents, young and old would be coming awake to herald another day of strict disciplinarian class-work!

Christian Brothers School, Sacramento, CA. (Boys only, grades 4-12)

Boys had been taught to pray a simple "Good morning, Jesus, guide me today" as their first conscious thought.

Wait a minute, thought Rex, *Today is Saturday. I don't have to get up.* He knew the day should be free, as this was the only "good-thing" he liked about this place. They worked the kids so hard during the school week, that weekends were times to be enjoyed and with clear conscience too.

Student weekdays started as early as 5:30 a.m., followed by an hour-long chapel, including daily Mass, then breakfast. Breakfast was always followed by an hour-long mandatory study hall before classes started at 8:30. The classroom schedule ended at 3:45, allowing outdoor playtime until dinner at 5:30. At 7:00 it was time for Vespers followed by another hour-long study hall. Lights out at 9:00 didn't allow much time for any personal endeavors.

Rex stretched again, vaguely realizing that there was something special about this Saturday, and that he should be thinking about getting up.

Ah, yes! awakened the thought, *Today is my 14th birthday. I'm almost a man!* And he toyed with the temptation of re-seeking the pretty young filly of his earlier dream.

"You awake, Rex?" It was Ron Martin, one of three other boys who shared this dormitory room, "Are we sticking to the plan for today?"

Ron Martin came to CBS from Hawthorne, Nevada where his mother and his aunt partnered in running a large dry-goods (Department) store. Ron had no father figure to influence his life, which caused worry to his busy mother. She feared that the small town influences of gambling, smoking, cursing, drinking, cheating and bullying was not good. In 1946, the Christian Brothers Catholic boarding school seemed to be the best of all options.

"Yeah," mumbled Rex, "Ice cream, baseball and a movie, in that order."

"By the way," said Ron, giving Rex a playful shove out of bed and onto the floor, "Happy Birthday, turkey!"

A brief no-win wrestling match followed.

An hour later, the two were standing in the Prefect's office, waiting for permission to leave for the day. Brother Felix looked down at the two boys and frowned. He was a large man, his size multiplied by the loose flowing black robe that hung all the way down to within an inch above his black shoes.

"It is my birthday," ventured Rex timidly.

"Yes, I know," answered Brother Felix, "Is that why you were wrestling in the dorm?"

"How'd you know about that?"

Brother Felix just smiled, causing wrinkles to assemble in his neck just above his too-tight white medieval clerical collar. The horizontal starched flats of the collar flapped like the wings of a bird as he spoke, "Have a good time and be back by suppertime."

The dormitory was quiet as they prepared to leave. Rex and Ron lived in their first floor room with two other freshmen, Pete and Tim. Rex and Ron were close buddies, going everywhere together and sometimes including Tim. Pete, on the other hand was somewhat introverted and pretty much left to himself by the other boys. Tim and Pete were both at home with parents for this weekend.

"Do you think we can sneak upstairs for a candy-bar?" ventured Rex.

"Sounds quiet enough," said Ron, "All the seniors usually go home for the weekend."

The dorm building was divided into three floors of about ten rooms per floor with four beds to a room. Freshmen were always relegated to the first floor, along with all the younger grammar school boys. Sophomores and juniors occupied the middle floor, while the upper class seniors lucked out on the top. The "Junior High" classifications had yet to be invented.

It wasn't because there were more seniors that they had a whole floor to themselves, it was that they needed more space, with only one or two boys to a room. They also had the extra privileges of a recreation room, complete with candy and coke machines, Ping-Pong and billiards table. And everybody knew the unwritten law that it was "slow death" for any under-classmen, if ever caught up on the senior's floor.

Ron and Rex had a few bruises to prove their bravery. After all, a nickel Hershey chocolate bar was worth more than the inconvenience of any pain. This time, however, they got their candy and made a clean escape.

It was a bright sunny day as they made the five block walk to their first stop: Ice cream a block away from the ballpark. Next door to the ice cream parlor, was a music store, and while the boys indulged in banana splits, the strains of the latest top-of-the-charts hit, *"I'm Looking Over a Four Leaf Clover"* drifted in and out of the shop.

Then suddenly, the music stopped and a crowd started to gather outside looking in the music store windows. Curious, the boys elbowed their way up to the show window. Inside, on a spotlighted pedestal was a small radio like contraption with a round lit-up snowy black and white moving picture. A sign informed them that it was called *"A Television"*, priced at an exorbitant $225.00!

The picture box looked strikingly like some twinkling green electronic device they had seen two weeks earlier, over Christmas vacation aboard a U.S. Navy ship of war.

Rex had invited Ron and Tim to spend a few days with him and his folks down at Hunter's Point Naval Station near San Francisco. It had been an especially real experience, a treat that they would never forget. Rex Franklin's dad was an officer serving aboard a U.S. Navy ship, which was currently in port. She was a large ship, the *U.S.S. Salisbury Sound*, used as a recovery vessel for downed aircraft at sea. Here in 1946, the world was just beginning to catch it's breath and recover from the horrible stresses and rigors of World War II.

Lieutenant Franklin had obtained Christmas dinner passes for his family and guests, who after an extensive tour of the ship, were treated to a fabulous dinner in the officer's wardroom.

Rex had seen it all before, the gadgets, controls and green radar-screens, but Ron and Tim were overwhelmed with the size and purpose of a major ship, just returned from war. It was a holiday not soon forgotten.

After Christmas, back at school, the ship tour was all the boys could talk about. All their peers were envious and throwing out a constant barrage of questions. It made it all the more difficult for anyone to concentrate on Caesar's Latin, or Catholic Dogma or First year Algebra, tough subjects under any condition.

The rest of Rex's birthday this Saturday was uneventful, except that the local ball club had captured their minor league pennant. The movie they saw was about some Canadian mounted policeman singing some mushy love song to an Indian maiden. Yech! Back at the dorm, they found that their friend and roommate Tim had returned.

"What happened to your weekend at home?" asked Rex.

"Oh, that idiot S.O.B. step-dad got in a big fight with mom, and they sent me back," explained Tim, almost on the verge of tears.

"Now, now!" scolded Rex, "We can't talk that way about our parents, no matter what kind of idiots they are."

Tim Caruthers was also the product of a single parent, living in Willows, California, and only an hour's drive north of the school. Perhaps this common thread was one of the reasons he and Ron got along so well together. Tim's mother had chosen to send him to the school for much the same reasons, after the small-town influence had caught him up in some petty-thefts. Neither Tim nor Ron were Catholic, but both mothers wanted a little more Christian influence and discipline in their lives.

On Tuesday, just after supper, Ron got a letter from home, and came screaming into their room, bursting with news to share.

"It's on! It's on! It's okay", screeched Ron, his obvious excitement stealing his breath away, "My mom says you can all come stay with us for Easter vacation." Catching his breath, he continued, "And those Indian brothers I was telling you about, say we can go see their gold mine."

It was Ron's chance to return the favor of Rex's hospitality at Christmas time, and it pleased his giving spirit very much.

Continuing, he asked, "Did I tell you fellows about the last time I visited that mine?" Not waiting for an answer, he said, "It was last summer, and I sure had a lot of fun, bumming around with Mr. Williams, the owner. He treated me like he really cared how I felt about not having a dad. I could almost wish that he could be my dad, but he's already married, and my mom doesn't care for him much, anyway."

"I know how you feel," offered Tim. "Anyway, tell us more about the mine."

"Yeah, how deep is it?" asked Rex.

"Deeper that the pits of hell," kidded Ron, "You'll have to say many "Our Fathers" and "Hail Mary's", to keep from falling down into it!"

"Aw-r, get serious," complained Rex.

At that point, they were interrupted by a loud bell, signaling assembly in the chapel for 7:00 p.m. Vespers.

"Dang it," exclaimed Ron, "This place is as bad as a monastery. I'll tell you the rest later, when that stupid bell gives us a break."

"Ha, it *IS* a monastery, don't 'ya know!" said Rex, as they grabbed book bags, which would be needed for the study-hall after chapel, and marched like little tin soldiers out the door.

Chapter 31 ~
Cold War Espionage

Lieutenant-Commander Robert Leslie Stotler, U.S.N.R. was beside himself. He felt that his naval career had been scuttled. He had been promised command of one of those new missal cruisers that were just starting to come off the line. Instead he had been sent to this god-forsaken "Hell-hole" in the middle of the "stinkin'" desert! Bob Stotler was not one to easily adjust to sudden and unexpected changes, and he despised the idea of navigating a desk for the next four years. His angry thoughts were interrupted by a loud knock on his office door.

"Enter!"

It was a Chief Petty Officer, he had not yet met, who spoke.

"Sir, I'm Chief Haddock, your assistant and orderly. Welcome to the Hawthorne Naval Ammunition Depot!"

He dropped his salute before continuing, "Here is an urgent post from Washington, and the Captain would see you at your earliest convenience." He handed over a thick packet plainly marked "SECRET" in huge bold red letters.

"Come with me to see the Captain," Cdr. Stotler ordered, "I'll be going up in half an hour, as soon as I check out this urgent pouch."

The door through which Chief Haddock exited was lettered "COMMANDER, N.A.D. INTELLIGENCE".

Hawthorne, Nevada, during World War II and the years following, hosted a huge military facility, a Naval Ammunition Depot, which boasted that it was the largest in the world. And it was. The United States military stored torpedoes, depth charges, artillery shells and floating mines. It was also rumored that the site included atomic bomb components. Signs posted everywhere in large red letters, read: "No Photography Permitted".

Nestled under snow-capped Mt. Grant, camouflaged ammunition bunkers stretched for miles in every direction, limited only by the shore line of receding Walker Lake to the north-east, and Lucky Boy pass twenty miles to the southwest. Miles and miles of wicked barbed and razor wire stretched everywhere, patrolled by armed sentries and mean guard dogs.

Near the exact center of this military complex, lay the two square-mile town of Hawthorne, the Mineral County seat, with a population of about three thousand people. The only other non-restricted real estate was the thin thread of U. S. Highway 95 as it dissected the valley south-east to north-west. Las Vegas was 333 miles to the south, Fallon and Reno to the north.

Miles away, to the west, in another "Restricted" area, the earth would shake with the explosions of obsolete munitions, which were being intentionally destroyed by the United States Navy. This was an almost daily occurrence, with the shock waves rattling windows in town with such severity that the Navy maintained a claims office with a staff of ten clerks, just to settle broken windows and damaged merchandise claims. Towns-people, for the most part, grew complacent and ignored the daily dish-rattling "bombings".

During the war, just ended, ordinance had also been exploded in Walker Lake, which had been an ideal testing ground for depth charges and submarine launched torpedoes. Schools of Lahontan chub, large-mouthed bass, landlocked salmon and huge record-breaking lake trout had been driven so deep by the bombings that, years later, they were still being caught bleached white, from lack of sunlight.

Walker Lake was twenty six miles long, six miles wide and had its own legendary sea monster, whose origins had been lost in time but probably had roots in Piute Indian legends. It had been further bolstered in the early 1920s when military depth sounding equipment could register no bottom, the depth then being in excess of a mile, far beyond the reach of earlier less-sophisticated sonar devices. Then, an enterprising photographer released a retouched photo post-card of a beautiful sea serpent swimming on the surface of the lake. It had been far better than anything promoting the famous Loch Ness monster in Scotland.

The big lie did accomplish promotion of the local Chamber of Commerce and created much needed tourist income, although the serpent was never "seen" again. It still exists, however, as the mascot of the Mineral County High School, whose sports competitions are conducted by the Hawthorne "Serpents".

Hawthorne's regulars were multiplied by thousands of base civilian workers, and military personnel whose families lived in a base-housing town by the name of Babbitt, and bussed several hundred children up to Hawthorne's already over crowded school system.

This transient nature of the temporary wartime labor force and their families was one of the many questionable influences that Ron Martin's mother had felt the need to protect him from.

"We've got a serious problem, sir", Cdr. Stotler began his meeting with the base Captain, "Intelligence from Washington has just intercepted some revealing photographs of ammo arrivals here, which were being channeled to the Soviet Union."

"There's too much super-sensitive stuff here," replied the Captain, "We can't allow the Communists to steal our secrets. Get a team organized under Lieutenant. Hamm, our Chief of Security and get it stopped!"

Miles to the south, overlooking the navy base, there was a high plateau between several mining properties, where a man was setting up a strange machine in a medium sized black box which he mounted on a collapsible light-weight stand. He hid his device in a small stunted Pinion-pine tree so that patrolling aircraft could not easily see it. The dim light was that of pre-dawn and the man would be gone long before the sun was up, leaving only his secret equipment hidden in the small tree.

At the base of the stand, lay another small box with wires leading up to the mounted box. If you were a passing horned lizard or a rattlesnake, you might have been able to detect a slight mechanical whir emitting from the box, followed by a loud click every half-hour. This caused an electrical charge to be sent up the wires to a remote control device, which activated another mysterious motor in preparation for the next half-hour's electrical impulse.

He was in no hurry to finish, as it was still an hour before sunup and he did not have far to go in order to be completely hidden from prying eyes; eyes that would not agree with, or understand his stealthy actions.

The man would return after dark, to retrieve his equipment, extract and process whatever data it contained, and then prepare the equipment for another day's work of stealing classified data at a different, but nearby location.

Well hidden from the man's view, in the dim light of early morning, the eyes of a curious female coyote followed every movement the man made.

Chapter 32 ~ Anticipation

The days to follow would be filled with boring Latin, Algebra and Ancient History for Ron, Rex and Tim. Memorization of at least ten verses out of one of the Gospels or The Acts of the Apostles was a daily requirement for freshmen Religion classes. Not everyone had to recite everyday, but two or three chosen at random, so all had to be prepared. Anytime a boy didn't recite it perfectly; it meant a crack over the knuckles with a 15" wooden ruler, which often was used with enough force to break the ruler. The Brothers must have purchased them by the gross.

Rex glanced around the quiet study hall. Brother Felix had stepped out for a moment, so he felt it safe to let his gaze drift over to where Ron was studying.

"Ps-s-st, Ron", he whispered.

"What?" answered Ron, glancing around nervously for fear of getting caught talking.

"When are you going to tell us more about the mine?"

Ron tried to shush Rex, but he was not quick enough.

"A-hah! Caught you! Ten demerits, each!" scolded Brother Felix. He had just sneaked in the back door, unheard. "When are you guys going to learn to follow the rules?" He then physically separated them for the rest of the study hour.

"Ten!" moaned Rex, later in relative safety of their dormitory room, "That's going to cancel our trip to the zoo this coming Saturday."

"Yeah," said Tim, "And if you guys get any more, you're going to screw up Easter vacation for all of us."

"Well, I didn't do anything to deserve those ten demerits," Ron complained, "I should be mad at you, Rex, but if I have to shut you up in order to protect myself, I'll have to finish the story."

"Hurry up, will you," interrupted Rex, "We only have twelve minutes until lights out."

Ron began slowly, wary of another unexpected interruption.

"The mine is 15 or 20 miles out of town, away up in the desert hills to the south. The road up there is a real terror. I've been up it twice, once in a five-ton dump truck and once in a jeep. If I had to do it alone, I'd never learn how to drive."

"How deep is the mine?" repeated Rex.

"You're not afraid, are you?" quipped Tim.

"Nah," answered Rex, "Just curious, that's all." He felt that the others didn't believe him.

" I think Mr. Williams told me it was 100 feet deep," continued Ron, "Not very deep at all, considering some we've studied about in Social Studies. There's an old two-room cabin and a compressor shack. He's got these neat little train cars that run on little tracks that you have to push to move rocks and ore around."

"Where do you move it to?" interrupted Tim.

"Well," Ron continued, "Down in the tunnels, it's moved from the blasting face to the shaft, where it is hoisted up on a big cable. Then, up topside, it is set back on the tracks and pushed either to a tailing pile to be dumped or to another place to be saved for later hauling to the smelter. There's even neat little track switching controls, just like real trains tracks."

"Wow!"

Ron could see he had the undivided attention of everyone in the room. Even Pete Smith, the loner, had put down his book and was listening. Two more boys from down the hall were standing in the open doorway.

"Sure wish I could go too," said one of them.

Word had earlier spread throughout the school that Ron had invited Tim and Rex to spend the whole Easter week vacation at his home in Nevada. Pete had also been invited, but had declined.

Ron continued, "Mr. Williams took me with him one time when he hauled gold ore up to a smelter in Virginia City. The ride in that old dump truck was a blast. The trip took almost all day. He gets upset when I call him Mr. Williams; he would rather be called by his first name, Forrest or "Chief". He was great to be with, had some great stories and jokes, and I always felt he really cared about me."

Ron paused briefly to wipe his eye, and continued, "On the way back home, he said that his dogs at the mine needed fresh meat, so for me to watch for fresh road-kill along my side of the road. Just then, he hollered 'Rabbit on the left!' and hit the brakes. The truck screeched to a halt, and before I could think about it, he was out on the road picking up a large jackrabbit, which he pitched into the back of the truck.

"As we started up again, he said, 'Now it's your turn! Keep your eyes peeled.'

"'Rabbit on the left, again,' I hollered. 'Do I get it, or you?'

"'I'll get them on the left side, but you'll have to get any on the right.'

"Later on, I had my chance to holler, 'Rabbit on the right!'

"By the time we reached the north end of Walker Lake, we had about ten big old dead jackrabbits. 'Won't they spoil,' I asked. 'Nope,' Forrest answered, 'Because I'll skin them and freeze them when we get home.' He also told me that he knew these were fresh, because the coyotes and vultures didn't allow dead or injured animals to lie around long enough to rot.

"Before he took me home, we stopped and filled up three big barrels with water and one with gasoline, which he would haul up to the mine the next day."

Just then, they were interrupted by the loud clang of the electric bell out in the hallway.

"Five minute warning," said someone.

"No more demerits for us, guys. We'll finish this later," said Ron, "Lights out and bed-check in five minutes."

The days dragged slowly by, and as the Easter vacation (or Spring break) approached closer, seemed to slow down even more.

"Jeez, I can hardly wait until Friday to get away from this place," announced Tim at supper midweek, "When you going to call your mom, Ron?"

He was worrying that something would happen to cancel the much-anticipated trip. Excitement was building.

Ron finished munching a corn fritter before he said, "I'll call her tonight for the last minute details, but you guys better cool it, because I'll betcha a wooden nickel that she won't pick us up until Saturday late in the morning. If she drives over Friday, it's too far to drive back the same day." It was over 260 miles of slow driving over Donner Pass, through Reno, down to Hawthorne.

Rex and Tim had long since cleared this trip with their parents, who, if the truth were known, were glad to be rid of them for a week.

"How much time do you think we'll be able to spend up at the mine?" asked Rex.

"Yeah," added Tim, "That's the main reason I'm going. What else is there to do for eight days?"

"Don't know," answered Ron, "Forrest once told my mom we could stay a whole week, but mom said, 'No way, one night only!' But we can work on her. Bring some money if you want to gamble, there's a nickel slot machine hidden away in a back room of the pool hall for kids to use. We can shoot pool and go to the movies. It's too cold yet to go swimming.

"Isn't the slot-machine illegal?" asked Rex

"Yeah, but nobody ever checks it."

Ron scraped his dinner plate clean into the scullery garbage container, and headed out of the dining hall, early, hoping to make a successful and rapid phone call home. But, as luck would have it, he heard mother Bell's operator tell him four times, "All circuits are busy, please try again later." He would sit in the tiny phone booth, wait five minutes and then try again. Outside, a waiting line was forming, as this was the only phone available to almost 100 boys. Anger was mounting as Ron connected finally with his mom.

The bell for Vespers rang, and the queue vaporized. Ron snuck into chapel four minutes late, fortunately unnoticed. He slipped quietly into a kneeler in the back row.

Later, during study hall, he sat within full view of the others, a secret smile on his face, but not daring to say anything. The suspense was murderous! A quick glance toward Brother Felix's desk confirmed his fears of being singled out. The Prefect was watching him like a hawk!

Ron had a unique sense of humor, which always surfaced under tension. As study hall was dismissed, the others immediately surrounded him.

"Did I ever tell you guys about the time my homemade raisin sour-mash dripped all over mom's car and ate the paint off it?"

"Dang you, Ron," said Rex, "Don't change the subject... What did your mother say about staying at the mine?"

"Okay," Ron relented, "Here's the skinny. Mom talked to Forrest and he said that he loves kids, and that we wouldn't be any trouble. In fact, he said he would put us to work to earn our keep. Then he told Mom that if we stayed in town very long, we'd probably get in trouble at the pool hall, anyway. That must have cinched it because mom said we could stay five days, or longer.

"Wow," exclaimed Tim, "I get to push the ore cars!"

"Grow up, Tim" chimed Rex, "You'll work where you're told to work; ain't that right, Ron?"

"Yeah, and you guys better be prepared for roughing it, answered Ron, "There's no electricity and no running water, and all you'll get to eat is bacon, beans and sourdough biscuits. And, when you work, you sweat, and when you sweat, you stink like old Burt, and four or more of us will be sleeping in one room."

"No showers?" queried Rex.

"Dream on! Only if it rains"

"Who is Burt?" asked Tim.

"Oh, haven't I told you about Old Burt, yet?" Ron smiled, "Now there's a character, right out of William Shakespeare's medieval history. I think he's Italian or Spanish or one of those old European's who talk funny, and he's just about the oldest old geezer I've ever known. Forrest told me that he's an alcoholic and lives up at the mine just to stay away from the booze. He doesn't have any teeth and he gums his bacon, but I guess he guards the mine property, and is an important person. I don't think he ever gets to take a bath, except when he goes to town to get drunk. He rolls his own smokes. He chews tobacco and spits a lot, but tells great stories. You'll like him a lot, once you get over the smell."

"Didn't you say that Mr. Williams was an Indian?" asked Rex

"Right, he and his brother are from the Nez Perce tribe in Idaho. They're only part Indian. His brother is named Skie, and he used to work at the mine also, but the last I heard, he had taken a job with the Navy."

It was time for lights-out, and the dorm settled down to an uneasy quiet, each boy seeking an elusive sleep because of the impending adventure. Who would be able to wait for the coming weekend?

Ron was imagining a changed life, a coming of age; he thought that one day he might experience the joys of being a father figure like his friend, Forrest Williams, such as he had placed so high up on a pedestal.

There were family ties and a seldom experienced deeply loved feeling that was missing in his life and that he was longing for.

Tim was wishing his mom would separate from that lazy, lay around, grouchy step-father, and that she would fall in love with a decent and friendlier guy. Ron's friend, Forrest Williams sounded like a good candidate.

Rex was unhappy with his home situation; although his dad was a great friend! He only wished that he didn't have to spend so much time away at sea. What worried him most was that he suspected his step-mom was ill with something really bad. He had learned to love and respect her after his real mom had died. Now he only wished that she would talk with him about her new problem. If she died and left him, it would be *déjà vu* all over again. He knew that he must pray more often.

All three boys were beginning to mature in many ways.

Chapter 33 ~ *On the Way to Adventure*

Friday dragged by like a night-crawlers marathon. At lunch, Ron repeatedly hassled the others about whether or not they had packed everything they would need.

"I've even got my fishing pole," said Tim, "Just in case!"

Brother Felix had expressed concerned about the child-labor laws, which might be different on the other side of the state line. But he finally reasoned that it wasn't his responsibility, because the boys were wanting and willing to go and probably wouldn't be paid anyway. Their safety was another concern, one shared by Ron's mom.

Friday night's study hall had been cancelled, as the dorm was almost empty. Besides, no teacher in his right mind would dare to assign homework over the long nine-day holiday.

"As long as you boys are still here, you'll still be required to attend chapel",

Brother Felix had warned during supper, "And we'll start early."

Supper that night was pretty meager; consisting of a peanut butter sandwich and some fish soup, with no seconds. Because it was Good Friday, everybody was expected to be penitent, to fast and abstain from treats in preparation for Resurrection Sunday.

This somber season was reflected even more in the chapel. All the statues and the crucifix were draped with black and purple cloth, which would not be removed until dawn on Easter Sunday. Only then, would the music of the organ peal forth with joyous chords, to celebrate Jesus' resurrection on Easter morning.

"Now what do we do?" complained Rex after chapel, "It's a long, long time until your mom picks us up in the morning." He was glaring at Ron.

Tim said, "That meal left me hungry. Do you want to sneak upstairs for a candy bar?"

"Do you think the seniors are all gone?" asked Ron, "I think that I saw two of them at supper."

"There weren't any in chapel," said Rex, "It would appear that they have taken off for their homes."

"Guess we can chance it, then. A candy bar or two and an ice cold coke really would taste good."

Cautiously, like thieves, they paused at the third floor landing to listen. After ten minutes or so, they ventured on up to the upper-classmen's recreation room.

Sighing with relief, Ron said, "Good, there's nobody around"

"Yeah, but look at that!" said Rex, his disappointment evident.

Both the candy and coke vending machines were plugged with a padlock looking device, and a taped on note, which read: "Sorry boys, remember, **it is LENT**!"

Dumbfounding!

"Well, if we can't eat," Tim said, "Let's shoot some pool."

"What if we get caught?" asked Ron.

"Ah, there's nobody around," offered Rex, "Rack 'em up!"

But they did get caught! Sedwick Cunningham heard the first break of the clay pool balls, and came charging into the recreation room. "Outa here, creeps!" he demanded, "Or I'll turn you in for demerits."

"I told you we should have checked every room," puffed Tim, as they fled back down the stairs.

"I wonder why he only threatened demerits," asked Rex, as they settled back in to their room.

"That's easy," explained Ron, "To keep himself out of trouble."

"What do you mean?" queried Rex.

"It's obvious, don't you see?" continued Ron, "We saw him at supper at the senior's table, but he wasn't at chapel, so that means that he has deceived Brother Felix into thinking he had already gone home."

"My, aren't you the detective!" chided Tim, "Now we've got a secret on old Sed, next time he gives us trouble".

Mrs. Jerry Martin, Ron's mother arrived at about 10:30 Saturday morning and was greeting with great waves of emotion. From Ron, because he loved his mom, and from Rex and Tim because she was the relief valve that they needed to let off the steam, caused by long waiting and anticipation.

"At last," exclaimed Rex, as they loaded luggage into the back of the '41 Ford sedan, "We're on our way to the mine!"

"I hope you boys aren't going to be disappointed," said Mrs. Martin, "That mine is nothing but a black and dirty hole in the ground."

"Mom," pleaded Ron, as they drove out of the parking lot, "We're terribly hungry. Can we stop someplace to eat?"

"Okay," she said, "I need a rest anyway. I've been driving since five this morning. I hope you guys appreciate all we're doing for you. And, what's the matter, don't they feed you at Christian Brothers?"

"It's "Black Saturday", you know, the day between Good Friday and Easter, and the Catholics believe in fasting. All we got for breakfast was half a banana, one piece of toast and some milk."

"Yeah,' said Rex, "And nothing but a sandwich and fish soup last night."

443

"We're starving," added Tim, "And they even locked up the candy and the coke machines."

Mrs. Martin pouted her lips and teased, "Oh, you poor babies!"

There was a new restaurant company springing up all over central and southern California which was called McDonalds. Their new signs claimed they had sold over two million hamburgers, and so that was the logical place for them to stop.

"We're going to eat in the car," instructed Mrs. Martin, "I have to hurry back to Hawthorne. Today is payday at the Navy base, and by 5:30 the department store will be very busy and need my help.

Motoring across the Sierra-Nevada, time moved much faster. Mrs. Martin had been a school teacher, and was at ease around teen age boys. She invented several good car-games, which kept everybody busy.

Somewhere a little after passing Reno, boredom began to set in, and Tim asked Ron to explain more in detail about the raisin sour-mash story that he had joked about earlier in the week.

"Boy, did I whip his butt for that," interrupted Mrs. Martin, "Can I tell the story?" she asked Ron.

Ron slouched down in his seat, wishing the tale had never been brought up.

"He called it *'Panther pee'*, I think,' she started.

Rex and Tim were shocked. Moms just never talked like that. They were beginning to like this lady, a lot. She spoke their language.

Mrs. Martin continued, "It was in the seventh grade science class, I think. They were teaching about fermentation and this smarty kid got the idea that he could brew his own booze. Unknown to the teacher, some of the boys got a recipe for a meade made out of raisins and sugar. Ron, here mixed up a big batch and hid it in the rafters of our garage, so I wouldn't find out. But, fermentation is stimulated by heat, and one hot day it happened; this gooey ooze dripped down all over my new car, and ate clean through the paint down to bare metal. To pay to get it fixed, I had to trade it in for this old clunker, and Ron's butt was sore for a week."

Secretly, she did see the humor in the situation, but knew that she couldn't let anybody know.

Ron slouched even further down in his seat and had little more to say until they reached home. It would be the last time he would brag about the "Panther pee" incident.

Later, slightly recovered, Ron announced, "We'll be home in about ten minutes."

Then he asked his mom, "When can we see Mr. Williams?"

"He'll probably be waiting at his house," she answered, "Wanting to check out the beefy muscles of your two friends." She snickered under her breath.

"I'll drop you off at home," she continued, "And you can walk over to Forrest's house from there."

As she pulled into the driveway, she handed Ron some money, and told him to feed the boys at the Home Café tonight because she would be too busy at the store to fix dinner.

"After you meet Forrest," she continued, "You'll need to all get a bath and a good night's sleep, as it might be your last for awhile." Again, she snickered to herself, knowing that these boys had many lessons to learn in the next few days.

"Let's eat, first," suggested Ron, leading the way to "downtown", four blocks away.

On the way, they passed the town's two movie houses. The Desert Theatre was featuring *"The Jolson Story"* with Larry Park.

"What's that about?" asked Rex.

"Another musical, I think," said Tim.

Across the street, The Cactus Theatre was playing *"The Yearling"* with Gary Cooper.

"Now that, would be worth seeing," ventured Ron, "It's about a young boy and his pet deer."

The Home Café in Hawthorne, Nevada was a Chinese Restaurant, and the boys were treated to an all-you-can-eat buffet, a real treat after the Spartan food served at CBS.

Ron had worked there as a busboy, and knew all the staff including the owner, Soo Ling. Even though the place was full on this Saturday evening, they were given a private room in the back and made to feel like royalty, or like a "Long lost Prodigal son" come home. It felt good to be back in familiar surroundings.

"Where is Soo Ling?" Ron asked.

"Oh,' answered the waiter, "He go back to China; sell out to Me Tsu, new boss."

As they were finishing dinner, a sound like an Indian war-whoop entered the room, followed by a huge bare-chested man with black stuff smeared all over his face, who was trying to imitate a war dance.

"Forrest!" exclaimed Ron, surprised.

"How!" grunted the man, "White men hav'um thick scalps. Me Chief Williams."

"Clown," scolded Ron, "Put your shirt back on!"

It was an action not at all unlike Forrest, who, like Peter Pan, had never really grown up. After he recovered his shirt and wiped some greasy makeup off his face (War-paint, he called it), he made the rounds, shaking hands with Tim and Rex.

His handgrip was strong, almost to the point of causing pain. But Ron, forewarned by his mom, knew exactly what Forrest was doing; he was sizing up these boys for strength and stamina.

It was going to be a hard week's labor, thought Ron.

Forrest confirmed this thought by his opening statement, "I've hired two extra men for this week, so with you three guys, and with Burt and me, that makes a crew of seven. We should be able to move a lot of ore in a week."

He told a few jokes, bought a couple of rounds of Coca-Cola, and eased Rex and Tim's concerns about too much work. He said they would learn a lot, and have plenty of time to explore, as long as they followed a few simple rules.

The rules he would explain tomorrow. "Everybody should be ready to go at 6:30 in the morning."

"Well, at least we're used to that," said Tim.

"Yeah," added Rex, "I thought this was supposed to be a vacation!"

"You'll have a ball," said Forrest, going out the door, "We'll all meet in the morning, just in time for Easter sunrise church."

"Well, what d'ya think?" asked Ron.

"I like him," said Rex

"It's gonna be fun," added Tim, "Now where's that pool hall with the slot-machines?"

"On the way back to my house," answered Ron, "I guess we've got about an hour. Mom said to be home in bed by 9:00 o'clock."

Rex's conscience was silently telling him, "No!" But, he didn't listen.

It was a typical pool-hall with a mostly young Saturday night crowd. They played some Rotation and Eight-ball, and stood in line for the illegal nickel slot-machine in the back room, which promptly relieved them of all loose pocket change.

The smell of stale tobacco smoke permeated their clothes and on the way back to Ron's house, Tim said, "What a stink! I'm sure glad none of us smoke cigarettes!

"Yeah," replied Rex, "It reminds me of Pinocchio's friend; what was his name, just before they turned into jackasses?"

"Sedgewick?"

"Yeah, something like that!"

Chapter 34 ~ Day One; Sunday

This morning, the desert air was clear and dry and the coyote continued sniffing morning air.

There was something...? Ah, yes, that vague exciting leathery smell! It was one she had detected before, but could never trace its source. It had eluded her and it was maddening! But, now she had another chance. Her God given instincts now automatically took over, and she slowed her pace. Crouching low, something warned her into a role of caution. Here, she blended into her background with a motionless camouflage that would be the envy of any army general.

Something was approaching, and the coyote emitted a low growl, heard only a foot or so away. All her senses were now on high alert, and she waited...

The man with the strange equipment was back again to set up for more data. He was looking for another good shrub in which to hide his gear before sun-up, but something else had caught his attention and he startled momentarily, at the flush of a hiding coyote.

He watched briefly as the animal loped off toward the now lightening eastern sky. Then he continued his quest.

Ten minutes later, his equipment was all set up, and he was gone.

It was two minutes after sunrise.

Far to the north, a great mass of air now poured down the east slopes of the Sierra-Nevada mountain range, southward and eastward, across the jagged tops of the mountains toward the hot lowlands. Now aided by the quick rise in temperature after sunrise, the wind suddenly was strong enough to start moving large grains of sand, all along the hilltops of west central Nevada.

At 6:30, Forrest honked lightly so as not to waken folks so early on Sunday morning. Ron and his guests crowded into the front seat of the dump truck, riding four abreast. Their gear had been thrown into the back along side the extra drums of water and gasoline.

"Sleep well?" was the first question Forrest asked.

"Okay, I guess," answered Ron, "These guys are too excited."

"Quite a wind has come up."

Last fall's dead leaves mixed with large sand grains, were swirling around in little whorls as they drove out of Ron's driveway.

Brief prayers and two short songs was all the blowing sand allowed to the small congregation who had gathered for an Easter Sunrise Service outside a local church. When the stinging sand forced the regulars inside, Forrest and the boys departed for the mine.

The road south out of Hawthorne was a smoothly paved highway for the first ten miles, offering opportunity for conversation.

"About the rules," Forrest started, "Mining is one of the most dangerous of all occupations. Use your common sense; brains, that is. No horseplay underground or around the openings. We'll fit you with a hard hat, which you must always wear around and inside the mine. Keep your ears open and obey instructions you hear from me or from any of the other men. Don't question anything you are told, just do it."

"Do you blast with dynamite?" asked Rex.

"Good question," replied Forrest, "Yes, we do. I'll show you where you must go, anytime you hear someone shout, '*Fire in the hole!*'"

"Can I push the ore cars?" asked Tim.

"You'll get your share," said Forrest, snickering under his breath.

They had been gently climbing, and now the entire Hawthorne valley with its saline lake and row after row of ammunition bunkers could be seen behind them.

Forrest slowed the truck, and said, "Here's where we turn off."

Sand was blowing horizontally across the highway, when Forrest turned the dump truck blindly into it. The boys wondered how he could see where to turn because the blasting sand cut visibility to nothing.

Forrest sensed their question and offered, "Gold is usually found near volcanic rock and I knew where to turn off when a milepost sign lined up with that old cinder cone to the left." Over the top of the low flying sand storm, they could see the tip top of a small volcano about a mile away.

"This is some blow!" exclaimed Forrest, as he searched for the twin ruts that now served as their roadway.

They continued to climb through a sandy salt-bush and sagebrush steppe toward the yawning mouth of a rocky canyon. The rolling, rocking motion of the big tires in the sandy ruts was beginning to be sickening.

"Just like an amusement park," said Ron, almost hitting his head on the ceiling of the truck cab.

"Yeah, and I hate roller-coasters," added Tim.

"At least you're sitting next to the window in case you have to barf," joked Rex.

The fine dust in the cab was thick and choking, when Forrest said, "We'll be out of the dust in a minute and you can roll down the window for some fresh air.

He drove the truck into the entrance of the canyon and stopped.

True to his prediction, the air was relatively clear, and they gulped it in with life-saving energy. The wind still blew, but with little or no dust.

"What happened?" ventured Rex.

"We just passed from desert sand onto pure rock," said Forrest, "And the canyon walls are sheltering us from the worst of the wind."

Ron was wiping grit from his eyes, when he said, "Yeah, and look at the road ahead of us now."

"Where?" interrupted Tim.

"Just follow the bottom of the canyon, don't you see it?"

"No!"

Tim could see nothing except a lot of strewn sharp rocks, some the size of boulders.

"Well, it's there, and old Eleanor, here will get through just fine." Eleanor was Forrest's pet name for his truck. It had been named for President Roosevelt's wife, Eleanor,

"But it's going to get a lot rougher, so fasten your seat belts," he joked.

(What seat belts? This was 1947).

Indeed, it got so rough, the boys were getting bruised, when not even their whitening knuckles could hold them from being flailed around inside the truck cab.

"It's only two more miles to the mine," offered Forrest. "Does anyone want to walk up the rest of the way."

While the offer sounded tempting, three boys remained silent, too proud (or too scared) to speak.

Presently, over the whine of the truck engine, they could hear dogs barking.

"That's Oscar and Ernie," explained Forrest, "They're my guards, and none too friendly to strangers. Keep away from them, until they get to know you as friends."

He stopped the truck on a little rise, about 200 feet away, overlooking a rustic old shack, which served as a cabin. Three blasts on the truck's horn seemed to signal somebody in the cabin. The dogs ran up to the truck and put up a fierce show, circling it several times.

"Don't get out," warned Forrest, "Or they'll tear you to shreds."

Presently, a bewhiskered old man exited from the cabin, looked up at Forrest, and then whistled for the dogs, who obediently ran back down to him. He chained them both to strong looking posts and then waved Forrest on down to park next to the cabin.

"Boy, ain't nobody gonna' sneak up on this place," observed Rex.

"Not a chance," added Tim.

"Where's your rifle, old man?" hollered Forrest, exiting the truck.

"Knowed it war you, seed ya comin' ten mile off," Whiskers replied, "'Sides you done tole me you'd be fetchin' young-uns up heyar tuday."

He walked up to the boys, "Howdee Ron, interduce yer buddies. I'm Burt," he added, extending a hand toward Tim and Rex.

"You look just like Gabby Hayes in all the Roy Rogers movies," offered Tim,

"Why, thank-ee very much," said Burt, "Who's this Rogers fella?"

Rex knew that he and Burt were going to hit it off good.

Meanwhile, Forrest was rummaging around under the seat of the truck for two half-thawed jackrabbit carcasses. "Here," he said to Rex and Tim, "Pitch these to the dogs, so they'll get to know you sooner."

"Coffee pot's, on!" hollered Burt, "C'mon in and stow yer gear."

"Coffee?" asked Tim.

"Yeah," Rex said, "It puts hair on your chest."

The cabin was indeed rustic. It consisted of two rooms walled with clap board and papered with old newspaper. Yellow stains spotted the paper, where rains had seeped in. The floor was of spongy boards with many cracks between, and looking up, the boys could see daylight shining through the some of the roof boards.

Burt, following their gaze, said, "That thar wind blew off'n the tar paper, and even tho this 'ear's the Lord's day of rest, we're a goin' to haf to fix 'er."

He then shuffled into the back room, and said, "This 'ears yer bedroom. Pick any unused bunk ya like." The room contained an old dresser with broken drawers and three sets of wooden bunk beds, outfitted with smelly one-inch thick straw pads, except for blankets and personal gear which covered two of the bottom bunks.

Yech! Dust was everywhere.

"Two more men will be returning tomorrow," he added.

The boys dumped their gear and sleeping bags on the remaining three top bunks, and returned to the main room.

"Where's the toilet?" asked Tim, "I gotta go!"

"Follow the trail up the hill, behind the cabin," answered Forrest, "And don't forget to flush!" he added with a laugh.

The main room was furnished as sparse as the other. One corner served as a kitchen with an old fashioned wood stove, complete with oven. There were a couple of cupboards, but much in the way of canned goods and bags were stacked on the floor.

The center of the room had a rickety wooden table and four chairs, held together with baling wire. Three kerosene lanterns hung on a nearby wall. The rest of the room was taken up with an old brass double bed, with a fairly decent mattress. Rubber pants hung on a wooden peg over the bed, and an old steamer trunk graced the foot of it, on which rested muddy boots and an old tin hat. Burt, being a permanent resident, deserved the best. A faded six year-old calendar hung in an honored position on the wall above his pillow. It featured half-naked Betty Grable from 1941.

"Suppose you guys want to see the mine, now," said Forrest, "But where's Tim?"

Tim had been gone over the hill to the outhouse far too long.

Ron, feeling responsible, said, "I'll go check."

He stepped outside, hollering Tim's name, to be answered only by barking dogs, which by now had finished their rabbit feasts.

"Tim!" he hollered again, "Where are you?"

No answer.

He started up the hill, followed closely by Forrest and Rex.

"You don't suppose he fell in the outhouse?" said Ron, jokingly.

As they reached the outhouse on the top of the little hill, there was Tim coming up the hill from the other side, still about 200 feet away.

"Tim," scolded Forrest, "No wandering around by yourself. You could fall into an old prospect shaft, and we never would find you."

Fifty Dollar Bills Caught Downwind from the Outhouse

Tim, out of breath, reached the others. His complexion was pale, as white as a sheet.

"Where'd you go?" asked Rex and Ron in unison.

Tim stuttered something unintelligible.

"What?" asked Forrest.

Tim just shook his head and managed a feeble; "I'm okay"

It was immediately obvious to Ron that his friend had seen something that he didn't want to talk about. Maybe he would be able to work it out of him later.

"You gave us a scare, you jerk," was all he could say.

Tim remained tight-lipped and shuddered imperceptibly.

Back at the cabin, Forrest said to Burt, "Let's fire-up the hoist and give these lads a tour of the mine."

"No jokes, either," he added with a wink. Ron caught the gesture and knew immediately what it meant. Poor Tim and Rex were about to be initiated, as Ron had been the year before.

Some 300 yards from the cabin stood a wooden head-frame, towering almost five stories into the cerulean Nevada sky. Nearby was a tin covered shack, which housed a gasoline donkey engine and compressors. Burt turned a key and the engine roared into life. In a short time, the engine warmed and settled into a quiet throb. Burt engaged a clutch, which caused a big wire drum to start spooling up a double steel cable.

The cables ran through two pulleys at the top of the head-frame, and then straight down into the dark abyss of a shaft running deep into the earth.

Burt disengaged the clutch, stopping the cables, and hollered, "Going down?"

A steel bucket, attached to the end of the cables had been drawn up so it was even with the level of the ground. Forrest opened a safety gate and climbed into the big bucket. "She'll only hold one man at a time," he told the boys, "I'll go down first, so I can help you get out of the bucket. You guys follow me down, one at a time." He reached for a signal cord alongside the bucket, and added, "One ring for up, two rings for down, and three for stop: emergency." With that, he yanked on the cord, ringing a loud bell twice in the engine house.

Burt engaged the gear and Forrest disappeared into the stygian darkness.

"Oh Jeez," said Rex, seeking his lost courage.

"You're next," said Ron, "And I'll follow after Tim."

After Rex had been sent down, Ron turned to Tim, and asked, "What happened back there by the toilet?" He motioned over his head, back up the hill.

"Can't tell you yet," said Tim, just finding his tongue, "I've still got to think about it."

"Come on," nudged Ron, "You can trust me."

: Maybe later," said Tim, "Leave it alone!"

"Hey," hollered Burt, "Yur bucket's a'waitin'"

As each of the boys descended into the cool blackness, they were assailed by numerous fears. Thoughts of falling into an unknown darkness were foremost.

Looking up, each could see the small square of blue sky getting smaller and further away. What kind of emergency could cause a three-bell code? *My gosh, where is that signal cord, anyway?* Peeking down revealed a tiny blue flame growing closer, and the bucket slammed to a stop at the bottom of the pit. All was total darkness, except for the faint blue light sputtering in the headlamp of Forrest's tin helmet.

"Welcome to the L'muma Mine," said Forrest, opening the safety gate, "Put on this helmet."

He rang the signal cord, sending the bucket back up for another boy.

"What does 'Lmuma' mean?" asked Rex.

"It's an Indian name for 'squaw', but means "Warrior's Joy!"

"Gosh, it's dark down here," complained Rex.

"We'll light your torch, as soon as we're all here," answered Forrest.

On the fourth trip, Ron opened his own safety gate, and stepped out of the bucket. "Let's light up," he said to the others.

"This stuff, here in this large white and blue can is calcium carbide crystals", he explained, "Screw off the top of your lantern, and use the spoon to fill it up with crystals. Now, who has the water canteen?"

"Me", offered Tim.

"Okay," continued Ron, "Pour some water into the crystals and screw the top back on tight. The water reacts with the carbide to create acetylene gas. When you open the valve and light it with a match, you'll have an old fashioned miner's lamp with enough light to last over two hours."

"Bravo," interrupted Forrest, "You'll make a good teacher, yet."

Then, they explored half a dozen tunnels, most fitted with little rails and cross ties. Occasionally, big timbers held up the ceiling, but mostly the ceiling was bare rock without any support. Sometimes they passed under wooden chutes, which came down out of cavernous cavities too large for their feeble lights to penetrate. At one such structure, Forrest stopped.

"This is where we will start working tomorrow," he explained, We'll bring down five or six ore cars, set them on the tracks, and roll them back here. Up above this chute is a muck pile that we blasted out of the vein last week. It'll be your job to shovel all the pile into the chute, fill up the cars, push them back to the shaft, hook them up to the hoist, and have Burt lift them out, dump them, then send them back down for another load. Meanwhile, I'll be up there, drilling holes for the next dynamite charge."

"Why do you work going up?" asked Rex.

"Simple," answered Forrest, "The stratum bends, so the vein of ore goes up, and we have to follow it. It's called a stope."

"Where's the gold?" queried Tim, "Can we see some?

"Sorry," answered Forrest, "It's all oxidized and in mineral form. We can't see it until the smelter processes it. Matter of fact, I never get to see any of it, because the smelter keeps it all and pays me cash.

"What's gold worth today?" asked Ron

467

"The price is up from last month," said Forrest, "We're getting $35 an ounce, at last count, and each full ore car will yield about a third of an ounce."

Back at the base of the shaft, Forrest showed the boys how to empty and clean out their carbide lanterns, so they'd be usable the next day.

"We're going out, now," he said, "The rest of the day is for play. Now, why did Burt pull that bucket up?"

He reached over and pulled the signal cord, twice, for down.

They waited...

Again, he pulled the signal cord, waiting a few more minutes but getting no response.

Back in the bowels of the mine, a low rumble began, loud enough to get everyone's attention. Ron glanced at Forrest, who smiled briefly and looked away. The rumble grew louder, followed by a loud pop, then a hiss and a rush of dust.

"Cave-in", hollered Forrest, "Get out, now!"

Horrified, Tim and Rex screamed, "Where? How?"

"Up that wooden ladder in the shaft, 50 feet straight up to the next level," demanded Forrest.

Rex looked at the ladder and started toward it.

"Enough!' exclaimed Ron, "It's only a joke."

Forrest was holding his sides, laughing.

Hearts were pounding and neither Rex nor Tim thought it was very funny.

"How'd you do that?" Rex asked, when his heart beat had slowed to under a hundred beats a minute..

"High pressure in the compressor air lines, caused an intentional blowout of a safety valve," Ron explained, "Burt and Forrest cooked it up for your initiation. They pulled the same gag on me last year, but I really did climb the ladder."

About that time, the bucket arrived and they started their ascent, one at a time.

The rest of the day was spent hiking around the hilltops in a now wind-less day.

Supper was bacon, beans, sourdough biscuits and strong coffee.

And later that night, Ron wormed the secret out of Tim. He had seen a piece of money blow by when he was at the outdoor toilet and had chased it down the hill, only to find three more bills caught on a big sagebrush. He'd never seen a $50 bill before, and now secretly carried four of them in his pocket. Where did they come from? Were they real? Were there any more?

And the coyote spoke wise words to the moon while the boys drifted off to sleep.

Chapter 35 ~ Work Starts

Tim woke before dawn, and lay quiet, internally gripped in one of the most major fights of his life. It was a moral battle, one which would not soon be settled. Who did that money belong to? His Christian ethics told him he must return it! But, to whom? Right now, he could only pray about it, and stay alert for an answer.

The small cabin was crowded with dark vague shapes of sleeping bodies; Ron and Rex in the other bunks, and the two buzz-saws sharing the double bed in the outer room. How anyone could sleep was beyond him. If Forrest and Burt were to square off in a snoring contest, it would be difficult to choose which one was the loudest.

Through the grime and fly speck covered window, he could see daylight beginning to lighten the eastern sky, and his bladder was again painfully urging him to action; to take a walk up the hill. Maybe he might find more money. The moral battle had returned to haunt him.

Quietly, he slipped into his clothes, but the sagging floor boards and rusty door hinges prevented him from passing unnoticed. The closing door caused old Burt to open a questioning eye.

More than half an hour passed before Tim returned, where he found everybody up and dressed. A fire was roaring in the wood stove, and the room was permeated with the odor of strong coffee, flapjacks and bacon.

Ron knew Tim had been gone longer than necessary and tried to catch his eye with a questioning look. But Tim kept looking away.

Forrest blew out the kerosene lanterns and opened the front door, flooding the room with sunlight.

Just then the dogs started a frantic barking.

"Comp'ny comin'!" announced Burt, "Prob'ly Jake 'n Henri."

"Who? asked Rex.

"The other two miners we hired earlier this month," answered Forrest, "Jacob Jones, my powder monkey, and Heinrich Heisler, a strongback laborer. They've been in town all weekend, and I hope they're not hungover."

A jeep pulled up and the dogs stopped barking.

"Yah, it's dem," said Burt, "Oscar and Ernie sez so."

"What's a powder monkey?" ventured Tim.

"That's slang for the man who places the dynamite charges and engineers the proper timing and layout of the fuses."

"You've always done that, yourself," Forrest," said Ron, "Why the change?"

Forrest let the question hang, unanswered as the room grew suddenly very dark, caused by the hulk of two huge men whose shadows fell through the open doorway. Three young men looked up simultaneously to see Jake and Henri's shadows flow into the room.

First impressions registered were not good.

Through broken yellow teeth and unkempt shaggy beard, Jacob Jones sneered, "Who're these little twirps?" He looked straight at Ron, Rex and Tim with a withering gaze.

Heinrich Heisler added his own contempt by asking, "Who needs whippersnappers?" He was greasy and overweight. Vomit stains were visible on his unwashed shirt. Both men had obviously been drinking heavily over the weekend.

Rex looked at Henri's oversized forearms and immediately thought of Bully Bluto of Popeye cartoon fame.

"Now, boys," interrupted Forrest, "You're going to get along and work together, or you'll have to leave." He looked squarely at Jake and Henri and added, "We were getting along just fine, before you two drunks returned."

You could hear a pin drop, and see the crimson creep up Jake's wide neck, but apparently, he thought better about making a fuss, and simply said, "Sure, boss, we didn't mean nothin' by it."

It was an uneasy truce, and Ron was wondering exactly where he and his friends stood. These extra, temporary employees had never been here like this before. Jake had shifty eyes and Ron wondered if he could be trusted. He would have to warn Tim and Rex to keep a close eye on their "back-trail".

Down in the mine, Forrest assigned the three boys to work together this first day. A train of ore cars had been lowered down the main shaft and parked on a little siding. The track switches were explained. Then the bucket slammed down and Henri climbed out.

"Henri is doing the same as you," Forrest explained to the boys, "Only he'll be working in another tunnel, moving his own muck pile. I've hung a large lantern at the branch where your tracks join the main line, so you'll be able to see each other coming or going."

"Bah!" I don't need no lecture," announced Henri, stomping off down the tunnel.

Next, he showed them how to unhook the bucket, move it aside, then roll an ore car under the hoist and hook it up. Easy enough! "And don't forget the hoist bell signals," he reminded them, "One for up, two for down, and three for emergency."

Back in the bowels of the mine, that low rumble was beginning again, but not nearly as loud as the "joke" of the day before.

"Compressor?" asked Rex.

"You're learning, lad," said Forrest, "Jake is starting to drill, and the compressed air operates his jack-hammer." He started back toward the noise, adding, "Time for us to get to work."

They followed him single file down the dark tunnel. Weird triple dancing shadows proceeded before them, in the retreating blackness, caused from the three carbide headlamps and one hand held lantern.

Past a lighted fork, the left tunnel where Henri would be working, they could smell the rotten cigar he would be chomping on.

"That's 'tunnel J'," said Forrest, "We work in 'tunnel D'."

They took the tunnel to the right and soon ended up at the chute below the stope where Jake was drilling.

"Take turns shoveling, pushing the car, and resting, in that order," instructed Forrest; "I'll be up in the stope helping Jake."

The morning dragged on with aching sore muscles beginning to take their toll. Three boys, each taking turns on the shovels and cars, were full-grown men still only in their minds. And after fifteen full ore cars, they were praying for the lunch break.

Rex said, "If this is Purgatory, I sure as h--- don't want to go to Hell!"

Ron could never get Tim alone long enough to ask him anything because either Jake or Forrest were always working overhead. And, Ron's question was burning a hole in his soul.

Forrest insisted that the mine be cleared completely during the two hour lunch break, allowing nobody to linger.

Above ground now, three very weary lads limped out of the shelter of the hoist.

"How many full ore cars did you send up?" sneered Henri.

"Fifteen", bragged Rex, "How about you?"

"Twice that, you snivelling twit," replied Henri, "But that's expected when boys try to do a man's work!"

"I don't think he likes us," ventured Tim, "Let's go eat."

The sneaky mystery man had never been out on the hillside in the daylight before. Today, he was cautious, frequently glancing at the sky and the horizons to avoid possible search aircraft. He was not carrying any machinery or equipment today, but walked slowly, as if looking for something; a small landmark, maybe? Then he continued his quest.

"Ah, here it is, just where they said they would leave it." he said out loud, and he stooped down, shining a flashlight into a cavity under a large flat rock, peering underneath he then uttered a groan of surprise.

His brief case was gone!

Examination of the soft ground revealed nothing in the way of footprints, as the wind had scoured the ground clean. Panic settled into the man's brain, and he rushed off, failing to notice the partially torn briefcase, less than fifty feet away from where it had been hidden, still full of money. It was right where the coyote had dragged it,.

"Beans, again?" complained Ron, as they sat down to lunch.

"Sop them up with sourdough biscuits," answered Forrest. The table had been set with seven tin plates and seven enameled tin cups for coffee, but only five were eating.

"Where's Jake and Henri," asked Burt, "Dere bean's getting' cold!"

"Oh. I forgot," said Forrest, "Jake said he was going for a walk because he had too much hangover to eat anything. I don't know where Henri is."

After lunch, Forrest told the boys that they could take the afternoon off.

"Jake and I will be setting charges, and will blast in three different places this afternoon. By the time the dust settles, it will be quitting time. Burt and Henri have some equipment to repair, so you boys stay together and keep out of trouble."

When they were finally alone, Ron faked a punch at Tim's arm and said, "Well?"

"Well, what?" faked Tim.

"Come on, turkey," asked Ron, "Did you find any more money?"

"Uh-huh, two more fifties."

"So, that makes six, altogether? That's three hundred dollars!"

"Uh-huh," agreed Tim, "And I'm more confused than ever."

Rex approached and overheard part of Tim's reply. He interrupted, "Sounds like you better let me in on your secret."

A sort of a haze, not gloom, settled over the boys for the balance of the afternoon. They experienced some peace resulting from the belief that their faith had placed the problem directly into the hands of their Lord, and they believed that God would fully care for them, and solve the problem one way or another. (1st Peter 5:7).

Chapter 36 ~ Day Three; Suspicions

Lt.-Cdr. Bob Stotler had been in meetings all morning, and his brain was exhausted. Logisticians had calculated the angle of the Russian spy photos and determined they had been taken with a very high powered telephoto lens from somewhere east on the Luning plateau, part of the Excelsior Mountain. Range.

He had assembled a team of six who were slowly working out all the details.

"What about time of day?" he asked Chief Haddock, "How much time has been spent figuring that out?"

"Analysis of shadows indicates all times of day, from sunup to sundown."

"Then the person is out there on the plateau all day long?"

"It seems so."

"Aerial surveillance indicates no hiding places," offered Lt. Richard Hamm, head of base security, "So a man would be seen by our air-patrols."

"How about caves?"

"Nothing visible from the air."

"Aren't there some active mines out there?"

"Yes sir, two; the Candelaria and the Lmuma"

"What do we know about them?" asked Stotler.

"Candelaria is too far south," said Chief Haddock, "But the Lmuma is the likely place to start."

"I know the owners of both," answered Hamm, "In fact, Forrest Williams of the Lmuma is my golf buddy, when he's not looking for gold. He's also a Lieutenant in the inactive Naval Reserves."

"That's gotta be it, then," said the Commander, "Get your butt out there and have look around, see if this Forrest fellow knows anything that can help.

"Who taken 'm water?" demanded Burt, in a loud threatening voice, which woke the other six occupants of the cabin, "I hauled in five gallon fer cookin' and it done walked off!"

Six weary miners woke, trying to shake out the cobs of sleep.

"It twer thayr last night," He roared, "Which one o' youse varmits done stole it?"

"Settle down, Burt," suggested Forrest, "We can get to the bottom of this without you scaring everybody into having a heart attack."

Everybody scrambled to get dressed.

To Ron and Rex, Forrest said, "Out in the truck there's two clean glass gallon jugs. Go fill them at the water drum, so we can start breakfast."

When the boys returned with water, Ron reported, "The gasoline drum was leaking, and we shut the valve off, but there's gas all over the ground, so watch the smoking."

"You're kidding!" said Forrest, "Let's go have a look-see."

Shoving a measuring stick into the gasoline drum, Forrest dismally reported, "Half gone!" It looked as if someone had cracked the valve to allow a slow trickle, or maybe as a cover-up to hide a gasoline theft.

"We'll need that gas to run the hoist," he continued, "Who would want to sabotage us?"

Gloom pervaded their meager breakfast, and there was little talk. Eyes searched faces and eyes shifted. Everybody was under suspicion.

The dogs, Ernie and Oscar now set up a horrible din, to which Forrest said, "Somebody is coming up the hill, get your rifle, Burt, and I'll go chain the dogs. The rest of you stay here by the shack."

He had the dogs well under control, when he heard the whine of low gear of some vehicle laboring up the last hill, then a "Beep-beep", which he thought he recognized.

Burt stood ready with his gun, when a U. S. Navy jeep rolled over the crest of the hill and started down the driveway to the cabin. In it were four armed uniformed men wearing "SP" arm bands.

"Howdy," hailed Forrest, "And what brings Lieutenant Hamm way out here?"

Burt lowered his gun and the boys heaved a sigh of relief.

Forrest walked up to the jeep and talked quietly for a few minutes with the Naval Lieutenant but was beyond earshot of the others. The jeep then drove on toward the mine's loading chute, where the sailors parked it, and then went tramping up into the hills behind.

"Wha' d'they want?" asked Burt

"Something about Naval security on the big base over the hill, and I gave them permission to look around."

Too many questions without any answers; something worry-some was happening, but what?

"Well, enough excitement," continued Forrest, "Forget the Navy; we've got work to do." Burt, Jake and Henri headed for the mine shaft and Forrest was alone with the boys for a few seconds and whispered, "The Navy has intercepted some restricted photographs of the ammunition base, which might be being sent to the Soviet Russians. Lt. Hamm told me that it looked like the pictures were taken from somewhere near here, but you guys aren't to tell anybody what I just told you, understand? Just keep your eyes open and tell me anything you see that's unusual."

"Jeez," exclaimed Tim, "A real honest to goodness spy search!" He looked at Ron with a questioning glance.

Work that morning was scheduled pretty much the same as the day before, with one exception: Forrest drilled alone in the stope where the boys were working.

He said that Jake was drilling in a new face down in a different tunnel.

After an hour or so, Forrest turned off his compressed air line, disconnecting the drill bit, and told the boys that he had something else he had to do.

"Finish hauling out last night's muck pile, then you can knock off early for lunch," he said, "It shouldn't take more than a dozen cars full." With that, he was gone, leaving the boys in total silence.

"Ye gads, I'm still pooped from yesterday," said Rex.

"I don't think I can push another ore car," complained Tim.

Ignoring them, Ron asked, "Isn't this silence eerie? Since the drilling stopped, I can hear my own heart pumping blood."

I'm wondering if the Navy is still up topside?" asked Tim, "And if that has anything to do with the money I found?"

"Yeah, and who's stealing the water and the gasoline?" queried Rex.

They hadn't moved any earth at all since Forrest left, and were enjoying the unexpected break.

"Sh-h-h!" hushed Ron, "Listen!"

"I don't hear anything", whined Tim.

"Shut-up, and listen," repeated Ron.

Very faintly, they could hear a motor running, unlike the hoist engine and nothing like the compressors. This noise was different, and very far away.

"Wonder what that is?" asked Rex.

"I've never heard it before," answered Ron, "We should ask Forrest. But right now, we better be for moving some ore. I don't want to miss lunch, even if it is the same old beans, bacon and biscuits."

Topside, two hours later, old Burt was still manning the hoist. "Gotta wait fer Jake 'n Henri," he complained, "Yuh awl go eat."

"Is the Navy gone?" asked Ron.

"Yup, dey left an' didn' say nuthin either."

Forrest had provided a tin basin and some real soap, so the boys could wash up for lunch, but the cabin was empty when they entered.

Beans were on the stove, biscuits in the oven and coffee brewed. It was just like cowboy fare on a roundup, right down to the grounds boiled in the bottom of the coffee pot.

"Hey," hollered Tim from the bedroom, "Someone's been going through my stuff!"

Sure enough, clothes and sleeping bags were scattered in a messy pile on the floor.

"Now, who would want to do that?" asked Rex.

"Yeah," added Ron, "I'm getting a real creepy feeling about this place."

More questions without any answers. And where were Forrest, Jake and Henri?

"Do you think Forrest might take us home early?" asked Tim, all the time thinking about the $300 hidden deep in his pocket.

They said their prayers of thanksgiving and ate lunch then waited to see what would happen next.

Obviously, these three young friends were not the only people who were worried. Some other unknown person was also very worried about the presence of these three boys. Some sort of secret or secrets needed to be hidden, and the unknown person was concerned the boys might stumble on to it, either by accident or by logical calculation. Why else would someone search through their belongings? And what could they be searching for? Was it for the mysterious missing money?

Forrest entered the cabin. Breaking up their question and answer session, and said, "I'm going to run a load of ore up to the smelter, anybody want to go along?"

Grasping an unexpected opportunity to get out of work, Tim and Rex simultaneously said, "Yes!"

"I've got to pick up more gasoline, too," he said, "And we won't get back until after suppertime.

"Do we get to play that game?" asked Tim

"What game is that?"

"You know, rabbits on the right and left."

"Maybe we'll have time," answered Forrest.

Burt came in just then, and Forrest asked, "What do you need from town besides fresh eggs and milk?"

Burt thought a minute and said, "That'll do."

"Where's Jake and Henri?" asked Forrest.

"I wait fer an hour," Burt replied, "An they nev'r cum up fer chow."

"Well, never mind, "said Forrest, "We have to leave right now, if we're going to make it back before dark. You ready boys?"

While Forrest was leaving instructions with Burt, Ron had a chance to ask Tim, "Are you going to tell him about the money?'

"Dunno," said Tim, "I'll have to think about it."

"Well, at least mention that somebody's been ransacking our stuff."

After they were gone, Burt told Ron to go down and check on Jake and Henri, then take the afternoon off. Burt explained that the reason he couldn't look for the missing men, was because Ron didn't know how to run the hoist.

"B'sides," he added, "They'r probly layin drunk down there somplace."

Burt had a melancholy far-off look in his eye, "C'mon, I'll drop yer bucket."

When Ron exited the safety gate at the bottom of the shaft, it was deathly quiet. He fired up his carbide lantern plus two electric hand lanterns for extra measure, and proceeded straight to the tunnel where Henri had been working. This was the first time Ron had been in this part of the mine, and nothing was familiar.

The tunnel branched twice more before Ron found the chute below the stope where Henri had been working. Ron's footsteps crunching in the rock between the tracks echoed eerily in the stillness. When he reached the end, he stopped, but the echo of his footsteps took longer to diminish. Then, in the deathly silence, he heard it again...

The motor that shouldn't be there sounded something like a generator running. And the sound was coming from directly over his head, from the top of the stope! "Impossible," he thought, shining his torch up to the ceiling.

The light revealed the typical air vent that is usually drilled into the top of a working stope, to provide circulation of fresh air. But this hole had been considerably enlarged and had the tail end of a rope ladder hanging partway down.

The sound was definitely coming through the hole, and there was something else, too; a smell, a sour smell, something vaguely familiar to Ron. He tried to remember what it was...? Like moldy apples soaking in vinegar? More mystery to worry about, and there was nothing more Ron could do, except finish the search for Jake and Henri. He backtracked, looking in every branch but found no sign of the missing men.

When he reached the base of the shaft, he knew Burt would be topside, waiting for his signal to lift the bucket. But Ron had a different idea. Leaving the signal cord untouched, he recharged his carbine lantern, and started up the safety ladder, straight up the shaft, fifty feet to the next level. He'd had to make this climb once before, and it still scared him. It was like being on the outside of a six story building with no safety line, climbing in total darkness.

The fifty-foot level exit tunnel cut through the shaft at the halfway point. It had been cut into the side of the mountain prospecting a weak vein, but was unused now, except for ventilation for the level below. Ron was glad when he reached it and climbed out of the shaft. He could see a hint of daylight in one direction, but worked his way around the shaft and started in the opposite direction, going deeper into the mountain.

He had to be very careful, as large boulders lay strewn about, and some deep, possibly bottomless holes broke through the floor. His passage would have been impossible without the benefit of the carbide lantern to see where he was stepping. Then, he heard it! The same motor as before, but this time he was sure it was a generator. But, before he could proceed any further, he bumped into a solid wooden door with a padlock! Now, here was something he would have to ask Forrest about.

The sputtering of his carbide lamp was warning enough that he must retreat immediately, and with no time to spare.

The fifty-foot escape tunnel exited at the outside chute where the dump truck was filled, so Ron climbed up the driveway to the hoist shack, where he surprised a sleeping Burt and told him that the mine was empty.

He kidded Burt by saying, "You slept so soundly that you didn't hear my signal, so I had to climb out the escape tunnel." Burt shook his head and wondered.

Ron had been thinking. There were too many questions, and not enough answers, and his logical curiosity kept growing.

The first thing he did was make a trip to the outhouse, studying the lay of the land.

"Now, let's see," he said aloud, "If Tim was standing here, and money blew by and landed down there, where we first saw him on Sunday, then the wind had to be blowing from over that hill." Ron took a long hike, searching for the source of the money. He walked all around the area of the cavity under the flat rock and found nothing except a lot of footprints. Could they be from the Navy men, this morning?

He left the area and returned to the outhouse, then down the other side of the hill to where Tim had made his find. He took his time, as he was under no pressure, and it paid off... handsomely! His slow methodical search was rewarded with six more bills, another $300.

Ron's methodical mind was still chewing on the clues when Forrest, Rex and Tim returned. They would have lots to talk about, tonight!

Chapter 37 ~
Burt is Missing!

Tuesday evening, when the boys entered the bunkroom, they were bubbling over with things to talk about, but Jake and Henri were already in the sack.

"You kids talk, and I'll stomp ya," said Henri.

The room was permeated with the smell of stale whiskey, so the boys had no choice but to crawl into bed and seek sleep. Each was burning with many questions, which would have to wait...

Wait until morning...

Ron awakened just as the eastern sky was beginning to lighten. He gently shook Rex, signaling "quiet," and then motioning "outside". He did the same to Tim, then quietly dressed and snuck into the outer room. It was immediately apparent that Forrest was in no snoring competition this morning, for Burt was already up, and probably at the outhouse. Sneaking through the front door, Ron was met by Tim and Rex.

"Whew!" exclaimed Rex, "If you lit a match back there in our room, I think it would blow up." He was referring to the strong smell of alcohol on the breath of Jake and Henri. "I wonder where they got all the whisky?" he added.

"Never mind that," said Ron, "We've got a lot more important things to talk about, such as your trip yesterday to the smelter..."

They had moved far enough away from the cabin and outhouse so that nobody could overhear their conversation.

"Okay," started Rex, "Tim here did tell Forrest about finding the money, and Forrest thought we should tell the Navy, but we didn't like that idea."

"But it happened anyway," interrupted Tim, "Because that Lt. Hamm was sitting down at the bottom of the road, standing guard on the road up to the mine, so I decided to go ahead and tell him. He seemed more interested in the denominations than he was in the amount, so when I told him they were fifty dollar bills, he said to just keep them for now, but not to tell anyone else."

"Forrest is really worried," added Rex, "Because a Navy staff car or a jeep, tailed us all the way to Virginia City and back. When Forrest stopped at the Home Café in Hawthorne to buy us some dinner they even parked outside, like we were spies, or something."

"Well, I did some sleuthing while you were gone," Ron told them, "And you'll never guess what I found."

He filled them in on all the events of the previous day, including the locked gate in the unused fifty-foot level, the generator sounds, the rope ladder in the air vent, and the money.

"Gosh, that makes $600 altogether," exclaimed Tim, "A fortune!"

"When are we going to tell Forrest?" asked Rex.

"Well, I've been giving that a lot of thought," replied Ron, "And I'm suspicious of everybody right now, maybe even Forrest."

"Suspicious of what?" injected Tim.

"Well," continued Ron, "Look at all the junk that's been happening. Don't you think there's something fishy going on up here? And who owns the place and should know more about it than anyone else? Forrest, that's who. But then, we have to consider the shifty eyes and bad tempers of Jake and Henri. Burt's about the only one I really trust, outside of you guys."

"Well then, I sure wish he'd hurry up and get outa the john," said Tim, "I gotta go, bad!"

"Yeah,' added Rex, "He has been up there a long time. Do you suppose we'd better check up on him?"

It turned out that Burt was not in the outhouse, or anywhere else on the property.

"He was here at 3:00 am," said Forrest, "I had to climb over him to get out of bed."

"Come to think of it," he added, "Jake and Henri were both up then too." He looked straight at Henri with inquiring eyes, "What do you know, Henri?"

"We don't know nuthin," answered Henri, blinking, "He was in bed when I came back from the john."

Jake looked away, "Yeah, me too," he said.

Now there was another mystery. What happened to Burt?

Forrest was obviously worried as he sent everyone out to search around and under the mine property.

An hour later, everyone gathered back at the hoist shack, all with negative reports. Burt was flat-out gone!

"We gonna work anyway?" asked Henri, "I can run the hoist."

Ron looked at Rex, "How could Henri be so cold and indifferent?"

Jake stepped into the bucket and announced, "I'm going to work, "Lower me down!"

Forrest shrugged, and said, "Okay, everybody move some rock, I'm going back to clean up the kitchen. It's only two hours 'til lunch."

Gloom settled over Ron, Rex and Tim, as they followed Jake down into the shaft. At the bottom, Jake spoke an unexpected kind word.

"Buck up, lads," he encouraged, "Burt could have walked in to town to get a drink. Take it from one alky to know what another one might do. The best remedy for you is hard work."

"I'll be working in "J" tunnel," he said as he walked away, "Let's have a race to see who can move the most rock; me or you three?"

The boys caught the spirit of competition and ran off into their own tunnel.

At lunch, the tally was twenty cars for Jake and twenty-two for the boy's team. Jake insisted that he had allowed them to win, but it was Henri who complained the loudest.

"You guys tryin' to kill me?" he growled, "Every car you send up, I've gotta' push down to the tailing pile, but before I can get it dumped, you're ringing up another car. You averaged a new load every three minutes, and I'm pooped."

Jake winked at the boys, then said to Henri, "You volunteered to run the hoist, remember?"

After lunch, the boys returned to work, in a much better frame of mind about Burt. It made sense that with all the boozing Jake and Henri had been doing, that the old alcoholic did just walk in to town. Forrest had agreed that's exactly what Burt had done in the past..

Afternoon work slowed considerably because the spirit of competition was removed. Jake and Forrest were both drilling for the next explosive charge, and there wasn't much ore left for the boys to muck out.

When they did have ore to send up, nobody answered the signal.

"Is Henri asleep?" asked Ron.

Just then, a deep rumbling explosion was heard. The concussion from it felt as if someone had just whacked their ears with a two by four.

"Ye-ow! That hurt!, screeched Tim, "What was that?"

"My ears are ringing too," said Ron, "That was dynamite, but there was no warning."

Forrest came staggering through a cloud of dust.

"Everybody here?" he shouted, "Where's Jake?"

"Dunno"

"Outa here, fast," he commanded, "Take 'em up the ladder, Ron."

Forrest grabbed the signal cord and jerked it the dreaded three times, while three boys scrambled single file up the emergency escape ladder, followed by their boss.

Chapter 38 ~ Last Day of Secrets

Tim was staggering with exhaustion and Ron's heart was pounding in his throat.

"How's your ears," asked Forrest, as everybody exited from the smoking and dusty escape tunnel.

"Ringing loud," panted Rex, "What happened?"

"Somebody set off a charge, probably by accident," Forrest explained, "And we've probably had a man killed." He was thinking about Jake who had been working in the "J" tunnel, because that's where Forrest assumed that the explosion came from.

With legs like rubber, caused from the stress, they climbed the hill around the tailing piles.

At the hoist shack, there was no sign of Henri.

Adding more worry, Forrest said, "Burt's missing and now this. Let's all gather back at the cabin to see what we can figure out."

Approaching the cabin, the four of them heard boisterous singing, and a light began to dawn.

Henri and Jake were both seated comfortably in the jeep behind the cabin, roaring drunk!

So, who set off the dynamite in "J" tunnel?

Forrest grabbed the bottle of booze and smashed it to the ground. "You deserted your post when we needed you," he glared at Henri, "We just had a blowup, didn't you hear the emergency signals?" He was mad. "I've a notion to fire you on the spot," he warned. Then, looking at Jake, he continued his tirade, "We thought you were dead, when did you come up?"

"Aw, shucks," drawled Jake, "Me 'n Henri been sittin' here for over an hour. I finished my drilling, 'n we figured you guys wouldn't be coming up yet for awhile."

"Who set off the charge?" demanded Forrest.

Shoulders shrugged.

Jake and Henri both showed expressionless faces and chimed together, "Dunno!"

"Well, did you pack any powder?"

"Nope!"

"Well," relented Forrest, looking seriously at Jake, "I'm glad you're not splattered all over the walls down there, like we thought."

Ron looked at Rex, and then at Tim, "Something is really fishy here," he whispered, "I think we need to talk about leaving."

"I need you here," pleaded Forrest, when Ron spoke privately to him later, "Just stick it out one more day!"

Forrest said he had some ideas, and that he might have some answers within an hour. Then, he wandered off on some errand.

With nothing better to do, the boys settled down with a deck of cards at the kitchen table, and Jake and Henri continued their serenade to another bottle of Southern Comfort.

Presently Forrest returned, a bright smile on his face, "Just as I suspected," he said, "Burt walked out, I found his footprints in the dust going down to the highway. It's six miles down to the highway and three more into the little town of Luning... and Luning has a bar, and a nine mile hike is nothing for an old alcoholic like Burt."

He looked straight at Ron, and said, "Let's go get him." He indicated that Tim and Rex were to stay at the cabin and finish their game of Gin Rummy.

Outside, he rousted Jake and Henri out of the jeep, warning them to be sober and ready to work, when he and Ron got back from Luning.

"Give me the other bottle," he demanded, "Or you both can leave right now!"

Once they were winding down the treacherous road away from the mine, Forrest flung the bottle out, grunting with satisfaction as he heard the glass shatter in a muffled waterfall against the rock walls of the canyon.

"Feel around under the seat for any more," he instructed Ron, "This boozing has got to stop!"

Ron found two more pints carefully wrapped in a large map.

"Let me see that," demanded Forrest, braking the jeep to a stop.

Forrest silently studied the map, chomping on a toothpick, sighed, and chomped some more.

"This is a classified map of the Navy ammunition depot," he finally said, "Now where in blazes did Jake and Henri get it?"

Ron wasn't too sure yet if he could trust Forrest, but his doubts were fading, "Do you suppose they're the spies and all that money was theirs?" he asked cautiously.

Forrest looked at him with a quizzical eye, and said, "It sounds to me like you know something you haven't shared with me." It was a question.

"Well... ," Ron hesitated.

"Maybe I'd better level with you, first," interrupted Forrest, "About a month ago, I got a surprise visit from the FBI, who told me they thought someone was spying on the base, from out here somewhere, and could I help keep an eye on things for them. So, if you have any doubts about me, forget it, because I am working for the government!"

This shocked Ron, who then decided to tell all, including the part about the generator sounds, the acidic smells and the rope ladder up in the stope at the end of tunnel "J".

"And, I've been giving that smell a lot of thought," he continued, "And think I have figured out what it is."

"Yeah?" Forest let out the clutch and the jeep continued slowly down the canyon.

"It smells just like the chemical baths we use in the photo lab back at school, to stop developing action and to fix photo images. They're called hypochloric and acetic acids," he said with a smile of pride.

"That makes sense," was all Forest said. Then, "Let's go rescue Burt."

"Rescue?" asked Ron.

"Yeah," said Forrest, "He'll probably be in the town drunk tank... The police chief and I are friends"

"And," he added forcefully, "Don't tell anybody about finding this map, not even Tim or Rex!"

Back at the mine, Ron helped tuck Burt into bed, so he could finish sleeping off his problem.

"He's going to have multiple problems when we start work in the morning," Forrest predicted.

"A hangover," said Ron, "And what else?"

"Sore feet," answered Forrest, "Sore feet; nine miles worth!"

He then looked in on Jake and Henri, who were also passed out in bed. Over his shoulder, he said to Ron, "First thing in the morning, we have to see what damage that blast did down at the end of "J", then we'll have a look see at that gate you found in the fifty foot level. From now on, I want you boys to stay together at all times, so I know exactly where you are."

"By the way," he added, "Where are Tim and Rex?"

"I didn't see them when we drove up," answered Ron, "And it will be dark soon."

Outside, they hollered and had an almost immediate response from Tim and Rex who were out below the outhouse, looking again for more money.

"Should have known!" exclaimed Ron, "Find anything?"

"Yep," answered Rex, "It was my turn anyway!"

"Okay, the Easter egg hunt is over," said Forrest, "We've got a big day tomorrow, so we've got to fix some supper and get to bed early."

After supper, Ron nudged Rex and asked, "How much?"

Rex ignored him.

"C'mon, turkey," Ron pleaded.

"Gotcha beat, turkey!" Rex answered, then turned over on his pillow and would say no more.

All three boys lay awake for a time, quietly considering all that had happened. Finally the snores of everyone around them diminished enough to allow them to drift off into a troubled sleep.

Lieutenant Hamm's jeep was still guarding the spur road leading to the Lmuma Mine.

Chapter 39 ~ Smoke Signals

Thursday dawned clear and bright. It was hard for the boys to believe that this was the start of only their fifth day in this place. It seemed like they had been here for an eternity.

"Burt, Jake and Henri are going to be pretty useless today," Forrest told the boys at breakfast, "Nobody will be allowed to do anything alone. You three stay together at all times, Burt and Henri will work the hoist together, and the rest of us will muck out the damage."

Ron was now feeling a lot better about things in general. He was glad that he had shared information with, and now fully trusted Forrest. He had been given permission to tell Rex and Tim that Forrest was in cahoots with the government and was assisting them in their investigation, but nothing was said about the map.

All eyes of suspicion were now turned toward either Jake or Henri, or both. That's why Forrest had separated them and assigned them to always work with someone else nearby.

On the way to the shaft, Ron finally worked out of Rex that he had indeed found nine more fifty-dollar bills.

"Ye gads," Tim exclaimed, calculating rapidly in his head, "That's a thousand and fifty dollars, altogether!"

Underground, Forrest led the way into the mysteries of 'tunnel J'. They found little damage and determined that only one stick of dynamite had probably been fired. One ore car and part of the chute had been blown to bits, but the loose rock could be hauled out in less than seven carloads. It took some back breaking shovel work to capture it, however, as it was all down in the floor of the tunnel. Forrest and Jake did the loading, while Tim, Ron and Rex pushed the cars and sent them up to be dumped.

In less than two hours, they had the job finished. No further evidence was found to determine how the blast had been ignited. Dynamite was never stored underground. Safety rules required its storage in powder bunkers topside, located a safe distance from any buildings. Solution to this mystery was topmost in Forrest's mind, as they walked toward the bucket, in preparation for lunch. Ron had pointed out the enlarged air duct in the ceiling of the stope, but there was no sign of the hanging rope ladder.

"That's big enough for a man to crawl through," Forrest had observed, "Right after lunch, we'll explore the other end of it."

He glanced around to be sure the others weren't close enough to hear. Tim and Rex had already gone on ahead with Jake.

"Other end?" asked Ron.

"Right! As near as I can figure," answered Forrest, "The gate in the fifty foot level, should connect within fifty feet of that stope where the mysterious dynamite was set off."

"Hadn't thought of that," declared Ron, "Do you suppose that there's a secret room up there?"

"I've not been in that part of the mine for years," Forrest replied, "My brother Skie always worked that part. There could be a secret room, maybe; but we'll soon check it out!"

"Then somebody might be using it as a base of operations to spy on the Navy base?" theorized Ron, "What d'ya think?"

Questions raced through his head as his bucket was hoisted to the surface. Everyone else was standing around in a tight circle when he walked up to the hoist shack.

"And lookee this side, there's sum more!" Burt was shouting and holding a chunk of rock about the size of a telephone. All eyes were on the rock. "Thut thayr is pure-dee gold!" he was saying, "That thayr blast musta opend up a glory hole."

"Alleluia!" shouted Forrest, "I knew it was down there someplace!"

It would be many hours before he could settle down enough to explain to the boys about rare pockets called "glory holes". In the meantime, Ron could see the spy investigation slipping deeper into the background. True, he was excited for his friend, but found it difficult to tolerate this further interruption and possible delay. This spy thing was really bugging him, and he was torn between leaving for the relative safety of home, or sticking around for answers in a dangerous environment.

After lunch, Forrest gained control of his gleeful emotions and of the situation, again, when he said, "Okay, Burt, I want you to get your gun and sit on top of that rock pile out there, making sure that the rich ore stays right where it is. I'll spell you every hour or so."

To Henri and Jake he said, "You fellas stay right here in the shack where Burt can see you. Me and the boys have a chore to attend to," and then he added, "Don't let anybody down into the mine."

He motioned the boys to follow him, and started off down the road to the dump truck loading chute, at the mouth of the fifty foot level.

Entering the tunnel, they found and lit some carbide lamps, then proceeded in as far as the main shaft.

"I want two of you to stay here," Forrest commanded, "And don't make any noise; no talking!"

It was Tim and Rex that he indicated, then said, "Keep your ears open for us, and if we're not back in fifteen minutes, go get help from above."

"And," as a second thought, he added, "This tunnel is really dangerous, so that's why I'm taking Ron who has been through it before."

He and Ron then started picking a cautious path through the rubble and proceeded deeper into the mountain.

"Be very, very quiet," whispered Forrest, as they neared the gate.

He suddenly stopped, and bending down, shone his light on a thin piece of fishing line which had been stretched across between two rocks.

"A trip wire," he whispered, "Was that here before?"

"If it was," answered Ron, "I didn't see it."

Close examination showed that the line was attached to a large cow-bell, set up only to make noise.

Stepping carefully over the line, they proceeded for another fifty or so feet to the plank gate.

It was a structure fashioned out of old mine timbers which effectively blocked further access into the tunnel. Only a small two by four foot door was hinged to allow access, and it was padlocked.

"Do you think someone's in there?" whispered Ron, "If they are, how could they get out?"

Forrest had knelt down and was closely examining the door.

"Look here," he whispered, "A sliding panel!"

Sure enough, a square-foot panel opened where a man could reach through from the inside, to unlock the padlock. It had been rigged to appear to be one way access only.

Forrest was peering through the opening, when he motioned for Ron to start back out. He silently slid the panel shut, and joined Ron.

When they were back at the shaft, Ron ventured his question, "What did you see?"

"Faint light, from around a bend in the tunnel," he said. "Someone's in there alright."

Forrest shushed the boys, and continued out of the tunnel, into daylight.

As soon they were back outside in the daylight, Forrest started issuing orders.

"See that pile of timbers over there?" he pointed, "Bring a dozen over here and stack them up on the edge of this tailing pile!"

"And Tim," he continued, "Run up to the hoist shack and bring down a five gallon can of gasoline. Hop to it!"

Then he got into the dump truck and backed it up into the mouth of the tunnel, effectively blocking it. After that, he helped Rex and Ron to build a pile with the timbers. A couple of old tires were thrown on top. When Tim returned with the gas, it was poured all over the pile.

Forrest hollered, "Stand back!" And he threw a lit match onto the pile.

In a whoosh, they had a roaring fire, sending up columns of inky black smoke, fed by creosote, gasoline and old rubber.

Back at the hoist shack, Burt, still guarding the gold, asked, "What's da big fire fur?"

Forrest replied, for all to hear, "It's a pre-arranged signal to bring the Navy, I think we've got an intruder bottled up, down inside the mine. The Navy has been looking for a spy, and it's probably him."

"D'ya think he heard us?" asked Ron.

"Probably not," said Forrest, "That secret room is deep enough in the mountain, that if he was sleeping, he'll still be sleeping, but whatever he's doing, there's no way out."

Presently Oscar and Ernie set up a fuss, and everybody knew the government was almost there.

The lead jeep was Lt. Richard Hamm, followed by two others filled with armed marines and some civilians.

One of the civilians came up to Forrest, and said, "I'm Special Agent Hovis of the FBI, bring me up to date!" And they huddled for five minutes, talking softly.

Meanwhile, Lt. Hamm asked Burt, "Can these other guys be trusted?" He had nodded at Jake, Henri and the boys.

"Yup, I tank so," said Burt, "We was not too shure about Jake n' Henri for awhile, but deys ok now."

Lt. Hamm made some assignments, one Marine to stay with Burt, who was to run the hoist. Two pairs of Marines were assigned to go down the shaft, guided by Jake and Henri. One trio was to make their way back to the tunnel "J" stope, the other was to climb up the escape ladder into the fifty foot level and wait.

Burt started lowering men down as fast as the hoist would run, one man in the bucket at a time. The rest of the party would enter the fifty foot tunnel, from the outside, just as soon as Forrest removed the truck from the entrance.

"Shucks," complained Tim, "That leaves us up here missing all the action!"

"Just our luck," added Rex.

"Well, we can always go play Gin-rummy," joked Ron.

He was struck simultaneously on both arms by clinched, but playful fists!

Chapter 40 ~
FBI Makes an Arrest

When everybody was in position, Agent Hovis gave the order for Forrest to move the truck.

With guns drawn, the rest of the Marines and Special Agents entered the tunnel. They moved slowly and stealthily along the side walls, so as not to provide a good target, silhouetted with daylight still behind them. After rounding the first bend, they moved more deliberately. Forrest had joined them in order to guide them around the various hazards that were strewn in their path. At the shaft, they met the other contingent of two Marines, who had climbed up from below.

"Where's my man?" asked Forrest.

"Jake was our guide," said a Marine, "But he stayed down at the bottom of the ladder. He said he would only be in the way, up here."

"Okay, move forward," commanded Agent Hovis, and the men crept deeper into the mountain.

Meanwhile, up topside, Burt and his assigned Marine were exchanging jokes, when the signal bell jangled a sharp tone, twice.

"Two fer down," said Burt, "But the bucket's already down!...? It's probly ol' Jake wantin' to cum up, an he's hittin' the bottle agin an furgot the signals." He released the clutch and the cables started pulling up the bucket.

Rex and Tim heard the hoist engine whine and looked out the door of the cabin, wondering who would be coming out so soon and what news they might bear.

As the bucket reached the safety gate, Burt got the shock of his life. In it was someone totally unexpected, someone he thought he recognized, a man with a gun, who immediately fired at the unsuspecting Marine guard.

As the guard fell against Burt, the man started running toward the cabin and the fleet of parked vehicles.

Thinking quickly, Ron ran and unchained Oscar and Ernie, the two guard dogs, who met the fleeing man with mean growls. Rex and Tim had ducked back inside the cabin, looking for old Burt's shotgun. One of the dogs lunged for the man's throat, and knocked him down and his pistol went flying, before he could get off another shot.

When Rex and Tim emerged from the cabin, the man was sitting on the ground, bleeding from his neck, Ron was holding the man's lost pistol and shouting at the dogs to "Stay".

He looked at Tim and said, "Go find some rope!" and then to Rex, "Is that thing cocked and loaded?"

"You bet," said Rex, "And I know how to use it too."

Burt had carried the wounded Marine into the cabin, laid him out on the bed and was inspecting his wound.

Tim and Ron got the groggy spy tied, hands and feet, and left him sitting in the dirt where he had fallen. No guns were needed because Oscar and Ernie were standing guard, growling and bearing their teeth at every effort the man made to move. Ron got a compress out of the first aid kit, and stopped the flow of blood from the man's neck.

"You're gonna have to get rabies shots," he kidded, "Because all we feed these dogs are dead, rotten, putrid road-kills."

He laughed to himself as the man shuddered.

"Stay close by with that shotgun," he told Rex, "I'm going to go see how the Marine is doing.

When Ron entered the cabin, the Marine was sitting on the edge of Burt's bed, holding his head.

"Don't got no ice," Burt was saying, "You got a nasty crease in yur skul-cap, 'n a mighty powrful headake tu go wid it, I'd bet." He was holding another compress over the skull wound.

"I can't run the hoist," suggested Ron, "If you think somebody might need it, I can stay here with this Marine."

"Shucks," said the Marine," I'm a little dizzy, but otherwise okay."

"We got the spy tied up outside, Ron told him, "And I need to get word to the guys down below."

"Get my gun, and drag him in here," said the Marine, "And I'll guard him while Burt goes back to the hoist, and you go for more help."

Before Ron could retrieve the Marine's rifle, the hoist bell was ringing, and he went to the shaft and hollered down.

"We've got the spy up here," he said, "Can you hear me?"

"Yeah," answered a distant voice, "We've got a wounded man down here, hoist him up!"

It was Jake, who had apparently been hit over the head just before the spy was hoisted up. He was conscious as Ron opened the safety gate to let him walk out of the bucket.

Ron picked up the Marine's rifle, then helped Jake limp back to the cabin. Meanwhile Tim and Rex had ushered their hobbled prisoner into the cabin, followed by two fierce dogs snapping at his heels.

"Well, I don't think this bird is going anywhere," said the Marine. We've got his pistol, my rifle, Burt's shotgun, big Jake and two mean dogs to guard him."

"And here's reinforcements," interrupted Lieutenant Hamm, "How'd you catch him?"

"A better question," interrupted Forrest, "Is, who is he?" He pushed his way into the crowded room where he got his first glimpse of the prisoner's face.

"Oh, my gosh!" he exclaimed, "You...? How...?"

Agent Hovis was right behind Forrest and as he snapped handcuffs on the man, he asked, "Do you know this man?"

'Yeah," said Forrest, "And so does Ron!"

Shocked, Ron queried, "Who?"

Forrest said, "Take off the blonde wig and remove the dark glasses."

"You are under arrest," Hovis said, as he pulled off the wig, "On espionage charges."

"Soo Ling!" exclaimed Ron, "I used to work for you...They said you went back to China. Why are you doing this?"

"I'm Japanese, not Chinese," he answered, "And you Yankees should never have won the war."

To the wounded Marine, Agent Hovis said, "You'll get a medal for this. Good work, soldier!"

"No, sir!" answered the Marine, "It was these three boys who captured him after I got shot. They deserve the medal!"

Hamm and Hovis dispatched Soo Ling in one of the jeeps, under the guard of two of the Marines and the other FBI Agent.

"Take him down to the brig, and book him," ordered Hovis, "We'll pack up the rest of the evidence, and join you later."

Hearts were pounding in the throats of the boys as they finally relaxed, and joined the circle of remaining adults. They were now an integral part of this adventure, and knew that they had earned the right to be involved in tying up loose ends and to hear the whole story.

"Soo Ling was sending many revealing photographs of the ammunition arrivals out to the Soviet Communists," Lt. Hamm was speaking. "We found where he had been setting up powerful telephoto lenses on cameras with timed remote controls. He used newly developed batteries which would take pictures every half hour all day long. His equipment would be hidden in small juniper shrubs or pinion pine trees."

Continuing, he looked straight at Tim and said, "His payment from the Russians was a quarter million dollars, in fifties and hundreds. It was hidden up on top of the plateau, but apparently a coyote, or some other animal was attracted by the smell of the leather brief case, and tore it open, trying to eat the leather. The brief case was dragged about sixty feet from where it had been hidden. During that bad windstorm, some of the fifties got blown away, and I guess we never will find them." He turned and winked at Tim and Rex.

"We took what was left of the briefcase", he continued, "When we were up here the first time. It turns out that all of the hundred dollar bills were counterfeit, but the fifties were real". Again, he winked at Tim.

"How'd Soo Ling get past all you guys?" asked Ron.

"Easy," said Agent Hovis, "He must have heard Forrest back up the dump truck to block the tunnel, so he slipped down his rope ladder into the 'J'stope, then he hid in the "D" tunnel until all the troops were in position. Then it was easy to bop Jake over the head and ride up the bucket to the top, where he planned to escape in Forrest's jeep. We're lucky you boys and those dogs were up here and had clear heads enough to know what to do." He hung his head briefly, and continued, "He totally outsmarted us!"

"Not me," said Ron, "When I heard two bells instead of one knowing the bucket was already down, I figured something was fishy and was halfway prepared to take action even before Burt hoisted him up. I only wish I could have warned them before the Marine got shot."

Hovis looked at Ron with new respect.

"Another question," continued Ron, "What did you find in the secret room?"

"Can I answer that?" asked Forrest.

Hovis nodded.

"You were right all along, Ron," Forrest continued, "He had a bed, candles, food, a Sterno stove, Geiger counters, and a complete photo lab. It looked like he'd been living in there for weeks, and walking out at night to set up his cameras. He processed his film and made enlargements, using a gasoline generator for electricity, and Burt's missing water!"

"He'd sleep during the day, while his camera was working, then he'd walk down to the highway at night, and hide his photos in a "drop" for his contact to pick up." said Lt. Hamm, "What he didn't know is that we already arrested his contact a couple of weeks ago, and we've kept the drop under surveillance ever since."

Forrest asked, "Well, how'd he find out we were up here, in the first place?"

Agent Hovis said, "I can answer that, but maybe you'd better ask Burt..."

"Huh?"

All eyes sought Burt, in the back of the room, questioning...

"Awr-r, I wuz hopin' thet wouldn't come up," Burt stammered, "I got drunk with Soo Ling about a yer ago, an' probly tole him."

By nightfall, all signs of government agents and military people were gone. They had radioed down to the base for an ambulance and two medium trucks. Marines and sailors had cleaned out the secret room and loaded all the evidence for transport back down to the base near Hawthorne. Jake had been diagnosed to have a minor skull fracture, so had been loaded into the ambulance along with the scalp-wounded Marine.

"Sure wish you had one of those powerful radios up here," suggested Ron to Forrest. "It would make communications a lot easier!"

"I don't see any need for that, now," said Forrest, "But, I sure wish I'd known Soo Ling was here, right under my nose..."

"Don't feel bad," he said to Burt, "We've all told people that we are up here. There's no way you could have known that he was working for the Reds."

Then he added, "Did you see anybody take any interest in our new gold?"

"Naw, I dun think those guys have a clue," answered Burt.

"Well, I got only one question," said Henri, "Where did that dynamite blast come from, that everyone wanted to blame on me?"

"Probably dropped through the air vent, by Soo Ling," answered Forrest, "Who wanted to scare us all away."

They ate a late supper, and talked well into the night.

"Pack up in the morning, boys," Forrest said as the last lantern was extinguished, "We're all outa here, except Burt."

Friday morning, they loaded the new ore into the dump truck. Oscar and Ernie, whined when they sensed the boys were leaving. They had all become really good friends. After packing their gear into the jeep, the small convoy headed for

Hawthorne, Forrest and Ron in the truck, followed by Henri, Rex and Tim in the jeep.

Mrs. Martin welcomed them home, first with much better good home cooked food, then with hot showers. Rex and Tim had never enjoyed warm water so much, in fact, they ran the hot water heater empty so Ron had to wait awhile for it to recover.

When they were all fed, clean and comfortable, she said, "I got a telephone call about you from the Navy this morning, and they want to see you this afternoon at the Administration building out at the base."

"Now what?" complained Tim and Rex in unison.

"You'll see," she said, leaving the room to make a telephone call.

At the base gate they were met by Lt. Hamm, whose jeep escorted them through the base, siren blaring, to the Administration building.

There was an awards ceremony, a band playing, and long speeches about the alertness of the youth of America. Everybody was there, from the Base Captain on down. The boys were each given a thousand-dollar trust fund toward college.

Puffed up and proud now, they soon felt a sinking feeling that they would have to return to the routine and boredom of school. At least there would be lots to talk about there!

Chapter 41 ~ Epilogue

Sunday, after a day of fishing in Walker Lake, the boys were on a train heading back to Sacramento. Ron's mother had driven them up to Hazen, where the Southern Pacific's main line from Chicago to San Francisco came closest to Hawthorne.

Forrest had surprised them with a monetary "bonus" for their "free" labor.

"Let's see," he had said, "Four days labor at $20 a day, that's..."

"Whoa," Ron had interrupted, "Even Jake and Henri don't make that much!"

"Yeah, I know," said Forrest, "And you won't tell them, either..."

"With a bonus," he continued, "That's $100 apiece."

On the train, now, Rex could feel the bulge of his wallet in his back pocket. It contained $550 in cash, more money than he could earn in a whole year. Tim had exactly the same amount, as the three boys had divided all the money found equally between them. Ron had left his money with his mother, to be put in the bank and saved for his college. He intended to obtain a

Bachelor of Science with a major in photography.

Tim had his eye on LaSalle College for a teaching degree. He would be the "Brother Felix" of the future. His mom would divorce again, but Tim considered it to be no loss.

Rex was still torn between a career as an officer in the Navy, like his father, or joining a fire department and obtaining a degree in Fire Science Engineering. His step-mom would die within a year of a cerebral tumor, but Rex had matured enough in his internal strength to be able to cope.

Three young men advanced toward maturity very fast in one week and learned a lot about the rewards of being honest. And they learned another valuable lesson, that broken dysfunctional families can still produce winners, in spite of the odds. Considering all that had happened, the bottom line of their successful lives was still basically the result of their own actions. A good prayer based faith in God never hurt, either.

Forrest made a trip to the smelter late in the week. His five ton truck load of ore yielded over sixteen pounds of pure gold, worth almost nine thousand dollars and aroused a great deal of speculation and interest statewide in his Lmuma[1] Mine. So much so, that he had to hire several armed guards, but then, within two weeks, the vein played out and was indeed only a pocket; a "glory hole".

Henri and Jake both went back to Tennessee to find work in the coal mines. They had never been asked to explain how they had obtained the classified map of the navy base, which was used to wrap up the whiskey hidden under the seat of the jeep. But every mystery must have at least one false clue.

Burt stayed with Forrest for another two years, until Forrest sold his failing mine to an eastern conglomerate. The last anyone heard, Forrest was working as a bouncer in the main casino of Hawthorne, the El Capitan Club. Poor Burt, after he was paid off, turned back to the bottle, which eventually consumed him.

The coyote walked slowly up the trail, which many footsteps had created, from the mine up to the plateau, her sensitive nose testing the air. She was hungry again, with a vague memory of things past. She checked the hiding place under the rock slab one more time, as she often did, and feeling only pangs of hunger in her belly; she turned and complained to the full moon.

THE END

---

[1] *Lmuma* is a Native American word for Warrior's joy (wife). In 1947, the property was called The Squaw Mine, but the author changed it to Lmuma, as "Squaw" is no longer a 'politically correct' word.